SISTERS IN YELLOW

ALSO BY MIEKO KAWAKAMI

Ms Ice Sandwich
Breasts and Eggs
Heaven
All the Lovers in the Night

SISTERS IN YELLOW

MIEKO KAWAKAMI

Translated by Laurel Taylor and Hitomi Yoshio

PICADOR

First published 2026 by Alfred A. Knopf

First published in the UK 2026 by Picador
an imprint of Pan Macmillan
The Smithson, 6 Briset Street, London EC1M 5NR
EU representative: Macmillan Publishers Ireland Ltd, 1st Floor,
The Liffey Trust Centre, 117–126 Sheriff Street Upper,
Dublin 1 D01 YC43
Associated companies throughout the world

ISBN 978-1-0350-2413-1 HB; 978-1-0350-9509-4 HB (international exclusive);
978-1-0350-2414-8 TPB

Copyright © Mieko Kawakami 2026
Translation copyright © Laurel Taylor and Hitomi Yoshio 2026

The right of Mieko Kawakami to be identified as the
author of this work has been asserted in accordance with
the Copyright, Designs and Patents Act 1988.

Originally published in Japanese as *Kiiroi ie* by Chuokoron-Shinsha, Inc. in 2023
Copyright © Mieko Kawakami 2023

All rights reserved. No part of this publication may be reproduced,
stored in a retrieval system, or transmitted, in any form, or by any means
(including, without limitation, electronic, mechanical, photocopying, recording
or otherwise) without the prior written permission of the publisher.

Pan Macmillan does not have any control over, or any responsibility for,
any author or third-party websites (including, without limitation, URLs,
emails and QR codes) referred to in or on this book.

1 3 5 7 9 8 6 4 2

A CIP catalogue record for this book is available from the British Library.

Printed and bound in the UK using 100% Renewable Electricity by CPI Group (UK) Ltd

This book is sold subject to the condition that it shall not, by way of
trade or otherwise, be lent, hired out, or otherwise circulated without
the publisher's prior consent in any form of binding or cover other than
that in which it is published and without a similar condition including this
condition being imposed on the subsequent purchaser. The publisher does not
authorize the use or reproduction of any part of this book in any manner
for the purpose of training artificial intelligence technologies or systems.
The publisher expressly reserves this book from the Text and Data Mining
exception in accordance with Article 4(3) of the European Union
Digital Single Market Directive 2019/790.

Visit **www.picador.com** to read more about
all our books and to buy them.

CONTENTS

1. Reunion — 3
2. Fortunes — 19
3. Grand Opening — 51
4. Premonition — 75
5. Springtime of Youth — 103
6. Touchstone — 123
7. One Big Happy Family — 165
8. Initiation — 225
9. Business Is Booming — 257
10. Borderline — 321
11. Blackout — 345
12. Back to Square One — 379
13. Yellow Falling — 411

SISTERS IN YELLOW

ONE

REUNION

1.

I used to think I'd never forget her, no matter where I ended up, no matter how many years passed, no matter what happened to me.

But once I saw her name in that article on the web, I realized I'd forgotten everything about her—her name, her existence, the time we'd spent together, what we'd done, and of course the fact I'd believed I'd never forget her.

Kimiko Yoshikawa.

For a second, I wondered if maybe it was somebody with the same name, but I couldn't shake the feeling that it was the Kimiko I used to know.

> Kimiko Yoshikawa, 60, an unemployed Shinjuku resident, appeared in Tokyo District Court on Dec. 23 for her first public hearing. Yoshikawa has been charged with blackmail, abduction, and battery. She allegedly confined the victim—a woman in her twenties from Ichikawa, Chiba—to a room in her Shinjuku apartment, where she battered the young woman over a 15-month period. During the arraignment, Yoshikawa invoked her right to remain silent. Her attorney entered a plea of not guilty on her behalf.
>
> In opening remarks, the prosecution stated that the vic-

tim moved in with Yoshikawa in 2017 after a period of prolonged housing instability. The two initially lived together without incident, but the defendant began to take control of the woman's personal belongings and social life, monitoring her movements. On multiple occasions, the defendant threatened the victim, telling her she'd 'never survive on her own' and subsequently breaking her will to escape. She was eventually locked in the apartment under the defendant's control and was repeatedly beaten and forced to follow the defendant's orders. The incident came to light last May, when the woman escaped and alerted the authorities.

I read the article three times, and once I had, I tried to exhale the huge lump that had formed deep in my chest. My fingers were trembling. It was her. Kimiko. It had to be her.

I searched the name "Kimiko Yoshikawa," which brought up one similar article, and another report just a few lines long, both detailed with only the bare minimum. My other returns were websites suggesting names for baby girls or offering fortune-telling based on the kanji in a given name. On the internet, my Kimiko didn't exist outside the information I'd already found.

I tried to put my thoughts in order. I went back to the page I'd first read and checked the date: January 10, 2020. Three months ago. And the article said the incident itself took place last year, in May 2019.

No matter how carefully I read, I couldn't wrap my head around that day, that year. I understood that it had been three months since Kimiko's first court date, but I didn't understand what that meant for the victim and the others involved. How had they been affected? How had everything unfolded in court? What would happen to Kimiko? Where could I go to find out?

I had no idea how police investigations or prisons worked. What came to mind were bleak gray cells, handcuffs, stone-faced judges, courtroom sketches—ham-fisted scenes I'd seen on crime shows or in the news.

And Kimiko's face.

Kimiko the way she looked those few years we'd lived together, back when I was young, some twenty years ago. The article said she was sixty. I couldn't believe it. Of course, two decades *had* passed. I was forty now, but attaching the number sixty to Kimiko's name seemed somehow unreal.

I closed my eyes and told myself I'd be okay. I had nothing to do with what had happened in Kimiko's Shinjuku apartment. There was nothing to worry about. I didn't know what Kimiko had been doing these past twenty years, we weren't in contact—in no sense did we have anything to do with each other. All that was long past, finished. Whatever else she'd done wasn't public knowledge—I couldn't find any articles on her besides the one about this incident. Not on the internet, at least. *It's okay*, I told myself over and over. *It'll be okay.*

When I finally looked up from my phone, I was surprised to find the room heavy with the deepening blue of evening, the shadows around me growing thicker. On my low table was a plate of spaghetti topped with boil-in-bag Bolognese—untouched. In the drawing gloom of night, the pasta no longer looked like food.

I kept waking up that night, and when morning came, I'd barely slept.

Backlit by the spring morning sunlight, my curtains looked like giant sheets of white construction paper. I closed my eyes against their brightness and watched colors appear and burst behind my eyelids. Dark blue, deep red, yellow—and then Kimiko's face appeared.

She gathered her long unruly hair in a black tail and said with a smile, I've got so much hair I bet I could hide a whole black cat in here. I laughed—we all did. That old house. Its small rooms, clutter everywhere except the entryway, which was always neat and tidy. The rule was you could only have two pairs of shoes out front because the entryway was where good luck entered and the bathroom was where it exited, which meant both of those parts of the house always had to be immaculate.

I closed my eyes and tossed and turned, trying to shake off the images in my head. But things I'd long forgotten to even remember came back to me one by one, as if linked hand in hand. The squeak of the warped hallway floors became our laughter and the swirl of the familiar woodgrain on the ceiling became someone's cigarette smoke. My memories were whispering to me.

Makeup left scattered in front of the mirror, cheap particle board furniture stuffed with clothes and underthings in the closet, baskets stacked full of cup ramen in our little kitchen. The images awoke even the scent of the days when we'd lived there.

I lay curled in bed worrying for about half an hour before I finally sent a message to our work group chat.

—*Good morning, everyone. This is Ito. I've had a cough since yesterday. I don't have a fever, but just to be on the safe side, I think I'd better take the day off. I hope that's okay.*

The person in charge of scheduling wrote back right away.

—*Understood. We'll be deciding on COVID policies at the beginning of next week, so I'll keep you updated. Given everything that's going on, I also need to let management know you're not feeling well. Feel better soon!*

—*Thank you! I think it's probably a normal cold, but if I get a fever, I'll let you know right away. Thanks again.*

Until the middle of last month, people still didn't quite believe how quickly the virus might spread. There were a lot of opinions flying around, and most people said it was basically the flu, so there was no need to be scared, no need to wear a mask. It felt like the world was suspended between nerves and bizarre excitement, but life was still well within the bounds of normalcy.

But between the end of February and beginning of March, as news from overseas grew more and more terrifying, rumors of Japan's own lockdown finally started flying.

And then five days ago, the government declared a national state of emergency, and the tension that had been gradually building burst. The virus was no longer just a story on the news—there was panic-buying in the supermarkets. Masks, hand sanitizer, disinfectants, and toilet paper vanished from the drugstore shelves, and soon after, people disappeared from the streets. All kinds of new measures were put in place where I worked. I had a part-time job as a salesclerk at a take-out deli run by a major supermarket. We had locations throughout the city, but my branch was in the shopping district a few minutes' walk from my apartment.

Ours was a small shop, with about thirty sides and salads in lines across the counter and in the cold case. Customers could choose what they wanted, and we'd pack their choices into plastic containers for carryout. We only sold the food—everything was made fresh off-site at a central facility each morning, so we didn't even have a galley kitchen, and the deli space itself was so small it couldn't fit more than four people at a time. In the three years I'd worked there, the menu had never once changed, and I began to wonder if the people who stopped by day in and day out—we had a lot of regulars—ever got tired of our food, but in fact, the monotony seemed to give them a sense of comfort. Our sales were good, and our shop was so popular we always had a line out the door at lunch- and dinnertime. By late last month, though, you could tell something was off: most of our customers disappeared, and when they did show up, they got into arguments about whether to wear masks—we even got phone calls complaining that we weren't taking enough measures to protect customers in the store.

Tucked into my futon, I thought about how maybe I shouldn't have messaged my coworkers that I had a cough. Why had I lied? What was I thinking, saying I had a cough at a time like this? I had no idea.

After a moment, I picked up my phone again, went back to the article about Kimiko, and slowly reread the whole thing. My mood grew even darker, and my limbs felt heavy. I decided I was glad I'd taken the day off, even if I hadn't used the best excuse. In my current state, I didn't think I could manage even something as simple as standing behind the sales counter.

I climbed out of bed, grabbed a bottle of barley tea from the fridge, and drank it down. Then I went to the closet and pulled a large shoebox down from the shelf.

The corners of the box were squished, and its lid was slightly torn; it was filled with old letters, notebooks, and datebooks.

Long ago, it had contained a pair of high heels my mother bought somewhere or other, but its sides, once dark blue, were now completely faded. I remembered my mother putting on those spotless white shoes and prancing around in them, not a care for the tatami mats. She was so happy that she kept wearing them, even once we sat down on the floor for our meal of instant ramen. I asked her for the empty shoebox and filled it with notes from school friends, clippings from manga and magazines, and stickers. Any time I found something I wanted to hold on to, I put it in the box. I'd moved a lot over the years, leaving things behind, losing them, but somehow the box remained. I didn't normally take it down to look through its contents, though. Seeing it now, I felt like it wasn't mine, that I'd inherited it from someone else, but something had compelled me to keep it all these years.

I opened the lid and found my navy flip phone and its charger in one corner of the box. The phone was what I was looking for, but seeing it made my heart skip a beat. Wondering if it would still work, I connected it to the charger and plugged the charger into an outlet. I waited thirty minutes and then held the power button. Slowly, the little screen brightened, coming back to life, and the phone chimed.

I'd changed my phone number and cut my old ties in the hopes that no one would find me, but I'd left my old friends' contact information in here. Maybe somehow I'd known that I might need them again.

There were only seventeen people in the address book.

Kimiko's name was in the K's. I scrolled down from there until I found Ran Kato and selected her name to see the phone number. Next, I went to the M's—Momoko. Momoko Tamamori. I made a memo of both numbers in my smartphone.

I didn't know where Ran Kato and Momoko Tamamori were or what they were doing now.

The last time I saw them was when they were leaving that house. We'd all been twenty, or thereabouts. I hadn't contacted either of them even once since then. If I hadn't stumbled across the article about Kimiko yesterday, I might not have even remembered they existed.

The time we'd spent together in that house came back to life, the voices and faces playing out on the screen of my mind, a mess of clips spliced together, dropping in and out of focus. I didn't think either of their phone numbers would still be working, and I didn't actually want to speak to either of them. But they were the only ones I could talk to about Kimiko. Only they could share the unease I was now feeling.

Because I was afraid that Kimiko might have blabbed about our time with her.

Maybe during the police investigation of Kimiko's apartment, they'd found evidence from back when we lived together, and even now, behind closed doors, they were making inquiries about Ran, Momoko, and me. The thought of it made me antsy. Nobody had come for me yet, but there was a chance they'd contacted Ran and Momoko for questioning first.

Logically, what we had done was probably already outside the statute of limitations. The punishment might not be all that severe. The three of us had been young, and we'd been acting under Kimiko's orders. But then what about Kotomi? Whose fault was it that she was dead? Could we really say we had nothing to do with her death?

The more I thought about it, the more an elusive, uneasy fear weighed down on me. Dread pressed silently down on me, like a giant sheet of iron, until tears threatened. What should I do? Should I pretend I never saw the article in the first place, lose Ran's and Momoko's numbers, and keep my mouth shut? Or should I maybe tell the police what I knew?

My imagination ballooned with worse and worse scenarios,

blotting out everything in sight. How were Ran and Momoko? What were they even doing now, and where? I knew their old phone numbers wouldn't work. But since they wouldn't work, there was no harm in calling . . . I set my phone down next to me and covered my head with the duvet as though that would erase everything. With the afternoon light blocked out, I blinked dimly, studying the humid, dark warmth of spring. And then I nodded off.

I know I dreamed, but the contents escape me—all I know is that it was a bad dream. Why is it, I wonder, that I always know it's a bad dream, even when I don't remember who I saw or what I did and only know that I dreamed. Like a dark, unstoppable wave, the nightmare chased me down. When I woke up, my chest and back were drenched in sweat. And then I called Ran Kato.

The phone rang six times before she answered with a bright "Hello?" I could feel my jaw trembling with nerves.

"Yes, hello. Is this . . . Ran Kato?"

"Yes," she replied in a voice that had grown deeper. It was Ran. I couldn't believe it.

"Oh, uh, this is Hana."

"Hana?"

"Yes, um, Hana Ito? We lived together, a long time ago."

After a shocked silence, Ran said, "Hana? *That* Hana?"

"Yes, *that* Hana. Sorry to call you out of the blue like this." I switched my phone to my other hand and pressed it hard against my ear. "I honestly didn't think the number would work. I really am sorry."

"What's happened? How did you get my number?"

"I had a copy of it in my old phone."

"Oh."

I heard her sigh.

"I'm sure this is a surprise to you. Sorry about that."

"No, it's not that . . . I just can't quite believe it. It's been so long."

"It has. Sorry. I'm actually calling you about Kimiko."

I could hear children laughing raucously beyond Ran. The sound of women chatting, too. The noises grew more distant, and I knew Ran was moving away from them.

"When you say Kimiko, you mean *that* Kimiko?"

"Yeah."

"What about her?"

"I found an article about an incident involving her yesterday."

"What?"

"On the internet."

"What exactly do you mean by 'incident'?"

"She was arrested. I was shocked, too. The trial's already begun, and I know it's a long shot, but I was worried it might have something to do with us, so I wanted to talk with you—"

"Hold on a minute," Ran interrupted. "What is this? I don't understand what you're talking about. Why was she arrested? And how would that have anything to do with us? Did she talk?"

"No, nothing like that, but Kimiko, apparently she was keeping a girl locked in her apartment, and she hurt the girl, and that's why she was arrested. It's probably . . . the same as back then, but this time she got caught. And if they start poking into her past, all of that might, you know, might come out. I don't know if that's actually going to happen, but it freaked me out." I bit the bullet and asked her, "Has anyone . . . contacted you? The police, or anyone like that?"

"Of course not." Ran laughed like she thought I'd said something stupid, but her tone was also faintly uneasy.

"I've been worried about it since yesterday, and I've been wondering if maybe I should go in and talk to the police."

"What?" Ran sounded surprised. "Talk to the police? About what?"

"About back then, about the things I know about Kimiko."

"You've got to be kidding me." Ran had lowered her voice, but somehow her tone was more forceful. But then I heard someone call Ran's name, and she called back "Okay!" in a cheery voice.

"Listen, I've got a guest who's just showed up."

"Of course. Sorry to have bothered you."

"Hana, where are you living? Tokyo?"

"Yeah."

"Maybe we should meet up and have a chat. I know it's hard with corona and everything . . . but I think it would be better if we didn't talk about this over the phone."

"Yeah, I think we should definitely do that . . . Oh, Momoko, I have her number, too, I don't know if it works yet, but I should call her, right, see if she can come?"

"Don't bother," Ran curtly replied.

"Why?"

"I'll tell you when I see you. But Hana? Don't, under any circumstances, go to the police. Okay?"

"Okay."

We picked a place and time to meet and then hung up.

2.

Ran carried herself differently now than she had twenty years ago.

She was still as small as I remembered, but she'd put on some weight, which made her body look somehow unbalanced. If she hadn't seen me first and raised her hand to catch my attention, I would have had a hard time recognizing her, even though there was almost no one in the café.

Ran wore a puffy cotton ecru tunic and a mask so large it hid almost half her face. Her low ponytail was dyed light brown, but white hairs at her hairline caught the light and glowed, revealing a haphazard root touch-up. There was still a hint of her old self around her eyes though, swept with a confident brown eyeshadow and a thick layer of mascara.

Her forehead was as narrow as ever, and I was reminded of one late night where the three of us—Ran, Momoko, and I—had measured and compared our foreheads, our eyes, all the parts of our faces. Ran had liked makeup even back then. I knew next to nothing about that sort of thing, and she'd laughingly wondered how her techniques would change the way I looked. She tried a slew of products on me, and when she was done, the three of us looked at my face and exploded with laughter. Seeing Ran before me now, remembering how we'd been back then, I was overwhelmed by how much time had passed, and I felt a twinge deep in my heart.

We didn't exchange the kinds of cheerful pleasantries used to greet an old friend. No "Long time no see" or "How have you been?" We just ordered our drinks. With her mouth hidden behind her mask, I couldn't make out Ran's expression, but she had the air of someone working to move not even a muscle, and in that stillness, we were silent.

After our two iced coffees arrived, I tried to start the conversation by saying I was glad Ran had recognized me, but she replied curtly that she knew it was me because I was dithering at the entrance. She'd been fidgeting with her phone, but now she stopped and removed her mask. Her brick-red lipstick had smeared on the inside.

"So, about Kimiko," Ran began, "what did she do? I tried to search for information, but I couldn't find anything."

Ran asked as though she was carrying on our conversation from the phone; she didn't seem particularly nervous.

"Was it on the news? Did it seem really bad?"

"Not exactly." I'd bookmarked the article on the website, so I pulled it up now and handed it over to Ran. She studied the phone intently, scrolled down, and then again gazed at the screen.

"How did you find this?" she asked when she was done, sliding the phone back across the table to me.

"I was reading an article about some other incident on Yahoo, and you know at the bottom it'll suggest all these articles about similar things, right? Same kind of content, stuff from years ago, links to local newspapers from places you've never heard of, and there were these links. And I was just clicking through the links over and over, and I came across this one."

"Shinjuku, huh . . . not Sancha." Ran furrowed her brows. "It said Kimiko was sixty. I guess that means she was forty back then, right. About the same age as us now."

"Yeah."

"Now that I look back on it, she was completely nuts," Ran spat. "I can't believe her. I mean, imagine if we started picking up twenty-year-old girls and living with them like that now. Absolutely crazy." She shook her head. "Back when we were living together—I mean, I guess we did do some pretty sketchy things. But we were what, twenty? It was a long time ago. I don't think there's any way it would come back to haunt us now."

"But what if her apartment, if there are things . . . like a stack of cards from back then, I was thinking if the police found those and asked her what they were. And if she talked, they might still question us about what happened, even if they don't plan on charging us with anything. We're probably past the statute of limitations, but what we did, it's . . . we don't know what might blow up into a problem."

"So you thought you'd go to the police and tell them you knew her way back when and that you have information?" Ran's eyes widened with shock. "You're overthinking things."

"You think so?"

"Absolutely. You're getting carried away. And it's not like what we did was that big of a deal, you know? That's what I think. Definitely not something you should be worrying yourself sick over two decades down the line. Kids now do way worse things than we ever did then."

"Are you sure?"

"Positive." She thought a moment and said, "And besides, she made us do it."

"But Kotomi died, and I still don't know what actually happened, but I feel like we got her involved, and with the way things ended—"

"Which one was Kotomi? Oh"—Ran nodded—"the hostess from that club in Ginza where you were side hustling."

"Right."

"No, no, that's got nothing to do with us. That was on her . . . Don't you remember what happened? I mean, her death was a shock, but . . . Wait, don't tell me you still think it was your fault."

"Well, no, but . . ." I shook my head.

"Of course it's not. Those people were crazy." Ran shrugged. "That's why you should just relax. Turn that frown upside down. Don't look at me like that. There's no point in worrying about something that happened so long ago it's already basically forgotten, dead and buried. Of course you were upset when you came across Kimiko's name. You weren't expecting to be reminded of her. And her keeping a girl like that, kind of a similar situation, I know. I get it. But I'm telling you, it's okay. If you're worried about a worst-case scenario, just remember the police already have her. I mean, that stuff from before, you're better off forgetting it. We were young and stupid, let's keep our skeletons in the closet."

"Keep our skeletons in the closet."

"Exactly. And shouldn't you be more worried about corona anyway? How's it been for you? My kids' school got canceled, and it's absolute hell. This whole virus is awful. You doing okay?"

"Well, I . . ." I took a deep breath through my nose. "I guess it's been fine for me. I live alone."

Ran stirred her iced coffee with her straw and nodded along. We were in a café in front of Jiyugaoka Station. Ran was apparently living somewhere along the Toyoko Line, and she'd told me this place was convenient because she could get here without any line changes, and the trains came often. The café was part of a chain, and its facade was floor-to-ceiling glass. Ran hadn't bothered to ask me where I was living, what I was doing, or what I'd done after everything happened.

"There's almost nobody out. Normally it's so crowded. I guess everyone's keeping themselves at home."

It was true that there were only a handful of people on the

street outside the café, though that might also have been because the sky had been heavy and overcast all day, throwing the whole neighborhood into sunken darkness.

"But time comes for us all. I mean, we're already forty. I didn't think I'd ever see you again. We said our goodbyes and kind of scattered."

"You never changed your number, so I was wondering, did Kimiko ever try and get in touch with you after that?"

"No," Ran said. "I can't say I remember everything from back then, and I don't want to either . . . Remember we were all so confused and flustered when we left? And that was the last time. But I feel like it must have been worse for you, Hana. You were the one she liked the most. I mean, can you imagine being trapped like that, terrifying. She was totally nuts. We were so young, just kids, really, and we had no idea what we were doing, it really is awful."

"Um, I know I mentioned it on the phone, but about Momoko . . . You said I shouldn't bother trying to get in touch. Did something happen?" I asked.

"Oh, Momoko." Ran shook her head. "Do you remember how she had that terrifying little sister. The one that was drop-dead gorgeous, but her teeth were so disgusting you wanted to die. She came by sometimes? Well, Momoko had a huge fight with her and her boyfriend over money, and after that, Momoko went missing, though I don't know all the details. I just heard the rumors. After we left, I kept in touch with Momoko for a while, but then she disappeared."

I sighed.

Ran's voice grew louder, as though she were practicing lines for a play or something. "We were mixed up with a bunch of crazy people, huh. We had no idea what we were doing." Her exaggerated voice rang through the café. Almost no one was inside, and the few customers they did have were alone, everyone wearing a mask. From a speaker somewhere in the ceiling came the faint sounds of bossa nova. From the sink behind the counter,

I could hear the clinking of plates being washed and the voices of the staff talking to each other. None of the other customers were speaking. An older man sitting in a chair a few tables down opened his newspaper with a loud rustle, and my eyes met his when he glanced our way. I took a sip of water and checked the mask dangling from my jaw with the tips of my fingers.

"Anyway, what's done is done. I'll say it again, that was a long time ago. It's in the past. You don't need to be worrying about it, okay, Hana? And Hana?" She met my eyes, unblinking. "Do not, under any circumstances, go to the police, okay? There's no point in it. I am a hundred percent sure it would be nothing but trouble for you. So I'm counting on you to not do it, okay? We're good, right, now that we've talked it over here today? So just forget about it, seriously."

I nodded.

"We're good, right?"

"Yeah."

And then we fell into a lengthy silence. Ran hunched over her drink, staring at a single spot on the table. I could see the fatigue in her expression. I felt like I must have something else I needed to tell her now that we were together again, something important. And maybe she was feeling that same need. But I didn't know what it was I needed to say or how to find the right words to say it.

"Well, I think I'd better head out. Oh, and Hana." Ran straightened as though to shake it off. As she readjusted her mask, she continued, "Could you erase my number? I'll be sure to erase my history of your calls and texts."

I couldn't speak, and in the face of my silence, Ran checked the receipt, left money for her coffee on the table, put her bag over her shoulder, and stood up.

"Well then, I'm off. Try not to get corona."

With those parting words, Ran left the café, but even once she was gone, I couldn't quite bring myself to leave. There were things I should have been thinking about, but my mind wasn't working. I didn't feel like eating, but I hadn't had anything since that morning, so I should've been hungry—I wondered if I should order something.

As I glanced over the little pictures on the menu, I heard something unexpected. A distant rumbling, as though something huge were trundling along, though what it was, I couldn't say. After a few moments, I realized it was a peal of thunder. Just as I glanced through the glass storefront, rain came pounding down, all at once. The raindrops were so large I felt like I could see each of them individually as they passed through my field of vision, and I watched as the people walking along the street covered their heads with bags or their hands and made a run for it. The rain grew even heavier, beating down on the asphalt and on the awning of the store diagonal to the café, bouncing back into the air again, sending up a faint white vapor.

TWO

FORTUNES

1.

It was summer when I first met Kimiko. I was fifteen at the time.

One morning, not long after the start of what was going to be my final summer vacation of junior high, I woke up to find a strange woman sleeping next to me on the futon where my mom was supposed to be.

I couldn't see her face. She was wearing my mom's pajamas, but I could tell right away that the woman snoring soundly with her back to me was not my mom.

Propping myself up on my elbow, I pulled away for a moment, then decided that it was no big deal and went back to sleep. My mom worked at a small bar not too far from where we lived, and this wasn't the first time she'd brought home friends and girls from work to stay the night.

The next time I woke up, the woman was nowhere to be seen. Instead, the pajamas she'd been wearing were neatly placed on top of the futon, which had been folded up. They were the same old pajamas my mom had been sleeping in for years, but now they looked pristine, like they were on display at a store. I couldn't take my eyes off them.

We always hung our clothes and underwear to dry on the curtain rod over the window, and we'd just grab whatever we wanted to wear when we needed them. Our room was messy and littered with junk, so the corner with the futon and the pajamas had a gravity all its own, like someone had taken a piece of pencil-smudged notebook paper and carefully erased one white spot.

My mom and I lived in a small town at the edge of Higashimurayama in a cramped, run-down tenement house hidden away from the main street.

In between a pair of detached houses facing the street was a gravel path about three meters wide. To find the entrance to our building, you had to head down that path and then turn left. The front was so old and dirty you could barely make out the writing over the door: "Evergreen Hills." The entryway always made me think of some ominous cave, and the hallway it led to was lit with nothing but a few dingy bulbs, so it was always dark, no matter how sunny it was outside.

Evergreen Hills was a two-story wooden building. Both floors had four identical rooms, but the only person living in the building, aside from my mom and me, was the middle-aged landlady, who occupied one of the back units upstairs. The sliding wooden doors separating the units were so flimsy even a child could kick them down, and each unit had a small entryway. Beyond that was a kitchenette, and then two rooms one after another, each about four-and-a-half tatami mats. At the end of the first floor was a communal bathroom, though we were the only people using it. We were surrounded by buildings on all sides, so even when we had the windows open, all we could see was a wall of concrete. We barely got any light.

Mom rented both units on the first floor: one to the right and one to the left as you entered the building. Most of the time, Mom and I were on the right-hand side.

The one to the left was supposed to be my dad's, but it never felt like anybody lived there. Other than a TV set and some bedding, there was nothing in there—only some clothes hanging in the closet. After all, my dad never stayed home for long, even when he was around.

At the time, I had no idea what he did for work. He was tanned and well-built, so he must have been working construction or driving trucks or doing some sort of day labor that called him away for long stretches. (I remember one time in elementary school I heard him call my name from some big truck as I was walking home.) For a while, he brought friends over—men dressed in the same kind of work clothes—and they'd have yakiniku, or maybe hot pot, and drink sake. But those nights soon came to an end.

Whenever my dad did come around, he was always nice. He'd bring me things: a badminton set, stuffed animals he must have gotten at an arcade, things like that. Sometimes he'd come home in the middle of the night, wake me up, and say, "Hey, you're gonna love this," and feed me pieces of sushi.

I didn't have anything against my dad. But I spent so little time with him that I never knew what to say—so when he was home, I'd get weirdly nervous and self-conscious. I couldn't wait for him to leave again. I also worried that he could tell how I felt. I knew he wasn't a normal father, but on some level, I felt like maybe it was unfair of me to think about him that way. The whole situation made me feel bad about myself.

By the time I was in my last year or two of elementary school, my dad came around less and less, then not at all. Where he went, what happened to him, to this day I have no idea. I only found out later on, but apparently he had another home, another family, somewhere else.

My mom was easygoing, so I could more or less do what I wanted, but she didn't offer me much in the way of family life. She liked having fun and drinking, even though she couldn't hold her liquor. She had lots of friends and always just went with the flow. Way back when, she went to a technical high school in the neighborhood, and after graduating, she started working full-time at a nylons factory. She used to brag about how she was the leg model when the higher-ups came from the main office to visit the factory. But she only stayed at that job for a few years. She found work at a hole-in-the-wall bar in town with some friends, then moved on to another, then another—that was when she had me.

Even as her daughter, I could tell she wasn't a typical mom. She was petite and looked a whole lot younger than the other kids' moms at school. There was something childlike about her face, and she was always smiling, optimistic, and upbeat, though every time she drank, it made her cry. Not for any real reason though. I guess you could say she was an emotional drinker, somebody who couldn't separate drinking, having a good time, and bursting into tears.

I never heard her complain or say anything bad about my dad. But she didn't seem particularly attached to him either. Even after he disappeared, she didn't seem fazed. Now and then, she'd tell me stories about how terrible her own mother had been before they stopped talking, but always in a lighthearted way, and only after she'd drunk enough to get sentimental.

What my mom liked was company. People were always hanging out at our place: hostesses from the bars where she worked, friends her customers had introduced her to, or local friends she'd known for years. When nobody else was around, and it was just me and her, I always got nervous. As a rule, we didn't see much of each other though. My mom slept while I was at school, woke up in the afternoon, put her makeup on, and headed out to work in the evening, then came home in the middle of the night.

There was only one other kid in the neighborhood whose home life was similar to mine, and we got along well. From the time we were in elementary school, the two of us didn't have a curfew like the other kids. Other kids had to be home in time for dinner or weren't allowed to go certain places—and their parents apparently didn't want their children spending any more time with us than they had to. Other kids were definitely not allowed to come over to our houses to play. I had another close friend at school, but she was always running off with the other kids as soon as the last bell rang. I remember I asked her why one time. At first, she was reluctant, but then she told me, "My parents said weird grown-ups are always coming over to your house. They say I'm not allowed to go because your family's not normal." Well, that wasn't some baseless rumor or horrible lie—it was the truth. And there wasn't anything I could do about it.

When I got to middle school, I started to notice things by my friends' faces, by their attitudes. I could tell right away which kids were from normal homes and which ones weren't. It was like we were wearing different-colored hats. In a normal home, you wouldn't wake up in the morning to find a woman you've never seen before sleeping in the futon next to yours. The sight of neatly folded bedding and pajamas probably wouldn't make you feel all warm inside. It wouldn't leave you so spellbound you wouldn't know how to look away.

I folded up my own futon, doing it the same way the woman had, then set it next to hers. I was alone in the room, and there wasn't anybody in the kitchenette either. I slipped into my sandals, hopped across the hallway, and opened the door to the other unit. Inside, the TV was on full blast. When I stepped in, I saw the woman sprawled out on the floor, back to the door, watching a talk show. The head of our ancient electric fan rotated slowly to the right, then back to the left, creaking loudly every now and then.

Noticing I'd come in, the woman turned her head and gave me a big smile, though she didn't get up. Her expression was so natural that I wondered if she was somebody I'd met before. But she wasn't—she'd apparently slept the whole night next to me, but this was the first time I'd seen her face. A second later, she went back to looking at the screen, her shoulders shaking as she laughed at the talk show. I stood still at the threshold between the kitchenette and the room, watching the TV, the fan, and the woman.

"Wanna eat something?" the woman asked me, stretching. The show was over. It had just gone to commercials. "I'm starving."

We went over to the kitchenette to make some instant ramen. She was taller than I was, and her arms and legs were really long. Her wild, raven-black hair was gathered loosely behind her neck, and the ends fanned out over her giant white T-shirt, which had something written in English on it. Standing at a slight distance, I watched the water heat inside the aluminum saucepan.

The woman ripped into the packages, tipped the noodles into the water, and separated them with a pair of chopsticks. Then she poured in the seasoning packets, mixed everything together, and divided the meal evenly into the two bowls I'd set out. She tried to peel off a wonton stuck to the edge of the pan, but couldn't manage with her disposable chopsticks, so in a cheery voice she said, "Forget it. I'll bring the whole thing over," motioning toward the room. I pulled over the stripped kotatsu that had been resting against the wall, and we sat down across from each other and slurped.

"It's summer vacation, right? You going anywhere?"

I hummed vaguely, not a real yes or no. I hadn't been feeling the summer heat a moment ago, but suddenly I broke out in a sweat. I reached over and turned the air conditioner on to high.

"You and Ai aren't going anywhere?"

Ai was my mom's name.

"Not really . . . we don't go places."

"Huh . . . Hey, what's your name? Mine's Kimiko."

"I'm Hana."

"Hana . . . Who gave you that name? Ai?"

"I . . . I don't know," I answered in a small voice.

"Oh, okay."

"You're, um, my mom's friend, right?"

"Uh-huh."

That's where the conversation stopped, and we went back to eating our ramen in silence. There was a game show on TV, and the old AC unit wheezed away. I heard the faint sound of an ambulance outside, drawing closer for a moment, then fading into the distance.

"How do you write 'Hana'? Do you have a Chinese character for that?"

"Just the normal one. Flower."

"For my name, it's 'ki' like yellow, 'mi' like beauty, and the usual 'ko,' like child."

I nodded, as vague an answer as before, and lifted my bowl to drink the broth. Bowl in both hands, I looked over at Kimiko. She had already finished eating and was resting her elbow on the table. Our eyes met, and I had to turn away. But again, I stole a few more glances at Kimiko's face over the top of my bowl. She didn't look like any other woman I'd ever seen before.

Obviously, every person has a unique face, but there was something so captivating about hers, something I couldn't quite explain with my middle school vocabulary. Even though she'd just gotten out of bed and was barefaced, she looked striking: full eyebrows, defined double eyelids, long, thick eyelashes, eyes and brows close together. I was drawn to her prominent nose and the wisps of hair from her temples down to her ears, damp with sweat and curled up in little rings.

More than beauty or a pretty face, what I saw in her face was strength.

She reminded me of the hero from a popular girls' manga series I loved to read in elementary school. Part of it was set in ancient Egypt, so the main character was a dashing young pharaoh. Watching Kimiko crack her neck and rearrange herself in front of the TV, I could almost see the pharaoh's lines appearing in a speech bubble over her head, the whole scene contained within an inky black frame. The thought made me smile.

"I could really go for a soda. Wanna come?" Kimiko asked when she came back from putting the bowls in the sink. We didn't freshen up to head out, just walked down the street to the nearest convenience store.

"You guys have two units, but you still sleep in one, huh?"

"Where we ate the ramen, we call that the TV room. We keep the futons in the other one, and that's where we sleep."

"So you have a separate living room, nice."

"It's not that fancy," I said, looking at the ground.

"Well, who wants to sleep alone, right?"

The rays of the summer sun were so piercing I had to squint, and I could sense the heat sinking deeper into my skin with every breath I took.

Evergreen Hills was right behind my middle school.

We followed the gray wall surrounding the school for a couple of minutes and turned left at the corner, toward the school's main gate. The convenience store was right across the street. Students weren't allowed to go into the store in our uniforms, but it was a rule that everybody at school broke. The bright leaves of trees planted inside the school grounds climbed over the wall and cast deep blue shadows on the narrow strip of sidewalk asphalt.

As we got closer to the school gate, I could see a group of people there, talking and laughing. Some students came to school over the break—for clubs and things—but that wasn't what these people were doing. They were the delinquents—the bad kids.

Two of them were third-years, same as me. There were a bunch of other juvies with them, too, including a guy in tobi work pants with hair bleached the color of straw, and a girl who'd already graduated, her bleached hair shooting up from the top of her head like a fountain and her eyebrows as thin as insect antennae. I knew who she was. She was a famous rebel at our school, and the other kids were her usual crew.

The girl with the fountain hair hadn't gone on to high school, instead apparently getting involved with a motorcycle gang and some local guys who worked construction. She was also known for wearing oversized socks—"loose socks," we called them—all the time, no matter what. Loose socks with baggy tracksuits, loose socks with flip-flops. Some kids even said she wore loose socks to bed. She had the names of all the guys she'd ever been with tattooed on her arm and had an older sister who worked at a famous boutique at 109 in Shibuya. She was the kind of person people feared and respected.

I did what I could to avoid making eye contact with them, but one of the girls from my year saw me and started shouting. I didn't say anything back, just kept my mouth shut tight and my eyes on the ground. Their lives at home weren't that different from mine, but I hadn't gone bad the way they had. At the same time, I was obviously nothing like the other kids who studied and went to cram school, who ate meals with their families and went on vacation. In school and out, I was the kind of kid everybody avoided and felt sorry for at the same time.

On top of that, our apartment was really close to school, so most of my classmates knew where I lived. Some of them even came to spy on me—just for fun—to see how old and dirty our building was. Of course, the kids at school weren't all from families with money. Lots of them lived in huge housing complexes or cheap apartment buildings, but there weren't any other kids who lived in a tenement house like mine, with a shared toilet and no baths or showers—at least not anybody in my grade.

"Friends of yours?" Kimiko asked with a smile.

"No, not really."

"I think they're talking to you."

"No, they're not."

"Oh, okay."

We went into the convenience store, and Kimiko picked out the soda she wanted, grabbed a basket, threw in some bags of potato chips and dried squid, then said to me, "Hey, get whatever you want. They've got ice cream." I was only tagging along so she could get something to drink, so I hadn't brought any money for myself. Besides, the heckling from the kids across the street had put me in a dark mood. I was surrounded by ice cream and juice, but I didn't want any of it.

"Hey, did your mom tell you she might not come home for a bit?" Kimiko asked as she riffled through the plastic packages lining the baked goods aisle.

"No."

"How do you guys stay in touch? Pagers?"

"Yeah, but I can call her at work if I need to," I said. "You mean, she's not going to be at work for a while either?"

"It sounded like she was going on a trip or something. She said she'd give you a call. Hey, what do you do for food?"

"Oh... um, there's ramen, and..."

"What do you do for money?"

"We have a can at home, and I just use what my mom puts in there."

"You don't run out?"

"No."

"You pay for electricity and everything out of that?"

"Yeah, when the bill comes in the mail."

When we left the store, the sun was beating down even brighter than it had when we'd gotten there.

There were more kids across the street now, and they were getting louder. For a second, I wondered if the scary guidance counselor was going to come out of the school and tell them to break it up, but it didn't look like that was about to happen. Some of the scarier teachers weren't afraid to rough up kids who got mouthy or gave them attitude, but even those teachers didn't mess with the kids who had gang connections or who actually fought back. With those kids, the same teachers would act like they weren't like other adults, like they got where students were coming from.

When my classmates saw me again, they started jumping around and laughing even louder than before.

"Hey, Bibinba!" they shouted.

I squeezed my eyes shut. I was naturally melanated and dark all year round, even though I didn't play sports and never went outside. Because of my tanned skin, some of the meaner kids at school called me Bibinba after a Sanrio character that had been popular in elementary school. (It didn't help that Bibinba sounded like *binbo*, which meant "poor," and those kids knew it, too.) When they saw me, in school or not, they'd hop up and down and act like they were holding spears as they gleefully chanted "Bibinba, Bibinba! Poor old Bibinbo!"

"Are they saying bibimbap? Like the food?" Kimiko asked me as she glanced in their direction.

I couldn't answer her—I couldn't even bring myself to shake my head. What they were doing was so immature, even elementary school kids wouldn't do it these days, but it still hurt me every time. In that moment, I was so embarrassed that Kimiko, somebody I'd just met, saw me for who I was, how I was treated, just like that. I was so ashamed that I wanted to vanish, right then and there. My face got hot, and I felt a prickle inside my nose. If I let go for even a second, the tears were going to come pouring out of my eyes. I walked on, staring at the toes popping out of my sandals, breathing out what I was holding inside, little by little.

"Bibinba! Hey, Bi-Bi-Bi-Bibinba!" One of them called, making a song out of it, and the rest of the kids burst out laughing. Normally they just ignored me. We lived in different worlds. So when they kept on coming after me that day, it came as a real surprise and I didn't know what to do. I kept on walking, pretending I couldn't hear them. I wanted to get away from them as quickly as I could.

When I finally reached the corner and snuck a look over my shoulder, Kimiko wasn't there.

Lifting my head to look back, I saw her crossing the street with the plastic bag from the store swinging in her hand. I was so shocked I almost jumped. What was she thinking? She walked right up to the group as naturally as if she'd been heading that way all along.

I gulped and craned my neck to try to see what was going on. While we were in the store, some other kids had shown up on motor scooters and custom bicycles with chopper handlebars. Some of them even seemed to be drinking or maybe huffing something and whooping excitedly. What if they beat her up? Or set her hair on fire with a lighter? How old was Kimiko anyway? My thoughts tangled up inside my head.

My heart was pounding so hard now I was sure it was about to pop, but the kids, who appeared skeptical at first, started to smile as if amused. Somehow, Kimiko looked like she was having a normal conversation with them. I couldn't see her face from where I was, but from the way she was standing, putting her weight on one foot, she seemed relaxed. A few minutes later, I even heard them laughing together. I started to wonder if maybe Kimiko knew one of them, but that couldn't be true.

I stood there under the bright white heat of the sun, watching as Kimiko and the kids talked and laughed, apparently enjoying themselves. It looked to me like they were welcoming this strange visitor, like they were enjoying having an adult show up and take an interest in them. They even looked kind of excited. After maybe ten minutes, Kimiko gave them a wave like she was saying, "See ya," then made her way over to where I was, shopping bag swinging once again. Behind Kimiko's back, I could see Loose Socks exaggeratedly thrusting her hands up, saying something that made everybody laugh. Kimiko smiled and waved back at them.

"Nice to be young," Kimiko said once she'd walked up to me, a grin on her face. "My soda's all warm now." She laughed loudly. Stray strands of her dark hair clung to her sweaty forehead and the back of her neck.

2.

I spent the next month living with Kimiko. It was my entire summer break.

My mom called now and then. She came home every once in a while, two, maybe three times. When she did, the three of us would eat sukiyaki together, then my mom would go off on another one of her trips.

She never really talked to me about it, but at the time she had a boyfriend, and she was staying at his place a lot. I didn't know his real name, but I knew that his friends called him Snoozy because he spoke and moved so slowly.

My mom had never been the perfect mother. But she'd never left the house for days or weeks straight before, so it scared me when Kimiko told me that she might not be coming back for a while. Kimiko was with me, though, so I adjusted to my mom not being around.

I couldn't tell if she had asked Kimiko to stay with me so she could go to her boyfriend's place without having to worry about me, or if there was some other reason Kimiko was there. Neither of them said anything about it. Three days after she showed up, Kimiko said she'd be back later and came back that evening with a big brown faux leather bag. That night, the two of us made pork belly on rice.

Kimiko and my mom had met out drinking a few years back, through Mama Junko, who ran the bar by the station where my mom worked. Kimiko and Mama Junko, who was almost sixty, had known each other for ages. I'd met Mama Junko a few times, too, but she always made me feel uncomfortable. Recently, Kimiko and my mom crossed paths again. Kimiko was thirty-five—two years younger than my mom. They'd never worked together.

I didn't really understand the relationship they shared, but it seemed to me like Kimiko looked up to my mom, and my mom was always looking after Kimiko. But maybe I only thought that way because I knew my mom was older. When I actually saw them talking, my mom was the one who was always complaining, venting about whatever was going on in her love life, gossiping about customers from the bar and the hostesses she worked with. She'd go on and on while Kimiko sat there, listening patiently and throwing in supportive comments. When they got together, my mom looked and acted even more childish and helpless than usual.

"Ai's the best, isn't she?" Kimiko said one night after we'd turned off the lights and gotten into bed. We put our futons next to each other and slept in the same room, just like my mom and I did. "She's so generous."

Before Kimiko, whenever my mom's friends and acquaintances came over and she wasn't home, every single one of them had said something critical about her. And they didn't just gossip about my mom; the things they said always made it sound like they felt bad for me, too. *You must be lonely, Hana. Ai's so fun, but she's not the most responsible person. It's not fair to you, Hana . . .* I never knew if these people had any kids of their own, but the lives they led weren't that different from my mom's. That's why they kept turning up at our house. But they all seemed to want to tell me that my mom was failing motherhood. And I could tell they were genuinely sorry for me, so I never knew how to respond.

Which is why I was caught off guard when Kimiko actually had something nice to say to me about my mom that night. I was tickled. "You . . . you think so?"

"Oh yeah," Kimiko said. "She's such a good person."

"A good person?"

"Yeah. And a good listener."

"I guess she is."

"Do you know what she's calling herself at the bar now?"

"She changed her name again?"

"Uh-huh. To Airu. 'Ai' is love, obviously, and 'ru' is tears."

"She's so picky about her names. But, wait, if she's going by Airu, that means people are still calling her Ai-chan, right? What's the point of changing it?"

"You're right, everyone's still calling her Ai-chan. But her astrology lady said that the number of strokes in a name really, really matters. Ai never messes around when it comes to that kind of thing, you know?"

"Yeah . . . What about you, Kimiko? Do you believe in stuff like that?"

Kimiko took a few seconds to think, then said, "Feng shui, maybe?"

"Feng shui? What's that?"

"It's the idea that all the directions, like north and south, have colors that are supposed to go with them. South goes with green, I think, and north goes with white."

"The colors have rules?"

"Yup."

"What happens when the right color goes with the right direction?"

"You invite good luck into your home."

"You do? To any home? What if it's a really small one, and not a real house?"

"I don't think it matters what kind of house it is," she said with a smile. "As long as you keep your entryway clean—and any rooms with running water, too. Oh, and don't forget yellow. When you put yellow in the west, that's supposed to attract money."

"The color yellow attracts money?" I said, bewildered.

"Sure does."

"Hey, Kimiko?"

"Yeah?"

"You have the character for yellow in your name, right? Do you think that gives you good luck with money?"

"I don't know," Kimiko laughed. "Maybe?"

"Do you think you'd be rich if you dyed your hair yellow and moved way out west somewhere?"

"I wonder."

Now I had to chuckle. The Kimiko I was picturing in my mind wasn't blonde. She had hair as yellow as the yellow in a box of crayons—like a kid's drawing of a lion, or maybe like a sunflower—and that made her eyes and eyebrows stand out even more.

In the dark, I tried to recall what colors we had around the house, but I couldn't remember any. It did occur to me, though, that the place had gotten cleaner and brighter since Kimiko came. Before, I only washed the dishes when the sink got full, and I left my dirty clothes on the floor until there wasn't enough space for me to lay out my futon. The landlady took care of the shared bathroom, and we never bothered to sweep the hallway. That was how we'd always lived. Kimiko, though, folded the clean laundry as soon as it was dry, and she always washed the dirty dishes and put them away as soon as we were done eating. The entryway looked a lot nicer, too. Whenever I got home and saw our sandals neatly lined up inside the door, I felt happy in a way I couldn't even express.

"Kimiko, do you think my mom and I should live somewhere else? Somewhere nicer?"

As I asked, I thought about the times kids from school followed me home to see where I lived.

"What do you think?"

"Sometimes I think we should."

"You do?"

"I know Mom's on her own, but I feel like we could make it work, if we tried harder, we could live somewhere else, somewhere more normal . . . a real apartment or something."

"Mmm."

"But mom is always spending money on other things. Like clothes. And drinking."

"Mmm, yeah."

"And her boyfriends."

"Hmm . . ."

"She doesn't care about where she lives. To her, a home is just a place to sleep. She hates moving, too. She doesn't see the point. This is what we've always had, you know? So why would we want anything else? But, yeah, home is the last thing on her mind. The very last thing. Well, she's never here anyway. She always has somewhere else to go. So I guess it makes sense for her, but . . ."

As I told Kimiko these things, things I'd never said to anybody, my cheeks grew hot.

Kimiko made a sound like she was waiting for me to continue, but I felt like I couldn't breathe and had to stop. I was glad it was night and the room was dark, so she couldn't see my face. I fell asleep without saying another word. In the morning, when I woke up, I saw Kimiko's folded futon and a wave of relief came over me. Then I closed my eyes and went right back to sleep.

The summer Kimiko and I spent together was like no summer I'd ever known before.

We fried karaage in the kitchenette, and she showed me how to add garlic to make it taste better. I'd learned how to make simple dishes so I could feed myself, but that was the first time I'd ever done anything with garlic. We held our fingers up to each other's noses, laughing at how smelly they were.

We took a lot of walks, too. Kimiko said she'd never spent so much time in my neighborhood before, even though she'd been to the bar where my mom worked lots of times to see Mama Junko. We'd walk to the station, which was thirty minutes away on foot, to look around the shops there, and when we were done, we'd keep going, down streets with nothing but houses on them, sweating away. No matter where we went, the summer sun was scorching, and if you were close enough, you could probably hear our skin sizzling under the heat. When we went out wandering like that, we'd stop by for a bath on the way back. We didn't have one particular place we went, though. It was fun to go to bathhouses we found while we were walking around. Kimiko would nod along no matter what I said, and whenever I told a joke, no matter how bad it was, she'd crack up. I'd always thought of myself as a shy, boring person, but when I was with Kimiko, I became somebody else, somebody happier. New, unexpected thoughts would pop into my mind, one after another, and I'd just keep on talking and laughing. At first, I felt like I was pretending to be someone else, but the more Kimiko smiled and laughed with me, the more I started to feel like maybe this was the real me.

We ate somen noodles a lot, or got bento at the store and brought them home. Sometimes Kimiko would take me to the izakaya by the station and let me eat all the yakitori I wanted. One time, she fed me sea grapes, umibudo, for the first time in my life. Kimiko never kept her money in a wallet. She carried her bills and coins loose in her pockets, and I was always worried they were going to fall out without her realizing.

Sometimes, when we were walking back from eating out, we'd go by the bar where my mom worked. We never went inside though. I could hear the karaoke music echoing through the walls, but I couldn't tell if it was Mom singing or not.

One night, the local shrine had a night market. I didn't feel like going because I thought I'd run into other kids from school, but Kimiko wanted to check it out, so we went.

As evening fell and gave way to night, the heat of the day faded and everything around me began to sparkle and shine. The red splotches of goldfish swimming in rippling water, the neon of the glow-in-the-dark bouncy balls, the soft clouds of cotton candy as sweet and fragile as memories, the sound of the pop guns at the shooting gallery, and the cheers from the crowd. The summer night filled the air with energy and a sense of wonder, and before I knew it, it had filled my heart, too.

Maybe because it was night and everyone was feeling carefree, kids from school were more friendly, coming up and actually speaking with me. All of us kids sat down on the stone steps together and ate shaved ice and other snacks we'd gotten from the stalls. When I first saw my schoolmates, Kimiko had nudged me to go talk to them and stepped away, but before long, she joined the group and started chatting with everybody like it was the most natural thing in the world. She bought the whole group juice and snacks and told everybody she and I were related. *So you mean Hana's your niece? You look more like a sister than an aunt . . . I always wanted a big sister like you.* The whole group looked at me with admiration.

Let's go get some yakisoba. When Kimiko made the suggestion, we headed over to the stall together. In the excitement of the moment, one of the girls hooked her arm around mine. Brimming with a pride I'd never known before, I laughed like I never had and told jokes that made them giggle and shriek. All I could think was how fun it was to have Kimiko there, and how I wished things could stay that way forever.

But that was just a dream.

When summer ended, on the first day of the new semester, I

got home from school and Kimiko wasn't there. Her big brown bag was gone, too. I waited and waited, but she never came back.

Around midnight, when I couldn't stand the hunger anymore, I went to the store to get something to eat. I kept an eye out on my way, thinking maybe I'd find Kimiko in the neighborhood. But I didn't see her anywhere.

When I got back to the room with my bento, my appetite had disappeared. I couldn't bring myself to touch the food.

Everything was in exactly the same place—the kotatsu, the unfinished walls, the lampshade, the TV, the electric fan—but it felt like everything had changed.

I got down in the corner and hugged my knees, listening for some sound, some sign—anything. Over and over, I imagined Kimiko opening the door and saying she was back. But that didn't happen. Every time I blinked, the weight in my chest grew heavier. It was like the whole room was plunging deeper and deeper into darkness and taking me along with it.

I pressed my palms against my cheeks and took deep breaths. Then I shook my head, as if I could shake away the loneliness and fear that were dragging me down. After a while, I realized I was incredibly thirsty. I got up and walked to the fridge to get some water, but as soon as I put my hand on the door, I knew something had changed. When I looked inside, I expected to find almost nothing, but the fridge was stuffed full of ham and hot dogs and kamaboko, cans of tuna and peaches, melon buns and juice boxes.

Still holding the corner of the door, I crouched down and stared at the food, unblinking.

It was Kimiko. She'd sent me off to school, then gone to the store to buy a feast. All for me.

She must have decided that she was going to leave that day and bought everything so I wouldn't be hungry. Item by item, she filled the fridge. For me. When I understood, my heart nearly burst. I stared into the faint yellow light from the back of the fridge, unable to move.

3.

After Kimiko left, my mom started turning up again.

It was almost too easy, how my mom and I slipped back into our old life, as if the month I spent with Kimiko had never happened.

I don't know how many times I asked my mom where Kimiko had gone, or how I could reach her, but she never gave me a straight answer. *Where did Kimiko live before? Why did she show up out of nowhere and stay at our house like that? And why did she leave without even saying goodbye?* My mom gave me vague answers like "She probably came here because she didn't have anywhere else to stay . . . Then she found a place, so she left . . . I don't know, Hana, I'm sure she'll be back soon."

I finally got my mom to give me Kimiko's beeper number, but no matter how many times I paged her, I never got a response.

On weekdays, my mom and I barely saw each other. Even on weekends, when we were both at home, we didn't talk much. I turned the TV room into my room, took my futon over, and started sleeping there. My mom and I didn't have that many meals together before, but now we never did.

Sometimes when I walked around the neighborhood and ran into those juvies, they would ask me what happened to Kimiko. Over the break, she and I fell into the rhythm of hanging out with them, talking and joking around every time we ran into them. One time, we lit some fireworks with them. Kimiko would buy them onigiri or croquettes from the store. Thanks to her, they'd started treating me like I was one of the gang. Loose Socks even gave me a pair of socks just like hers. When they saw me on the street, they'd call my name and wave. When the kids at school saw that, the ones who used to call me Bibinba stopped making fun of me.

"So what, she's never coming back?"

I didn't know what to tell them.

"Damn, that sucks. She was pretty cool."

Then they moved on, laughing out loud at something one of them had said.

The empty days blended together, and so did the months. When spring came, I went to a public high school about twenty minutes' bike ride from Evergreen Hills, a place that didn't need any exam prep or high scores. It was the kind of school where it didn't really matter if I showed up or not—probably third from the bottom out of the ten high schools in my district.

That same spring, after two years with Snoozy, my mom broke up with him and started seeing somebody new—an older guy with a job in real estate. His main office was in Saitama, but he apparently had a branch office not too far from the station by us.

Even though the man had met my mom as a customer, he didn't like her working at a bar, so he asked her to quit and work for him in his office—that's what I heard her saying to her friends one day, when they were drinking together in my mom's room like usual. "Yeah right, like you could do that kind of work," one of them said. "I could, though," my mom replied. "You wouldn't know it from looking at me, but I'm really good at math." Then another friend said something funny, and they started laughing.

I wanted to leave home as soon as I graduated from high school, so I spent all my time working to save up money. If I wasn't at school or at the bathhouse or sleeping, I spent every second I had working at a family restaurant by the station.

As soon as I was done at school, I got on my bike and headed to work. I rode so fast that people on the street did double takes. Once I got there, I'd wait tables until ten at night.

Every time I had a break from school, I worked as many hours as I could, from dawn to dusk, until my manager started protesting that he didn't have enough shifts for everybody else. I was making ¥680 an hour, and when I got paid for the first time, I got so emotional I almost broke down and cried.

It had never occurred to my mom to save money or to have some kind of financial plan. Ever since I was little, she just stuffed cash into a round cookie tin whenever she remembered. Sometimes it was more, sometimes less. When the money ran out, she'd fill it up again. She didn't have any savings. She didn't even have a bank account. Whenever we got bills or notices in the mail, I'd go to the store to take care of them. All the money we had in the world was in my mom's wallet or in that tin.

I was so happy to be able to work, to make my own money. I felt like I'd become stronger. The first time I got paid, I bought a wallet with a zipper and put ¥5,000 in it so I could pick up things I needed or go to the bathhouse. I put the rest of my pay in an envelope and hid it at the bottom of the navy blue shoebox I'd been keeping things in since elementary school.

School was boring. There was nothing fun about it. The restaurant wasn't exactly fun either, especially when another student around my age started working there. I had no idea what I'd done to offend her, but she was always mean to me and pretended like I didn't exist. Things got harder with her there, but I told myself I was there to make as much money as I could. I kept my head down and stayed focused, not letting her get to me.

Before long, I started my second year of high school.

I never studied outside of school, and even in class, I was always falling asleep. I barely ever opened a textbook, and my grades showed it.

Almost all my classmates were in the same situation; only a handful of kids were actually trying to go to college. A lot of them wanted to go to trade schools to become cooks or accountants. A couple of the more artistic ones had their sights set on design school, and the rest were too busy talking about their favorite celebrities to think about what they were going to do when high school was over.

Working nights and falling asleep in class during the day, sometimes I wondered what I was doing in school. I had no real friends. I couldn't see the point of it. I knew that even a school like this would give me a diploma if I stuck around and graduated, and having something like that would be better than not having it. But what good did it do exactly?

I couldn't imagine getting a real job anywhere in a year and a half, and I hadn't given any serious thought to my future. All that was in my head was putting in my hours at the restaurant and saving up enough money to move out.

I could hardly wait for summer to start. My manager would probably laugh at me for asking, but as soon as the break started, I planned to pack in my shifts again, dawn to dusk. Or maybe I could find another job that paid better. Daydreaming about better-paying jobs always made me feel more hopeful.

Finals came and went, and the semester was going to end in a couple of days. Usually, I went straight from school to the restaurant, but that day I'd forgotten something I needed, so I had to go home first. I was getting a raise, and my manager had told me to bring my family seal so we could take care of the paperwork.

But when I parked my bike and saw the entrance to our building, I knew something was off.

Whenever my mom had friends over or was talking on the phone, I could always hear the sound coming from the unit on the right, what we used to call the sleeping room but was now my mom's room. That day, though, the sound was coming from the unit on the left, from my room. There were two voices, my mom's and a man's. They were arguing so loudly that I was immediately on guard.

When I opened the door, my mom was standing in the middle of the room with her arms crossed. We locked eyes, and then the man who was facing her turned around to look at me. I didn't recognize him. At first, I thought it was her real estate boyfriend, but he seemed too young for that. It looked like the two of them had been facing off for a while now.

When I looked down and saw the man's dirty heel stepping on my cushion, rage boiled up inside me. I wanted to yell at him, to tell him to get the hell out of my room, but I was so shocked by the whole situation that nothing came out. "Why are you in here?" I finally managed. My voice was so small, and my hands trembled.

"My air conditioner's busted!" My mom was scratching the side of her head frantically, like she was about to snap. The man took a full-body breath, as if trying to calm himself down.

He had a haircut I'd never seen before: short above the ears, but long around the nape. His dark, grimy-looking pants were sagging, and there were chains and other things hanging from his belt loops. The arms sticking out of his T-shirt sleeves were skinny and veiny, and he was so short that from where I stood it looked like I might be taller than he was.

"Go outside then, or just go back to your room," I said, then rushed into the other room. I dug through all the junk in the drawers, found our seal, then went back to my room. They were still there, staring at each other in silence.

"Could you please get out," I said, trying to stay as calm as I could.

"I know," my mom growled. "I heard you."

She was pulling at her hair with both hands now, like she was on the verge of exploding. She liked to have a good time with her friends, and she didn't care about much of anything, so she was usually in a good mood, never emotional. I'd never seen her like this before. Come to think of it, she'd only brought over her girlfriends before. This was the first time I'd seen a guy in our house, and that probably meant that this guy, whoever he was, hadn't been invited. Maybe that was why she was so upset and angry. Because he'd just shown up out of the blue.

Wait, could this be Snoozy? The guy she had broken up with?

"Sorry, Hana, but like I said, the air conditioner is busted! We'll be out of here soon."

I took a step back, floored by the snap in her voice.

It was definitely hot—my armpits and back were covered in sweat—but this was the first time I heard anything about the air conditioner being broken. Maybe she didn't want to let Snoozy into her room. All I knew for sure was that things were going well with the new real estate guy. My mom had looked so happy lately; having Snoozy show up at our house had to be the last thing she wanted. I didn't know what was going on, but it made sense that she wouldn't want to let somebody she didn't love anymore into her room.

"... Okay, fine, just make sure you leave soon."

I didn't want to be late for work, so I rode my bike to the restaurant. At first, I was worried about leaving my mom with that guy. What if the situation got worse? What if Snoozy got violent? But, I told myself, I didn't have a kitchen knife or anything like that in my room, and plus, it didn't feel like things would get to that point. I figured she would be okay.

I didn't know how long they'd been standing there, but they'd clearly been fighting since before I showed up. And Snoozy was so scrawny looking that I thought even if things did escalate, my mom was more than capable of fending for herself. When I got home from work that night, I peeked into my mom's room and found her lying on her futon reading a weekly rag, laughing like everything was completely normal. So that was how my summer started; I poured more of myself into work than ever before.

My mom quit her job at the bar and started working at the real estate guy's office by the station, just like he wanted her to. She gushed about how he treated her more like a personal assistant than an office worker, how he drove her around to view properties with him, even asking for her opinion about some new residential development in Tokorozawa.

But when my mom quit the bar, she made an enemy out of Mama Junko. My mom just left one day, without giving any kind of notice. On top of that, the real estate guy had been a customer at the bar. She'd broken the code of nightlife and the people who worked it, and at least one friend really hounded her for it.

"Well, you know what they say, Hana. People are going to be jealous. They can't handle it when somebody they thought was their equal, or somebody they thought was beneath them, catches a lucky break. They don't like feeling like you got the better of them."

Another friend apparently stood up for my mom and told her

as much. I was over on my mom's side of the hallway, cooking hot dogs in the kitchen while she drank and mused. "Life's full of surprises, huh? Been runnin' up that hill, been going through the mill, but now we're through . . . Hey, you catch that rhyme, Hana? God, I'm so glad I changed my name to Airu. I haven't had it easy, you know. I really haven't."

Mom went on dreamily, her cheeks flushed.

"Things are about to change. I can feel it."

But it wasn't my mom's life that was about to change—it was mine.

I didn't know what had happened—what was happening. I had no idea what I was looking at. I couldn't comprehend.

My money was gone.

At the end of July, when I got paid and rode my bike home, I put ¥5,000 in my wallet like I always did, then opened the box to put the rest of my money away. Except it was all gone. The envelope was missing.

My money—it's all gone. How? Why? I didn't understand.

I put my hand on my throat and took a few deep breaths. My heart was beating like crazy. Then, trembling, I took another look inside the box. The only thing in there was my pay stubs; the envelope was nowhere to be seen.

Did somebody break in? No way. Who would break in to a dump like ours? Besides, everything else in the room was exactly like it had been. *Was it Mom? Did she take my money? No, Mom would never do that. She has the real estate guy, and plus, she wasn't strapped for cash. Then who? Who would take my money?* Then it hit me like a metal club to the back of my head: Snoozy.

It had to be him. It couldn't have been anybody else. It was him; it was Snoozy. It had to be. I was in such a shock that I almost blacked out, and I groaned like I'd never heard myself groan before. I went screaming into my mom's room.

"What, Hana, what's wrong?"

"What's wrong?! Where the hell is Snoozy?"

"What, what are you talking about?"

"You know what I'm talking about! My money! He took it, all of it!"

"Calm down, Hana! What money?"

"My money! The money I saved! All the money I had! He took it!"

I was screaming, crying.

"How do you know it was him? How much money are we talking about? Where was it?"

"A lot of money. A lot! It was in the box in my room. It had to be him! What happened that day when he was here? I told you to get out, and then I had to go to work . . . What did you do after that? What happened?!"

"Nothing!" she said, eyes wide.

"What do you mean nothing? How can you even say that?"

I was crying louder, screaming louder now.

"Just hold on, Hana. Lemme think, okay?"

Once she finally realized how serious the situation was, she frowned, squeezed the sides of her head, and started muttering under her breath.

"What happened, what happened . . . We already broke up, you know? But, that day, he showed up saying how he wanted to get back together . . . Then we fought, and you came home . . . After you went to work, he just kept going on and on and wouldn't stop, and I . . . I couldn't take it."

"But what did he do?"

"I don't know. I just don't feel that way about him anymore . . . I already moved on, you know? I chose a different life. What was I supposed to do?"

"But what did he do?"

"Well, he wouldn't leave. He was a total mess. Seeing him like that, it really made me wonder what I ever saw in him . . ."

"But what did he do??"

"I mean, I had somewhere else I had to be, so . . . I left . . ."

"And him?"

". . . He stayed here."

I put my hands over my face, fell to the floor, and cried. Then

I started punching my own thighs. I did it again and again and again. *Thud, thud, thud.* I kept hitting myself, each dull thud amplifying the rage and regret building inside me.

"Stop it!" my mom yelled. "Don't do that to yourself, okay?"

"Don't tell me what to do! You have no idea how I feel!"

"I do, Hana!"

"Like hell you do!"

"I'm telling you, I do!"

"How could you?! How could you?!"

"Fine! I don't! I don't understand, but . . ."

"But what?"

"You earned all that money by working, right? So you can just do it again."

I stormed out and slammed the door shut with everything I had, so hard the whole building shook. I ran back into my own room, pulled the covers over my head, and sobbed.

I was so upset, so hopeless, so lost. I was so scared; I didn't know what to do. Furious at the world, at myself. I was hyperventilating, and my head hurt so bad I thought it was about to split open. I kept crying and crying. The tears wouldn't stop.

I didn't sleep at all that night.

4.

After the incident, nothing made sense anymore, and I ended up quitting my job at the restaurant.

My manager asked me if something had happened, but I couldn't tell him the truth. I just told him I had things going on at home and thanked him for everything he'd done for me.

Unsurprisingly, Snoozy vanished without a trace. I guess my mom felt responsible, at least a little, because she started asking around, talking to anybody who knew him to see if she could track him down. But he was gone.

The ¥726,000 that had taken me a year and a half to save was gone, too. It had disappeared with Snoozy, and it didn't seem like it was ever coming back to me.

That summer, in my hot, dim, musty room, I stared up at the ceiling as thoughts and memories passed through me. I thought about all kinds of things, like how my dad used to lie here like this, too.

But none of what came to mind seemed important. I didn't have any memories worth looking back on, and I didn't know how to figure things out either. I just lay there, eyes open, unmoving, unsleeping, as the images marched on.

They made me feel alone somehow, but not in an entirely bad way. I let them run across the patterns on the ceiling, float over the stains, shimmering in the dim light. I couldn't quite put them into words, but I got the impression that they were things I normally couldn't see—smells or textures or feelings—that had somehow become visible. Every time I blinked, though, those images transformed, faded, or ran away, so I tried to keep my eyes open until they started to sting, until tears formed in the corners of my eyes and trickled down my face.

It was late August, and the fact that school would start in a week and a half had me depressed.

I didn't want to stay at home like this forever, but my dream of saving up and getting a room of my own was as good as dead. I didn't have the energy to find another job either. I had nowhere to go.

I went to the supermarket or convenience store to buy food with the money my mom left in the tin and ate nothing but somen and karaage.

In the morning, I listened to the wood pigeons cooing, and later in the day, I heard the buzz of the cicadas filling the air like a thousand tiny bells. I thought about going back to work at the family restaurant. I could still feel it in me—the motions of stacking the plates and wiping the tables down in big, sweeping circles, the speed of my fingers as I tapped on the register, the unexpected grip of the linoleum as I strode across the floor. But that was all over now. I remembered I still had my spare blouse from the restaurant. *It's already washed, I should take it back.*

That day, I walked through the sweltering heat for nearly thirty minutes. I would have taken my bike, but the chain had come off a while back and I'd never gotten it fixed.

When I got to the restaurant, they told me the manager wasn't in that day. I was relieved. He was a kind and funny man. He had to be forty or so, and no matter how early he came in, his hair was always neatly parted and teased up like a greaser. He had a habit of muttering jokes under his breath, almost to himself, and it made everybody else groan, but I actually liked it. If he'd been there that day, he would have asked how I was doing, what I was going to do with myself now. There wasn't anything I could have told him, so it was just as well that I didn't see him.

In the break room, I ran into a part-timer I'd known for the past year or so, and we made small talk for a while, as if nothing had changed. She had a daughter who was getting married in the fall, and she moped as she told me how expensive the wedding was turning out to be.

When I got up, I thanked her for always looking out for me. *Hana*, she said, *you're a real hard worker, and so responsible for your age. It's wonderful to see.* I thanked her again and left.

The AC was cranked up so high in the restaurant that the second I left, every pore on my body opened up, making my skin tingle. It had already been two weeks since I stopped working there, but now that I'd returned my blouse, I felt like that part of my life was truly over. I was even more alone.

The sun was still high in the sky, and its heat was sinking into me through my eyes and my skin. As I walked down the shopping arcade by the station, everything waved and blurred with the heat. We hadn't had rain in days, and even though it was humid out, the street was dusty. I had nothing to do with any of the people around me—not the person smiling in front of the shop, not the one coming out of the bakery, not the one on the bike coming toward me. *Is this what being in a desert feels like?* I wondered. Ever since I started high school, all I ever did was bike between home, school, and work. So walking around like this, aimlessly, I got this funny feeling, like I was in a dream in which time and place had ceased to exist.

As I walked, I glanced over the bento shop, the drugstore, the pachinko parlor.

Up ahead, on the right, was my mother's old bar. I remembered how she said she'd had a falling-out with Mama Junko, and I wondered if they'd managed to patch things up. But what did it mean to patch things up? To ask for forgiveness, to be forgiven? What did it mean to forgive somebody? I thought about Snoozy. I didn't forgive him. I never would, not as long as I lived. But what difference did that make? It's not like I was going to get my money back, and it's not like he was going to suffer or repent for what he did. I was starting to feel dazed from the heat. With the back of my hand, I wiped away the sweat dripping down my forehead again and again.

Just as I walked past Mama Junko's bar, the door swung open.

I saw who was coming out, and I froze.

It was Kimiko.

A gust of wind blew between us, and Kimiko's long black hair billowed as she stood before the door, looking at me.

Kimiko.

We stood there like that, staring at each other for a few seconds.

"Hana."

She brushed away the hair clinging to her face as she called my name. I couldn't reply.

"Hana."

She called my name again.

"Hana, can you hear me?"

"I can hear you," I said. My voice was shaking, but I felt weirdly calm. I was looking right at her. I blinked, and a shudder ran through me. Kimiko was here. Two years ago, on a hot day like today, she showed up out of nowhere, and then she vanished. Now here she was, standing in front of me.

All those scenes came back to life, like clouded ice beginning to gleam with meltwater.

Paging her again and again, walking around town trying to find her. How dark the night was, but how green and bright the trees were. The color of the karaage we cooked together, the white of the somen we ate, the comic-book speech bubbles, how we laughed. Those shifts at the restaurant, the uniform I wore, the missing envelope, crying like crazy, how I slammed the door, my mom, how she cried, the pale-yellow glow emanating from the back of a fridge full of ham and hot dogs.

"Hana," Kimiko said my name again and smiled. "You look so grown up."

I couldn't say anything back. I looked down and rubbed my eyes, then hid my face behind my hands and wiped away the tears as they ran down my chin and the sides of my neck. Was I angry? Was I shocked? Hurting? Sad? Happy? I had no idea what was making me cry like this.

"Hana," Kimiko called my name again, her voice louder this time.

I lifted my face and looked at her.

"Do you want to come with me?"

"Yes," I said. "I want to come with you."

THREE

GRAND OPENING

1.

Kimiko and I spent several days debating whether the bar's name should be written in Chinese kanji characters, rounded Japanese hiragana, or angular katakana.

The kanji had a certain majesty to them, and that seemed like it would be cool, but we hesitated because the characters were so uncommon people might not be able to read them. In fact, Kimiko and I had never even written the characters at all until we looked them up for the bar. And the katakana reminded us both of a bottle of dish soap sitting next to the kitchen sink.

We tried to imagine what we would do if we were customers looking for a nightcap, passing by our bar sign—would it be kanji or hiragana that made us want to come in? That's how we settled on the hiragana "Lemon."

I was the one who first suggested the name.

Lemons were yellow, which tied the bar to Kimiko's name, and even though we debated how to write "lemon" for a while, when I imagined an actual lemon, I was sure the name was a good idea.

It was easy enough to ask a contractor friend of Kimiko's to make the sign for us. A few days later, he showed us a bunch of designs, and Kimiko and I picked the one we liked best.

"This one is nice. It's got this cute little lemon on it, too."

The background was a frosted black that looked gray from certain angles. The hiragana "Lemon" was written out in fine yellow lines, and underneath was a drawing of a lemon styled to match.

"It kind of looks like a potato," Kimiko said with a chuckle.

"A potato? But potatoes are lumpy."

"Well, I guess it is sitting right under the word 'lemon.'"

"Yeah. And it's yellow, the best feng shui color," I said with a knowing air.

"Well, yeah. But that doesn't matter. I just like it."

"Lemon?"

"Yeah. You chose a good name, Hana."

All our energy went into the final push of preparing for Lemon's opening week. Not that there was much to prepare. Until a few months ago, the space had been a bar, so we left everything—the decorations, the lights, the karaoke machine, the glasses—more or less the same. Only the name on the sign changed.

We didn't need to move or carry in anything heavy, but when we turned the lights up to full brightness to inspect the place, everything was shockingly filthy, especially the places that got damp, like the galley kitchen and the restroom. The carpet was worn in some spots and faded in others, spattered with stains.

Ideally, we would have hired professional cleaners to come and give the place a good once-over, but we didn't have enough money for that, so we pulled on rubber gloves, hauled in cleaning supplies, and spent days scrubbing from dawn until dusk—we polished down to the last glass, even the last karaoke laser disc.

Lemon was in a small, multi-tenant building just off the main drag, only a few minutes' walk from Sangenjaya Station.

A restaurant called Little Heaven, run solely by a woman named En, occupied the first floor, the second floor was a tattoo parlor—I could never figure out when they were open—and Lemon was on the third floor.

A run-down building, cramped, with only one business per floor. An ancient red lantern hung above Little Heaven's door, and next to it was an entrance with three nameplates, one on top of the other. The entrance led to an elevator the size of a matchbox that rattled ominously as it went up and down. The neighborhood was filled with narrow buildings like ours, bunched so closely they almost leaned against one another, holding each other up. The buildings to either side of ours were plastered with garish signs large and small, advertising bars and watering holes. This part of town was already busy during the day, but at night it grew even more raucous and lively with the drunks who came in.

Kimiko fell into running Lemon more or less by accident.

She frequented the bar that was there before Lemon and was friends with the previous owner, an easygoing, friendly woman from northern Kyushu, maybe fifty years old, named Mama Atsuko. Mama Atsuko came to Tokyo when she was twenty. She started working at a bar in Kameari, and after that, one in Tamachi, then Shimbashi, until finally she opened her own place in Gotanda. About ten years ago, she moved her business to Sangenjaya, and she was hoping for another ten years, but then she got diagnosed with breast cancer. For a few years, she struggled to stay open while she got treatment, but it was impossible, so she decided to move back to Kyushu, where her younger sister and brother-in-law still lived.

After Mama Atsuko vacated the shop, the building's landlord, Jinno, wanted to fill the vacancy as quickly as possible—he didn't want to have to pay the taxes on the place if he could help it. But there are all sorts in the city, and no matter how run-down the building, he knew if he went through a real estate agency, he'd get lots of lookie-loos and weirdos with questionable backgrounds. And even if he found a tenant, he was worried he'd wind up with mountains of trouble from them subleasing or running illegal businesses—it had happened to him before. To avoid the headache, he asked Mama Atsuko if she knew anyone—preferably someone who wouldn't bother him about keeping the building up to fire and earthquake code—who could just take on the lease from her, and that's how the offer came to Kimiko.

Jinno had actually met Kimiko several times and remembered her. He'd liked drinking with her and thought she was a good person, so he was enthusiastic about the idea. He even sweetened the deal, dropping the rent and maintenance fee from ¥157,000 a month to ¥147,000 and making the security deposit five months' rent instead of six.

I never asked Kimiko for details about where she was from or what kind of work she did. But I guessed that, like my mother, she'd been working nightlife ever since she was young.

All my mother's friends were women who worked nightlife, and no matter their beauty, personality, or age, they shared some indefinable quality, something I couldn't begin to explain but could always recognize.

Kimiko had it, too. It wasn't in her eyes or the way she talked or her routines, in her clothes or her spending habits, not in the way she laughed, not even in her scent. What was it, that thing that sank into our home, into the women I lived with, and refused to let go?

Kimiko's explanation of how she got the lease was jumbled, and I had a hard time understanding it, but I managed to figure out that Mama Atsuko acted as a go-between for Kimiko and Jinno, and the end result was that Kimiko didn't even have to pay a deposit or anything—she even got to keep the register, the telephone, everything that was still usable from the previous bar.

Two months before the old bar closed, Kimiko joined its staff as a part-time hostess to start building connections with the regulars. If a customer had purchased a bottle-keep with Mama Atsuko, Kimiko kept that same bottle, so the regulars could come by to drink their alcohol, same as always. The two other part-timers moved on, but Mama Atsuko took Kimiko around to all the noteworthy neighboring bars and introduced her. After that, they went back to each one several times, letting the owners and customers all know when Kimiko aimed to open up shop. "Mama was good to me," Kimiko said with a smile.

In the middle of August, she finally got the keys. And only a few days after that, I ran into her on my way home from dropping off my uniform.

Lemon's opening day was only a week away, the last Monday of September.

Kimiko and I lived in the nearby heights—from Lemon's corner, we made our way back to the main thoroughfare, crossed at the light, and went straight down Chazawa Street to our building on the right-hand side. Our apartment was in a cozy two-story walkup, and most of the neighboring apartment doors didn't have nameplates, only rusting mail slots. Kimiko had been living there for two years.

Our peeling white door was the first on the landing, and when you opened it, you came in on our kitchenette, our combination bath and toilet, and an eight-mat Western-style room with a metal bar for drying laundry hung over the window—no veranda.

The building was shabby on the outside, but when I first entered our apartment, the wallpaper was so blinding white it stung my eyes. I'd never seen wood floors or a combination bath and toilet before, and I felt like I'd stepped into an apartment from some TV show or manga or something. It was so different from the home I'd grown up in, and when I realized I'd be living there, I felt something, something like joy or embarrassment but somehow neither. The furnishings were spare—a TV, a small cabinet, a folding table—and the apartment was neat and tidy, everything in its place.

"Can't believe it's the day after tomorrow," I said. "I'm kind of nervous."

Saturday afternoon found Kimiko and me watching a talk show while we ate beef-and-rice bowls she'd picked up from Yoshinoya. On the show, they were talking about the new cell phone models—they were featuring one that came with a program you could use to compose your own ringtones. The next story was about how people were running scams reselling Tamagotchis for huge payouts, and the commentators joked about all the demand for the little toys.

"You don't need to be nervous," Kimiko said.

"You sure?"

"Being a waitress is harder."

"It is?"

"It is. You have to stand the whole time, and you have to remember everything, right?"

"You don't have to remember things in a bar?"

"Not really. You just kind of roll with it."

"I didn't know that."

"It's true."

"I've only ever worked as a waitress," I said, "but I like working."

Kimiko hummed thoughtfully and looked at me.

"And with the bar, there's no hourly pay. See, with restaurants, you always get the same amount of money no matter how hard you work. And they'd only give me so many shifts, and there was no bath waiting for me at home, and then there was school the next day. But now I can work as much as I want—I don't have to care about punching in and out."

"I suppose."

"And the more I work, the more money I'll make."

"That's true."

"I think I'm going to be amazing at this job."

On Sunday, we set out in the morning to give Lemon yet another scrub, and also to check if we had stocked enough of everything we would need—snacks, bottled beer, all-you-can-drink whiskey, several brands of cigarettes.

The bar looked much cleaner than it had when we first started, because Kimiko and I had polished each and every surface. I was proud of all the work we'd done. In the corner of our little bar was a telephone box with a door, and it had a light that flashed when the phone rang. I'd never seen anything like it before, and I used Kimiko's cell phone to call the box several times.

I took in everything—the three booths with their fuzzy dark-brown bench seats, the curve of the dinged-up counter, the glass shelves lined with glassware and bottles of whiskey and brandy—and felt myself growing attached to it, even before we had our first day of work. Today, Kimiko's thick hair was gathered up, and she was checking corners we might have forgotten to clean, just in case. She also made sure the towel-warming machine was working and the ice machine was making its ice.

Two hours in, I was feeling hungry—*What time is it?* But I couldn't find a clock.

I didn't have a watch, either, so I asked Kimiko, who said it was just after noon.

"Is it okay that we don't have a clock?"

"Most bars don't."

"Why?"

"It's better if the customers don't know what time it is."

"Why's that?"

"The longer they're here, the more they'll drink. That's why we don't need a clock. There are customers who would go home if they realized how late it was."

"Oh."

Just then, the automatic door opened, and we both turned at the noise.

A man stood in the door, bowing just a touch before he entered. I stood.

"You're here early. We were just about to go get lunch," Kimiko told him. She raised her eyebrows and smiled.

My eyes met his, so I bowed my head, and he made a shallow bow again. Kimiko and I stood side by side, facing him. He wasn't much taller than me, and I was only 163 centimeters. He wore a slightly wrinkled black shirt unbuttoned at the collar, black trousers held up by a brown belt, and he clutched a black leather pouch at his side. His hair was buzzed close, and the way the thick black strands stood on end like grass reminded me of a stray Kai Ken I'd known growing up.

I'd loved dogs ever since I was a kid, and back then, the town was always filled with strays. I wished they could live with us, but I knew there was no point in asking my mom if we could have one. When I first went to elementary school, I used to give them crumbs of leftover bread from my school lunch, or if it was raining, I'd lead them to covered bicycle parking outside apartment buildings and make them impromptu cardboard box beds, but as I got older, the dogs just seemed to disappear.

Sometimes in the school library, I looked at picture books of dog breeds from around the world. Elegant dogs, dogs with flashy patterns, dogs with purposes and jobs, multicolored dogs, clever dogs, designer dogs, dogs of all sizes, dogs with special features—they all had homelands and breed names. The book said the dogs I petted around the neighborhood were mutts, but I couldn't see how they were any different from the dogs in the section on Japanese breeds. Among those was the Kai Ken, which looked exactly like the pitch-black stray named Ponta that I'd fed for a while. Maybe Ponta was a Kai Ken. In my young mind, staring down at that picture, I was sure he must be. And now the man before me reminded me of that Kai Ken, of that jumble of memories.

"This is Yeongsu," Kimiko told me.

"Mr. Yeongsu," I repeated, and he nodded, though he avoided my eyes.

"An Yeongsu. You write it with the characters for 'peaceful,' 'reflection,' and 'water.'"

Each character appeared one by one in my mind's eye.

"Yeongsu is my friend. He's helped me out a lot."

"Nice to meet you."

Kimiko walked behind the counter, pulled a spare key out of the cupboard beneath the register, and passed it to Yeongsu. He put the key in his pocket, but he made no move to sit, so I stayed standing, too. Instead, he moved to the center of the bar and gave everything a once-over.

"Have you had lunch, Yeongsu?"

"Not yet."

Though his answer was curt, his voice was so striking I couldn't help but study his face again.

His voice had a mysteriously deep quality, smooth and clear, and I felt less like I was hearing him with my ears than that he was carefully and meticulously placing words down in the quiet places of my mind. I wanted him to speak again, to make sure I wasn't imagining it, so I waited with bated breath for him to say more, but he didn't.

We left Lemon and headed for a diner in front of the station. Kimiko and I ordered curry. Yeongsu seemed uninterested in the menu, but when Kimiko asked him if he'd be all right with the same, he nodded, scratching at his neck.

The diner was crowded with the lunch rush. Manual laborers, young people, couples dressed in matching outfits, white-collar men in suits, and down the narrow aisle between them, two waitresses ferried food and water without pause. This diner wasn't the only busy place—Sangenjaya was always lively and noisy with people and business. It was a far cry from the neighborhood where I was born and raised. Until now, I'd spent virtually my entire life in that town on the borders of Higashimurayama and Saitama. My experiences of Tokyo boiled down to a social-studies field trip to the National Diet and the Tokyo Metropolitan Government Building, one trip to Ueno Zoo with my mom and her friends, and one trip to Shinjuku to see a movie—one of my mom's customers had given her and her coworkers tickets, so we had gone together.

The movie had been *Kiki's Delivery Service*. The story was about a girl who could use magic, and she left home on a flying broomstick with her cat in tow so she could start up a delivery service at a bakery in a new town. After the movie finished, I remember my mom and her friends smiling and wishing they could fly in the sky like that, but I didn't want to fly. I just thought about how amazing it would be to leave home and work as much as I wanted, the way Kiki did.

On the way back to Higashimurayama, and even after we got back home, my heart burbled with the excitement of my first movie theater experience, and I didn't sleep well that night. As I replayed the bright, shining colors and scenes in my mind, my heart sank deeper into darkness. It reminded me that no matter what I watched, no matter how the magic glimmered through the film, it didn't have anything to do with the real world. Nothing in my own life would change.

"Kotomi said she's coming by tomorrow," Yeongsu said. Just like back at the bar, his voice struck me.

"Oh?" Kimiko said as she fixed her hair. "I wonder what time. She has work tomorrow."

"She'll probably come by before her shift."

Our three curries arrived, so I stuck my silver spoon in my glass of water and then scooped my first bite of rice. I was copying Kimiko. She told me if I dipped my spoon or chopsticks in water, rice wouldn't stick to them anymore. Yeongsu, too, stuck his spoon in his glass and swirled it around. The man in the neighboring seat glanced over at the clatter of our spoons in our cups but quickly returned to his own meal. None of us said much of anything as we dug into our curries. Both Kimiko and I were fast eaters, but Yeongsu was faster still. Silently, we bolted everything down, and then Kimiko paid the bill and we left.

"Yeongsu, we're going to need two more keys. One for Hana, too."

Yeongsu nodded, extracted a white envelope from the pouch at his side, and handed it to Kimiko. She took it without checking the contents, folded it in half, and stuck it in her pants pocket. I was sure it must be money. I felt like I should pretend I hadn't seen anything, though Kimiko made no attempt to hide what she was doing.

"I'll call you soon, Yeongsu."

He took the stairs down to the subway, and we stood at the threshold, watching him go. We remained there, unmoving, until he disappeared from sight.

2.

"You don't need foundation. Just a little powder, and then brows, eyes, and lipstick."

Kimiko sat before me and told me to close my eyes. It was Lemon's opening night. We were preparing to go to the bar for the evening.

I had never closed my eyes while someone else was staring at me before, and my heart started to race. Kimiko patted a nice-smelling powder on my forehead, nose, and cheeks, and then she carefully traced a pencil over my eyebrows. The tip of the eyeshadow applicator passed back and forth over my eyelids and then cool fingertips pressed down the corners of my eyes while chilly metal pinched my eyelashes—it made my eyelids sting and quiver. Kimiko chuckled, apparently amused.

When she told me I was done, I opened my eyes, ran to the bathroom, and peered at my face in the mirror over the sink. My eyes were bigger, my eyebrows darker and thicker, drawn in a permanently surprised arch.

When I was little, I'd stood at my mother's side every day, watching her do her makeup, but I'd never been particularly interested or wanted to try it for myself. The look Kimiko had given me was simple enough, but it still made me feel like I was seeing myself for the first time, like my face was brand new. I turned this way and that, studying how different angles affected my bold brows and the shadow of brown over my eyelids. When I went back to the main room, Kimiko handed me a tube of lipstick and told me it was okay to wait to do that until we were at the bar.

Once she was done with my makeup, she gathered her own long, black hair and began separating it, like fronds of tangled seaweed, efficiently making several sections and running a brush through each of them. Then she wrapped each section around hot curlers and did her makeup while she waited for the heat to do its job. I'd never seen her deck herself out before. Even under normal circumstances, Kimiko's face was striking, but when she used brown eyeshadow and a pencil to carve out her already strong eyes and brows, her features became even sharper still.

She's so cool, I thought. Her mascara lifted her lashes to a lush, long angle, and her red-painted mouth looked like some kind of sigil to me. Kimiko removed her array of curlers, and once she'd loosened and fluffed the mass of curls, she brushed them again, smoothing the strands from hairline to tip, following the sides to the back, fluffing and brushing the same way you might a long-haired animal. Then she unleashed a cloud of VO5 so thick I couldn't see her face for a moment, and I coughed. From the white mist of hairspray, Kimiko's hair rolled forth in waves, expanding, growing, undulating, and shining even more under the light of the fluorescents.

"I have so much hair you could practically hide a whole cat in here without anyone noticing."

"Yeah, it's like a cat and a forest had a baby."

I watched the way Kimiko smiled with her eyes and remembered how she looked two years ago as she ate instant ramen in that sweltering summer kitchen. The young pharaoh in ancient Egypt from the manga. Kimiko had been barefaced then, just like she usually was around the apartment, but now—it was strange—seeing her face contoured and her hair done, she seemed more like Kimiko than any version of her I'd ever met before.

Though the sun was setting, the stifling heat of day lingered. We walked to Lemon, sticky with sweat. Kimiko had given me a rayon dress, which was now plastered to my back, so I pinched at the front and flapped it, trying to cool myself. Kimiko wore a shiny white blouse and trousers flecked with narrow lamé threads.

When we arrived at the bar, I went to the restroom and applied the red lipstick. I gaped at the way it instantly changed my face. It wasn't that it was too flashy or didn't suit me, I just looked weird, funny even, though Kimiko smiled like she didn't see anything wrong with it. For the first thirty minutes or so, the gunky feeling of the lipstick on my lips put me on edge, and

I kept going back to the bathroom to look at my own face, but after about an hour, I got used to it.

We powered up all the bar's appliances, put cash in the register, and did all the necessary prep. Kimiko's cell phone rang just as we hit one hour till our eight o'clock opening.

"Hello? Well, now we're . . . Yeah, go straight there, and it's at the end of the street . . . Yeah, it might not be open yet, but there's a place called Little Heaven on the first floor and . . . Yeah, third floor."

Kimiko yeah-ed a few more times, hung up, told me to get two sets ready, and then went to the bathroom. I prepared an ice bucket, two ten-ounce tumblers, paper coasters, an ashtray, and two little plates of snacks—dried seaweed and kaki-pi crackers—and carried everything to one of the booths. The door opened just as I set everything down.

"Hi," I said, turning to find a woman standing there.

She was small and slender and wore a matching jacket and flared skirt made of some fine, shiny material—maybe silk—that was either white or very pale pink. When she saw me, she smiled. Her uniformly white teeth flashed between her plump, glossed lips. Her bangs were parted in the middle, and the rest of her short chestnut hair was slicked back, which drew attention to her smooth, rounded forehead. Beneath her flawlessly arched, penciled eyebrows, her huge, dewy eyes caught the light, while the rest of her features gathered in perfect proportion on the lower half of her face. She was so stunningly beautiful that the light seemed to touch her differently. She looked like a TV star—I had to take a step back.

"Kotomi!" Kimiko called as she returned from the bathroom.

"You weren't kidding, this place is hard to find." Kotomi laughed as she turned to look behind her. An older man sedately followed her in.

It was almost ceremonial, the way he walked in, and we solemnly watched him.

Even I could tell at a glance that his clothing was high-end. He wore a blue-gray suit with a goldenrod-yellow shirt and a skinny, chic silk tie—though I couldn't figure out what color it was. His thinning white hair was combed back, and deep wrinkles carved through the sunken, drooping flesh of his age-spotted face, but paired with his sumptuous outfit, even the signs of aging seemed somehow elegant and luxurious on him.

The man tucked himself into the booth furthest from the door, and Kotomi slid in next to him, spreading her hands wide to introduce him to Kimiko.

"Gon-chama, this is Kimiko. Kimiko, this is Gon-chama." Atop her lap, on her beautiful silk skirt, Kotomi held a huge, deep green alligator-skin wallet, likely Gon's.

"Gon-chama, welcome," said Kimiko with a smile.

"Humph, hm humph."

I couldn't understand a word Gon said and began to panic. I looked to Kimiko for help, but she was smiling and nodding, not looking worried in the least. Gon sank onto the bench and crossed his legs, which drowned in his crisply pressed trousers, like a teddy bear whose stuffing had been squished and lost over the years. He looked at least two sizes smaller sitting than he had standing.

"What will you have, Kotomi?"

"Gon-chama will have some hot tea, and I, hmm, I think I'll have a beer. I'm parched from the walk."

"The walk? Surely you took a car."

"Well, yes, but we still had to walk from the curb."

"It's less than a minute!" Kimiko laughed. "Hana, a beer. One of the big bottles. And another tumbler. And some hot tea."

I prepared the drinks and the glass and returned to the booth, where we all toasted. Kotomi poured me a beer without a second thought.

One night when I was little and my dad was still around, he'd had some work friends over for a hot pot or something, and as a joke, I had a sip of my mom's beer, my first taste of alcohol. But this was my first real beer. It tasted bitter and made my throat tingle, but I didn't mind it. This second sip tasted pretty much the same, but now I also noticed a lingering flavor that I hadn't caught before. *Ah, so this is why you keep drinking beer. This faint mouthwatering aftertaste takes over and then gets enhanced by the bitterness of the next sip, and round and round it goes, the both of them together making you want the next sip.* I put the glass to my lips again as I considered the flavor. And then I wondered if maybe I was one of the lucky ones who could hold their liquor.

"You gave this one a cute name, too. Lemon."

"Hana picked it."

"And you're Hana?" Kotomi asked, peering at me. She tilted her head at an angle, fluttered her left eyelid once, and sat up straight again. What? A wink. An honest-to-god wink, so perfect it blindsided me. I'd only ever seen people do it in manga, but those were all drawings—I'd never actually seen someone wink in the real world. And so sudden, too, from a woman so beautiful I barely knew where to look. I had to lower my gaze, overcome with shyness and embarrassment.

"Do you like lemons, Hana?"

"Um, I don't hate them, they're fine, but um, I like their color," I said, flustered.

"So you like yellow?"

"Yes, it's cheery. And strong."

"I like yellow, too."

"And it's supposed to be good for feng shui."

"Feng shui, that's that thing with cardinal directions and colors, right?"

"Yes. Yellow is for prosperity. Plus, yellow is in Kimiko's name, too."

"Of course. And so you chose lemon."

"Yes."

"But, if yellow is good for business, why not just name the bar Yellow?"

"What?"

"I'm joking," Kotomi laughed. "Kimiko, since today's a celebration, shall we . . . Gon-chama?"

Kotomi laid a hand on Gon's skeletal knee and smiled at him, and he mumbled happily and nodded in response.

"Okay then, we'll have Lemon's finest, please!"

Kimiko brought out a hefty bottle of Hennessy X.O, though when she'd prepared it, I had no idea. She handed Kotomi a silver permanent marker, and Kotomi used it to write "Gon-chama★La Belle Kotomi" in curling handwriting on the glass.

"Look, Gon-chama. Now La Belle Kotomi will have to earn her keep."

"Hmm humph."

"She's going to make it big-time, just like me!"

"Humph!"

The automatic door sounded again. It was the woman who owned Little Heaven, En, and she'd brought along a man in a baseball cap and workmen's clothes, some construction company's name embroidered in white on the breast pocket. "Sorry we're a bit early," En said. Kimiko and I ate at Little Heaven quite a bit while we were getting Lemon ready, so En had gotten friendly with us.

En had been running Little Heaven for twenty years. She was a lovely, cheery woman who spoke with a thick Kyoto accent. Her white hair was dyed purple, and she could have told me she was sixty or seventy, and I would have believed either. Kimiko stood and walked over to greet her.

"Would you like me to get some water for your brandy?" I asked Kotomi shyly.

"Oh, no, that's fine. We won't be drinking this," Kotomi said. "It's just for the celebration."

"Oh, of course."

"Are you good with beer, though, Hana? Do you want something else?"

"Oh, beer is fine," I said, raising my glass and taking another gulp. I'd drunk about two-thirds, so Kotomi laughed and topped off my glass.

"Nice. Another round, then?"

I poured from the fresh bottle into Kotomi's glass, and we toasted again. The beer was still bitter, and when I drank, something in my throat put up a token resistance, but beyond that bitterness and reluctance, I sensed something else, something new, a rush of exaltation, and I hurried to meet it. Gon had not yet touched his tea—instead, he closed his eyes and sank back into the booth, mumbling from time to time like he had only just remembered he was supposed to be making conversation.

"You're living with Kimiko, right?"

"Yes."

"And it's going well?"

I nodded.

"How old are you again?"

"I'm supposed to tell you I'm twenty, but I'm actually seventeen."

"So young. That's about how old Kimiko and I were when we first met."

Kotomi pulled a cigarette from her bag and lit it with a golden lighter. She exhaled the smoke like a sigh, squinting as it drifted up, and then pulled the ashtray closer to flick off her ash.

"You've been friends that long?"

"That's right. Yeongsu was here yesterday, right?"

"Yes."

"An Yeongsu."

Kotomi peered through the smoke as she uttered his name.

"We've all known each other since we were that age."

"Were you all in school together?"

"No, of course not," Kotomi said with a laugh. "We didn't go to school. We met at a bar. Way back when we were all working in Kabukicho. Where are you from again?"

"The far end of Higashimurayama."

"Oh. So you were at Mama Junko's place, right? What was the name of that bar again . . . it was really long?"

"Yes. The Lullaby of the Madonnas. My mom worked there, but I was still in junior high."

"That's right, 'The Lullaby of the Madonnas.' What a mouthful. Junko named it after that song you know, the Hiromi Iwasaki one. She used to work in Kabukicho, too, and that's what she always sang at closing time. No one could go home until she'd sung it. Do you know it, Hana?"

"Yes, my mother used to sing it, so I can, too."

"Such a funny song."

Kotomi gracefully extinguished her cigarette against the edge of the ashtray and raised the corners of her lips in a smile. I again thought how she had the face of someone who should be on a poster or on TV.

"Have you always"—I gulped once and continued—"been, um, like, this pretty?"

"My face? Or my clothes?"

"Both."

Kotomi laughed out loud. "It's fake, all of it. If I wash my face, I look ridiculous, like a dried sardine. I wear tracksuits around the house. I only look like this for work. I have a shift tonight, actually."

"You're going to work after this?"

"Yep. This is Kimiko's grand opening, right? That's why I asked Gon-chama to come along. We had dinner in Ginza before this, and after this, it's back to Ginza."

"Is that where you work?"

"That's right, at a gentlemen's club."

"What kind of club is that?"

"'What kind?'" Kotomi repeated, chewing the words over. "Well, there's alcohol, it's spacious, there's a grand piano, all of the girls have their hair done every day, wear gowns and kimono, and day after day rich customers come in to drink."

"So a club is different than, for example, a bar like this one?"

"Well, the drinking is the same, but the prices aren't. And in bars like this, the working girls aren't supposed to sit right next to the customers, right? But in a club, they get up close to their customers to serve them. So remember, Hana, even if you're escorting a customer, you don't have to sit next to him, you can sit across from him like this."

"What do you mean by escorting?"

"You know, when you meet with a customer for dinner before your shift and then you escort them to the club?"

"It's okay to do that?"

"'Okay' has nothing to do with it, it's part of your job."

"Do all hostesses do it?"

"All the ones who work at clubs. We have quotas."

"So you escort guys every day?"

"Of course. I'm getting older, so I really need them. I usually escort two a night, or even three. Because I don't have dedicated clients."

"What do you mean?" I was so intrigued, I found myself leaning in, pelting her with questions.

"You really are interested. You make me feel like I'm talking to a news reporter or something, how fun. Okay, so a club is like a company. There's an office that manages everything, and Big Mama works there, and then, since our club is so big, there are four Mamas under Big Mama. Our four empresses. And every month, those four compete for the largest take. And in addition to them, there are hostesses who have a dedicated clientele, and all of that is, well, it's management. Not just hourly or daily wages—the system is designed so that the better you manage your clients, the more you get, because our take depends on how much our clients pay for their drinks. So it's kind of like, like we're renting a space in the club and doing the sales ourselves? And then there's the help. The girls who work under the Mamas and hostesses and hang out with the clients for hourly wages. There's about thirty of them, and then maybe about seven men, the suits. They have their pecking order, too—the president, the division head, the section chief, senior staff, and then the newbies at the bottom. And I'm the fairy godmother. I go where I'm needed. I used to have my own clients, but then they ran out on me, and things got rough for a while."

"Ran out on you?"

"Yep. There was a time when I was working a ton of clients. My take was so good it looked like I might make Mama, but all of a sudden, a bunch of my big spenders ran."

"Cut and run?"

"You could say that." Kotomi smiled. "See, clubs are members only, so normally we do things on tab. Each member is on individual credit, so they just sign their tab and pay later. We have to sell as many drinks as we can to turn a profit, but all that responsibility falls on the women who manage the clients."

"You mean the women pay for it all?"

"That's right. All the drinks. And there are clients who stop taking your calls or go bankrupt or never plan on paying in the first place—they just hand over someone else's business card and then disappear. Then there are hostesses who band together with clients and plot against other hostesses to bring them down. There are all sorts, I guess. But if you can't collect on the bills, then you have to pay the club back for the drinks because it was your client. So you have to get all your ducks in a row. The champagne and wine are so expensive, you wouldn't believe."

"They really cost that much?"

"They do. And the bill comes two months later, kind of like a two-month deferral. But then that two months' worth slaps you in the face, because it's just, it's a lot of money. And it happened right around my birthday, so I was riding my high horse, drinking all this Romanée-Conti and Moët & Chandon, so the bill was just outrageous."

"But when something like that happens, don't the other people working there help you out?"

"At first, they'll go out and help you collect from clients, or if you have a partner, they can go negotiate for you. Men are usually more effective for that, anyway. But if a client won't pay, he won't pay. There are limits to how far you can push people."

"But the club won't give you a discount or forgive some of the debt?"

"Absolutely not," Kotomi said with a laugh. "Once they confirm you've been ditched, they come right after you. That's why hostesses run, too, sometimes, or if they don't have the guts to run, they'll start working a new club and ask for an advance to pay back the debt. But then you're just up to your ears at the new place."

"Does that happen a lot?"

"It happens enough."

"If a hostess decides to run, what does she do?"

"Well"—Kotomi looked at me—"she disappears."

"Disappears?"

"Disappears. To a place where no one can find her."

I clammed up and drank my beer. Two booths away, En was chatting up a storm, her gestures expansive. Kotomi glanced at the gold watch on a chain band around her wrist and then finished the rest of her beer.

"I know it wasn't long, but I have to get going. They've really been on us lately about being late."

"Of course. Let me call Kimiko over."

"No, that's fine."

Kotomi lifted the glossy alligator-skin wallet from her lap and showed it to Gon-chama, opening the clasp and peering inside.

"Can I use any of them?"

Gon nodded, and Kotomi joked, "Eeny meeny miny mo," before extracting a gold card and handing it to me.

"Could you make it twenty?"

"Twenty?"

Just then Kimiko arrived and sat next to Kotomi, and the two of them talked in hushed tones before Kimiko took the card to the register.

"Gon-chama, dearest, shall we? Gon-chama? Thank you for the celebratory bottle. Thank you, too, Hana. You should come to ours for a bottle of champagne sometime."

Kotomi picked up the signed, unopened bottle and held it up beside her face.

"To the ongoing success of La Belle Kotomi. She's a cutie, isn't she? And so strong!"

"Wait, when you say 'La Belle Kotomi,'" I asked, "don't you mean yourself?"

"No, a horse, a pretty little horse!"

"What?"

"Gon-chama keeps racehorses. He's got a lot of famous ones. He just got a new mare, and he named her after me. Her debut is soon. Both Kotomis are going to make a killing, isn't that right, Gon-chama?"

"Hmmph!"

Kimiko thanked Kotomi and gave her an itemized receipt and the duplicate credit card receipt. "No need to see us off," Kotomi told Kimiko, so instead I escorted Kotomi and Gon down to the first floor.

Kotomi took Gon's arm and matched his slow pace, and I followed behind them. When we emerged onto the boulevard, we found the world shrouded in the dark blue of night, and a huge, glossy black car was waiting at the curb. The driver dashed out and opened the rear door, tucking Gon in as though he were folding him up. Kotomi followed, and the driver bowed deeply to her until every last bit of her was in. Only then did he quietly close the door. Then the smoked glass car window rolled down with a sound unlike any I'd heard before, like pure comfort itself, and Kotomi stuck her head out.

I was starting to bow, but she beckoned me over.

"Hana?"

"Yes?"

"I'll come again."

"Okay."

"Be good to Kimiko, okay?"

Kotomi held my gaze for a few seconds, smiling with only her mouth. It wasn't until the car had borne them away that I realized how boisterous everything around me was, and I turned to look, wondering if a fight had broken out nearby. But nothing was happening. Crowds of people moved through the night, laughing, joking, same as always, as the cars rushed by. The blinding white of the driver's gloves was burned into my retinas, and it glowed under the light of the glistening traffic signal. For some reason, loneliness closed in on me, so I ran back to the bar.

That evening, the neighboring bar Mamas and their employees brought their own clients over to Lemon, making for a busy opening night. The landlord made an appearance, too. Customers paid their bills and left, only to show up again an hour later with friends in tow. With around thirty square meters, Lemon was packed hot and close all night. Midnight came and went, and the air grew thick with cigarette smoke, but we kept drinking, and people sang karaoke one after another, we gossiped about this and that, listened to people talk about their lives, laughed at their jokes, beat tambourines, and drank more until two in the morning.

It turned out I could hold my liquor, just as I'd suspected. I probably put away about five big bottles of beer, but they only made me more giggly and relaxed. I didn't feel sick or uncomfortable at all. My wits and memory were still sharp, too. Kimiko was plastered, so I put her arm around my shoulders, and together we walked back to the apartment, laughing and talking at the tops of our lungs. The take for the day was ¥263,500—it would've taken four months of working at the restaurant for me to make that much.

FOUR

PREMONITION

1.

I first met Ran Kato out on the street.

Whenever I went outside to see a customer off or to go home after closing up the bar for the night, there was always a group of girls by the main drag, handing out fliers and pulling in customers. Ran was one of those girls.

She was petite and always wore the same pair of rhinestone-studded hot pink platform sandals. Her hair was bleached, almost blonde, and she had a narrow forehead. Her eyebrows were plucked thin, and her makeup stood out, too, her eyes accentuated in a dusting of white shimmer.

"Hi there," Ran said to me one night in early December. "Cold, isn't it? I've seen you around."

"Hi. Is it just you out here today?"

Kimiko had asked me to go to the drugstore to pick up a bottled energy shot. It was around nine.

"Yeah, all the other girls have customers. Except for me." Ran was wearing an oversized white bomber jacket and a strappy black dress that hugged her body. "It's kind of dead around here today, don't you think?" she asked with an exaggerated shiver. "You work around here, too, right?"

I turned to point toward our building and told her I worked at the bar on the third floor. Just then, En came out of Little

Heaven to see a customer off. I waved. She waved back, then ducked inside.

"A bar? What's it called?"

"Lemon."

"Lemon? I don't think I've heard of it."

"We're still pretty new. We've only been open a couple of months."

"I'm over there, down the street. You know that big building? The one with the huge atrium? I work on the second floor at the cabaret club."

"There's a club over there?"

"Yup. We probably don't have the same customers though."

A gust of cold wind blew between us. I smiled to let her know I was heading back, and Ran, arms crossed and hunched against the cold, shook her whole body like she was waving me off.

"Hey, Kimiko, did you know there was a cabaret club around here?"

Back upstairs, I handed the energy shot to Kimiko, who was slumped down in one of the booths. She twisted off the cap with a heavy sigh, then drank it slowly. She'd been under the weather for about a week now, making it through the nights with over-the-counter medicine and energy shots, and spending her days lying in bed.

"Ugh, why does this have to be so syrupy . . . Uh, what were you saying? A cabaret club? Yeah, maybe . . ."

"I was chatting with one of the girls from there just now."

"Huh. I guess it's a quiet day for everybody."

"How are you feeling?" I asked.

"All achy."

"Kimiko, if you don't get better by next week, you should see a doctor."

"Yeah, I know."

At the end of December, it would be a full three months since we opened. I was getting used to the job, and Lemon was doing all right. We inherited more than a few customers from Mama Atsuko, and got some new ones, too. Maybe sixty percent of them were older men who were Sangenjaya locals. Thirty percent were younger men—first-timers who happened to come in one day and came back every once in a while. The other ten percent were people who worked at other clubs and bars in the neighborhood. In that sense, no one was really a stranger. We had a good number of regulars who showed up at the bar like they were stopping by their local café to read the newspaper.

Customers had a few options for how they spent their money. Some went with our all-you-can-sing, all-you-can-drink option, which cost ¥4,000, plus the drinks they bought for us. So if they stayed for two hours or so, they'd pay about ¥6,000. Some bought bottles to keep at the bar, so they only paid for the mixers each time they came, but they tended to come a lot—some maybe three times a week. Then there were the people who ordered what they wanted à la carte. For them, the cover charge was ¥3,000; then they'd pay for karaoke and drinks on top of that. They were the ones who ended up spending the most.

I'd developed a taste and tolerance for beer, so I got straight to work whenever a generous customer came in and encouraged us to let loose. A medium bottle cost ¥800, so if they ordered three, that came to ¥2,400. At the restaurant where I used to work, that would have been almost four hours of work. It seemed too good to be true—to be able to make the same amount of money by just sitting there and drinking beer all night. On a good day, it wasn't unusual to make ¥10,000 or even ¥20,000 off a single customer.

Each day was different, like the weather or your mood, but on average, Lemon was pulling in around ¥30,000 a night. On top of that, Kotomi came by maybe twice a month, bringing her fancy customers from Ginza, and they were on a completely different level from our normal crowd, spending way more money than any of the regulars. And that meant that we made a lot more each month.

Plus, there was something special about the people who came to Lemon.

It was like they were all members of the same group, even the other bar and club workers from the neighborhood. Everyone got along and enjoyed each other's company; no one seemed to mind when Kimiko and I spent our time at other tables. We had four bar stools and three booths, so even at full capacity, we only had about a dozen customers in the place. Maybe that's what gave Lemon such a community feel. Once in a while, some first-timers would get angry about not getting enough attention from us and demand their money back. But Kimiko never seemed bothered about it. She always knew how to get those customers to calm down and go home. "Just forget about them," she'd tell me with a smile, but when that kind of thing happened, it always weighed heavy on me, and sometimes I'd stay awake all night thinking about it.

"Hey, Kimiko, I know we've kept everything under control so far, but I was thinking . . . what happens if one of us gets sick or something? What do we do then?"

"Are you saying we should hire some help?"

"Yeah . . . maybe one more person, like somebody to work part-time? We've been getting more customers, too. It feels like a missed opportunity when they leave unsatisfied. Who knows, maybe they could have become regulars. It's probably too close to the holidays for us to find somebody now, but maybe in the new year?"

"Maybe, yeah."

I tried bringing up the idea of hiring help with Kimiko a couple more times, but she never seemed that interested. It was the same when it came to money. I'd get all excited and tell her how much we'd made that month, and she'd smile and act happy, but it never seemed like it brought her the same kind of satisfaction it brought me.

So I ended up being in charge of the finances, too, taking care of things like paying our bills and keeping track of our profits.

It just sort of worked out that way, and plus it wasn't that complicated. All I had to do was go to the bank every month and pay our bills in cash: rent for Lemon and the apartment we shared, alcohol expenses and hot towel service for the bar, and our utilities. That was it. We never really talked about how to divide our earnings either. We had a bowl we kept next to the TV where we'd put money for day-to-day expenses, just like my mom and I used to do. Whenever we ran out, we put more in. I always made sure I had ¥5,000 in my wallet, and Kimiko still kept small bills and loose change in her pockets.

I kept the rest of our money in a sturdy cardboard box with a lid. Ever since the Snoozy incident, part of me thought it might be safer to put our money in the bank. But all I brought when I left home were some clothes and underwear, and my navy shoebox. I'd never had a bank account, and I didn't have an ID either. Kimiko said she'd forgotten the PIN to her bank account, and she'd lost her family seal, too. So the bank wasn't an option for us.

I didn't feel like there was any need to worry, though. People weren't coming and going into our apartment like they did when I lived with my mom. Still, on the way home from Lemon one night, I found a big, flat, round stone—like the kind people used to weigh down vegetables in a pickling barrel—and brought it home. I scrubbed the stone clean in the bathtub and placed it on top of our money box, just to be safe.

December was flying by. In the rush toward the end of the year, the city, the people, and time itself were all buzzing with a hectic energy. Everywhere I went, things seemed to twinkle and shine, and lively music filled the spaces between the shimmering lights. *So this is what the holidays are like in the city*, I thought. It wasn't like holidays in the town where I'd grown up, even the busier shopping districts I'd known as a kid were never like this. *And if this is what it's like in Sangenjaya, just imagine Shinjuku or Shibuya*. Those places were only a few train stops away, but they still only existed as concepts to me—place names and images of busy intersections I sometimes saw on TV. Whenever I thought about that lavish, unreal world, it made me think about Kotomi and the fancy club in Ginza where she worked. I didn't know the first thing about Tokyo—I didn't even know how to get to Ginza on the train if I wanted to. Whenever Kotomi came to Lemon, towing along men who spent huge amounts of money without batting an eye, she practically glowed like she'd been sprinkled from head to toe in fairy dust. *Is Ginza full of people like her? It has to be*, I thought.

In the clubs in Ginza, expensive champagne and brandy flew off the shelves, each bottle worth what normal people spend a month struggling to earn. And not just in one business either—it was happening in countless bars and clubs all at the same time.

Beautiful women, laughter, music from the grand piano, big bills everywhere. Gleaming black marble surfaces, effervescent champagne bubbles streaming out of long-necked bottles—scene after scene, soaked in wealth and luxury, whirled together in my mind. All I could do was sigh.

Lemon was nothing like a Ginza club, of course, but we made it through our first Christmas well enough and closed up for the holidays a couple of days later. Kimiko and I didn't have anywhere we wanted to go or anything we wanted to do, so we would have been fine keeping the bar open. But our hot towel service and liquor supplier were closed for the holidays, and we figured nobody would show up anyway, so we decided to call it a year.

"Are you going back to Ai's place for New Year's, Hana?" Kimiko asked as she ran a dustcloth over the wall.

She said she was doing the big end-of-year cleaning, but there wasn't much for her to do. We didn't have a lot of stuff to begin with, and she was always cleaning. As Kimiko wiped the walls, I lay against my folded-up futon and watched her making little circles with one hand.

"Nah, I'm not."

"Have you talked with her recently?"

"No, I don't have anything to say to her, so why waste money on the call? Doesn't she call you sometimes?"

"Nope."

"Huh . . . That makes sense, I guess."

I hadn't spoken to my mom since I left home at the end of the summer.

That day—the day I ran into Kimiko on the street—I left home and started living with her. And back then I was excited to be leaving, but also afraid—like maybe I was making a huge mistake. My mom was always off in her own world, doing whatever she wanted, and that was exactly why I worried about her. Moving in with Kimiko, I felt like I was abandoning my mom—maybe she wanted out just as bad, and here I was leaving without her. I was torn with guilt.

If my mom begged me to come home, what would I do? I gave it some thought, but the more I thought about it, the more confused and upset I became. Was she going to be able to make it on her own? What if she got caught up in some kind of trouble? Was she worried sick about me? I blamed myself for making the huge mistake of leaving without even telling her where I was going.

But it turned out I'd been wasting my time worrying. My mom didn't even realize I was gone until more than a week later.

When Kimiko got a call from her and handed me the phone, panic welled up in me. On the other end of the line, my mom started talking like normal, like everything was the same as always. She went on and on about how she was thinking about getting her driver's license, about the different options for driving school, about the cats she'd seen in the display window of some new pet shop. The longer I listened, the harder it got for me. When I couldn't take it anymore, I blurted, "Mom, I'm going to live with Kimiko from now on." Without missing a beat, she replied, "Sure, Hana, if that's what you want"—like I was asking her what she thought of my new hairstyle. She didn't ask me if I would keep going to school, or what I was going to do for money. She didn't ask me anything about my life. I half expected her to tell me it was out of the question, or that I should come home first so we could talk it over. But no. She wasn't sad, she wasn't angry. "You've always been so responsible,

Hana. And you're an adult now. Besides, you've got Kimi there. If you need me, you know where to find me, okay?" She said it all so cheerfully—then she hung up.

"The holidays sure are long," I said, faking a huge yawn. "What do people do anyway?"

"I don't know, go home to spend time with their families?"

"What about people who don't have families to go back to?"

"Go out with friends, maybe?"

"What if you don't have friends or the money to go out?"

"Hmm . . . Hang out around the house?"

"What if you don't have a house?"

"I guess New Year's wouldn't make any difference then."

"Maybe."

"Definitely."

Kimiko turned the cloth over, folded it neatly in half, and carefully polished the kotatsu tabletop. Then she took the top off, propped it up against the wall, yanked the blanket from the kotatsu, and tossed it over me. As the warmth overtook me, I squealed, "This is the best."

"Feels good, huh?"

"Yeah." I let the feeling of warmth and comfort envelop me, dispelling all the guilt and tension I'd been feeling about my mom. I let out a deep sigh. I was happy.

"Kotatsu burrito."

"Kotatsu burrito?"

"Yeah, you know, all wrapped up like a burrito. Mmm, I love it."

I closed my eyes and curled up under the blanket. It smelled like home, like warmth and comfort. I stayed curled up like that for a while.

"Plus," I said, popping my head out from under the blanket, "I have you, Kimiko."

She stopped what she was doing, looked over at me, and smiled faintly. "What's that supposed to mean?"

"I mean . . . don't I? I have you, Kimiko." Feeling embarrassed, I threw the blanket off, turned over on my back, then snuck a look in her direction. "I do, don't I? It's the two of us, right?"

"Sure it is."

"And we have money, too."

"Well, sure, for now."

"What do you mean 'for now'?" I asked, pouting. "We always will. Forever. I mean, if we keep this up, we won't have to worry about money ever again."

In my mind, I saw the ¥860,000 stashed in the box. That's what three months of hard work at Lemon had gotten us. The idea of that money made me feel proud and safe, but the combination of box and cash also reminded me of what happened with Snoozy. I couldn't even think of his name without clenching my jaw. Snoozy . . . Anger and hatred whirled up inside me until I found it hard to breathe. Whenever that happened, I'd drag out everything closing off my windpipe—the memory of his stupid hair, his dangling wallet chain, his filthy foot on my cushion—and stomp on it. Then, I'd smash it to pieces with the big round stone I'd put on top of the cardboard box.

"Oh, hey, Hana, guess what?"

"Huh? What?" I sprang up and looked at Kimiko.

"Yeongsu got you a cell phone."

"Seriously? Yesss!"

"He said he can bring it over tomorrow."

"That's awesome!"

"Why don't we make a hot pot tomorrow and invite him to dinner? He's pretty funny when he drinks."

I'd seen a lot of Yeongsu since Lemon opened. Sometimes we had lunch together, and sometimes he popped into Lemon when we were open. Every time he showed up, without fail, he handed Kimiko a white envelope, just like he had that first time. The last time I saw him, we started talking about how cool his phone was, and Kimiko, remembering that I'd been wanting one, asked if he could get one for me. And he actually did. I'd given up on the idea of ever having my own phone because I didn't have a guardian or any kind of ID, which meant I couldn't fill out the paperwork. I don't know what kind of magic Yeongsu pulled. I had no idea who I'd call or if anyone would call me, but as soon as Kimiko told me the good news, my excitement set my body tingling.

"Must be the power of yellow!" I said as I turned to look at the Yellow Corner—a collection of yellow knickknacks on a shelf I'd set up against the wall on the west side of the room.

I'd been buying all sorts of yellow things from hundred-yen shops and other stores around the neighborhood. A piggy bank, a stuffed animal, a pair of chopsticks, a makeup pouch, a pencil case, envelopes, notepads, stickers, a ball of yarn, a bunch of boxes in all different sizes, a keychain, fake flowers, a spool of ribbon, and even a yellow good-luck cat. Every time I added something new to the already crowded shelf, I felt like it made our future just a little brighter—like it was bringing us more good luck, one step at a time.

In our collection, there were dark yellows and light yellows, warm yellows and greenish yellows. There were so many kinds of yellow, so many shades. But yellow was what brought them all together. Simply by being yellow, they held a special power, giving us courage and comfort.

The next day at seven in the evening, Yeongsu came over to our place. He took one look at me and held out a silver cell phone. I jumped up from the kotatsu and ran over, grabbing the phone and the charger. When I saw my own number on the display, I couldn't contain my excitement. I barely noticed the hot pot cooking in front of me as I tried out all the buttons, then tried them out again.

"Yeongsu, how do I pay you back for this?" I asked when I finally came back down to earth.

"It's taken care of," he answered.

"No, I mean, not just the phone but . . . it costs money every month, right? Can I give you money when I see you?"

"You don't have to worry about that either."

"What, you mean you're going to pay for everything?"

"Well, not me personally. But you don't have to think about that."

"What do you mean? Who's gonna pay for it?"

"Don't worry about the details." He laughed, making a small grimace. "It's easy enough for me to expense it, along with everything else."

"Expense it? You have a business, Yeongsu?" I couldn't stop asking him one question after another.

"Hana, if he says it's okay, it's okay," Kimiko cut in. "The meat's ready. Hurry up and eat. You, too, Yeongsu."

"But . . . you're sure? It's really okay?"

Yeongsu nodded without looking at me, ladling the steaming food into his bowl. As I watched him eat, deep satisfaction bubbled up inside me. I'd never felt joy like it before.

It wasn't just the phone that made me so thrilled. It was somebody going out of their way to help me, somebody watching out for me and telling me I didn't have to worry. It made me feel safe and grateful, like I was being protected somehow . . . I couldn't quite have the words to describe it.

I thanked Yeongsu, over and over, from the bottom of my heart.

"It's no big deal. It's just a phone," he said, almost laughing.

"But it is a big deal," I said, barely able to get the words out.

I was so overwhelmed that I didn't even notice what was in the hot pot, but I dipped the meat and vegetables in the ponzu sauce, and everything tasted incredible. As the three of us ate, I yammered on and on, but before long, I picked up the phone again so I could put in Kimiko's and Yeongsu's numbers. As soon as I did, I called them both and joked about their ringtones, which made them laugh. Kimiko was having a beer, which she almost never did at home, and Yeongsu was sipping the makgeolli he'd brought over. The room was nice and warm, and we were enjoying ourselves. Some flashy news show was running on TV, a look back at the biggest stories of the year, working up to the ones with the biggest shock value: the handover of Hong Kong, the downfall of a major securities firm, the death of Princess Diana and her lover in a car chase. I didn't read the newspaper growing up, and whenever I watched the news on TV, everything always seemed like it was happening in a faraway place. Tonight, more than ever, all these major news stories seemed irrelevant to me.

"Got any ichimi?" Yeongsu asked.

"Shichimi okay?" Kimiko asked back.

"I'll go out and get some," Yeongsu said, getting up. "I'll go grab some beer, too."

"Wait, I'll go," I volunteered.

"You stay right there."

"No, I want to. Ichimi, and any beer will do, right?"

"Oh, grab some rice crackers for me, will you? Yuki no Yado," Kimiko added.

"Got it!"

I grabbed my phone, threw on a jacket, and rushed out. With my own phone in my pocket, our ordinary street transformed into an illuminated airstrip, leading me to some new place I couldn't wait to be. I was almost bouncing as I walked along.

When I got to the supermarket, I noticed Ran handing out fliers not far from the entrance. Her pink platform sandals and white bomber jacket made her stand out, almost floating in the crowd. I practically skipped over to her.

"Hi there! You still working today?"

"Oh, hi!" Ran broke into a smile when she saw me. "Yup, it's our last day today."

"Wow, you guys are serious, huh? We're already closed for the year."

"Makes sense. I guess it's already the twenty-eighth. You live around here?"

"Uh-huh, over on Chazawa-dori."

"I'm nearby, too. On the other side of Kannana-dori, three stations away. Sometimes I walk home after work."

"I don't think I've ever been that way. Hey, when does work start for you in the new year? Around the fifth?"

"I guess? I don't know actually. It's my last day there. I'm quitting."

"What? Seriously?" My voice came out louder than I expected, and I looked around to see if anybody was staring. "But why?"

"All kinds of reasons, I guess. But the minimum is too much for me. Maybe cabaret clubs aren't my thing. All the other girls get customers. I don't."

"So you're going to do something else for work? Or find another place?"

"I dunno . . . I haven't made up my mind yet. I've kinda been down in the dumps. Anyway, it's the only kind of work I can do . . ."

"Hey, I don't know anything about clubs, but . . ." There were more people going in and out of the supermarket now, so we moved toward the street to get out of the way. "How much do you make working there? If you don't get customers, do you get less money? Does that change your pay?"

"Um . . ." Ran smiled uncomfortably. "I mean, I don't know if this is what you're asking, but yeah, all you get is the base pay, which is like, seven thousand yen? On really good nights, like miracle nights, I've gotten something like twenty thousand, but that hasn't happened in a while. It's different for the other girls, though. They make a lot. It's just . . . customers never pick me. Maybe they can tell I don't really want to be there."

"You don't?"

"I mean, I do, but it's just not a good place for me. All the other girls, we don't really get along. It was a lot better where I worked before."

"So every club is different?"

"Well, yeah."

Just then, a group of men walked by, and one of them turned and yelled something at us, though I didn't catch what. Another guy smacked him on the head, laughing, and slurred, "Apologies, ladies." Every one of them was drunk. With a big smile on her face, Ran went around handing each guy a flier. When she smiled, her narrow forehead grew even narrower, and I suddenly remembered the one good friend I had in elementary school.

Ran didn't look anything like her, but the memories came flooding back all the same: the two of us walking around after school until it got dark, our backpacks swaying from side to side, hours after the other kids had left because their moms were waiting for them. I remembered how we used to sit on stairs around the neighborhood—the housing complex, the shrine, fire escapes.

The guys stumbled past us, grabbing and shoving each other as they made their way to the main street.

"Hey, gimme your phone number. You have a cell phone?" I pulled mine out to show her. "This is mine. Let's meet up, over New Year's, or after that. We're practically neighbors."

"Okay!"

"Hey, what's your name? I'm Hana, as in flower. Hana Ito."

"I'm Ran—Ran Kato."

Ran, like an orchid. I noticed Ran had a bunch of cute, colorful charms dangling from her phone. *Wait, I have one of those, that fluffy one on the yellow shelf. I should put it on my phone tomorrow.*

"I'll call you, okay? I gotta go grab a few things from the supermarket. Good luck with work tonight."

"Thanks, Hana."

The supermarket was white and frosty like a freezer, so I zipped my coat all the way up. There were shoppers everywhere—maybe because the other stores weren't open so late. I headed straight for the ichimi, grabbed some beer and a package of Yuki no Yado, paid at the register, and left. By the time I got back out, Ran was gone. Maybe she'd found one last customer.

I was still buzzing with joy because I had a phone. I clutched it in my pocket, traced the buttons with my fingers, pulled it out again just to watch the screen light up, and cycled through all the menus as I walked back.

Back home, I found Kimiko watching TV. Yeongsu was gone.

"Where's Yeongsu?" I asked.

"He got a call and had to go," she said. "Right after you left."

"Was it work for that business he was talking about?"

"Maybe."

"I got him the ichimi, though."

"We can save it for next time."

"But it's the end of the year. He still has work?"

"Maybe things get busy at the end of the year?"

Kimiko was buzzed. She had her legs tucked into the kotatsu with the blanket up to her waist, grinning with her eyes closed. I had a little more hot pot, then switched the burner off.

There was a variety show on TV. Every time someone said something, the people around them cracked up and clapped. It made me wonder how many TV celebrities there were in the world. How much money did they get for one of these shows? I couldn't begin to imagine. I kept my eyes on the screen for a while, but I soon got bored, so I lowered the volume and changed the channel. TV shows seemed pretty much the same to me.

"Hana," Kimiko said sleepily. "I'm gonna take a quick nap. Wake me up in like an hour, okay? I'll get up and take care of the dishes."

"I can do that."

"No, no, I got it. There's a trick to it."

Then Kimiko went to sleep—right where she was.

Kimiko was particular about how the apartment was cleaned, and she didn't like it when I tried to help. No, it wasn't that she disliked it—it threw her off. The only exception was when we were getting ready to open the bar; for that, we split things up, but as a rule she wanted to do everything at home herself. I told her it would go faster if we worked together, but she insisted there was a specific way of doing everything. I'd grown up in a messy house, so I'd never learned how to clean, and I wasn't very good at it. I had no idea what Kimiko meant when she said there was a trick to it. Whenever she had the chance, she grabbed her dustcloth and wiped down different spots around the apartment while we talked or watched TV. An orderly apartment was new to me, but it was a pleasant surprise to live with somebody who constantly paid attention to our living space and took care of it. Kimiko wasn't as interested in doing the laundry though, so I made sure to hang our clothes out to dry and fold them up nice and neat.

She was snoring softly.

I snuck over as quietly as I could. Her mouth was hanging open, drool glistening on her lip. When I saw it, I had to turn away, to keep myself from laughing. Then I took a deep breath and looked at her face again.

What if I hadn't met Kimiko two summers ago? What if I hadn't found her again this year? I tried to imagine it. Well, I'd still be living with my mom, riding my bike to a school I didn't care about, working all day to save up money at a job where I couldn't make more than a thousand yen an hour. It wasn't difficult to recall the building where I'd spent my childhood, my whole life up until this past summer. I remembered every single detail: the cracked walls, the bare bulbs hanging in the dim hallway, the small, flimsy doors on both sides, the faded Evergreen Hills sign. All those things were still very real to me, so real that I started to feel suffocated by the damp air that filled that place. I shook my head and looked around the room. Four blindingly white walls. I was used to it now, but I remembered how the first time I came to this apartment, the pristine glare hurt my eyes.

As I looked at those walls, a strange thought overtook me—*What if I'm only imagining that I live here with Kimiko, and the real me is still living back in that building? What if I'm still stuck in that TV room, staring up at the ceiling with nowhere to go? After Kimiko left me, and Snoozy ran off with my money—what if I am just lying there, and everything that happened after that is a dream, just a fantasy created by my desperate imagination?*

No, no—I'm here. I'm here now. Kimiko's sleeping right here, and this is the real me. I pressed my hands against my cheeks to make sure what I felt was real. *Besides, it isn't summer now. It's winter. There's only one me, and this is where I am, where I exist, this place, right now—there's no other me, no other place.* I exhaled deeply, emptying my lungs of air, and nodded to myself as if to confirm my existence. Then, I took a good look at Kimiko's face one more time.

With her eyes closed, Kimiko looked less guarded than usual. I could see tiny sunspots that I didn't normally notice, and fine lines between her eyebrows, under her eyes, and around her mouth. For some reason, looking at her made me emotional, like I was about ready to cry, and I thought, *I have to work harder, to make sure Lemon keeps going.* Not like I hadn't been trying up until then, but I wanted to try even harder. A whole lot harder. I sat there for a while, watching her sleep, but when I got up to go to the bathroom, I noticed the white envelope off to the side of Kimiko's head.

It was one of those envelopes Yeongsu was always giving her. This had to be from today—and Kimiko had just left it lying there.

I stared at the white rectangle for a while, then looked back at Kimiko's face. She was deeply asleep. I gulped and reached for the envelope. It wasn't sealed. When I looked inside, the sepia tone of ten-thousand-yen bills jumped out at me. I counted the bills. Fifteen total. There was a piece of paper in there, too, and when I opened it, I saw someone had scribbled down names with numbers next to them: "Yusuke Ochi 5. T. Yama 7. Yoshimi 3." I'd never seen Yeongsu's handwriting before, but I could tell right away it was his. I guessed that the numbers were breakdowns for the ¥150,000. I slid the money and the note back into the envelope and quietly put it back where I'd found it.

2.

Ran and I met up on January 3. She seemed different somehow—her makeup was the same, so maybe it was what she was wearing or just the fact that it was daytime.

She wore a short, fluffy black coat over a satin shirt, a miniskirt, and white platform boots that made her even taller than the sandals she wore for work. We met at Sangenjaya Station to get on the subway together and go to Shibuya. We'd talked on the phone a few times after we exchanged numbers, and at some point, Ran suggested meeting up to see *Titanic*.

We had to wait in a long line to buy tickets, and the movie was really long, too. When it was over, we squeezed ourselves into an elevator full of women sighing for Leonardo DiCaprio. "Oh Leo, my prince . . ." "I need to see him again . . ." "What a hottie . . ." Then the doors opened, and we were swept up into a wave of people. We weaved through the crowds and made our way across the intersection to the arcade across from the theater, where we waited about fifteen minutes for a purikura photo booth to open up so we could take pictures together. Then we walked past the 109 building, where clerks were shouting "Sale! Sale! Sale!" at the top of their lungs, and moved on to Center Gai, where there were even more people. We got in line at McDonald's to have a late lunch. We were still talking about the movie. "That giant iceberg looked so real, huh?" "I think it's based on a true story." "Do you think you'd survive if you were on that ship?" As we sat there chatting, more and more people came in, and I found it hard to stop watching them. Everyone was talking and laughing so loudly that I couldn't tune them out. I was tired and irritated. My whole body was tense, so much so it hurt.

I couldn't even enjoy my Coke, though I kept sipping. I started to realize the awful tension reminded me of something—something I'd felt before and knew well. Then it hit me: school. Everybody in the McDonald's was young, and the energy they were giving off made me think of being in school. Their voices, the way they spoke, the color of their hair, their makeup, their clothes. They each had their own characteristics, but deep down they were all the same.

The air around us was electrified with a defiant, in-your-face energy, the peculiar mixture of boredom, excitement, and guardedness that came from multiple groups of kids occupying the same space. I was an only child, and I'd spent most of my life in a cramped apartment with my mom and her hostess friends. For someone like me, who had never been comfortable at school or around anyone my own age, the crowded McDonald's wasn't just overwhelming—it was downright torture.

"Uh, Ran, do you come to Shibuya a lot?"

"Yeah, I guess so. When I go shopping for clothes and makeup. It beats Shinjuku, for sure."

"So you're okay with, um, big crowds?"

"I guess? I don't know. I've never really thought about it before."

"Yeah . . . Hey, when we're done here, do you want to go back to Sancha? There's a McDonald's there, too, and it's always empty. That way we'll be closer to home, and we can just relax."

"Sure."

Once we'd taken the subway back to Sangenjaya, I was finally able to let go of all the pressure I'd been holding inside, finally able to breathe deeply. Once we got aboveground, we headed straight to the McDonald's, ordered orange juice and Coke and fries, and found a table.

"Sancha's the best," I said, and I meant it.

"So did you, like, grow up here?"

"No. I'd never been here until last summer."

"Really? Where did you live before that?"

"Higashimurayama. What about you?"

"I'm from Satte."

"Satte? Where's that?"

"Yeah, nobody ever knows where it is. It's this tiny city at the edge of Saitama. That's where my parents are, and I used to commute from there. I dropped out of high school and started going to this beauty school in the city."

"Beauty school, huh. Oh hey, how old are you?"

"Eighteen. Turning nineteen this year. What about you?"

"I'll be eighteen this year. I quit school, too. Well, I guess I didn't actually quit. I just stopped going. So . . . you go to classes during the day?"

"Not anymore," Ran said, looking down at her straw. "I

stopped. I kept up early on, but it was so far. I'd get up at five in the morning, ride my bike to the station, get on the train to go to school. Then I'd hang out with friends after school, you know? So by the time I got home and took a bath, it'd be like one in the morning. Three hours a day, just to commute. I thought I could do it, but when I actually tried, there was just no way."

"Three hours is a lot."

"Yeah, seriously. I wanted to get my own place in Tokyo, but my family didn't have that kind of money. They were totally against me going to beauty school, too. They were like, where do you think you're gonna get the money for that? And they told me if I was gonna quit high school, I should just get a job back in Satte. I begged my grandpa, though, and he agreed to pay my tuition. So I couldn't complain about how hard the commute was, you know? Plus, all my friends at school were loaded. They always had money to buy new clothes and makeup. I was the only one who couldn't."

"So your friends, their parents were giving them money?"

"Yeah, probably, none of them had jobs. Most of them were from the city. I dunno, they had money. And every time I went out with them, they'd just spend and spend, and I was like, what should I do? That's when I started working nights, once a week at first, and only till the last train."

"You mean after school was over?"

"It was a total side gig at first, but then I needed money, so I signed up for more shifts. The money was good, you know? Back when I quit high school, I worked some temp jobs in Satte stocking shelves at the drugstore, doing checkout at the supermarket, things like that. But I couldn't make more than a hundred thousand a month. The cabaret club was a different story. Of course I got some guys I couldn't stand, you always do, but it's not like you don't get creepy customers working regular daytime jobs. Anyway, once I started doing three nights a week, it didn't make sense to commute all the way from Satte anymore. It was too far, and all I did there was sleep. It made no sense, know what I mean?"

"Oh, completely." I nodded earnestly.

"I mean, what's the point? So I started staying over with a friend who had her own place. But clothes cost a lot of money, you know? I didn't want to stick out at school. And I wanted to go out sometimes, too. For a while, I tried doing both: days at school and nights at work, but I couldn't keep it up for long. I started oversleeping, missing classes. Then I flunked all my tests. Once your grades get that bad, you really don't feel like going to school anymore. Plus, I was the only one working at a club, so of course I didn't fit in. My friends stopped asking me to hang out. I could tell what they were thinking—that I was tacky, that I was a loser for working at a club. So I quit. I guess if I was still in school, I'd be taking the national exam in a couple of months."

"What did your parents say when you quit?"

"Oh, they tore me apart. They said I was stupid, that I can't do anything right. But I could tell they were actually relieved. Beauty school isn't cheap. I got the feeling they were happy that they wouldn't have to pay for another year. I mean, it was grandpa who agreed to pay, but in the end it's all family money. They asked me what I was going to do. I could tell they weren't that worried, though, not really. I told them I was going to stay in the city, work part-time and split the rent on a place with a friend I met at beauty school. They didn't try to stop me."

"So you're living with your friend now?"

"No, my boyfriend."

"Wait," I said in disbelief, "you have a boyfriend?"

"Uh-huh."

I sipped my Coke, swallowing slowly, feeling what was left of the fizz tingle against the insides of my cheeks. I was caught off guard, though I didn't know why.

"We've been living together for like eight months now. I don't think I can take much more of him, though. He's kinda controlling."

"And . . . what made you want to go to beauty school?"

"I don't know . . . I guess I figured I needed to pick up some kind of skill, so I could get work. It was either that or pet grooming. That's what everybody else was doing. And I guess I thought something would work out if I was in Tokyo. Or more like, nothing would work out unless I came here. Why'd you decide to move to Sancha, Hana?"

"Well, I didn't really, um, decide . . ."

As simply and quickly as I could, I told Ran about where I'd grown up, about meeting Kimiko two years ago, about finding her again last summer and leaving home.

"Wow, that's so cool," Ran said, like she was blown away. "So her name's Kimiko."

"Oh, you know her?"

"I've seen her with you a few times. You always walk home together, right? She's kind of tall? So she's the Mama at the bar?"

"Sorta? It doesn't really feel that way, though. We kind of run the bar together. Well, actually, she mostly leaves it up to me. I'm the one who chose the name Lemon, too."

"That's amazing," Ran said, sounding impressed.

"Yellow's our lucky color. Have you ever heard of feng shui? The way it works is, if you put yellow things in the west, like knickknacks and decorations and stuff, you get this boost of good luck with all your finances. Plus, Kimiko has the kanji for yellow in her name, and lemons are yellow, too, right? It's a super powerful color."

"Yeah, I've heard of feng shui. I think maybe I saw something on TV about it? What was it . . . Oh, you know. Dr. What's-his-name, he was really selling it, right?"

"Um, I dunno . . . I think that might be something else," I said, clearing my throat.

"Oh really? I could've sworn that was it," Ran said, tilting her head. "Do you not watch much TV?"

"Not really. Kimiko likes to leave it on during the day, though."

"What about music? What's your go-to karaoke song? What magazines do you read?"

"I don't know anything about music. I listen when customers sing at the bar, but I don't actually sing myself . . . I'm terrible at it. I don't read magazines either. Kimiko does, sometimes, so we have some lying around. Weekly gossip rags, stuff like that."

"Wait, so what did you do with your friends before you left school?" Ran asked almost teasingly.

"I worked. I didn't have any friends. I've never been to a purikura photo booth before today. It was really cool."

"Seriously?"

"Yeah, seriously."

"I don't believe that. I mean, you're so funny."

"Me? I'm funny?" I was surprised.

"Totally."

"You're kidding, right?"

"Not at all."

"How am I . . . funny?" I asked nervously.

"I mean, you just are! You're also kinda different, you know? You don't wear makeup. Your hair's not dyed, and you probably don't do anything with your eyebrows, right? Plus, working as a bar hostess is kinda rare these days. And your fashion . . . I don't even know how to describe it. Hey, are there any celebrities you like?"

"No, I don't know any."

"So what do you do for fun, when you aren't working? What do you like?"

"I don't do anything. I like . . ." *I like, I like . . . What do I like?* "I like working . . . I mean, I like making money."

"See?" Ran laughed out loud. "You're hilarious."

"Um, I guess . . . But you have to make money to live, right?"

"Definitely. You do need money to live, you're right about that. Hey, I like your phone strap. It's yellow, too, your lucky color. So, does it work?"

"Oh yeah, it does, one hundred percent," I said as I stroked the furry charm attached to my phone. "We opened Lemon at the end of September, and it's been going really well so far."

"The customers are okay?"

"We have lots of regulars. Sometimes new people come, but

the ones who come every day are the old guys who've lived in the neighborhood forever. They actually spend more than you'd think. I mean there are some skinflints, but mostly they're good."

"The locals, huh?"

"Uh-huh. They're like, landowners? There's a lot of them like that."

"Oh, yeah. I know what you mean." Ran nodded.

"You know the guys who own those places that look like they don't do any business, but they never close down either? All their goods are dusty, and it's all random, like, mugs and rubber slippers and stuff? The owners tell me they don't care if the shops make money. They keep 'em open for taxes, or because it's too much of a hassle to shut down. They get enough income from leasing their land to buildings and shops and apartment complexes. I remember I was walking around Sancha one day and I realized I was seeing the same name on house after house. At first, I thought it was just a coincidence, but then I found out they all belonged to one of our customers, his whole family—all his relatives, too—have been living there from way back. In the hugest houses, too. It's crazy, right?"

"Totally."

"But then he comes in and he's like, 'This is the only place where I feel at home. My son's in charge now, and I don't have anywhere around the house where I can be myself. My daughter-in-law is always nagging me, and my grandkids never shut up.'"

"Huh. We never got people like that at the club. Or, I don't know, maybe I just never sat with them."

"No, I mean, I bet clubs and bars like ours have different customers. These guys have been coming to the bar for years, way before we took over. It's like . . . we're a community center, but with booze and karaoke. I can't complain, though, because they're decent customers, and they spend money," I said as I reached for the fries, "but it really is crazy. These guys make tons and tons of money every month, and they don't have to lift a finger. They have their land, and it's gonna stay that way until they die. They can live their whole lives without worrying about anything. What does that even mean? Land is land. It didn't belong to anybody in the beginning, right? So how did they get it?"

"Seriously. From what I hear, when the war ended, some people were just like, 'From here to here is mine now,' and that's how they got rich. Know what I mean?"

"But why do you think some people were able to do that and other people weren't?"

"Maybe they were just smart about it and grabbed what they could when they had the chance?" Ran said, cocking her head.

"I wonder what it would feel like to be born into a family like that, where you can live every day of your life without thinking about money."

"I guess we'll never know, huh?"

"But I mean, are your parents poor, Ran?"

"Oh yeah, they are. Our house is super small and literally falling apart. My dad got hurt really bad on the job a few years back. Now he's unemployed and bedridden. My mom works multiple shifts a day, and we've got no savings. Flat broke. They're living off the insurance money, and living with my grandpa, so no rent. That's the only reason they can scrape by. I have two little brothers, too. The last time they called me, they told me I didn't have a room at home anymore. I mean, that room was the size of a closet to start with. I guess all I'm saying is, I don't have a place to go back to now."

"Damn."

"That's right," Ran said and laughed.

"I guess our situations aren't that different after all," I said and laughed, too.

"You know, I don't think I've ever told anybody about my family like this before."

We didn't say anything else for a while. Just sat there sipping our drinks and picking away at our fries. There was a guy sitting at the table next to us, dressed head to toe in black, swaying to the music on his headphones. One table over from him, a woman still in her coat sat with her arms folded. She hadn't moved the whole time we'd been there, and her bangs were covering most of her face, so I couldn't tell if she was asleep or not.

After a while, I asked, "What are you going to do for work now, Ran?"

"Well, there's not much else I can do, so I guess I'll have to find another club. Get an interview. I wish I could stay in Sancha, but there aren't that many options around here."

"Hey, why don't you come and help out at Lemon until you find something else?"

"What?"

"It's just us right now, Kimiko and me, and we're getting really busy. I'll talk to Kimiko about it. We can come up with an hourly rate, too. Just till you find something else."

"That . . . that'd be really great, but . . ." Ran hesitated. She was flushed, and she chose her next words carefully. "You guys don't have minimums? And there's no one else? It's just you and Kimiko?"

"No minimums. Just me and Kimiko. Oh, but how well do you hold your liquor?"

"Pretty well. I mean, I was the strongest drinker at my last job."

"No way!" I said giddily. "I'm the one with the tolerance at Lemon. Kimiko gets drunk super quick, so it's all down to me. But if you were there, we could go all night."

"Oh yeah we could."

"You're not exaggerating, right?"

"I've never even had a hangover."

"Wow. I have a feeling you and I are gonna be killer," I said. "I'll talk to Kimiko and call you, okay?"

We ordered chicken nuggets and more Coke and spent the next two hours talking away—about how Ran did her ganguro-style eye makeup and plucked her eyebrows, how the millennium was only a couple of years away, and how Nostradamus and his prophecies were all the rage when we were younger.

When we finally left, it was completely dark out. In the crisp winter air, the traffic lights, shop lights, and streetlights sparkled and glimmered, brighter even than usual.

I had never spent the day with a girl my own age like that, and I was having so much fun I didn't want it to end. We crossed the main drag and followed it down, peering inside the shops.

At the bookstore, Ran pointed at a stack of paperbacks on display. "Hey, look! It's that feng shui guy. See?"

I took a closer look and sure enough, on the cover were the words "#1 BESTSELLER" and a photo of a middle-aged man called Dr. Copa flashing a toothy smile. I picked up the top copy and flipped through.

According to Dr. Copa, feng shui could bring you a whole lot more than money: it could bring you good luck in health, family, career, relationships, romance, marriage, you name it. But what I needed—what Kimiko and I needed—was money. Nothing else mattered. Once I confirmed that yellow was all we needed, I put the book back with a renewed sense of confidence.

When I got home, Kimiko wasn't there. I filled the tub and took my first long bath in a while. Kimiko had told me not to wait up because she was going to see Kotomi and wouldn't be back till late. Without Kimiko around, I was antsy, but after spending the whole day doing new things, I must have been more tired than I thought—I fell asleep instantly.

That night, I dreamed about Leonardo DiCaprio.

We were standing at the very front of a luxury passenger ship drifting across a dark ocean and talking about the end of the world. I called him Leo, my prince, and I was trying to explain to him about Nostradamus's prophecies, waving my hands dramatically to make my point. Leo looked at me with kind eyes, which made me want to keep talking. I wanted him to know everything I felt in my heart. *I'm about to go fall in love with that spoiled rich girl and die, but that's not something I chose myself,* he confessed to me. "What do you mean?" I asked. *No one in this world gets to choose the life they live. I was brought into this world to make people understand that . . .* "I think I see what you mean," I said, nodding.

Believe me, that girl's not the one for me. Not even close. She doesn't know the first thing about life, about what it means to be human. She's got cotton candy for brains. I could never fall in love with someone like that. I didn't know what to say. Leo's crystal blue eyes sparkled; then he looked right at me. *I know what a hard worker you are, Hana. And I know how incredible and smart you are. I see you.* His words rang through every part of my body. I shook with pleasure and tears brimmed in my eyes. "Leo, my prince, please don't die," I pleaded. "I don't know who decided you have to die, but you don't have to. Aren't you scared? It's freezing out there. The water, it'll kill you in an instant." *Thank you, sweet Hana. You're so kind. But I'm not afraid of dying. Everyone has to go sometime.* Then he reached out and caressed my cheek. I watched his rosy lips as they drew closer to mine, and then I—I woke up. Ejected from the dream, I had no idea where I was or how I'd gotten there. For a moment or two, I just lay in a daze. Then my heart caught up and started pounding. I knew it was only a dream, but it was so weirdly real that I didn't know what to do with myself. I had the strongest urge to go and see *Titanic* again—right away. But then, I went back to sleep and forgot all about it.

FIVE

SPRINGTIME OF YOUTH

1.

The police showed up at Lemon in the middle of February. It was an hour before opening, and Kimiko was vacuuming while I was counting the till. We turned at the sound of the automatic door to find a big man in what could only be a cop's uniform. "Beg your pardon," he said, lowering his head and then peering around. Behind him there was another officer, one size smaller, his expression somber.

"Sorry to bother you while you're getting ready. I'm Officer Sano, we're stationed at the Sangenjaya Police Box."

Kimiko met them at the door, so I stepped out from behind the counter to join her. I'd passed by police officers on bicycles or seen them through the police box window plenty of times, but I'd never been so close to them before. Real police officers—my pulse began to race, and I couldn't stop blinking. And then it popped into my head: *They know.* What they knew and about whom, I had no idea, but they knew.

"And are you the Mama?"

"Yes," Kimiko said, the same as she'd say to anyone else, but I sensed a hardness in her voice.

"You may already be aware, but we're here today regarding an incident in the tattoo parlor on the second floor."

"The tattoo parlor?"

"Yes, yes. Last Sunday they were robbed. The burglars entered when no one was there."

This was the first we'd heard of it, and Kimiko and I looked at each other with surprise.

"There's been a rash of burglaries lately. Is your bar closed on Sundays?"

"We are, yes," Kimiko said.

"I see. We don't know yet what time the burglars entered, and we're still taking inventory of the damages, as well as what's gone missing."

The officer, Sano, despite his intimidating build, spoke with a friendly tone, like he was just making polite conversation. His attitude made me relax, and I slowly exhaled the breath I'd been holding.

"Have you already arrested the thief?"

"No, no, not yet. That's all in the future, but as you know, this building is rather tucked away. And there's only one business per floor. No security cameras." Officer Sano gave us a troubled smile. "And this building already had an incident not too long ago. A customer punched the owner of the tattoo parlor. And the assailant ran off before we could catch him. We don't know yet if that same man was involved with this robbery."

"What?" Kimiko hummed. "How frightening."

"Of course, it sounds like you're not witnesses, but if you think of something, anything at all, that might have something to do with the robbery, please do give us a call. We're also asking that you make sure your security is in order, maybe beef up your locks or get a camera. Be sure to lock up when you leave. I'm sure you're careful, but there are a lot of shop owners who tuck the keys in the gas meter or stick them under the doormats outside their shops. Which, of course, is an invitation to burglars."

Kimiko kept her arms crossed in front of her chest and nodded.

"We're also making a list of contact information for our patrol officers. If you'd like, we can put down your name and number so that if anything happens, we can be here right away."

"Maybe next time," Kimiko said with a smile. Officer Sano nodded readily, as though this was all part of the routine, gave a sharp bow, and then left with his partner.

Even once the police officers were gone, Kimiko and I remained where we stood. We were still frozen there when the automatic door opened again, startling me.

"So they came here, too?" En asked, standing just where the officers had stood.

"You scared me, En," I said, holding my chest. "Really, really scared me."

"Why'd this happen?" En stepped in, shaking her head as she made her way to a booth. She sat down with a sigh. "You're not open yet, right? How 'bout a beer?"

Kimiko and I sat across from En, and the three of us had a beer together. En said that the Sano duo had stopped by her place about thirty minutes ago to give her the news, and she was shocked to hear there'd been two incidents in the same building where she did business. It was still early, but En had been drinking even before she came up, and her eyes were red-rimmed.

"Do you know the person who runs the tattoo place?" Kimiko asked.

"No, not really. But all the same, frightening, isn't it? First, the guy was beaten, and then he gets burgled."

"I suppose."

"Sure, they went for the second floor this time, but it could have been me or y'all. Thought makes me sick."

"But nothing happened to us," Kimiko said.

"Maybe we just got lucky! He said it was Sunday, right. They could have broken in, for sure. Not that there's much to steal from Little Heaven, not anything that'd put me out, anyway. Imagine if I'd stopped on by though. Sometimes I do on Sundays. He'd want money, but I don't have any, so for payback he'd punch me, maybe even kill me. A lot of people get killed that way. Thinking about it scares me down to my bones."

"Well, that's just weird," Kimiko said with a laugh.

"Nothing weird about it. Aren't you frightened?"

"No, not really. I don't get it."

"But there was a fight and a burglary right next door!"

"Well, yeah, but nothing happened to *us*."

"But I'm telling you, that just means we were lucky. It could've been me. It could've been y'all. And that's what's scary."

"You're making it so complicated."

"Well, you're—never mind." The moment she said those words, En's expression darkened, so she piped up again, as though to banish that darkness. "Hana, give me another."

"How far do you think the police will go?" I asked as I topped off her glass. "Do you think they'll actually catch the burglar?"

"Doubt it," En said. "There was a break-in a couple years ago on the other side of the road. Back then, they took fingerprints, asked questions. But that was it. Forget about it, case closed."

I remembered when my money had been stolen, how it never even crossed my mind to go to the police. But even if I had, I'm sure nothing would've come of it. It's not like my name was written on the bills, and I couldn't prove how much I'd had. Even if they'd dusted for fingerprints, Snoozy had probably wiped the place down with the hem of his shirt, and then what? Honestly, it had taken a while for me to realize the money was missing. Who's to say they wouldn't have blamed the whole thing on my mother. My only option was crying myself to sleep—my heart sank into the darkness of that thought.

"I'm getting fed up with life," En said with a sigh. "Am I living to eat or just eating to live?"

"En, you're bringing yourself down," Kimiko said.

"Of course I am. You're both still young; your bodies can do anything. When I was your age, I didn't think about a thing. But nothing good ever happens anymore. Only ever the bad stuff. And it's not just me. Everyone, the whole world, is going crazy. Just think about that huge earthquake not too long ago, did you see? The whole Hanshin Expressway completely flipped over, and the city was a sea of fire. And the crazies are getting together and spewing poison left and right. Nothing makes sense anymore. The world is just crazy. I feel like I'm living in a manga."

En always got chattier the more she drank, but tonight, there wasn't a trace of her usual cheer.

"They say Japan still has money, that it's a safe country, but they're wrong. Worse things are going to happen, awful things. Countries are like people, you know. The good times don't last long. The springtime of youth, when you don't have to worry and you can laugh everything off, it only lasts a second. Gone just like that. Sure, we live longer now, but the longer you live, the more your head fuzzes out, goes blank. Look at me, how many more years can I run my restaurant? One injury, one illness, and it's all over. No pension, no savings. No family either. In fact—" En finally paused to take a breath, sighing deeply. "I had this customer, Yosshi, came in all the time, but then I realized I hadn't seen him in a while, and it turns out he's dead."

"What?" I asked, surprised.

"Died in his house. Alone. Just as he was getting out of the bathtub."

"He lived alone?"

"Guess so. A vein popped in his brain, and that was it. I've known him twenty years. But the last time he came, we had a fight, if you can believe it. Well, we fought all the time, but I thought we'd make up like we always do. And now he's dead."

"What did you fight about?" Kimiko asked.

"He told me I was seasoning the stew too strong these days, getting the flavor all wrong, just little complaints of his, and I told him I hadn't changed a thing about the recipe, and then he joked my food's all messed up cause I'm a drunk. Then I lost my temper, and he said this and I said that and he said this again, and next thing I knew, I said, 'Get the hell out,' and he said, 'You bet I will.' And that was that."

En sighed again.

"But you know, Yosshi was right. I'm a drunk, and I can't taste what's good anymore. My head's no good, neither is my tongue. I asked my other regulars, and at first, they didn't want to tell me, but eventually they did. 'The food's been off for a while now,' they said. And of course it has been, how could it not be, with me day drinking all the time. Anyway, that was the last I saw him. Well, I guess it's better than getting really sick and suffering for years and years before finally dying. That's the only silver lining, or at least that's what I tell myself. After he died, there was no one to take care of things, to plan his funeral, see, so they ended up putting him with a bunch of other people who died around the same time. Cremated him and that was that. Burned right up."

Neither of us said anything, just drank our beer.

"I know I shouldn't be saying this to you two, but working the nightlife is plain miserable. Sure, it's fine when you're young. But everyone gets old, that's life. I didn't understand it until I finally got old myself. I've put my everything into work, and I've got nothing left."

"Come on, En, cheer up," Kimiko said.

"I'm gonna tell it to you straight, girls, make sure you start saving up right now. Or find yourself a rich guy and live the easy life . . . No, don't do that. There aren't hardly any decent rich guys out there. Save your money, all your own, save it and save it, and just sip off the top to make ends meet, that's all you need. 'Cause there's no guarantees or promises in this life. You can have friends, and you can have buddies, but if you don't have money, they all fall through. The second you're poor you lose your edge. People die, and the ones that don't, they end up all alone. Do you know how awful it is when your time comes and you don't have money? People'll tell you you can't take it with you, but who says you need to? Whatever's left can stay right here. People get old and they die, but money, money doesn't."

The phone box light started flashing, so I got up and answered it. It was Ran. Ran had been working at Lemon since after the New Year's holiday, but she'd gotten a fever last weekend and hadn't been able to come in this week. She sounded better on the phone, and I was relieved. Her fever was down, but her voice was still shot, so she asked for today off as well, just to be safe. She promised to call tomorrow, and then we hung up, and I went back to En and Kimiko.

The dim light of the bar robed En in gloom, and Kimiko watched her in silence. At last, she asked if En would like another drink, but En said no, she had to get back to the restaurant, and she stood. She tried to pay for the drinks with change from her coin purse, but we both smiled, said "No need," and promised we'd come to Little Heaven for dinner early tomorrow evening.

"The food tastes like shit," En said with a feeble laugh.

"It's always delicious," Kimiko said, and I nodded.

The elevator arrived with a rattle, and En slowly packed herself in. Under the faint gray elevator light, she turned back to us and hit the button, smiling for just a moment before she closed her eyes. As the elevator door slid shut, I couldn't help but think of a coffin. I tried to shake the image off. That day, we only had two first-timers, and the take for the night was ¥14,600. Those two left right after eleven, and we could tell that no one else was coming, so at midnight, we gave the bar a quick clean and headed home.

When we arrived, Kimiko declared that she was hungry and vacantly watched TV over a cup of seaweed ramen. I lay in my futon and played with my ringtones, and then we took turns showering. Just after two, we both settled down to sleep.

In the dark, I spoke up. "Kimiko? En was really down, wasn't she? Because her friend died."

"Yeah, I think she was in shock."

"I mean, I was, too. When the cops came . . . I thought for sure they knew."

Kimiko was silent for a moment, and then said, "About what?"

"I don't know. It just popped into my head." Nerves gripped me as I tried to explain. "I was trying to figure out what while we were working—I guess that I'm underage, or that I ran away from home."

"But nobody knows that." I heard her turn over.

"Well, yeah . . . I've never been so close to a cop before. They have guns, right? I kept thinking about them after, wondering if they were wearing bulletproof vests under their clothes."

As I talked, I remembered the envelope Kimiko got from

Yeongsu whenever we saw him. The paper with the names and amounts written on it. What was that money for? I almost asked Kimiko about it, but I couldn't tell her that I'd peeked inside one of her envelopes—I had a feeling I shouldn't ask, especially right now. Kimiko had never hidden the envelopes. But she'd never said anything about them either. I couldn't imagine how she might react if I asked her about them. Would she be annoyed with me? Would she ignore me? Or would she laugh and tell me everything? Or maybe, for the first time ever, she'd get angry at me. My mind started conjuring one scenario and then the next, and they weighed on me, heavier and heavier. On top of that came the memory of the cops at the door and the shock I'd felt seeing them, and En sounding so cornered as she talked about getting old, about money.

We all get old. And getting old means you need money. And if you get hurt or get sick, that's it. Nobody's gonna come and save you. There's no security in this kind of life, just misery. En's voice and face had been so raw, her words so bitter and fierce, and the way she'd made me feel lingered, even now, because she'd skewered me through with the obvious truth of what she was saying. Frightened, I called out to Kimiko. She grunted sleepily.

"Kimiko," I asked, "aren't you scared?"

"Of what?"

"What En said today . . . I'm terrified. The burglary was frightening, for sure, but I'm more afraid of being poor, of the future. I didn't feel like I was hearing about someone else's problems, I felt like I was hearing about mine. We've still got decades to live, but how are we gonna survive? My head's full of all these dark thoughts. I mean, we have the bar, and we'll do the best we can, but what I'm worried about feels deeper somehow . . . You don't think about stuff like that?"

"Nope."

"Why not?"

"How should I know." She sounded irritated. "I don't know about all that hard stuff."

"Hard stuff?"

"Yeah."

"Like what?"

"I just said, I don't know," she snapped, and I was taken aback. I waited for her to pick up the conversation again, but after a while, I heard her breath even out in sleep.

I felt abandoned. I was confused by how deep the hurt was, how I could almost feel the sharp pain of it in my heart. Kimiko was annoyed with my questions, no, with me, and her attitude, her irritation, that was what hurt.

Kimiko's sharp reply echoed through my mind again and again. I'd wanted her to ask me about the fear and anxiety that hounded me, and I'd wanted to get her to talk about what our future might look like, about all the important things, and how she was feeling about it all, but her tone had said she didn't care about any of it and that she was pissed at me for even asking—it tore right through me. She'd stabbed me right in the heart. At first, sadness squeezed my chest tight, but then my face grew hot, and I choked up. The sadness transformed into a mix of frustration and anger, and hot tears welled in my eyes and trickled down into the hollows of my ears. I lay next to Kimiko in such pain, and there she was, sleeping on, indifferent. I glared at a point on the ceiling in the pitch dark and waited for my feelings to calm.

2.

About ten days after the cops showed up, toward the end of February, we had a pair of early-bird customers. I shared a glance with Ran when the two of them walked through the door, because I didn't know what to make of them.

We saw plenty of other nightlife workers, so it wasn't strange for a man and woman to come in together, but one half of this pair was a girl in a high school uniform.

She wore a navy blazer and a loosened red tie, and her shoulder-length hair was so shiny and black that it caught a perfect ring of light all the way around. She was shorter than me, solidly built—her tartan miniskirt showed off two stocky, muscular legs. Long bangs obscured her face. She wore knee-high navy socks and loafers, and the bag hooked on her shoulders was so bedecked with charms—one was a Hello Kitty head almost as big as a lunch box—that she could have gone into business selling them. The man ordered the all-you-can-drink deal and asked the girl what she'd have. She asked for oolong tea.

"Has this place always been here?" the man asked me.

"No. The furniture is the same, but the lease changed hands."

"I knew it. I was pretty sure I'd been here once before, but it had a different name."

"We've been here since last autumn."

"Right, right."

Once Ran delivered the drinks, he exclaimed, "Cheers!" and he and the girl clinked their glasses. She toasted him back and crossed her legs, which made her skirt ride up. I couldn't stop staring at her enormous thighs, dotted with bug bites here and there. Her school uniform made me remember how I, too, had been wearing a uniform until less than a year ago.

"You two should drink with us," the man said.

"All right, we'll have some beer then, please."

The man was plump, and his skin was as white as mochi, and his raven black hair was tied in a tiny bun. He had almost no eyebrows, but his eyes were wide and bright, and he had on a red sweater that, even from a distance, I could tell was wearing out—I couldn't decide if the overall effect was flashy or homely.

"Wait, aren't you too young? How old are you?"

"We're both twenty," I said stiffly.

Ran and I always said we were twenty when anyone asked.

"Wow, that means they're three years older than you, Tamamori-chan," he said, looking at the girl beside him. The girl angled her head to get her bangs out of the way, slurped at her tea, and nodded.

"You two run this place?"

"We have a Mama, but she won't be in until later tonight," I said.

"Oh, no need to be so formal, relax. At least with me." He rustled through his nylon bag and handed each of us a business card with white writing on a black background—"Tomcat Nagasawa, Writer." "What are your names?"

"Ran."

"Hana."

"Ran-chan and Hana-chan. Ran and Hana. Ranbana . . . Hey, it kind of sounds like the lambada! Now that makes me sound old, doesn't it! Ha ha ha! But girls call me Tommy-cat, so you can, too!"

With that, Tommy-cat downed his beer and poured more for Ran and me, urging us to drink.

"This here is Momoko Tamamori. She's a bona fide high school student, almost a senior!"

Tommy-cat seemed like an overfriendly, hyper kind of guy—he put his drinks away fast, and he never stopped talking. He was thirty-one, apparently, and he'd worked in publishing until not too long ago, doing editing and production on magazines and books. But now he was independent, a freelance writer.

He dropped a bunch of names—wrote in this magazine, planned this special issue, ghostwrote that bestseller, knew those guys before they made it big in the music industry when they still worked part-time at an izakaya—but I'd never heard of any of them.

Tommy-cat wasn't the kind of writer who showed up on variety shows on TV, but he was apparently a specialist on all things cool, creators in the subculture who were popular not only among the young Shibuya crowd but also well-respected among certain intellectual circles. Even experts and critics tipped their hats to him.

He told us the details of how he decided to go freelance and summed up, with a sheepish grin, "It's what the world wanted me to do, you know?" Then he downed another beer. Ran and

I kept pace with him, which put another two big bottles of beer on his tab. Overjoyed, he cried, "More, more!" and started talking even faster about what he was writing. He told us that, more than anything else, he was interested in the idea of "the death of the high school girl." For close to ten years now, high school girls had been all the rage, especially in cities, but soon the boom would end, and someone had to start recording it before it disappeared.

I'd heard the words "high school girl boom" on TV and in the weekly gossip rags my mom read, but I never knew what they were talking about. I was a high school girl then, and technically I could still be one now, but it seemed to have nothing to do with anything I knew. Ran apparently agreed. "We graduated not too long ago, but we weren't really part of that stuff."

"Of course not, the mass media can call it a boom all they want, but what they're up in arms about is almost always a localized phenomenon. Just a complete minority," Tommy-cat explained. He waved his hands around as he listed more and more so-called booms: telephone dating clubs, pager dating, girls selling used panties to burusera, compensated dating, existentialism, internal ethics, the right to self-determination, self-discovery . . . He jumped between things I'd heard of and things with words so difficult I had no idea what he was talking about.

Finally, Tommy-cat paused to catch his breath and then said, "And now, I'm thinking of writing a novel."

"What, really? That's so cool!" Ran and I buttered him up.

Tommy-cat smiled and nodded. "I have so much respect for these girls . . . I think they're true warriors. All these old guys, these high and mighty windbags who cling to tired postwar binaries and only know how to lecture us from on high, they think they're using these girls, buying them off, but it's the girls who are using them, and they're clever about it, too. Those girls are kicking them right in the balls, their self-flagellating, openly opportunistic view of history, a justified *le sentiment* existing on the borders between reality and fiction—basically these girls succeeded in overturning values on a societal level once and for all."

"What does that mean?" I blurted before I could think better of it.

"Well . . . it means exactly what I said." Tommy-cat cleared his throat and continued.

"Anyway, what I'm saying is I want to write the truth. I want to grasp it . . . Of course, everything about girls' culture and burusera and compensated dating has already more or less been said, there's a shit ton of books and data. Yeah, the data's great and so's the analysis . . . but all those, you know, those super smart, super confident nihilists? Those superstar sociologists and researchers? They can keep grinding away, 'cause I'm not interested. What I want to do is, how to describe it . . . put my whole body into it. And for that I need fiction, and so does the world, you know? What I mean is, there's this essence to our existence, the truth of our generation, and you can only begin to sketch it through imagination. I want to get as close as I can. As a high school girl."

"As a high school girl?" I asked.

"Yep . . . I want to write as a high school girl, not as thirty-one-year-old Tommy-cat. As a high school girl with a finite endpoint . . . I don't want to be one of those guys who's speaking *for* the younger generation. I want to get tangled up with them, melt into them, until I resonate with their very souls. I've already got the pen name and the author bio. Rough draft for the first chapter, too. And more than anything, I hope that girls will pick up my book. I want to give birth to moments where those girls discover a truth they didn't even know they knew. When I first started writing, I couldn't believe it, how in sync we were. Those guys, when they saw *Evangelion*, they hopped on Shinji's side, right? Doing the same tired 'self-discovery' shit? But what's important is 'self-erasure.' That's why I'm on Rei's side. I'm with the girls. Of course, I have to write the rest of the novel first. I can talk all I like, but it's the details that bring a novel to life. That's why I'm having Tamamori-chan here help me out, teach me about her reality."

In the face of Tommy-cat's fervor, all Ran and I could do was nod along, with some exclamations thrown in here and there. We filled the silence that followed with a drinking game where we each downed a bottle of beer in one long chug. Even though Tamamori-chan was supposed to be helping him out, she barely said a word, just hummed and smiled along and occasionally checked her pager. *Oh, she has a pager, not a phone*, I thought to myself.

Suddenly, Tommy-cat yelled, "Man oh man." His eyes grew big. I hadn't been able to tell when he was talking before, but now I was sure he was completely plastered, his pale face blotched with red. Then he told us why he'd come here today.

"You know the tattoo parlor on the second floor? They got robbed. The owner's helped me out a lot." Tommy-cat grew gloomy. "What a disaster. Getting robbed, getting beat up. They took all the electronics and machines, just awful, right? And now my friend, his nerves are completely shot, he's in the hospital."

"That's awful," said Ran.

"I stopped by here 'cause I got thirsty, but I have his key, and I'm supposed to take care of some things for him. Anyway, I'm gonna go downstairs. What do you want to do, Tamamori-chan? You want to come with? Or you want to wait here?"

"I'll wait here," Momoko Tamamori said.

"Okey dokey smokey. I'll leave my bag with you, then." And then he left.

Momoko Tamamori fiddled with her pager a bit, and I got the impression that she didn't want us bothering her. But even if she was a high school student, she was still a customer, so we couldn't exactly leave her alone. It was Ran who struck up the conversation as she topped off her oolong tea.

"I like your socks. They're really fresh. Are loose socks on the outs now?"

Momoko Tamamori looked up and smiled slightly. Beneath her bangs, I spied a bad case of acne, some of her zits so red and swollen they looked infected.

"Some girls are still wearing them . . . It's about half and half between Ralph Lauren and Hanes, I think?" Momoko Tamamori's voice was bright and cute, not what I expected given her solid build.

"Mr. Tommy-cat, he seems to have a lot of energy," I said, chuckling.

"Yeah . . . um, you can relax around me. You don't have to treat me like a customer."

"Oh, okay . . . He said you've been teaching him a bunch of stuff. Have you known him long?"

"Three months, maybe? He's been interviewing a bunch of girls, not just me."

"Interviews, huh. Cool."

"Not really? Not cool at all."

"The stuff he was talking about sounded pretty awesome though. Not that I understood it."

"Not really? Tommy-cat's not that awesome," Momoko Tamamori said quietly. "But I'm chunky and ugly, so guys like him are the only ones who bother with me. I basically only tell him lies."

Ran and I didn't know what to say, and an uncomfortable silence fell over the bar.

"It's okay," Momoko Tamamori said, laughing. "I'm used to it, making fun of myself, I mean."

Relieved, Ran and I started asking Momoko Tamamori about her school and her spring break and her friends—happy things. But her replies were all vague and short, and after a while, she murmured, "I'd rather hear about you two? And maybe I want a beer?" So we poured her a beer and traded jokes as we each gave her our stories.

Poor and penniless, dad who ran off somewhere, dad who's bedridden, juvie girls and Bibinba, dropping out of beauty school, never getting customers at the club and pretty much being fired, mom's ex-boyfriend stealing the money, our special color yellow, Kimiko . . . keeping our stories up got annoying, so we dropped the act and told Momoko Tamamori that I was actually the same age as her, and Ran was a year older.

"Just wow," she said solemnly. I thought there was more fire in her eyes now, though maybe I just hadn't noticed it before. "Might be the first time I ever heard anything like that in real life."

"What's your family like?" I asked.

"My family . . . basically kitsch all around. Total cliché. I live with my grandma and my younger sister in Aobadai, and my parents are at their summer house in Karuizawa all the time."

"What do you mean kitsch?"

"Well, they've got about six signed Christian Lassen screen prints hanging on the walls, and my mom only wears Issey Miyake, so no matter where you turn, that house is traumatisch."

"What's 'traumatisch'?" Ran asked.

"A wound in your soul that never heals," Momoko Tamamori said with a smile. "New slang."

"A summer house, so that means your family's rich, right?" I asked. Momoko Tamamori shrugged and said that her parents had inherited their company and their land and basically stuck with the family business.

Then she gave us her story. She started off each new detail with "This'll sound really stupid, but." How she and her sister were forced to go to some private, Christian all-girls school in the city, a school anyone could go to for six years as long as you paid the tuition. How her parents didn't get along, but they wouldn't divorce either, partly out of spite and partly to keep up appearances. How, unlike Momoko Tamamori, Shizuka, her sister, was a bombshell, so she always brought boys to the house in Aobadai whenever she wanted, which Momoko Tamamori thought was super annoying. But Shizuka never brushed her teeth, so she had a mouth full of cavities and awful breath, and if you ever said anything about it, she went absolutely postal. How their grandmother was starting to go senile. How one time, when Momoko went with some of the prettier girls in her class to check out a burusera shop, no one was interested in Momoko, so she got left alone in the waiting room, playing a Sega Saturn the whole time, and the other girls started making fun of her after that.

Her nickname changed from Gorilli to Gorilli Saturn, and no one would hang out with her after school, and now just about the only person who would was Tommy-cat. Though Momoko Tamamori spoke haltingly, Ran and I were totally absorbed in her story—we felt like we were actually there, experiencing each episode in turn.

"You are super interesting, Tamamori," Ran and I declared.

"No, you two are way more fresh and cool," Momoko Tamamori said, shaking her head. "Nobody's ever told me I'm interesting. Nobody hangs out with me."

"I don't really have friends either," I told her. "I work here every day with Kimiko and Ran, and I see them on my days off. You, too, right, Ran?"

"Yeah. Hana's basically my only friend."

It didn't seem like we'd get any more customers. We kept drinking beer, and the conversation was so easy I almost forgot I was at work—my body felt warm and fuzzy. Eventually we started up the karaoke machine.

We laughed and chatted: *What do you like? What'll you sing? What, you have to set up the laser disc by hand? This belonged to the bar that was here before, and it's super expensive to rent the automatic ones.* Then Ran, now tipsy, put her all into Namie Amuro and then Dreams Come True and then Tomomi Kahara while Momoko Tamamori and I swayed along, following the lyrics and cheering and clapping when each song ended.

"What do you like, Tamamori?" Ran asked.

"I . . ." She shook her head reluctantly. "You're gonna think it's weird. The last time I tried to sing it at karaoke, everyone thought I was creepy, so I don't really . . ."

"Aw, come on, sing it," Ran and I begged.

"No, I don't think I can."

"But why? We want to hear."

"No, you don't."

"We really do, come on."

"Please?"

Finally, resigned to her fate, Momoko Tamamori picked up the thick karaoke book and studied its pages, flipping through until she found what she wanted. She scribbled down the number on a memo pad and handed it to Ran. After a moment, the title appeared on screen: "'Kurenai,' by X Japan." The song opened like a ballad, with a heavy, bittersweet instrumental. Slowly the lyrics appeared, all in English, and Momoko Tamamori began to sing. The moment we heard her voice, Ran and I looked at each other in disbelief. It was so beautiful I almost said "No way" out loud.

I didn't understand the English, but I couldn't look away from the screen, gaping at the magnificence of Momoko Tamamori's voice. The ballad intro faded away, and just as I wondered what would happen next, the speakers sent up the most vicious drum solo I'd ever heard—and then Momoko Tamamori was truly unbelievable.

The whirling storm of music was impossible for me to understand, but Momoko Tamamori's voice cut through, sparkling and crystalline and fleeting, but in spite of its fragility, there was an iconic menace to it, as though a thick, silver pipe extended from her throat straight into forever. I didn't know what the performance style was called or what instruments were playing or what genre the song was, but every single sound, every bit of Momoko Tamamori's voice, slammed directly into my brain and shook my body.

As the lyrics ran across the screen, a scene came to me, something I'd seen on TV when I was a kid—light shining down as the massive walls of the ocean parted before Moses or Christ or whoever it was. And in that moment, a galaxy spread across my heart.

You run like something's coming for you
Don't you see me? I'm right beside you
. . .

There's no one to comfort me now
Dyeing in this crimson

When she was done, Momoko Tamamori oh so gently set the mic on the table. Ran and I were dazed—all we could say was "Holy shit." It wasn't just her amazing voice, though. The lyrics on the screen were burned into my eyes now, and they wouldn't go away. My brain screamed "so cool" fifty times maybe. "Don't you see me? I'm right beside you." I turned the line over in my mind until my heart throbbed. I'd felt this ache before. That night the cops came, when Kimiko treated me like I was nothing, when she turned her back on me and went to sleep, leaving me behind. It was the same pain.

"Seriously . . . Tamamori, that was so, so amazing." I was floored.

"Thanks . . . I'd like it if you called me Momoko."

Momoko sang first one song and then the next, and Ran and I watched the screen, mesmerized. Every song Momoko chose was by X Japan, and every last one of them moved my very soul. According to Momoko, the band had just broken up, which was tragic. Their metal songs were amazing, and the ballad "Endless Rain" brought tears to my eyes. I never wanted the song to end. Momoko's voice was like a swan song when she sang the only Japanese lyrics in the chorus—*Kokoro no kizu*, "wounded heart"—a guitar that held me tight, smiling as it bled out, and finally, the intensity and sorrow of the drumbeat as the song neared its end. I held my breath in the moment—I felt like I was watching a soul trying to claw its way back to life even as it lay dying.

Eventually, Tommy-cat reappeared, finished with his tasks, and he and Momoko went home. Their bill was ¥23,000. All three of us, Momoko, Ran, and I, were drunk and overwhelmed, and before Momoko left, the three of us clung to each other right in the middle of Lemon.

The next week, Momoko came again, alone this time, to hang out at Lemon with us, and every week after, too. When it came time to pay the bill, I was hesitant to take her money, but she told me not to worry since it wasn't really hers anyway. "It's not like Grandma's checking the accounts," she said as she handed me a credit card. Every visit, she paid ¥10,000. I became obsessed with X Japan, so I went to a secondhand shop and bought a CD Walkman for ¥800, as well as some of their albums—used of course—and when Lemon didn't have any customers, I'd sing "Kurenai" to myself, swapping out every "crimson" with "yellow."

And we became friends. Ran and I started spending time with Momoko outside of Lemon, hitting up purikura photo booths, hanging out at McDonald's, chatting about whatever wherever. Kimiko had dinner with us, too, and Kotomi sometimes joined us when she had a day off. (She looked nothing like a dried sardine on her days off.) In the middle of the night, when Sangenjaya was sparkling with light here, there, and everywhere, and the five of us were walking down the street after dinner at some 24/7 restaurant, contentment would wash over me, and I'd have to stop and put my hands to my chest. *This*, I thought, *must be what they mean by the springtime of youth.*

SIX

TOUCHSTONE

1.

I had a nightmare.

Kimiko and I were walking along the edge of an oversized tennis court where four strangers played a doubles match. The stands were filled with onlookers, and the two of us walked just next to the court, so close we could see the players' sweat as they swung their rackets and grunted. I wondered if we should move back, but then the court became a beach. As I watched the white surf roll and froth up the sand, I thought, *The ocean is alive, but it doesn't know it's alive.*

The sky was cloudless and sunny, and it was hot, and there was no one but me and Kimiko, which made part of me nervous. Kimiko crouched down and toyed with the sand, the wind billowing her jet-black hair in waves.

We were looking for something, so we dug deeper and deeper into the sand until at last we found it—the dustcloth Kimiko always had at home. She gave a happy little cry, shook the sand from the cloth, and then clutched it to her chest. I was happy, too. But somehow the dustcloth in her hand became a kitchen knife, a silver blade, and when I noticed it, Kimiko shoved it in my gut.

I staggered and fell onto the beach. Kimiko said nothing. I couldn't tell if she was looking at me or not. I'd never been stabbed before. The way the blade was lanced inside me, something about its size and substance, it was all wrong, and it made me feel sick to my stomach. That awful feeling spread and spread like fire, and I felt my body grow hot. I pressed both hands to the wound. Blood welled and flowed, but I didn't feel any pain, only fear of the fact that I had been attacked and that I was slowly losing the ability to move. Then Kimiko changed her grip on the blade so it pointed to the sky, and she came close again. I thought maybe she'd mistaken me for someone else, so I tried to call out, to tell her *Kimiko, it's me, it's Hana,* but the voice that should have emerged from my throat spilled from the wound, flowing out with the blood. I tried to stop the flow with my palms, and that's when I woke up.

Checking the clock, I saw that it was just after eleven in the morning. My neck was damp with sweat. Kimiko wasn't in the room; her futon was folded neatly next to me. After a couple seconds, I remembered that she'd said she was going out this morning. Kotomi was thinking of moving, so she'd asked Kimiko to go with her to the real estate agent's office.

The fear and pain from the nightmare lingered and put me in a funk—I showered, slowly drank a glass of barley tea, and then went back to my futon. The scenes and sensations of the dream reappeared one by one, and I tossed and turned.

What the hell was that dream? I almost never dream. Such a terrifying, terrible dream. What to make of it? Did it have any meaning? Questions popped into my head one after another. The images felt too raw to be a dream, and each time I remembered them, my heart rate spiked. Me and Kimiko. Walking side by side like we always did, and then the tennis court becoming a beach, the waves frothing, and Kimiko's dustcloth becoming a knife. And her, stabbing me in the stomach.

Did it mean anything? Maybe it was a hint or an omen. I wasn't sure, or maybe a message? I thought about possible interpretations, but I didn't have any ideas, and with each remembered scene, my unease only got worse. I studied the Yellow Corner. And then I changed clothes and went to the bookstore in front of the station.

There was hardly anyone in the store, and I headed for the spot where Ran Kato and I had found the feng shui books back when the weather was still cold. I found the corner display soon enough. The whole thing had been spruced up since I'd last seen it. Fortune-telling by blood type, Four Pillars of Destiny, tarot, name-based fortune-telling, rokusei senjutsu and numerology, palmistry and physiognomy, astrology and standard card deck divination, extrasensory divination—every imaginable book on fortune-telling packed the shelves and display plinth, and every blurb on every cover was plastered with flashy phrases like "Take Hold of Your Happiness," "The Best Fortunes," "Unlock the Key to Yourself," "Astonishing Luck and Fortune," and "Illuminate Your Future."

At the edge of the shelf were a few books on dream interpretation, and I picked up a ridiculously thick one called *The Dictionary of Dream Analysis*. The blurb on the cover read, "Deluxe Definitive Edition! Complete analysis from more than one million dreamers. Discover your truth with more than eight thousand dream types!" The book cost ¥2,800.

I wasn't sure if a million people or eight thousand dream types were a lot or not, but I didn't think it would have anything as specific as a tennis court in its pages. When I flipped through, though, I was surprised to discover that not only did they have images related to tennis, but they had several detailed scenarios: playing tennis with your lover, winning a tennis tournament, tennis rackets that never feel right in your hand, loud crowds at a tennis match. I supposed it only made sense, given the thickness of the book, so I searched down the line of entries looking for "tennis courts" until I found a scenario that matched my dream perfectly.

"Tennis courts represent relationships or the workplace. The size of the tennis court reflects your heart. The larger the area of the court, the more good luck is headed your way." The tennis court I'd dreamed had been huge. So this was saying I was bighearted, and that as far as my relationships from Lemon—basically my whole life—were concerned, everything was about to change for the better. I tucked the meaning of the tennis court into my brain and then searched for "beach."

"A beach represents a rise in fortunes, and indicates you are overflowing with enthusiasm and energy. If someone was walking on the beach with you, this is proof that you've built a good, strong relationship with that person. It also indicates that you are not isolated, and you are at peace. If anything emerged from the sand, this indicates that you are fully prepared to accept the truth of things, their fundamental nature. Beach dreams indicate great fortune." What? So beaches were good, too? I'd been walking with Kimiko, and stuff had come out of the sand. Did that mean I was about to discover my true self? My cheeks grew hot. But there was more to read.

"Beaches may also indicate that a chance for you to grasp your true power is on the horizon. You will soon find new work or take on a position with more responsibilities." Grasp my power, new work, position with more responsibilities? I couldn't imagine what that might mean. Was there really nothing bad in the dream? Did everything in the dream actually mean good luck? I grasped the dictionary in both hands and glanced around, nervous. And then I searched for the most memorable image, that terrifying scene. Being stabbed by Kimiko. The dictionary contained a section labeled "Stabbed by a blade," so I started to read. With the first words, I nearly gasped out loud.

"Dreams in which you are stabbed by a blade are a sign of extreme monetary fortune. They are an indication that you are carving out your future and will soon find something new, which you will surely succeed at. They may also indicate a prosperous marriage. However"—the page ended, and I hurriedly flipped to the next—"if you bled from the wound, this can either mean money will flow out or flow in. Additionally, dreams where you were stabbed but felt no pain indicate that you are possessed of a cool discernment. Even if you are pursued by choices that seem like they might pull your life off track, have faith in yourself, and things will turn out fine. If, in the dream, you were stabbed by someone of the opposite sex or someone you are fond of, this indicates that your bond with that person will deepen all the more."

I reread the entries on tennis courts and beaches and stabbings until I'd basically memorized them, and then I returned the book to the shelf. I took a step back and looked over the whole display. It was decorated with handmade decorations and a large sign that declared, "Learn to love yourself! New Age Healing Corner."

I walked away, puzzling over each of the meanings I'd learned from *The Dictionary of Dream Analysis* and trying to imagine what they might signal together. No matter how I fit the reading to my own life, it always boiled down to "It's been a tough ride, but you're about to hit the big time." That had to be it.

The signs of good fortune banished my gloomy mood, and I breathed a sigh of relief; I was so glad, I nearly started skipping. Of course, a dream is just a dream, and fortune-telling is usually so vague it matches up to almost everyone in the world. I was also worried about the bleeding and how that meant money might flow out, but still, so many strong symbols of good fortune in one dream—I was sure it must mean something. After all, the book had said it gathered its analysis from over one million people. Besides, I wouldn't be able to prove if the predictions were right or wrong until the future came, which meant I could believe what I wanted and set aside the bad parts. It was the same with our Yellow Corner—it's more important to believe, to let your belief sustain you, because then you can tell yourself that everything's going to be okay. When I first woke up from the dream, I was so down, but now I was on top of the world. Every part of me—hands, eyes, feet—was bursting with energy, and I let it carry me through the neighborhood in front of the station.

I took streets I'd never taken before, wandering into shops, or else looked at clothes and knickknacks in stores I'd passed but never gone inside, picking up things and inspecting them. There were some chokers with cute charms on them, and I thought it would be nice if Ran, Momoko, and I could wear them as a matching set, but then I realized our tastes in fashion didn't match, so I bought Ran a super popular eyebrow pencil and Momoko a little pouch with Hello Kitty on the front. I even had the clerk gift wrap them. Then I had a beef bowl at Yoshinoya, and took off again, enjoying the sights. I went into Carrot Tower on a whim and caught sight of my reflection, alone in the huge glass doors. But that reminded me of Kimiko, and I grew lonely.

There was no reason for me to be feeling lonely, but I froze, staring at my own bluish reflection.

The day had only just begun. I regretted not going with Kimiko. But she'd promised to be back by nightfall. I thought of her at En's, eating the same thing she always had: konjac twists in a salty-sweet sauce. Her favorite. I was a terrible cook and wasn't sure I could handle even such a simple recipe, but I thought Kimiko might be happy if she came home and found I'd made it for her, so I went to the supermarket, bought a block of konjac, and went home.

A lot happened over the spring and summer of 1998.

A newbie showed up to Lemon and got so blackout drunk we had to call Yeongsu to come take care of him. Then the pipes burst. And changes were coming to the heights where Kimiko and I lived—we'd need a new place. Yeongsu was the one who told us. We paid the rent, but Yeongsu had lived in our apartment before us, and before that, it was his friend who'd signed the actual lease. The owner of the heights was a friend of Yeongsu's, so even though the apartment kept changing hands, he'd always let it slide.

"There's no way around it," Yeongsu said. "I guess they're going to tear the building down."

"When do we have to be out by?" Kimiko asked.

"They didn't say exactly, but I expect by the end of the year."

Kimiko hummed and nodded, but the unexpected news made me anxious. How much did it actually cost to rent a place? Could we even manage it? I was still a minor, more or less a runaway, and even my cell phone was in Yeongsu's name. I hadn't even known it wasn't our name on the lease, or even Yeongsu's for that matter.

What would we do next, would Kimiko rent a new apartment under her own name and sign the paperwork—even as the thought crossed my mind, I doubted Kimiko could do any of this. But why did I think she couldn't? We'd saved all our money, never wasted it, and Kimiko was an adult; she was the one who'd opened Lemon, so there was no reason why she wouldn't be able to rent an apartment like any other adult. Why did I immediately assume she couldn't?

"Kimiko, what will we do?" I asked, trying to keep my voice neutral.

"About what?"

"You know," I said, surprised. "I mean, Yeongsu just told us, the apartment."

"The apartment. I suppose we'll have to look for a new place."

"Well, yeah, but . . . will it be okay?"

"Will what be okay?" Kimiko repeated, sounding surprised. I fell silent.

"Don't look so down in the dumps, it's not like you have to leave tomorrow. There are always rooms for rent," Yeongsu said, chuckling.

"I suppose," I said, smiling, forcing myself to try and match their tone.

That was the end of April. And then the world, and Lemon, too, hit the long holiday of Golden Week, which was when I got a call from a sobbing Momoko. Through tears and sniffles, she managed to tell me that she was in front of the station, but she didn't have any change, so the phone might cut out at any moment. I was with Ran, so we rushed off to pick her up.

Momoko was trying to hide her tear-stained face behind her

bangs, but when she saw us, she dashed over, buried her face into our shoulders, and wailed.

She told us Hide, the former guitarist for X Japan, was dead. Ran and I didn't know what to say, so we took her back to my apartment.

After a glass of water, Momoko calmed down enough to piece the story together, sniffling as she haltingly explained what had happened. She found out about Hide's death around sundown—there was a breaking news report on TV. At first, she didn't understand what the ticker was telling her. She was sure it must be a practical joke, a lie. But then other TV programs started saying the same thing, and her knees started knocking. She tried first paging and then calling a friend she'd made at the Tokyo Dome during X Japan's reunion concert at the end of last year, but nobody answered.

Next came tears of shock and fear, and Momoko sat in front of the living room TV, at a loss. That's when her sister, Shizuka, came home, her friends in tow, and they started laughing at her, teasing her for crying. Then they told Momoko to go to her room because they wanted to play a video game, but she refused. The only way she could be connected to Hide was through the information on the TV, and she didn't want to let go. She and Shizuka fought—*You're in the way, bitch. So? Get lost! I can't*—until Shizuka sneered, "Probably suicide, what a loser, disgusting." Momoko had, in that moment, shoved her sister to the ground, and they started wrestling. And then Momoko fled her house and walked all the way from Aobadai to Sancha.

"It's not suicide, he'd never do that."

Momoko was insistent, swearing it couldn't be suicide, and we nodded in agreement. Every nightly news and TV program was about Hide, and even though we told Momoko it might be better for her not to watch, she couldn't tear her eyes away. She kept a towel pressed to her cheeks to catch the tears. Kimiko came home, and we told her what had happened; she comforted Momoko and stroked her hair. Then she asked if we were hungry. Momoko said she hadn't had anything since a slice of toast at breakfast, and Ran and I hadn't eaten either, so we ordered delivery from a neighborhood soba place.

Momoko said she didn't want to go home, so Kimiko said, "You should stay here."

"What'll you do about school? You still have to go, right?" I asked.

"I don't know," Momoko said, her voice trailing. "But I don't want to go home."

Momoko stayed with us for a while after that. The day after Hide's death, the news reports about him heated to a boil, and Momoko didn't move from her spot in front of the TV. Her sorrow made me feel guilty—it was thanks to Momoko that I first learned about X Japan's killer songs, but by then, the band had already broken up, and I didn't know much about the members. I felt like I didn't have the right to mourn alongside Momoko, and I didn't know what to say to her. Ran came over after lunch, and the four of us sat in front of the TV listening to eulogies from people who'd known him and watching footage of the vigil and funeral service. More than fifty thousand fans traveled countless kilometers to say goodbye, and they crowded in around the temple, clogging the surrounding roads. A reporter babbled on about how the situation was getting loud and chaotic. It seemed like all Hide's fans were there offering flowers, but Momoko said she couldn't bring herself to go.

In silence, we watched the images repeat on the talk shows. Thousands of people shaking and crying, falling in the streets, crawling, wailing his name, hunched over, wringing their lungs for every last bit of volume. Every one of them was suffering, so devastated they could barely stand it, and when I saw how real their sorrow was, I started crying, too. Every person the reporters interviewed broke down sobbing, saying how Hide had saved them, how they'd been able to keep going because of him. Listening to their stories, I realized that their thoughts and feelings and burdens were revolving around, had revolved around, this one person, and I knew I was witnessing something that was both amazing and terrifying.

And the people on TV were only one part of an even bigger whole—how could one person take on all that unstoppable, incalculable energy? How could they bear it? How do feelings like this happen? Why does a song move us to tears? How is it that someone we've never met can save us, make us courageous, make us want to be part of something bigger than ourselves? As I watched the screen, my thoughts piled up on me, but I didn't know how to put them into words. I didn't know much about X Japan's band members, but I liked their music. Compared to the depth of Momoko's feelings, though, mine amounted to a grain of sand—but still, I wondered if my feelings, too, were connected to this man who was dead, or maybe they weren't; maybe they were worlds apart. I couldn't stop turning the thoughts in my mind.

That weekend, Momoko went back to her home in Aobadai. She went to school for a while after that, but toward the end of June, she started skipping school more and more, showing up at Sangenjaya still in her school uniform, spending her afternoons with us. Momoko's mantra became "Everything sucks—home, parents, school. I could just die." Ran was miserable, too. She and her boyfriend had argued about cleaning their air conditioner, and that turned into an actual fight—it was the first time he hit her.

"It was the heat of the moment, I know it was," Ran said darkly, "but it was my face. Can you believe it?"

"Unbelievable. What happened then?" Momoko asked.

"I think he surprised himself, but then he panicked and blamed me, said I made him lose his temper."

"Asshole. What does he do again? For work?"

"He's got a part-time job at an izakaya right now. Says he's their 'star waiter.'"

That's how that summer began, the summer we became real friends. The three of us went to the local pool, ate dinner at En's with Kimiko, and hung around at McDonald's like always.

I had Ran teach me how to do makeup. I'd never gotten a nice haircut either, but she suggested a shag, so we went to a nearby salon and looked at the magazines and got new haircuts. I always tanned nut brown—before, I was self-conscious about it, but somewhere along the line, I realized it had stopped bothering me. Momoko showed us her brand-new cell phone—she'd had her parents buy it for her—and when I asked why she didn't already have one, since her family was so rich, she said it was complicated. "Not everyone at school has a cell phone. So when someone like me has one, people call me a poser, and it's super annoying, so I got a pager instead," she explained as she applied steroid cream to her acne. "But I decided I don't care anymore."

Once summer vacation started, Momoko came to Lemon all the time, helping out behind the counter, and after closing, she spent the night a lot. (We bought an extra futon set at the local big box supermarket.) Not everything was perfect, and Ran and her boyfriend were always fighting, but things were starting to look up. Momoko cheered up little by little, and when Ran was with us, it was nonstop jokes and laughter. We were having the time of our lives. One day, we went over to Kotomi's new place. It was a huge, white apartment with brand-new furniture. While we were there, the dry cleaners even stopped by to deliver her laundry—I was amazed.

With all of us there at her apartment, laughing about nothing, I daydreamed about how it would be nice if we could live together. Although apparently Kotomi had a man (there were leather loafers in one corner of the entryway, and one of the items the dry cleaners delivered was a necktie), if we did live together, I figured it would be Kimiko, Ran, Momoko, and me— the four of us. Kimiko and I had to leave our apartment by the end of the year, so maybe we could pick out a place where we could live together? Ran's boyfriend would probably complain, though. And Momoko had school and parents to think about. But Yeongsu could come over sometimes, have dinner with us. And there would always be Lemon.

Each time my daydreams ballooned out, reality barged in

to burst them, but imagining was fun. I kept collecting yellow knickknacks, and while the rawness of the dream I'd had in the spring faded, the predictions from the dream analysis book were carved into my brain. Sometimes I went to the "Healing Corner" display in the bookstore, pulled out *The Dictionary of Dream Analysis*, and read it to reassure myself. My favorite parts were the beach and the stabbing. I would know the truth of things, grasp my power, and explosive wealth would rain down on me, just like if I'd married a rich guy like En said. I felt like it had been promised to me, and I wanted it all to come true, wished for it with all my heart. Even now, I don't know if my wishing was a good thing or bad. But in the end, everything I saw in my dream did come to pass.

2.

It started with the eel kabayaki.

Right before the Obon holidays in August, En came over with a bag of eel kabayaki in hand. It was the kind you heat up in hot water, really high end: one vacuum-packed portion was more than ¥2,000. She brought it up to Lemon and said, "A new customer gave 'em to me, but I can't eat all that fatty stuff anymore. You lot have it, it'll give you life." I put the packs in Lemon's fridge and then accidentally forgot them there. I only remembered the last day of Obon, a Sunday. Since it was the last day of the holiday, I could have waited until Monday, but once I remembered that precious eel, it started to bother me—I felt like we had to eat it that very night. It had been nearly a week since En gave it to us, and maybe it would have been fine, but I was worried about it spoiling.

Kimiko got up around eleven, had an instant coffee, and started her usual dusting. She told me she was doing her Obon grave visit in the afternoon. "Whose grave?" I asked. "My dad's," she said. This was the first time I'd ever heard her mention her family, and I almost asked about her mother, but our conversation fell dead. Come to think of it, it wasn't just Kimiko's family I was clueless about. By now, I'd exhausted almost everything I had to say about myself, but Kimiko almost never talked about herself. What did we usually talk about? I thought for a while and couldn't come up with anything. We just lived together, ate, worked, slept, laughed over nothing with Ran and Momoko—I thought that was enough.

Walking to Lemon on a Sunday afternoon felt somehow novel. Everything changed in the light of day. All the details normally hidden by the dark of night leapt out at me now: had that building always been so run-down, and look at the random trash stuck to the street, somehow so colorful, and oh, look at that narrow alleyway with a bicycle, its seat missing, shoved in alongside a teetering mountain of glass bottles. The metal shutter over Little Heaven was rusting brown at the bottom, and I imagined En, early and late, reaching up, raising and lowering the shutter with all her might.

Inside, I pushed the button for the elevator and heard the clattering of its descent; idly, I thought, *I've got time, maybe I'll practice singing a little, it's been a while.* I hummed to myself as I climbed inside the elevator, hit the button for the third floor, and let my mind wander—*Did that eel come with sauce? I think En gave us four, I wonder if Ran would come over if I called her.* I emerged onto the third floor, turned the corner down the short hallway, put the key in the lock, turned it, and in that moment, I sensed something was off.

I paused, confused, as the automatic door opened, and I caught a glimpse inside.

Lemon was on the other side—of course it was—but it wasn't Lemon as I knew it. The scent of tobacco smoke rolled over me like a solid mass, and in the farthest booth, I saw a man I didn't know. He was huge and wore a gaudy shirt, and next to him, there was another strange man. They were both talking loudly into their cell phones. The man in the colorful shirt met my gaze, but he didn't put his phone down, just kept talking with the same intensity as he stared at me. I stood frozen until at last, as if to cut me off, Lemon's door swooshed shut again.

I couldn't comprehend what I'd seen. I don't know how many seconds I stood there before I realized I should probably run. I didn't know their purpose, but I knew that two terrifying strangers were in the bar. And then I remembered the cops who had come around in winter, and the blood drained from my face. I dashed to the elevator and hit the call button again and again. Behind me, I heard Lemon's door open. I was sure the huge man was coming, that he would grab me, but then someone called my name. It was Yeongsu.

"You should drink your tea before the ice melts," Yeongsu said, pointing at my glass where it sat untouched on the table. We'd been silently sitting across from each other in an old café near Lemon for quite a while. I stared at my hands where I held them clasped between my knees. I was calmer now, but the aftertaste of my fright still lingered.

"Where's Kimiko?" Yeongsu finally asked.

"She said she was going to visit her dad's grave."

My voice was colder, lower, than I'd intended it to be, and I drank some water. And then I sighed again—how many times had I sighed now, sitting here?

With each sigh, a mix of emotions swelled within me like a wave, but the most prominent was disgust. I felt like I couldn't breathe. I didn't know what Yeongsu was up to, though I was sure he was going to tell me, but more than that—our Lemon, there in our Lemon, where only we should be when the bar was closed, now there were men who sat there like they owned the place—the shock of it. Even remembering it made me feel sick to the very pit of my stomach, and I ground my teeth together.

"Where's the grave?"

"Don't know."

"Oh." Yeongsu stuck a straw in his iced coffee and sipped. The ice had watered down the brown at the top of the glass. No matter how used to Yeongsu I'd grown, every time I heard him speak, I was still struck with how beautiful his voice was, but now, it made me so angry.

"What you saw before," he said, "that was work."

"What work?"

"Well, my work, obviously."

"No, I mean, why are you doing *your* work in Lemon?"

There was silence again, and Yeongsu scratched his brow. I sensed he was trying to figure out where to start. Questions and fears whirled and caught in my throat, but I waited for him to speak.

"Today, that was . . . I suppose you could call it running the books, something like that."

"Running the books?"

"Baseball. Running the books on baseball."

"What?" I frowned. "What does that even mean?"

"It's baseball season now, right? Every day, on TV? Professional baseball. The Giants, Hanshin, Yakult, they're playing games, right."

"So?"

"So we take bets on the games. Collect money."

"And that's your work?"

"Well, that's part of it."

And then we were both silent again. "Running the books on baseball." I'd never heard that phrase before.

"So that's different from, like, a game, or something?"

"You could describe it as a game, that wouldn't be wrong, but it's not exactly right either."

"Whatever it is, it's underworld stuff, right? Bad people? Crime?"

"Maybe," Yeongsu said, tilting his head. "I suppose it depends on your point of view."

"No, it doesn't. Whatever it is, it's shady. It's fine, you can tell me. Those guys I saw in there, they didn't seem normal at all," I continued. "They seemed like really bad dudes. Because what I'm thinking is, I don't really care about your work, the thing that pisses me off is that you're using Lemon. Who said you could? I had no idea! Seriously? Since when? This is the worst. Does Kimiko know? I mean, I might be talking about it fine now, but I was terrified back there. What would you have done if I went straight to the police?"

"Hana," Yeongsu said, "don't get so worked up. I'm trying to tell you everything. Just give me a minute."

"Like you gave me a minute?" I said, looking right at him. What exactly was running the books on baseball? Even without an explanation, I had a feeling it wasn't on the up-and-up, that it was bad, but how bad was it? That was the most pressing question, but the fact that he'd used Lemon for it—I was furious that he'd made me feel so terrified.

Yeongsu glanced at his wristwatch. Then he stirred his watery iced coffee with his straw and scratched his brow again. The straw revolved in the little whirlpool of the glass and slowly came to a stop. He gave me a resigned look and said we should go somewhere else.

We left the café and followed the back alley until it emerged on another thoroughfare, where we found an island-themed izakaya that was open all day. There were a bunch of fake palm trees at the entrance, and they were playing loud, lively music. A smattering of colorful tables sat outside, and a group of college students were there, drinking and having a good time. We went inside and sat at the booth farthest from the door. A woman with huge dreads wrapped in colorful fabric danced her way to us, moving in time to the music, and Yeongsu ordered a beer on tap, so I ordered the same. The beers glinted under the lights, and I found myself frowning. We didn't toast, just started drinking in silence. Yeongsu finished his first stein quickly and flagged down the waitress to order two more. He unclasped his hands from where he'd clenched them together in his lap and glanced at me for about two seconds. Then, he scratched his forehead again, tracing the line of his eyebrow, and started talking.

3.

Yeongsu was thirty-six, two years younger than Kimiko and Kotomi. He was born and raised in the eastern end of Tokyo, in the working-class districts. His parents were both Korean nationals, but they were born in Japan, too. He had a brother five years older than him. No one spoke Korean at home, and none of them had ever been outside Japan.

When he was little, Yeongsu realized that his grandparents didn't speak Japanese very well, and when they did, they had accents. At the time, he thought it was weird that even though they were blood-related, his grandparents spoke a different language than him, and sometimes he wasn't sure they knew what he was saying. Both his grandparents were sickly and bedridden, so Yeongsu assumed, as only a child could, that their illness was what made their language funny.

It was Yeongsu's own name that first made him realize that even though he was born in Japan and only knew Japanese, he was not Japanese. He was Korean—not like the other kids in his school and neighborhood.

Then he started noticing things in his grandparents' house: their loudly patterned, glossy blankets, the foods they ate, the plates, bowls, and chopsticks they used on New Year's and other holidays. There was something fundamentally different about Yeongsu's grandparents—in his own house, everything was Japanese-style.

Yeongsu's father worked at a factory, and his mother cleaned office buildings and cafeterias. They were poor, and though his parents worked long, hard hours, their lives never got any better. "We didn't have much, but our house was still cramped with all our stuff, and my brother and I usually slept curled in balls because there wasn't enough room," Yeongsu said with a small smile.

His parents paid for everything—not only their house and food and clothes but his grandparents', too, and they were also paying off his grandparents' massive debt. His grandparents came to Japan when they were young, and they opened a restaurant with some friends in eastern Tokyo. They were known for their naengmyeon, and in just a few years, they were the most popular Korean restaurant in the neighborhood. They were generous with their customers, and their business provided work and a place to hang out for locals. But then came the long war. It was a blow to the restaurant, and they never recovered. Eventually, sunk in debt, they closed up shop.

There were a few months in second grade where Yeongsu didn't even have money for school lunches, and kids bullied him about his ratty clothes, his ramshackle home, his name. He brooded, wondering why his parents kept paying for his grandparents' debt, even though they were so poor. Once, he dared to ask his father how long they'd have to keep taking care of them. Yeongsu's father was usually a quiet, calm man, but he could also be hard on his sons, and on their mother, too. Sometimes he beat them all to make a point. It had taken courage for Yeongsu to question him, and he expected a blow, but his father didn't even look at him, just said, "Children work to take care of their parents. That's how it is." And then he left the house for the factory, same as always.

Since his parents were both working themselves to the bone, it was Yeongsu's brother, Ujun, who looked after him.

"I was a pipsqueak and a crybaby, but my brother was different, big, and a good fighter, always sure he could do anything he set his mind to," Yeongsu said. Whenever Ujun found Yeongsu crying because some neighborhood kid had called him "Kimchi," his response was to tell Yeongsu that next time he should hit his bully and call him a "stupid pickled radish." Then Ujun would wrap an arm around Yeongsu and take him to the kitchen, where he'd boil water and make Yeongsu something hot to eat. Until he became a teenager, Yeongsu had bad asthma, and whenever he had an attack, no matter the hour, Ujun would carry him piggyback to the neighborhood doctor, knock on the door to get some medicine, dose Yeongsu, and then put hot compresses on his chest. When Yeongsu couldn't sleep because of his coughing, Ujun rubbed his back and told him about his day, the idiot things his friends had done, anything to help distract him.

Yeongsu's grandfather and grandmother both died in summer, his grandfather when he was eight, and his grandmother when he was ten. Ujun was fifteen by then. Both funerals were supposed to be small, so Yeongsu was surprised by the crowds of people who came. He'd thought no one but his family cared about his grandparents. It was bizarre to him, all these people he'd never met before crying and going on and on about how his grandmother and grandfather had taken care of them. Why hadn't any of these strangers said anything when his grandparents were still alive? They'd never come to visit his bedridden grandparents or to ask after his family; they'd never helped out when his family was desperate for money. Yeongsu didn't see the point of saying these nice things now that his grandparents were dead. Their last moments had been miserable. With no money, they couldn't get any good medical treatment, so they collapsed into death, like ratty cardboard boxes broken down for trash. And even once his grandparents were cremated and nothing but bones, ash, and smoke, their debt remained. One of Yeongsu's teachers once told him that all earthly things disappear in time, returning to nothing, but that was a lie. Money never died, and it didn't disappear either.

Yeongsu's father started drinking. Sometimes he brawled with his longtime coworkers at the factory. When he was drunk, he'd make Yeongsu's mother sit in front of him while he spent hours railing senselessly, scolding her and complaining, and if Yeongsu's exhausted mother dared to say anything, his father exploded into a rage.

More and more, his father hid himself away at home, and his mother grew sicker and sicker.

Ujun and Yeongsu had been raised to believe that a father should be the most important and powerful person in a household and to go against him was unforgivable no matter how outrageous his behavior. So even when their father stopped going to work, even when he took their mother's paltry couple-hundred-yen-an-hour wages and used them on booze and pachinko instead of food and clothes, even when he was drunk and furious and spitting hateful things at them, they endured. They still remembered how their father had ground himself down working to support the family. But one day in a drunken rage, their father hurled a bowl of ramen, broth and all, at their mother, and before he could think better of it, Yeongsu grabbed his father's arm and threw him to the ground. His father yelled and slapped him, then tried to grab at him, but Ujun punched his father's shoulder to stop him. Their mother burst into tears as her husband and sons proceeded to wreck the house.

Ujun stopped going to school after junior high—that had always been his plan. He started hanging out with other local boys, and Yeongsu tagged along. When you're hungry and penniless and the cupboards are bare, stealing is the only natural option. So they stole. Boxes of bread that suppliers had piled up early in the morning in front of supermarket loading docks, and drinks from vending machines, because a child's hands were small enough to wriggle inside. They went to neighboring districts, and places that were farther away, too, to bully money out of school kids in pressed uniforms, and they pickpocketed on the trains. They stole anything they thought they could sell and turned it into money. At first, it was just Ujun and a few friends, but soon there were more, like a gang. Other good-for-nothings from other neighborhoods got wind of them and showed up to pick fights and punch it out. With each fight, the bonds between Ujun, Yeongsu, and their friends grew deeper, stronger.

Ujun and his childhood best friend, Jihun—also Korean—became the leaders, and all the troublemakers and small-timers in the neighborhood knew them and respected them.

Though Ujun was strong and had no mercy for his opponents, he always looked out for the ones he cared about, listening to their stories. Everyone idolized him. Jihun was just as strong, but he was a contrast to Ujun. Where Ujun burned hot, Jihun was cool, almost gentle, and he could temper Ujun's heat. Like Ujun, Jihun had been there for Yeongsu as long as he could remember. He told Yeongsu stories, taught him songs, played with him, and treated him like they were really brothers. Yeongsu was proud of both of them.

Three years passed that way, until Ujun and Jihun were both eighteen and Yeongsu thirteen. Ujun ordered Yeongsu to at least finish junior high, but whenever he bothered to show up to class, he was always bored. None of his teachers paid attention to him, and though his classmates kept their distance, knowing how powerful his brother was, Yeongsu knew that they were calling him a useless piece of goldfish shit behind his back. He almost made friends with another boy once, but the first time they disagreed about anything, the other boy spat, "You're just some stupid Korean." And anytime Yeongsu got in trouble, people always said things like, "This is why Koreans are useless." With time, Yeongsu learned he had nothing to say to Japanese kids whose money protected them from the things his own family had to go through. He knew there was no place for him at school.

That summer, a man they recognized from running the stalls at shrine festivals and night markets, a tekiya, invited Ujun and Jihun along. Soon the boys were mingling with tekiya. Things had been getting bad—they started having run-ins with the cops, fighting small-timers, or getting into shakedowns, and some of the younger members started showing up with bruises and cuts. Motorcycle gangs from distant parts of the city and kids with juvie rap sheets started coming round and jumping them. But even so, Ujun and Jihun's boys still weren't a real gang; they didn't even have a name. They were just doing what they needed to stay in the neighborhood, to keep on living the way they best saw fit.

What they were getting invited into was a whole other world. That world was completely alien to them—they couldn't shake the fear that something new, something darker and harsher, had opened its maw and lay in wait for them, that soon it would swallow them whole.

Tokyo was a big city, and enemies kept coming. Each new attack or incident forced the boys to acknowledge that there was always someone stronger, someone smarter, someone more wicked out there. They didn't know what to do, what would happen to them. Ujun and Jihun had to protect themselves and their friends. And to do that, they needed to be stronger. But what did that mean? Ujun insisted they should keep doing what they were doing, beating down anyone who came sniffing around, growing their crew numbers, but Jihun said that wasn't the answer. Strength, he said, wasn't in more members or thinking up new petty crimes or fighting and winning against anyone who came looking for a bruising. He thought strength was one part money and one part allies, namely the kinds of adults who would make the boys' enemies hesitate, just knowing there might be retaliation from a bigger fish.

The tekiya men were foulmouthed and rough around the edges, but they also had an unmistakable fire in them. Their clan consisted of an Oyabun at the top and a bunch of guys who followed his orders, and there was money like they'd never seen before. The tekiya men taught the boys their exhaustive set of etiquette and cleaning procedures, and how to fill their bellies without stealing. They learned the fundamentals of buying and selling, of running street stalls.

They were assigned an older brother, a twenty-one-year-old named Naru, and they spent every day grilling squid with soy sauce. Through the tekiya, they met all sorts of people. Men with missing fingers, men who were all smiles, men who always reeked of alcohol, men with traditional tattoos on their backs and arms, silent men, Koreans, Chinese, men who spoke in dialect, men who watched your back, men who didn't, men they only met once, and men they met again and again. The only thing these men had in common was an understanding that you didn't ask about anyone's past. There was an unspoken rule that, even if you were drinking together, joking, laughing, even if your companion seemed like an open book, you didn't ask personal things like "How'd you lose your finger?" or "Where were you before here?" or "How's your family?"

Three months after Ujun and Jihun started working for the tekiya, they went to a "Divvy," a meeting between all the tekiya to decide what stalls would be where for a big upcoming festival. This was the first time they met their Oyabun, and his intensity impressed them. Even though he only sat and watched over the proceedings, his presence transformed the usual festive atmosphere—everyone in the room moved differently, looked differently, focused more. The boys' skin tingled with a sense of urgency, like even though things looked calm, something big might happen at any moment. It was then that Ujun and Jihun realized just how conceited they'd been, how small their world actually was. The Oyabun didn't say much to them, only asked them for their names and ages.

Yeongsu stopped going to school and instead clung to his brothers, trailing them as they learned the stalls. All three of the boys watched and learned the business until it was muscle memory. Their older brother, Naru, was missing a few front teeth, but he was a funny guy, and even when he was telling them something very serious, there was always something cheeky about him. He took care of Yeongsu, too, sometimes giving him a little spending money or treating him to dinner. Once, Yeongsu and Naru went to the public baths early one morning, which was how Yeongsu discovered that on Naru's back was a traditional tattoo of an ogre riding a cloud. While they sat side by side to wash, Yeongsu mumbled his way through thanking Naru, but Naru said, "Don't mention it, kid. Once you join the family, you're in for good. It becomes your true family, with the Oyabun at the top. And Ujun and Jihun are my brothers, right? That means you're my brother, too."

He smiled. "Those two, they're an interesting pair. Complete opposites, inside and out. Have they ever had a real fight?"

"No," Yeongsu said. Naru smiled again and dumped hot water over his head.

"They're both big boys, but Ujun, he's got a temper and the muscle to back it. Jihun, though, he's got a face like a woman. And he's sensible. Takes his time with his words. Is he a good fighter?"

Yeongsu said they both were, and Naru nodded and grinned. He said, "I never was. But neither of them have been in the clink, right? Well, so long as they can get by with just nights in the pig pen, they'll be all right." Then Naru told Yeongsu about the fights and robberies he'd been part of, the time he spent in juvie after he got caught, and how he wound up with the tekiya clan, and every story was filled with plenty of jokes and thrills. Then Naru started kicking around in the bath, flailing his arms and legs like an octopus and singing, "You gotta live, you gotta give!"

With the tekiya, Yeongsu didn't hide himself in the corner anymore; if there was so much as a rubber band on the floor, he was there, carefully picking up the trash, and he did his best to help around the stands and hawk their wares. The tekiya men told him he showed promise, and he was overjoyed by the praise, blushing. If someone asked him to, he'd do ingredient runs, dashing from the bright lights of a festival down to the unlit streets where the trucks were parked. There, he often saw kids even younger than him playing around the trucks' tires or trailers like shadows. He figured these kids must move around a lot, following the festivals. Because festivals weren't only during the long summer holidays—there were spring, autumn, and winter festivals, too. Once, Yeongsu grew curious and asked the kids what they did for school, but they hunched in like they were embarrassed and said things like "I go sometimes," "Not me," or "I don't know." Then they retreated into the darkness.

Soon rumors spread that Ujun and Jihun had sworn themselves to the tekiya, and Yeongsu started to notice changes. The boys in the crew kept following Ujun and Jihun's lead, clearly happy that they had stronger backing now, but that didn't last long.

With their money, Ujun and Jihun could treat everyone to extravagant meals and liquor, and they still spent time laughing and joking around, but it was clear that little by little, they were falling out of sync with their crew. Less than a year later, the toughs and gangs from other neighborhoods disappeared, but Yeongsu began to hear whispers of new, younger men's names. Any time there was a serious fight, he didn't hear about it until long after the fact. The generations were passing their torches.

Working for the tekiya was grueling. There were days when Ujun and Jihun worked themselves so tired they couldn't get up the next day. Working under the Oyabun came with its own kind of stress, and there were lots of fights below the surface. They grew used to things after a while, though, so much so that they could be big brothers like Naru. And that's when Yeongsu and Ujun's father died.

He fell off a bridge in the middle of the night, drunk off his ass. There was no way of knowing if it was an accident or suicide. It was the dead of winter, and Yeongsu was sixteen, Ujun twenty-one. Both of them had been couch surfing, staying at Jihun's or at the tekiya's main office or with other clan members, but they did go home once in a while to give their mom money, which meant they also had to see their father. After that big blowout, though, the boys never spoke to him. They held their father's wake at a community center on the edge of the neighborhood, and all their dad's friends from the factory gathered, bowing their heads and talking about how hardworking he was, how terrible it was that he died so young. After the guests left, Ujun and Yeongsu and their mother talked. Jihun was there, too, pouring out drinks for the family.

After the tears, after the long silences, Ujun asked, "What do you think his last words were?"

"I don't think he had any," their mother said.

And then they were silent again. Under the fluorescent lights, their mother's face was gaunt, almost skeletal. She looked like a crone, like a complete stranger who had somehow wandered in among them. The thought cast Yeongsu into even deeper darkness.

"I slept through the night, and when I got up, I went straight to work. I didn't find out until that evening when the cops showed up."

"Do you think he killed himself?"

"I don't know. But it's not a time that you'd go out for a walk. And all he ever did was drink and sleep."

"We were bringing you money, so it wasn't money problems or anything, right?" Ujun asked.

"No, I don't think so."

"And he hadn't been losing his temper as much lately, right?"

"No . . . That was thanks to you. After he wrecked the house that one time. After that, he really calmed down. When I got home from work, he'd eat whatever little thing I managed to make, and once he'd had his booze, he didn't even complain. 'Course he'd been drinking more and more for years. He started first thing in the morning. Oh and one time, I saw him crying at night." Their mother sniffled. "I couldn't understand him 'cause he was drunk, but he was talking about his mother. Your grandmother. Something about her memorial services. And how pathetic he was. He got violent sometimes, but you know, most of the time he was just scared."

"I think he must have fallen," Jihun said as he poured another round. "That bridge has a really low railing. You can't see it at night. No streetlights. One of my friends fell off it just messing around. And he was sober. He fell off sober and broke almost every bone in his body."

"He didn't die?"

"He had enough fight in him to swim, apparently. It was early in the morning, and the people passing by just avoided him, so he walked himself to the hospital sopping wet, bones broken. What else was he supposed to do?" Jihun grinned. "I mean that canal is filthy, right? And he drank a bunch of that shit when he fell. Made him puke and puke, and he had diarrhea so bad he was sure he was gonna die. He said that part was way worse than the broken bones."

"Fuck, man," Ujun said, grinning, too.

"I'm glad he survived," their mom said with a small smile, raising her eyes to look at them. "You've gotten so big, Jihun."

"You think so?"

"You were just a kid the last time I saw you."

"Well, Ujun and I are twenty-one now."

"So you are. Amazing," she said, still smiling, shaking her head. "I guess it's true, for everybody, kids, adults, you grow up, grow old, in the blink of an eye."

When Yeongsu's mother slipped into the room where they'd put their futons, the boys went outside for some fresh air. Without even discussing it, they started walking. Jihun lit up a cigarette. The white smoke curled out and out into the sharp winter air, but soon it dissipated.

"It doesn't make sense," Ujun murmured to himself.

"What do you mean?" asked Jihun.

"I mean . . . our old man, he worked himself to the bone day in and day out, but he was poor as fuck his whole life, lived in a place no bigger than a doghouse, turned into a drunk, and in the end, he died like *that*, so I guess that's what I was thinking."

Jihun nodded.

"He wasn't dad of the year, that's for sure, but he was a hard worker. Never cheated anybody, just worked at the factory, kept his mouth shut, kept everything simple. And this is how he dies? I don't think he thought much of us, thought we were gutless, pathetic half men with no real job or nothing. And I just, I don't know . . . It makes me so goddamn angry, and angry at what, I don't even know. At everything, I guess."

Their footsteps crunched down the gravel path, the only sound.

"Hey, Jihun, maybe there's no point in asking," Ujun said, "but do you think it would've been different if our dad was Japanese?"

"I don't know."

"Would it have been better, a better life?"

"What do you think, Ujun?"

"I think . . ." But there Ujun fell silent, glaring at the darkness before him.

Eventually Jihun said, "There are plenty of guys who aren't Japanese who are doing good."

"Yeah, I guess. So what the hell did we do wrong?"

Jihun didn't answer, flicking the ash from his cigarette. The cherry drew a red spot in the darkness and then disappeared again.

"Times like this, what's the take here?" Ujun asked Jihun. "Are we supposed to think, well, we're the scum of society and there's nothing we can do about it, or do we go ballistic, say, one day we'll get all you fuckers, just wait and see."

"I don't know."

"Or maybe it's smarter to give up, because from the start, money, luck, they had nothing to do with us."

"I don't know, man, but I do know that some things are set from the start. You can't choose the big things—your parents, where you're from," Jihun said. "Yourself."

After a pause, Ujun said, "Who gives a fuck about blood? People have been telling me it's the most important thing ever since I was born, but I think it's fucking bullshit. What the hell is it, anyway? Dirty blood, clean blood, rich blood, does any of it really exist? What are they trying to say? Say there really are different kinds, how do you tell them apart? The food you eat? The place you were born? Your parents, your parents' jobs? Your face? Or your name? What the hell is it?"

"I don't think anyone knows what they mean," Jihun said. "That's why they can say whatever the hell they want."

"The fuck? How can they say whatever the hell they want if they don't even know what it means?"

"It's when you don't know anything, that's when you start cruising."

"Cruising?" Ujun tilted his head, looking at Jihun. "What's cruising got to do with it?"

"I mean," Jihun said, laughing. "It comes down to attitude. People don't need reason or truth. See, when you're cruising, you feel like everything is going great, like it's all good. People like feeling that way. That's how the cruisers get the people, the money, the luck, too. And power. The guy who knows the least, he's cruising the most, and whatever he says becomes the most true thing in the world, at least for that moment."

"I never know what you're saying," Ujun said, scratching his head. "If those guys get all the good luck, just when are you and I gonna start cruising? How do we do that? I want a taste."

"Ha! It's impossible for guys like us."

"But why?"

"Because of everything," Jihun said with a laugh. Ujun still didn't look convinced, but after a moment the frown lines on his face relaxed, and the three of them laughed.

They spent the entire night wandering around the neighborhood they'd been born and raised in, and they went to the funeral not having slept at all. They bore the coffin. While they waited for their father to finish burning up in the neighborhood crematorium, Ujun had their mother sit down in the waiting room so he could rub her shoulders. Jihun told Yeongsu a bunch of stories and fables. Yeongsu didn't remember the details anymore, but they were stories with animals in them. The time came, and he listened as the attendant explained what each bone scattered among the white ashes was, and he thought about his father's smiling face. When his father had laughed, his eyebrows descended, and you could see his snaggletooth. Yeongsu recalled those moments of laughter, the happy moments. He also recalled how, when he'd been a child, he would come home from school and stare at their crooked house and think about how when he grew up, he was going to earn a lot of money and buy his parents a huge house. Once when he was very little, their family took a walk to see a dam. They ate the onigiri his mother packed and skipped stones from the riverbank. On the way home, it started pouring, so their dad gathered Yeongsu and Ujun under his jacket, holding them tight on either side, swaying from left to right and laughing as they walked along. It must have been early spring. Yeongsu thought about that moment as he trailed Ujun, who held the paulownia box with their father's remains inside. The four of them, Yeongsu, Ujun, their mother, and Jihun, made their way back the way they'd come. In the dazzlingly clear winter sky, Yeongsu noticed a scrap of cloud appear, like a tiny, frozen breath.

Yeongsu took a breath as he finished telling his story. "It's been more than twenty years, but I still think of that night, walking with Ujun and Jihun. The morning of the funeral, too. About how it would have been better if we'd just gone on like that, working for the tekiya or even getting a job someplace close to home. But I didn't know back then. I was a useless brat with shit for brains—I guess I still am—and I thought if I just followed Ujun and Jihun, so long as we were together, that would be enough. I thought we'd be okay. Not that it's worth much, wishing now. But still, I think about it."

Yeongsu put his lips to his glass and drank the last of his beer. "I've been rambling, haven't I? I've never gone on like this before, even drunk as a skunk," Yeongsu said, smiling self-deprecatingly. "Guess I'm useless once I've had a few. I knew that, though."

I nodded and kept my mouth shut. I glanced at the clock on the wall and saw it was nearly three. When had we arrived at this place? I couldn't remember. Maybe two hours ago, maybe even more, but I was totally absorbed in Yeongsu's story. The whole time he'd been talking, I felt like my arms and legs weren't quite here, in this place, in this time, on this seat. We'd ordered two refills while he was talking, but the glass stein in front of me was empty yet again. When he asked if I'd have another, I nodded. Yeongsu called the waitress and ordered refills.

"I didn't meet Kimiko and Kotomi until after," Yeongsu said. "We'd left our own neighborhood by then, had a source in Shinjuku. Kabukicho wasn't a mess like it is now, things were easier to understand back then. You could still see a man's face."

"Were Kimiko and Kotomi already friends by then?"

"They were working at the same watering hole and living

together. Ujun, Jihun, and I were at a nearby casino. We got to know each other, started hanging out together."

"Casinos, you can get arrested for those, right?"

"Yeah."

"So you moved from the tekiya to a casino?"

"Maybe six months after our dad died, the family started fighting. The tekiya clan, I mean. Small fries like the three of us never got all the details, but there was a huge fight about who would succeed as clan head. Everything took a complete one-eighty, and we didn't want to wind up the same. Sure, we got beat around—that was normal—but the biggest reason was that the guy we were reassigned to beat Naru half to death. And yeah, Naru had messed up, but we thought the punishment was too harsh; beaten down by a guy we barely knew, no brothers to watch our backs, it seemed wrong. Naru decided to leave the clan—he had other brothers in Shinjuku, guys from way back, so he called his big brother there and started working for them. Our Oyabun finally decided who would take his place, so we thought it was the right time to leave, in every sense. Plus, Shinjuku's on a whole other level. There were a lot of terrible things about it, but we figured there are terrible things everywhere. And we were excited by the idea that we'd get bigger hauls. That's how we wound up sourcing in Shinjuku.

"Naru's brothers hooked us up with a gambling den boss who worked for a big organization. That's how these things work. A lot of tekiya are tied up with the yakuza. It wasn't all new to us. But we'd come out of a backwater tekiya, and kids like us were a dime a dozen. We moved into a shitty workhouse, and when the casino was open, we worked the kitchen and the main floor, hauling stock and money, standing on lookout. That was the only kind of work we got at first. But soon enough, they started sending us out on collections. When I first went along, I honestly thought we were in hell. I couldn't believe half the stuff they did to guys who didn't pay up. No way I could do that myself. Of course I was still a kid, so I was never directly involved with a lot of the work, but Ujun and Jihun got sucked in right away. Naru, too, in a way.

"The organization, they paid for our room and board, our driver's licenses and cars, all the money was taken care of, and the three of them got involved with yakuza women, too, and soon it was impossible to get out. And before long, it wasn't just baccarat—they had lots of sources. They started with the big collections, getting experience, getting results. Soon, people knew Ujun and Jihun's faces, the people around them doubled, tripled, friends and enemies alike. We probably should have stopped somewhere along the line, called it quits, gotten out. But where? I wonder even now, but if you said I could go back to one moment in time and change it, I don't know when that would be."

"So Ujun and Jihun became yakuza?"

"They started visiting headquarters, and then, yeah, they pledged their cups and joined."

"Did you join, too?"

"I didn't pledge," Yeongsu said. "I wasn't even eighteen yet, and Ujun and Jihun ordered me to stay respectable. I loved being with them, and I hated that they treated me like a kid, but part of me understood what they were saying. I didn't have any talents or resources I could offer the yakuza. So we just kept on same as always, with me trailing after the two of them, scrimping sources here and there and making a half-assed living. But little by little they left me behind. The people around them changed, the kinds and amounts of money they moved changed, and then the people changed again. My brothers got pushed along at a speed even they hadn't imagined. Soon they were moving money outside the city, too, and sometimes they didn't come home for weeks or months. And then Naru disappeared. Ujun and Jihun wouldn't tell me the details, but apparently, he'd been doing speed for ages, and he started stealing from the yakuza—product and money both. Less than two years since we first came to Shinjuku. Disappeared, just like that. As for me, they could only give me odd jobs, so I ran lookout for the casinos, brought in people to work the pachinko machines, collected protection money from bars, hot towel outlets, prostitutes, wherever. I kept an eye on the guys selling knockoffs, too."

I nodded and sipped my beer.

"I took on the crappy jobs and bummed around town. And I went over to Kimiko and Kotomi's place for dinner."

"So you got along right off the bat."

"Back then, Ujun and Kimiko were dating, and Jihun and Kotomi were together, too, so I was basically everybody's little brother."

"Really?" I exclaimed.

"What?" Yeongsu said, surprised that I was surprised. "Don't act so shocked."

"It's just that," I said, sitting up straight. "I didn't think Kimiko was ever involved with anything like, you know, that."

"Why?"

"Um, I dunno," I said, taking a long swallow of beer.

"We didn't have cell phones back then. If you wanted to get ahold of someone, you had to call their home or their work. So when the casino was closed and I had free time, I watched the phone at Kimiko and Kotomi's place. They didn't know when Ujun or Jihun might call, and they never left messages on the answering machine."

"So I guess they were just, like, normal lovers."

"Yeah, I guess. But whenever they got together, they always ended up in huge fights, never made nice. Well, not all of them. It was Ujun and Kotomi. For some reason, they always wound up fighting, and then Jihun and Kimiko would try to smooth things over. I used to think they'd messed up who should be dating who," Yeongsu said, smiling. "Kotomi's calmed down a lot since then, mellowed out, but back then, she was fiery, and she had such a mouth on her. Jihun was always chill, he'd just say, 'Okay, okay,' and smile, would never engage her when she wanted to fight. But then Ujun would butt in and say, 'You've gone too far. Jihun may be your boyfriend, but don't forget he's my brother first,' and then Kotomi would lose it and start up the fight. That was always how it went. And then once they'd had their fill of fighting, we'd all head out for dinner."

"You were close, huh," I said with a smile. "And Kimiko and Ujun didn't fight?"

"I never saw them go at it," Yeongsu said. "But Kimiko is Kimiko, and she's got her own stuff to deal with, right? My brother was always worried about that."

"Her own stuff?" I asked, and Yeongsu caught and held my gaze, sipping his beer. "What do you mean?" I asked again.

"Well, you know . . ." he said, rubbing his brow. "Hana, has she told you anything about . . . anything?"

"No."

"Hmm. Nothing about her mother?"

"Her mother?" I asked. "No, nothing. She said she was visiting her dad's grave today, but that's the first time she's ever mentioned her family."

"Well, I suppose it's not that important."

"What?"

Yeongsu stared down at his fingertips and then bluntly said, "Kimiko's mom is in jail."

"In jail?" I repeated. "Right now?"

"Yeah."

"Alone?"

"Everyone's alone in jail," Yeongsu said with a worn smile, and then he looked at me. "Though there's plenty of people in there."

"Right. Sorry." I pressed my lips together.

"No need to apologize. But anyway, her mom's in jail. For a long time now. Whenever she gets out, she winds up right back in, over and over."

"What did she do to get arrested?"

"Most recently, I think it was shoplifting or speed," Yeongsu said. "The first time it was speed, theft, and arson."

"Arson?"

"She wasn't going around and setting people's houses on fire for fun. She didn't have a choice. Her dealers told her if she burned a place down, they'd clear her debts. They said the store was in on the whole thing, they were going to split the insurance money, so no one would get hurt—but that was a lie. Kimiko was maybe ten years old, and her mom took her along and had her help start the fire."

I stared at Yeongsu.

"Her dad was already dead by then, and she didn't have any relatives, so after her mom was arrested, she was raised in the system, one place and then the next. Her story's not uncommon. You can imagine what kind of childhood she had, right? She went without food a lot. And with Kimiko the way she is, I'm sure horrible things happened to her."

"What do you mean exactly?"

Yeongsu blinked at me. "I mean—" But then he cut himself off and looked at the wall. The reggae music seemed to grow suddenly louder.

"I mean, you can feel it, right? You live with her, so I think you already know. She's a little off."

I studied him closely, trying to understand what he was telling me.

"She's normal enough, at least on the surface, but I don't know—there are moments, right? When you don't know if she understands what you're telling her. Times when you wonder why she acts the way she acts."

"Yeah," I said without thinking.

"And there are plenty of things she just can't do, right?"

I remembered all the times when conversations with Kimiko had felt unsettling or when I'd questioned her actions and reactions. I pressed my fingers to my eyes.

"Right?"

"Right."

"She's not really capable of thinking about the future—money, savings, things like that, you know."

"Yeah."

"She's not doing it on purpose," Yeongsu said, "and I don't think you could just chalk it up to her personality either. She is how she is. I bet you knew people like her, back in school. There are a lot of people like Kimiko working nightlife or working in the underworld, too. They come through plenty. And to *crooks*, people like Kimiko, men and women alike are just money trees."

"Money trees?" I whispered.

"Yeah. People like Kimiko, you can make them do anything, do anything to them. No family, no connections to the normal world, no real ID. If they disappear all of a sudden, nobody cares. There are lots of folks like that working in the dark, and to some people, they're just *things*. Things you can use. Because they're so easy to get rid of, to sink. That's what I mean."

I stared at Yeongsu, wide-eyed.

"And then there are guys whose job is to find people like Kimiko. It's a way to get real cash real quick. Society pretends people like Kimiko don't exist, so they can't speak up for themselves, and even if they could, no one would listen. These guys will find folks wandering around, and it only takes a few sweet words to get them to do anything. These guys, they pretend to be friends, shackle people in debt, and suck them dry."

At some point, I'd put my hands to my mouth, but now I lowered them.

"She's been through a lot," Yeongsu said, holding my gaze. "She was about eighteen when we met her. About the same age as you. She was already with Kotomi by then. And I've stayed by her side and looked out for her ever since, so she hasn't been forced into anything since then. Just worked the nightlife, hasn't found herself in hot water. Her childhood must have been horrible, though. Not that she'll ever talk about it."

"Before," I said, asking each question as it came to me, "in winter, you came for hot pot, right, and you, I mean, you're always handing her envelopes, and the envelopes, they're, I mean, money."

"Yeah."

"She's never told me, but I looked, without her permission. And there was cash in the envelopes."

"Yeah, to pay off her mother's debt."

"Her mother's?"

"Yeah."

"Is it money from you running the books? The baseball thing?"

"No, from somewhere else," Yeongsu said. "I've got a lot of sources."

"Is Kimiko involved?"

"No. I just hand her the money, nothing else."

"Which means you're repaying her mother's debt."

"Yeah, I suppose I am," Yeongsu said, scratching his brow. "But that's nothing, I mean, it's just insurance money. Injury insurance. With insurance agents and clinics."

"What do you mean?"

"Well, a whole bunch of people take out an insurance policy and pay a couple thousand yen a month for it, right? And then they get themselves a little injury, and they go to a hospital that accepts the insurance policy. And each time they go for treatment—well, it depends on the policy—but they might get about ten thousand a day or so. It's like going to a part-time job each day. But if you go, there's always a record. So you go until you hit your payout limit. The goal is usually two months, sixty days. And then when the insurance pays out, everyone splits it."

"And if you get found out?" I asked.

"The doctor who issues the prescription and the insurance agent who clears the claim are in on it. They're each handling a couple of groups, making sure things don't overlap, and they change members in and out, and if the insurance agent's contact puts a stop to it, they stop. The money I give Kimiko comes from that."

"And if you get caught?"

"Well, we're not talking that much money, so, you know."

We fell into silence and drank our beers. For a moment, I wanted to ask if Yeongsu had ever been caught, but I sensed I shouldn't, so I didn't. The silence was a long one.

"Is her mom's debt really bad?"

"It's a lot, things can add up if you're hooked on speed. Her mom used to owe loan sharks, too, but Kimiko took care of those. She's been taking care of her mom's debts ever since she was a kid."

"So Kimiko"—I exhaled all the breath in my lungs and kneaded my cheeks with my palms—"she's been living like this ever since she was a kid?"

"You've seen the big mark that looks like a mole on her right hand, right?"

"No. I didn't know she had one," I said, looking up.

"It's there. On the base of her thumb. She's never been able to tell right from left, no matter how many times someone teaches her, so when she was little, they inked that mark on to remind her. Used a sewing needle. So she could tell just by looking which hand was right."

"Who did it?"

"Her mother and whoever she was dating back then."

I didn't know what to say.

After a moment, Yeongsu said, "Hana, I know Sancha doesn't look like much, but you never know what might happen. You gotta be careful what you say about yourself. Don't tell people you're a runaway or that you're not in touch with your folks. You never know who might be connecting the dots. Don't be a money tree, don't call attention to yourself."

There was a searing pain in my temples, as though my brain had been running too long or not running enough. It was all I could do to nod. Yeongsu finished the last of his beer and looked at me again. Then he suggested we head out. I nodded silently. Yeongsu raised a hand to signal for the check, and the woman with the bright fabric hair wrap came and handed him the bill. I pulled out my wallet to pay, but Yeongsu stopped me and paid for both of us. The waitress grinned and cheerfully thanked us. Even though she was the same woman that greeted us when we first got here, the same person who'd brought us all those beers, I felt like she was *someone else*, that somehow another person had taken her place, and somehow everyone knew but they'd agreed not to say anything about it.

Outside, it smelled like the end of summer. Through my brain fog, I wondered how I knew this scent, where I'd experienced it before. Yeongsu walked beside me. We automatically turned toward the station. How strange that seasons have scents. Who decided what season it was? What defined them? Flowers and leaves? The wind? Things outside the world of people. Did a season always smell the same, no matter how old you were, no matter where you were? My brain rattled on and on with no direction.

"Kimiko's coming home, right?" Yeongsu asked.

"Of course she will," I said, looking up. "Why would you say that? Has she not come home before?"

"I didn't mean anything by it. I was just wondering what time she would be back." Yeongsu peered at me. "What is it?"

"She didn't say what time," I said, sounding pitiful and helpless. "But she'll come home."

"I'm sorry again about the betting," Yeongsu said. "You were startled, of course you were. I was, too, but you were probably even more startled than I was."

I didn't respond.

"We're in transition right now. Not that this kind of work has a transition period. But today was a one-off. We were just borrowing Lemon."

I watched the sky between the buildings where a small flock of black birds flew up and then dipped away again, swallowed into nothing.

"What does your brother do now?"

"He's dead," Yeongsu said. "He died when he was twenty-seven. The young ones die first."

We arrived at the stairs that led down to the ticket gate. Yeongsu grinned and said, "We really drank a lot, can't believe how well you hold your liquor." He fiddled with his pouch, shuffling it from hand to armpit and then back again.

"What about Jihun?"

"Jihun." Yeongsu sighed and scratched his brow. "He disappeared without a trace. He's not in jail, but I never heard rumors of him dying or getting offed either, so I don't know. It's been a long time. The last I saw him, he was working credit unions or banks or something. Jihun was good-looking, and you don't get guys like that in the yakuza a lot, so they thought his looks were useful. The yakuza boss, he liked Ujun and Jihun both, so they got in deep, too deep, in the money and the organization both. Well, who knows, maybe Jihun got lucky and got out, might be working a respectable job by now. But it's not that easy. I don't know. Either way, I've never found him."

"You're looking for him?"

"Well," Yeongsu said with a smile, "he is my brother."

After Yeongsu and I parted, I wandered Sangenjaya aimlessly. I probably should have crossed the road, headed down the shopping district, and just gone home, but for some reason, I couldn't. I followed the gray road stretched before me, and when I hit a dead end, I turned right, turned left, over and over. Before I knew it, it was dusk, and I was back in front of the station again. It wasn't full dark yet, but there was a feverish excitement in the people who milled on the boulevard, as though they were already welcoming the night. I didn't know where to go next. My body grew heavier and heavier, but still, I dragged myself along, and two traffic lights later, I found myself in a new shopping district. This I passed through, too, until I came to a park filled with huge trees, where I found an empty bench and sat. Kids, old people, couples, mothers rocking their babies, all sorts of people—in the waning light of a Sunday afternoon, they seemed faded to me. I felt like there was something I should be thinking about, but what that was, I couldn't begin to guess.

I stayed in the park until night fell. When I got home and opened the door, Kimiko was there. She was wiping down the walls with her dustcloth, same as always. When she saw me, she stopped what she was doing and came to the entryway.

"Hi, Hana!"

"Hi."

"I got us some takoyaki."

"No way!" I said, forcing cheerfulness. I couldn't meet Kimiko's eyes.

"When I went to my dad's grave, there was a festival at the temple, so I bought some."

"That's awesome." I went to the sink to wash my hands, taking care not to meet Kimiko's eyes. Once I got hold of myself, I went into the main room.

"Let's eat once I'm done cleaning up."

"Okay."

I watched Kimiko's back as she wiped the walls single-mindedly, her arm churning in circles even though there wasn't a speck of dirt. She became a child before my very eyes, again and again and again.

"Okay, Hana, let's eat."

Kimiko spread out the takoyaki boxes on our folding table, and on her right thumb, just as Yeongsu had said, there was a small bluish oval, almost like a bruise. I crammed two takoyaki into my mouth. "Mmm, it's really good."

"Oh, Hana, why are you crying?"

"What are you talking about?" I lied. "What, am I crying?"

"You are," Kimiko said. "You're crying. Did something happen?"

"Nothing. These are just so delicious."

"Okay." Kimiko smiled. "The ones from street vendors are always the best. Oh remember? Me and you, we had some once, at a night market, when was it?"

"We did!" I said, my mouth full, tears still dripping down my face. "The two of us, together."

I felt like we were in that distant summer night again, eating takoyaki. The scene unfolded before me, every summer, that summer—glistening crimson candy apples, cotton candy, orange fluttering goldfish in their pool, colorful bouncy balls, the scent of earth, the aroma of sauces, the press of jabbering people, all having the time of their lives, the endless smoke of the grills. The night stretched out and out.

Children running around, dark shadows against the darker

edges of night. Adults warning them, it's scary, don't go over there, but they only laugh and laugh. They don't understand it's night, don't understand anything about it. But then, on the path ahead, there's a faint light spilling from a gap between the hot dogs and melon buns and canned goods. When next I blinked, I realized Kimiko was watching me.

"Kimiko," I said faintly, "don't disappear like you did before."

"I did do that, didn't I." She laughed.

"Don't laugh," I said. "Stay with me, forever."

We ate the rest of our takoyaki and watched TV. Then we took turns showering, turned out the lights, crawled into our futons, and chatted for a while. I told Kimiko I'd stayed home all day and then gone out for a walk just before dusk, and she told me about the stray cats she saw at the graveyard. Soon Kimiko fell asleep. I lay, staring at the blue shadows that fell softly into the corners of our room, and listened to the sound of her breathing. I didn't sleep well that night.

SEVEN

ONE BIG HAPPY FAMILY

1.

"Come on, let's take a break already, I'm totally starving over here."

Ran did a full-body stretch, like she couldn't take any more and then flopped face down on the tatami. Already that time, I wondered, but when I checked my cell phone, sure enough it was almost two in the afternoon. It'd been a long time since our morning onigiri from the convenience store. As if in agreement, my stomach rumbled. I hadn't even noticed I was hungry, too focused on working with everyone to clean our new house.

"What should we have?" Kimiko asked, setting down the heavy cardboard box she'd been carrying. "What does everyone want?"

"Anything's fine as long as it's quick," Ran said, rolling onto her back. Momoko and I agreed that anything was fine.

"Okay, let's walk down to the station and decide from there."

We walked for fifteen minutes through the still-unfamiliar streets lined with houses, crossed the highway, and emerged in front of Sangenjaya Station's familiar facade. There, we wandered around, peering in restaurant windows, wondering what to have, until eventually we settled on our usual Chinese place. The sliding door rattled as we slid it back, and the scent of the grill and gyoza and sizzling fat washed over us—I started salivating, hunger twisting my stomach like it was wringing out a rag. We all ordered the daily special plus two plates of gyoza to share. Our beef stir-fry came almost instantly, and we tucked in, silence falling. After a few minutes, Momoko laughed.

"This is hilarious, we're eating like pigs. I don't think any of us is planning to enter an eating contest anytime soon. I mean seriously, the rice is gone already."

"I mean, I am *obsessed* with rice," Ran joked.

As I savored the way the beef drippings and garlic chives melded into the rice on my tongue, I hummed, "*Obsessed*. Why is rice so delicious anyway? I could just keep eating it forever." The waitress approached with our gyoza, fresh and crisp from the grill. She thunked the plates down in front of us, and we murmured appreciatively.

"We're almost done with the cleaning," Ran said, dipping her gyoza in its sauce. "It's just the curtains on the second floor, right, Hana? We already put the futons in the closet."

"Yeah. I was worried we got the wrong size curtains, but they look all right. And we bought enough screws for the rails, too."

"We're sleeping in the tatami room, right? And the room next to that can be for storage for now. We probably have a lot of clothes, between the three of us."

"Yeah. I feel like it's better to have more room for us in the bedroom. Oh, did you see the tile around the washbasin? It's pretty beat-up, but don't you think it's kind of cute? The pattern, the color, like, it's giggly."

"It is super cute," Momoko and Ran agreed.

Once we'd filled our bellies, we stopped by a convenience store to buy drinks. It was a bright and sunny November Sunday. From time to time, the breeze picked up, carrying the pleasant scent of the coming winter chill. Since the weather was nice, people were out in force. The whole neighborhood felt alive, everyone more cheery than usual. We weren't done with the moving cleanup yet, but we decided to mix into the flow of people around the station, walking aimlessly.

It'd been more than a year since I first moved to Sancha. I

already knew the shops, but on that day, I found myself noticing the places that sold home decor, the vases and shelves and chairs and mirrors, the things you'd put in a house. Everything was glowing, like it was welcoming me with a smile. I could look at all the furniture and decorations I liked, and if it wasn't too expensive, I could buy it, for my own home—just the thought filled me with a slow-blooming joy. I couldn't help but grin. Life certainly wasn't worry-free, but this was the first time I'd ever tasted triumph.

It was back in April that Kimiko and I found out we'd have to leave the heights, and we thought we'd have plenty of time to find a new place, but life never slowed down. Before we knew it, summer had come and gone, and the deadline for finding a new place was bearing down on us. I knew we needed to think about it, that finding a new place would take effort, but there was Lemon to look after, and Kimiko came down with horrible stomach flu, and Ran and Momoko and I were spending a lot of time together—my days were so busy, I just kept putting it off.

To find a place, we had to go to a leasing agent. On my way to work or on my days off, I marched around town, pressing up against the glass of every leasing office in the neighborhood and intently studying the layouts and figures on each of their for-lease ads. But I could never bring myself to go inside. All I could do was look longingly at each ad in turn.

Our funds were fine. We were saving, and while Lemon wasn't making a killing, it wasn't failing either, so we'd have no problem paying the rent. I was sure we could make a go of it and not cause the landlord any trouble. But the truth was, we couldn't even get to the starting line—we didn't have any credit. I was still a minor and didn't have an ID or a way to prove my monthly earnings. And even though Kimiko was an adult, she was in the same boat.

Ran and the boyfriend she was living with were still having terrible fights all the time, and last month, there was a whole mess where he'd started hyperventilating or something, and that turned into seizures, and she ended up having to call an ambulance. Setting aside his health and mood swings, the fact of the matter was that they both got so worked up that they were at each other's throats; sometimes they even got physical. Ran had started talking about how she was reaching her limit. And Momoko was Momoko. She never went back to Aobadai unless she absolutely had to. She wasn't going to school either, which meant she was fighting with her parents, and her relationship with her sister, Shizuka, was only getting worse. Momoko spent almost all her time with Kimiko and me, either at our apartment or at Lemon.

So when the two of them heard that Kimiko and I had to find a new place by the end of the year, they got excited and were quick to suggest we should find a place together. That's all it was, though—enthusiasm. None of us had a concrete plan for how to go about actually carrying out the idea.

Ran and I couldn't rely on our parents, and Momoko's family might have been wealthy and well-to-do, but they had nothing to do with us, had never even met us. "I wonder if we can get my grandma to help out," Momoko said, half-joking, but that idea didn't have any teeth to it. We were alive, living in the real world, but without IDs, we didn't exist; we were only half-alive. With each day, I realized more and more that the way we existed in the world wasn't normal. Maybe that's what being a kid meant, but maybe age had nothing to do with it. Because Kimiko was in the same boat.

One night, Kotomi came to Sancha to have dinner with the rest of us—one part of the evening sticks out in my mind. Kotomi liked to have a smoke and a coffee after dinner, and that night, there was a moment where she exhaled the smoke like a sigh, and our eyes met. She gave me this Mona Lisa smile like she always did—I liked how even when she smiled at me, there was still something so lonely about her, it made me want to cry. But that night, when I saw her smile, a spasm of anxiety I'd bottled up surged through me, and I panicked, sure I wouldn't be able to stop myself from spilling my fears and worries. But Kotomi was already helping us out a lot—she brought in her Ginza customers twice a month to spend money at Lemon before she took them to her club—so I didn't think I could ask her to help us find a place to live on top of that. Somehow, I managed to squash the urge to tell her everything.

Maybe if Kimiko had asked, it wouldn't have been so awkward, but the thought apparently never crossed Kimiko's mind. And I thought it would be wrong of me to urge Kimiko to ask Kotomi for help. It seemed impossible.

I felt like I couldn't ask Yeongsu for help either. That day—the day when I found him with the baseball gamblers, his story had sunk roots deep into my heart. I remembered each and every scene, and they left me feeling bitter and heartbroken, even though none of it had happened to me. Nothing about Yeongsu had changed—he was still quiet, always coming by to spend time at Lemon. But his presence or absence didn't matter, because I'd started thinking about his story all the time. I remembered the people and places he'd talked about, imagined the things he must have seen and felt. He and Kimiko went way back, so maybe he would've helped us out, but I was already borrowing a cell phone from him, and I didn't feel like I could ask him to take on more of our expenses. And even if we got his help, I was sure whatever deal he found wouldn't be on the straight and narrow, so Yeongsu had to be our last resort.

Maybe I should go back to Higashimurayama and figure out some kind of ID. But what? What would prove I existed? There was nothing. IDs were useful for more than just renting apartments, too. Say, for example, I was in an accident or I got sick, what then? Could I go to the hospital? Without insurance, could I even pay the bills? A massive black hole yawned before me, ready to suck me up completely, face-first. I shook my head, trying to banish the image. No, I wasn't sick or hurt, what I needed to do was find a place to live. What was I going to do about that?

If worst came to worst, Kimiko and I could probably live at Lemon for a while. Could we use the bench seats for beds, turn a booth into a closet, hide it with a sheet, and eat the loss?

Or could we have Momoko tell Tommy-cat what was going on and ask him if we could borrow the key to the tattoo parlor, put down our futons, and secretly live there for a while? From the time I woke up until the time I went to bed, I thought nonstop about where to go, until I felt like I was going to lose my mind. Kimiko kept on same as always, rag in hand, wiping down the walls. Ran and Momoko both seemed optimistic—they apparently hadn't noticed how worried I was about finding a place. In fact, even though they'd suggested we could live together, they didn't seem to have their hearts set on it. More like they thought it would be nice if it happened. I couldn't tell anyone how cornered I felt. I had to do something. I had to figure something out to protect this life I'd built with Kimiko. But how? I spent weeks feeling like I was packed in a shoebox, my oxygen slowly running out, but just when I reached my wit's end and was sure I'd have to ask Yeongsu after all—my savior came from a place I hadn't imagined: Lemon's landlord.

"I've got a place in Shimouma."

Jin-ji, whose real name was Jinno, was born and raised in Kansai and spoke with a lilting Osakan accent. He liked Lemon and came to hang out about once a month or so. Our building was run-down, yes, but the fact that Jin-ji owned it meant he was probably well-off. He never acted like he was above us or said anything nasty, though. (We had plenty of regulars who were rich or landlords, and they never bothered to hide their selfish egos.) Jin-ji was a good customer, and on the days when he came, Kimiko and I, Ran and Momoko, we felt like he brought a bit of cheer with him.

Given that he'd introduced himself as Jin-ji—old Jin—it was no surprise that his hair was pure white. Anybody would've called him a grandfather with that hair. But his skin was still dewy with good color, almost like he'd put on blush or something. And his posture was perfectly straight, his movements precise—he was brimming with life. Jin-ji always called before he stopped by to ask if the booth farthest from the door was open, and he always started with a beer—not just for him, but us, too. After that it was on to whiskey with water, and once he was feeling it, he'd move on to karaoke. At first, he sang songs he already knew, but then he'd pull a memo pad and reading glasses from his breast pocket to check the names of songs he wanted to try. Every time he came, he always tried something new; the night he saved me, he'd challenged himself with JAYWALK's "What Can I Say to You . . . ?"

Once the song was done, Jin-ji took a breather. He noticed my sour mood and asked what was eating me. So I went on and on about how we were going to lose our apartment and about trying to find a place. "I've got a place in Shimouma." This announcement was so amazing, at first, I thought I'd misheard. The bar was full that night, and the customers were rowdy, but when Jin-ji said those words, all sound disappeared. His voice pierced through me, like a ray of sunshine breaking through the clouds and banishing the darkness.

"It's a mess, but it's there. Haven't been by in a long while," he told me, picking at his salt kelp. "Who'd I put in charge of it? Well, whoever it is, they haven' contacted me 'bout it in a long time. Long enough I figured we weren' gonna find any renters. Been thinking about bulldozing it and selling the land, but honestly, I forgot I even owned the thing. You'll 'ave it." The first step had appeared before me, the solution to this unspeakable problem that had been eating away at me, nauseating me—my cheeks warmed with hope, and I bent toward Jin-ji.

"But here's the thing, I don't have an ID. I can't sign any contracts or anything."

"Wadja do for this place?"

"Wa, wadja?"

"I've got too many, can' remember wadja do for this place."

"Oh, I came in after the place was already set up, so I dunno, can' be sure." I was starting to get worked up, mimicking Jin-ji's thick Osakan accent without meaning to, but I licked my lips, sure I couldn't let this chance go.

"Well, yeah, but things were done right, 'less I miss my guess. I think it went smooth."

"Done right?"

"Think so, 'cause of the thing with Kimiko and Mama Atsuko, the lady who ran this place a long time. Mama Atsuko liked 'er a lot. And she introduced us. I don' like complete strangers. 'Cause they'll mess a place right up sometimes. Nothing you can do 'bout it either. You're good on your rent, but it's the cleaning really. Your cleaning's top-notch. Don' think there'll be a problem, 'less I miss my guess. It comes down to the shitter."

"The shitter?"

"Tha's right. Anyone can talk sweet, talk pretty. But doesn' matter if I'm buyin' a car or lendin' money, I always check out the shitter. And yours, it's always clean. Business is built on the shitter." Jin-ji licked the salt from his thumb and pointer finger. "It'll be you and Kimiko, right? Go on then."

"Oh, it won't just be us though, Ran and Momoko are moving in, too. We've decided to live together and split the rent."

"Wonder if that place is big enough—been so long . . . Hmm, two rooms on the second floor, living and tatami on the first? Wadja think, though. It's been around a while, empty a long time, fallin' apart for all I know."

"It's a house, though?" I asked in wonder.

"Yeah, how big was it? Only about sixty square meters, 'less I miss my guess."

"Is, is the rent high?"

"Hmm," Jin-ji said as he returned his reading glasses and notepad to his pocket, "what cost was it, don' really remember. I'll have someone call you aboudit tomorrow. Don' imagine it's much. Could even roll it right in with the rent for this place, if you want. I'd bulldoze it if I could be bothered, so you go on and do whatever you want with it. But you'll want to go and see it first, 'less I miss my guess. You're thinking 'bout living there, yeah? Oh, the keys. I'll call 'bout that, too."

It wasn't only my face that was hot, now. My hands, my feet, my neck, my back, everything was burning, and I bowed my head and thanked him over and over.

"You'll break your neck, you keep doing that. I get rent oudda the deal, so go on then." Jin-ji sipped at his whiskey and water. "Oh yeah, mention it to Yeongsu, too. An Yeongsu, you know 'im, right."

"Of course."

"Have 'im come pick up the keys for you."

With that, Jin-ji went home, and I turned around and immediately called Yeongsu. But he never picked up, no matter how many times I rang him. After the twelfth call, I finally gave up, deciding I'd call him tomorrow morning as soon as I woke up. But all day the next day and late into the evening, I never did get ahold of him, which meant I came to work in a huff. Over our dinner of bento, though, Yeongsu finally showed up. Before he had a chance to say anything about my phone calls, I gave him a sharp look that said, "Not here," and then I asked him to go to the convenience store with me. I still didn't know if we would actually get to rent the place, and I didn't want to get everyone's hopes up with any half-baked ideas only to disappoint them if it fell through. Ideally, I wanted to surprise them, to just take them to the house and throw up my hands and shout "Ta-da!" And then they'd tell me how amazing I was. That's what I imagined anyway. Yeongsu and I left Lemon and headed for the convenience store. I explained the situation as we walked, and while he looked skeptical at first, his eyes slowly widened with wonder. When I was done, he sank into silent thought.

"You think something's off?" I asked.

"No, honestly, I never imagined Mr. Jinno would come to the rescue like that. Now that you bring it up, I guess you don't have much time left on the lease, do you?" Yeongsu absently looked up at the sky. "I've had a lot going on lately, been running around all over the place."

"It's okay. I was in panic mode, too. I thought we were done for, but then Jin-ji mentioned this place. He said he knew you, though, from way back. He said you should come get the keys. I know you're super busy, but I'm begging you. Please," I said, putting my hands together.

"Okay. Where did he say the house was?"

"In Shimouma. Not as far as Setagaya Park, but nearby. He said it's been empty for years, and it's really old. But that doesn't matter, it's still a house. I'm worried about the rent, but it's got three bedrooms and a living room, so the four of us can definitely be comfortable there. A real house. I've never lived in one before. I can't even imagine. What's it like to live in a house with stairs and everything, I wonder." I knew I was talking faster than usual, fueled by excitement and anxiety.

"I'll ask him about the house and the rent," Yeongsu promised.

"I hope it's not too high."

"Well, it's Mr. Jinno. I don't think he'll do you wrong. He's loaded already. When we worked up the contract for Lemon, he basically said yes to every request we made on the paperwork."

Yeongsu's words reminded me of something that I'd been wondering about off and on. "Oh, so . . . when Kimiko rented the space for Lemon, you took care of the paperwork, right?"

Yeongsu nodded, watching me.

"Oh, I mean, that's great," I said, staring at the toes of my shoes. "Of course you'd do that sort of thing. Yeah, that's . . . it's all good." After Yeongsu told me about Kimiko's upbringing, everything clicked into place. That feeling roared back to life. More than a year ago, when I first came and started cleaning up Lemon with Kimiko, I hadn't known a thing. And back when I'd first lived with her in Higashimurayama, too—no, even a month ago, I hadn't known anything about Kimiko. I pictured the blue wound on her right hand and felt heartsick.

Three days later, Yeongsu gave me a map with the house marked on it, the floor plan, and the keys. I studied the blueprints so intently I should've burned a hole in the paper. Just imagine everything we could do with a house. The six-mat tatami room on the first floor would be Kimiko's bedroom, and the six-mat tatami room on the second floor would be for the rest of us. We could put dressers and shelves and all our clothes in the smaller room next to it. Should our Yellow Corner go in the most eye-catching spot upstairs or in the living room, where we'd spend the most time? The kitchen was tiny, so we could probably only get a small table in there, but still, it would be nice if the four of us could eat together, and for that, we'd need chairs—Chairs! I'd always lived on the floor up till now. I'd never lived in a place nice enough to have chairs. *Maybe the first thing I'll buy is a chair. A chair. My first chair.* I was so happy I couldn't stand it. After going back and forth for a long time, I finally decided I wouldn't go alone to check out the house—we should go together, the four of us, opening the door on the count of three.

That Sunday was pleasant, sunny, much like our move-in day, and I invited everyone to go to the park in Setagaya with me.

We usually just bummed around at a McDonald's or in the apartment or around the neighborhood, so everyone thought my invitation was weird, but we grabbed some onigiri from the convenience store, sat on the grass, and chatted—the whole day kind of felt like a holiday. On the road home, as the shadows began to lengthen, I pretended we were taking a nice walk and guided us into the residential area. I was so excited to surprise everyone, but at the same time I was shivering with anticipation and nervousness—I didn't know what kind of house it was or what it looked like. What if it was a complete ruin? What if there wasn't even a house there? But at last we arrived at the spot, the one I'd memorized from the map, right next to a small parking lot—and there was the house.

"What's wrong, Hana?" Ran asked. I was frozen, staring. "What? What's wrong?"

The house was completely ordinary, the kind you'd see anywhere. It had a triangular tiled roof, and the building was square, the way all houses are. Completely forgettable no matter how many times you saw it, nothing special about it. But it was my new house. Mine and Kimiko's, everyone's—our new house. Wide-eyed, I took it all in.

Inky black cracks ran around its foundation, though I couldn't tell if they were deep or shallow. When I glanced down, I noticed the weeds that had sprung up between the gate and the entryway.

Advertisement flyers littered the flagstones, melted and congealed by the rain, and to one side of the path was a huge potted aloe plant, shriveled and brown. There was a weather-beaten wooden bat tossed on the ground next to the pot. *And there's supposed to be a small garden in the back, too,* I thought, remembering the faded blueprint.

The house's walls reminded me of a pair of gym sneakers I'd worn in elementary school. After months and months of dust and mud, the shoes had turned a dull, spotty gray—I couldn't even remember what color they'd been originally—and no matter how many times I washed them and set them out to dry in the sun, the gray stubbornly remained.

On the second floor was a small window with a black frame, staring silently down at us. Directly below it was a door nestled beneath an awning. The metal was the color of bitter dark chocolate, the kind that comes dusted with cocoa powder. Between the door and where I was standing was a chest-high aluminum gate, tucked into a concrete wall that surrounded the entire house. On that wall was a faint rectangular ghost where there had once been a nameplate, and above it was a crooked, rusted-out mailbox.

"Haa-naa." Momoko came and stood next to me. Still, I said nothing. I didn't move, so she turned her eyes to the house suspiciously. Kimiko and Ran came closer, too, until we stood in a line, gazing up at it.

"Everyone," I said, still taking it in. "This is our home."

At first there was only baffled silence, the three of them unsure what was happening, then Ran glanced at me. "What are you talking about?"

"We're going to live here."

Momoko waited about three seconds before squeaking, "What? Wait, wait, Hana, what do you mean 'our home'? What, you mean this place?"

"This place," I said, nodding.

"Oh my gosh, Hana, when did you even—"

"No way, Hana. Are you serious? Wait, Kimiko, Kimiko, did you know?" Ran cried, cutting in.

"I didn't know," Kimiko said. She sounded puzzled, but when she looked at me, her expression was neutral, as if nothing out of the ordinary was happening. I grinned at her and looked back to the house.

Ran and Momoko were locked in each other's arms, making a racket, but eventually they calmed down. Then Kimiko sneezed loudly, and they laughed. I gripped the sleeve of Kimiko's jacket, the one she was always wearing.

"This is our house."

Above us, the sky had darkened to shades of navy, with the furthest corners of the sky softening into night. I could hear crows cawing somewhere, and their voices waxed and waned as they slowly moved away from us. Somehow, I could smell the salt of the ocean. But soon, that, too, disappeared. Silently, shoulder to shoulder, we gazed at our home.

2.

Lemon's rent was ¥140,000, plus our business and utility expenses: gas and electric, booze stock and hot towels, plus wages for Ran and Momoko. All of that came out of the month's sales, but after, our takeaway was usually about ¥400,000. We worked our asses off to make sure we never made less than ¥30,000 in a night, and we were open twenty-six nights a month, which added up to about ¥800,000 total. We also had the special big takes from Kotomi's customers, so though Lemon was a small bar, I thought we were doing well. What was left after Lemon's bills went to our apartment rent, utilities, and the things we absolutely needed. And the rest always went in our big cardboard box of savings.

It'd been a year and two months since we first opened Lemon, and I had saved about ¥2.35 million. Jin-ji let us rent the house with a verbal contract, and he didn't ask for a security deposit, which meant I didn't even have to touch our savings to get the lease. I was so relieved. The rent for the new house was ¥120,000. Kimiko and I together put up ¥70,000, Ran did ¥30,000, and Momoko did ¥20,000.

¥2.35 million was truly an amazing amount of money to me.

I kept the fact that I hid our savings in the house secret from Ran and Momoko. It wasn't that I didn't trust them—I did—but why would I bring it up in the first place? And even though the money was technically mine and Kimiko's both, it felt personal; it wasn't anyone else's business. I didn't know if Ran and Momoko had any savings, but that didn't matter. Just because we were living together didn't make it my business to know. Kimiko was the same as ever, completely uninterested in how much business Lemon was doing, what our profits were, how much was in the savings. Sometimes when it was just the two of us, I tried to talk to her about it, but she never said much besides "That's great."

About a month after we'd moved into the house, on the first Sunday of December, Momoko invited Ran and me to go to a new pastry shop in Shibuya—some place with a really long name where the head chef was French-trained. Momoko didn't really have any close friends, but she did sometimes chat on the phone with a girl she'd known since elementary school. They'd been in the same class several times in middle and high school, and even though Momoko had stopped going, they still kept in touch. She was the one who told Momoko about the pastry shop. Ran was game, and I told them I wanted to go, too, but that I needed to talk to Yeongsu about the house, so they should go on without me, and I promised I'd go next time. Kimiko left late that morning to meet Kotomi at the salon to get their hair done. Ran took her sweet time with her makeup, chatting away, making sure I was really okay with them going without me, and Momoko took forever picking out her outfit—but at last I saw them off, watching until they'd walked down the street and turned the corner, and then I went back inside. And I searched every corner of the house for a place where I could hide the money.

Unlike the tenement house I grew up in or the apartment Kimiko and I had shared, a real house had depth, in more than one sense of the word.

Houses were full of empty spaces and gaps and holes, places where things didn't quite meet, and soon I found a hiding spot. While there were plenty of candidates in the kitchen, the entryway, and the downstairs closets, I decided on a place right under everyone's noses, in the closet in the bedroom I shared with Ran and Momoko.

The house was old enough that its closets were Japanese-style, with sliding wood and paper doors and enough space to store all three of our futons, so I climbed onto the upper shelf, and when I pushed on the ceiling, one of the boards popped loose. Peering inside, I could see the roof joists and the wide-open attic stretching in every direction. We usually kept our futons on the bottom shelf of the closet, but I decided that starting tomorrow I'd put them on the top shelf. That way during the day, it would be stuffed with mats and blankets, and at night everyone would be asleep, so Ran and Momoko wouldn't be climbing in here and opening up the ceiling. Not that I expected them to do that, futons or no.

I went into the next room where we'd shoved the boxes we hadn't unpacked yet, but I knew exactly where I'd placed the cardboard box, mixed carefully in with everything else. I found it and lifted its lid, taking out the money. The box was too big for a bunch of loose bills, and I wondered if I should switch to a paper bag. I'd been weighing down the bills with the pickling stone I'd found on the curb, but when we moved, I'd put the stone back where I found it, saying a little prayer of thanks for its help.

We kept a bundle of paper bags in the kitchen, so I grabbed a sturdy one that looked like it would be water-resistant and placed the ¥2.35 million at the bottom. I peered down at the money. And then I changed my mind, returned to the other room, and grabbed the blue shoebox I'd had since childhood. I liked the heft of the lid whenever I took it off or put it back on. Inside were envelopes and clippings, bits and bobs. I pushed them aside until the bottom of the box was exposed, and that was where I tucked my precious money. I double-checked to make sure the lid was back on tight and then put the box in the attic and pulled the loose board back into place.

Ran and Momoko had left just after twelve and got back at dusk. They told me Shibuya was packed, and they'd waited in line thirty minutes just to get in the door, but even with as popular and busy as it was, they said the atmosphere was good, and the pastries and cakes were delicious. Together, we tucked ourselves under the kotatsu in the first-floor living room and drank beers and cassis oranges, chatting about everything and nothing. The kotatsu table was from our apartment in the heights, but after we moved, we bought a new blanket for it at Seiyu. The fuzz covering every inch of the blanket felt new and fresh and amazing. We talked about our customers, regulars and newcomers, about our new menu, and then about the customers again. Ran especially had been putting a lot of effort into entertaining them, but lately, one guy had started demanding she go with him to Odaiba on her day off. We tried to think up ways she could put him off without offending him. At one point, Momoko remembered they'd gotten me something, and she pulled a small package out of her bag. It was a friendship bracelet woven in different colors of yellow.

"I can't see anything yellow without thinking of you, Hana," she told me.

"Wow, thank you!" I set down my beer and took the bracelet. "I think this might be my first friendship bracelet ever. You're supposed to tie it on and just let it fall off on its own, right?"

"Right. You make a wish and tie it on your wrist or your ankle, and when it falls off, then the wish comes true."

"Okay. What do you think, wrist or ankle?" I asked, holding the bracelet up to each.

"Oh, hey, guess what," Ran said. "We ran into one of Momoko's friends from school."

"In Shibuya?"

Ran looked over at Momoko. "Yeah. She was at the pastry shop."

"Did you get a chance to talk to her?"

"No. I don't think she saw me," Momoko said, cracking open another cassis orange. "But she was definitely with her sugar daddy."

"What?" I blurted. "How do you know?"

"Well, she was wearing her school uniform, even though it's a Sunday, and the guy was an older dude in this hideous rat-brown sweater, and he was all pressed up against her. What else could he be?"

"You're at an all-girls school, right, Momoko? Is everyone doing it?" I asked, remembering Tommy-cat. He'd been back to Lemon several times, drinking beers and chatting up a storm, but not recently. "We haven't seen Tommy-cat lately. Have you heard from him?"

"I'm trying to keep him at arm's length. I don't know. I feel like he's just gotten to be a pain in the ass," Momoko said, then she drained her cassis orange like she thought it was a pain in the ass, too. "Tommy-cat's not a bad guy. I don't mind meeting up with him to talk, but about two hours in, I'm just done, you know? I don't know how to explain it. He's kind of . . . sketchy. You know what I mean?"

"I think so," I said, nodding. "He doesn't give me the creeps or anything, though."

"Yeah. But he's always so over-the-top, like he's trying too hard. He's not a liar or anything, but he *is* a poser. He talks like he's known all this shit for decades, even when he's talking about something he learned yesterday, and it pisses me off. This book is this, and that movie is that, he knows such and such famous person, he was at so-and-so's party, you know? He'll half-ass some famous person's name into the conversation just to make himself look good. I mean I've learned a lot from him, so it's not all lies. A liar and a poser, they're different, right? You know what I mean?"

"I don't," said Ran.

"Well, they are."

"How are they different?" Ran asked, puzzled.

"Forget it," Momoko said, giving Ran an icy look. "Anyway, that friend of mine, the one we saw, I couldn't believe it. I mean a sugar daddy? Now? It's so uncool."

"Uncool?" I didn't know much about that sort of thing—the news called it compensated dating—but I'd always figured it was a big deal, so it surprised me to hear Momoko dismiss it as "uncool."

"Or maybe just gross? When I was a second year in middle school, the high school girls were all doing it. That's when it was all the rage. But those girls were super cute, and their hair was so perfect you could die and so was their makeup, and they were just so, so cool. A lot of men asked them out and gave them a ton of money, and they got attention all the time. They were super popular, you know? Basically, celebrities in Shibuya, they knew everyone. You had to be at least as beautiful and perfect as those girls, or you'd just embarrass yourself trying to get a sugar daddy," Momoko explained. "We all wanted to be them."

"Wow," I said, awed. "It's kind of different from what I imagined."

"Oh?" Momoko stuck out her lower lip and huffed arrogantly. Her bangs fluttered. "I guess it felt like they'd found the secret to adulthood, like they'd leveled up, you know? There were these clubs, only people like them were allowed to go in. They stayed out all night and went straight from the clubs to school."

I sipped my beer and asked, "But don't you get a sugar daddy for the money? I mean, those girls wanted money, right? They were doing it 'cause they needed cash?"

"No way," Momoko laughed. "This isn't like some prostitute plot out of the 1700s or something, money had nothing to do with it. Of course, they weren't going to say no to money, but everyone who goes to that school is already rich, so it wasn't about that. It was the challenge. They were bored, and it was fun, that's why they did it."

"Really?" I asked, surprised. "But isn't a relationship like that, kind of, I mean . . . it's something you have to put up with, right? Like, there's this guy you don't know, and he's buying you, so he can do whatever he wants to you. I feel like you must have to put up with so much."

"No," Momoko said, tipping her head, "I don't think they're 'putting up' with anything? If they think a guy's not worth it, they can pass on him. They get to choose. It's not like anyone's forcing them to do it. I think mostly they're just trying to have as much fun as they can."

"I've never sold my body, but I kind of get it," Ran said as she walked back in, a fresh beer in hand. "I mean, think about if you have a boyfriend where the relationship's gone sour or he's just gotten to be a pain in the ass, but you have sex anyway. You're not all lovey-dovey anymore, and you think, 'Well, I've got nothing else to do, might as well.' Lie back and let it happen, you know? It's totally pointless. And then after, you feel annoyed, and you just want him to get the hell out of there, right? If you're gonna feel the same way either way, might as well get money out of it. I get it."

"I don't think it was that way for those girls in my school," Momoko said, tracing the corners of her eyes. "They were having fun, always so psyched about it."

"Seriously?"

"Yeah . . . I mean, I guess I don't know what they were really thinking, but from where I was standing, that's what it looked like. All those guys giving them so much attention."

"Wait, does that mean you wanted to try it, Momoko?" I asked, and my heart sped up.

"Well, yeah. I told you guys about it before, right, about the time when me and my friends went to the burusera, but nobody wanted my underwear because I was so ugly, so I ended up in the waiting room? But I wonder what would've happened if I'd looked more like those girls. My life would be so different. And that girl we saw before? She and I were basically on the same level! That's what I'm getting at. My nickname was Gorilli Saturn, right? Well, hers was Poltergeist! Better a gorilla than a creepy ghost! The fact that it's taken her this long to get a sugar daddy? So uncool. The moment's passed, come on, get a life. And besides, well, this is off topic, but"—Momoko peered at me through her bangs and smiled—"Hana?"

"What?"

"I'm just guessing but . . . you haven't done it yet, have you?"

"Oh, is that what we're talking about?" Ran asked, flashing her teeth with glee, pointing at Momoko with both pointer fingers.

"No, I haven't." I was surprised the talk had suddenly turned to me, and I answered honestly. "I've never even dated anyone."

"Well, it's not like you have to date a guy to have sex with him." Momoko laughed, waving her can of cassis orange back and forth. "Right, Ran?"

"But most people do have their first with someone they're dating," Ran said with a smile. "Come on, there must've been someone you liked, what about him?"

"Someone I liked," I repeated. "I'm not sure I know what that means."

"What? A boy you like is a boy you like! You never kissed a boy or anything?"

"There wasn't . . . any boy I liked," I said, serious.

"You're funny, Hana!" The two of them looked at each other and laughed. "There's something about you, you're kind of mysterious! But come on, there must have been at least one, like, one nice guy?"

"Hold on, let me think."

I massaged my legs under the kotatsu, stretched my back, and tried to remember if I'd ever felt like that at any point in my life. But no matter how hard I thought, all that came to me were the rough-textured walls of my childhood home, the faded Evergreen Hills sign over the entry, my mother wearing her white heels indoors and eating ramen—I tried to remember the boys from school and couldn't even bring up a single face or name.

Just when I was about to tell them so, I remembered someone—the Egyptian pharaoh who'd been the main character in that manga I'd been obsessed with as a kid. His hair was black, his eyes cool and determined. What was his name? . . . Right! Memphis. Memphis, from *Crest of the Royal Family*. But if I mentioned a manga character, I was sure Ran and Momoko would tease me. He wasn't real. So did that mean there wasn't anyone? No one I'd thought was nice, no one I'd liked? Had I really never felt that way about a boy? I took another sip of beer, and then someone did come to mind.

"The manager at the restaurant where I worked," I said. "I guess he was nice."

"So there is somebody!" The two smiled.

"But I didn't *like* like him. He was nice to me, that's why I thought of him."

"But if he was nice to you, doesn't that mean he was crazy about you?" Momoko said, teasingly.

"Definitely not," I said.

"Oh, he definitely was, you know he was." Momoko laughed, and Ran joined in.

"No, I don't think so."

"He must've been wild about you," Momoko said with a grin. "He definitely wanted to sleep with you!"

My entire body zinged with confusion, like someone I'd been having a good time with suddenly glared down at me with hatred. At the same time, I felt disgusted—truly disgusted. That feeling was as vivid as black ink splashed on a white paper screen. I slowly exhaled through my nose and stood to disguise my trembling. "I'll, I'll put the bracelet here," I said and went over to the Yellow Corner, trying to remove myself from the conversation.

I took the time to pick up each object in the Yellow Corner and then put it back in its place, and then I did it again, trying to calm myself. I counted them from right to left and then left to right, forward and backward. The two-tiered shelf was crowded with knickknacks, fifty-three in all. Only once I was done counting did I try to understand why the conversation had made me so upset, why it had hurt me so deeply. It had nothing to do with the manager. I wasn't mad at Momoko either. I wasn't even angry. It didn't seem to have anything to do with my heart or my feelings. More of an immediate sensation, like something repulsive had touched me, my skin. I went to the kitchen and washed my hands. I could hear they'd turned on the TV in the living room, the noise from the variety show drifting in. Or maybe the TV had already been on. I couldn't tell the difference between the laughter and exaggerated reactions from the B-listers on TV and the ones from Momoko and Ran. I stood silently in front of the sink for a few minutes, calming myself down, and then called out, asking if anyone wanted cup ramen.

Ran and Momoko joined me in the kitchen, commenting that it was too cold, too much of a pain to go out for dinner, so we each took our favorite ramen flavors from the basket where we stocked them and boiled some water, returning to the kotatsu with our slowly steeping cups. We hadn't gotten a table or chairs for the kitchen yet.

After a bit, Ran asked, "Was Kimiko supposed to be late tonight?"

"She's with Kotomi, so I bet they'll eat out," Momoko said, ripping the lid off her ramen. "Those two are really close, aren't they? How old are they again? Same age?"

"I think they'll both be forty soon," I said.

"That means they're only three or four years younger than my mom. I can't believe that." Momoko's eyes grew rounder. "Kotomi is so young! She's always so beautiful, so graceful. She's nothing like my mom, unbelievable."

"Right?" Ran smiled. "I haven't seen my mom in a long time, but she's so country. When I see her at home, I don't really notice how frumpy she is, but when I'm out with my friends and I see her, I can't believe how shabby she looks. Her clothes, her face, everything about her is just so old, and it feels like the world is telling me, 'This is your mother, so this is how you're going to look one day.' So depressing. And scary. But your family is rich, Momoko. Is it the same for rich people? I mean, can't you get all the facials you want?"

"Even with money, it's basically the same. Plus, my mom kinda went off the deep end a while ago." Momoko scrunched her face and rattled her disposable chopsticks around in her ramen. "I've always thought that no matter how much money I have, I'll do anything not to be like my mom. She's so selfish, so self-obsessed, and she treats me like I'm a piece of jewelry she can show off."

"What do you mean?" I asked.

"Anything and everything—people, money, stuff—she thinks it's there just for her. She lives to show off. Her life's purpose is to hear the words 'What a lovely house, what a beautiful family, you're so wealthy, you deserve it, I wish I could have your life.' As long as I can remember, she's been telling us, 'You girls are born special, so you better act like it.' I never knew what the hell she was talking about. She made us take all these stupid lessons, hauled us all over the place, got us these creepy tutors, forced us to wear these hideous, expensive clothes. And for what? It was so dumb."

Momoko left off her stirring and lifted her cup to slurp a bit of broth.

"And, you know, she doesn't know the first thing about art, but she'd take us to art museums or get the best seats in the house for classical concerts and operas, and we'd go just to look good. Then on the way home, we'd eat at some famous, fancy restaurant in Akasaka, all because my mom is a total snob, through and through, and she just wants to show off how much money she has, how she stinks of it. But it's not like she earned the money herself. My parents are trust fund babies. My mom and dad live by the grace of my grandparents, even though they're grown-ass adults. And they don't even think that's embarrassing. And they wanted to send their daughters to a famous private school no matter what, so they hauled us off to prep schools before we could even write, but the both of us are dumb as fuck, and there wasn't anywhere they could send us, so they used their connections to find us a school, but neither of us could keep up there, either, and we both had to quit and ended up at the lowest of the low. Mom still nags both of us all the time about the fact that we couldn't get into a school she could be proud of. 'How many times do I have to tell you, why don't you get it, why can't you do what everyone else can, after all I've given you, after all I've done for you?' She'd get mad and hit us all the time, too. She'd go on and on, like, 'Don't you feel bad for me? I gave birth to you, and all I ever wanted was to set my beloved daughters on the path toward a good life! I've done everything for you, put my whole heart into it, so why won't you show some gratitude?' And then she'd start sobbing. What a joke."

"Seriously," Ran said, slurping her noodles and laughing.

"And I mean, we're both about the same level of stupid, Shizuka and me—I told you her name was Shizuka, right? My sister? Anyway, she's completely gorgeous. Her face is so perfect she could probably be a model."

"Wow, she's really that pretty?" I asked.

"Bombshell. Our mom is, too. I mean, pretty for an old lady. That's another reason why she thinks she's so damn special. And Shizuka looks like her. She took after Mom, I mean. And I took after Dad, so I've got the big bones. I look just like my dad's mom, and she was a boulder." Momoko smiled wryly. "When we were kids, Mom pushed both of us around, but she was usually harder on Shizuka because she was cute, and people spoiled her wherever she went. It didn't really make sense, but that's how it was, probably because my mom was jealous? I was ugly, so she was nicer to me—she probably felt bad for me, at least for a while. But then, she did a one-eighty, and Shizuka was her favorite. For Mom, Shizuka's pretty face was basically her last hope. You can't fix stupid, but if you use your pretty face, do it right, you can marry a guy with money and power, right? So then, Mom got obsessed with turning Shizuka into a perfect catch. And then she'd look at me, and it's a total wake-up call, you know? She used to ask me, totally serious, 'What exactly do you plan to do with your life, looking like that?' What the hell am I supposed to say to that, you know? Like suddenly I'm supposed to stop being ugly? But she'd be like, 'I worry about you because I love you, time is ticking, don't you see?' She'd tell me no one would ever love me if I didn't put in more effort. Like, that's super fucked-up, right?"

"That's awful," Ran said.

"And the school we went to, it's the absolute worst, right, so all the students are stupid like us. It's a place for idiots with money who have nowhere else to go, so everyone just gets stupider, like, at the speed of light. From elementary school on, everyone's like that, so by the time we hit middle school, everyone's turned into a perfect idiot, complete dyed-in-the-wool morons. Shizuka started smoking and partying at clubs, going out with boys and much older guys, too. The teachers would call her out on it, and each time, it drove our mom up the wall. She started tailing Shizuka out so she could figure out who the guys were, and then she'd ambush them and rant and rave, and back home, she and Shizuka would fight, sometimes they even got in fistfights. Meanwhile, I just got uglier and fatter, like someone hit fast-forward on me or something, acne all over my face. People bullied me, so I started hiding in my room, not talking to anyone, listening to 'crazy music' and reading 'creepy books.' So in the end, not a single one of my mom's dreams came true, and eventually she lost it."

"Lost it?" I asked.

"Well, she started counseling, therapy, all that shit. I mean, she did stop talking, and she'd spend all day in bed, and she did look depressed, but even that, she was just drunk on herself, you know? Her therapist was some hotshot who wrote a bunch of books and gave talks and shit, so before we knew it, she was back to being full of herself. It's unbelievable, how she stays the same. And that 'amazing' doctor told her, 'You've done your best, you haven't done one thing wrong, the fact that you're suffering right now is proof of just how much love you've poured into your daughters.' That became her one and only truth. Because it felt super super super super good. And my dad's my dad, he's always had a woman on the side, and she's an old hag, just like my mom, can you believe that? Just this chubby, boring, average lady. I've seen them together plenty of times. He's wanted to divorce Mom for ages, and they always fight over it. They don't even love each other anymore, but my mom says she won't stand for it, having both her daughters be failures and then, to top it off, getting cast aside by her husband? No way. She brought in a lawyer and everything, they've been fighting about it forever. And then, you remember that whole thing with that cult, Aum Shinrikyo, right, the sarin gas attacks? And the earthquake, too? Made Mom snap."

"Snap?" Ran asked.

"Totally snapped. Just like that. Now she's super gung ho, like she suddenly started volunteering all over the place, changed her whole look—hiking boots, poncho, backpack, emergency whistle—and went off to the disaster zone in Kobe. She started putting her energy into raising money for charity and made a huge fuss about wanting to raise the kids who'd lost their parents. Wanted to do it all by herself. Like she even could. Now all she talks about is the real meaning of life, how she's found true happiness, the harmony between humanity and nature, global warming, how we have to be better to the planet. And then someone introduced her to this fortune teller, and she told my mom to buy this piece of land in Karuizawa, so she did, and then she built a house there. I think the real reason is that she wanted to force my dad out of Tokyo. She basically threatened him into coming with her."

"Jeez," Ran said, and we both groaned.

"Shizuka and I still had school, so our grandma came out to the apartment in Aobadai to live with us. But she's really getting up there, and I never know what she's talking about. She's totally going senile."

"But your sister's a real piece of work, too, right?" Ran said, laughing.

"Yeah, she is. She's as crazy as my mom, seriously, but the

worst thing about her is how dirty she is. Like, unbelievably filthy. They always fight about it—she never brushes her teeth, almost never bathes, never cleans or lets anyone clean her room either. And her sheets—they're so yellow you can tell they're gross even with the lights off, and she has guys over? In that bed? Who in their right mind? Makes me sick, like I want to throw up. Oh, and she wears the same underwear for days on end. And when they've reached their limit, she just takes them off and throws them in a corner of her room and puts on a fresh pair."

"Why?" I asked, shocked.

"She just doesn't care." Momoko gave a lopsided smile. "Also, our mom hates it. I mean, I hate Shizuka, and she hates me, but we're united on one thing: if Mom hates it, we'll do it. That's when we're on the same side. We've never talked about it, but we both know. Mom can say she loves us all she wants, but really, she does it for herself. After everything she made us do just so she can look good, she abandoned us, ran off to do her own thing. That's why we'll both try anything, so long as our mom hates it."

In the silence that followed, we slurped our noodles. Ran sipped her broth and chewed and said something at the TV, something I didn't quite catch, but I laughed along with her. The door in the entryway opened, and Kimiko was home.

We twisted around to say "Hey" as she appeared in the living room. She set a box of pork buns on the kotatsu and told us to dig in.

We said thanks and each took a bun—they were still a little warm. Kimiko took off her jacket, hung it on a hook on the wall, and then turned on the space heater, saying it was really cold out. She joined us at the kotatsu, and we dug in to the pork buns and ate them plain. Around the square kotatsu we settled, one to a side, our legs under the blanket, toasted by the heater. We fit so neatly that I felt like we hadn't chosen to be here of our own free will, but that each of us was part of something larger—a single creature, the four of us and this house, each with our own parts to play. It was like staring at a word on the page so long that its meaning and component parts collapsed, and I could no longer understand it. The things I normally never doubted, the size of my body, the sensation of my arms and legs, they had all somehow slipped sideways. I tried to regain my sense of reality through touch, through sight, blinking, biting my pork bun, chewing it slowly. Kimiko's hair was huge, curled into waves, the same way it always was after a visit to the salon, and I tried to focus on its shape and texture. The perfumed scent of some hairstyling product reached my nose, then mixed with the scent of the pork buns, and I got confused all over again.

We watched TV late into the night. The channels overflowed with the bustle of Christmas and New Year's. I thought about where I'd been one year ago. It'd been more than a year since I'd moved to Sancha and we'd opened Lemon. On the screen was some police documentary—drunks and juvies, people whose faces were blurred and their voices mechanically distorted. The police questioned them and yelled at them as they tried to make excuses, run or scream, show remorse or fight back.

Momoko and Ran laughed through the whole program, but I couldn't focus. I glanced at Kimiko, and she was watching TV with her chin perched on her hand, but she looked like she was thinking about something else entirely, or maybe nothing at all. We bathed, said our goodnights, and Momoko, Ran, and I went upstairs to our room. After we'd already crawled into our futons and turned out the light, Momoko said, "We should go to my apartment in Aobadai sometime. There's a lot of stuff in there."

"Sounds nice," Ran said. "Will we meet your crazy mom?"

"No way. Although she might stop by for the New Year, so we should wait until after that. I have stuff from there I want to bring here, anyway."

"Okay."

Ran and Momoko chatted a while longer, but slowly their voices faded away, and at last, I heard their breathing deepen into sleep. I thought about Momoko's story and tried to imagine her mother's face—a rich woman who'd once been young and beautiful, and whose daughters hated her, stuck living in Karuizawa with a husband she didn't even like. But I couldn't come up with an image. Instead, I thought of my own mom's face. When was the last time I'd talked to her? Maybe summer. Not this past summer but the summer before. I hadn't heard her voice in more than a year. I wondered how she was doing. She'd worked in bars ever since she was young, drinking, entertaining drunks, hanging out with her hostess friends in our crumbling tenement house, laughing. That was her whole world, and she'd raised me in it. My mom and Momoko's had something in common: both their daughters had run away from home. But my mom didn't have money. She could never afford to live in Karuizawa, and I couldn't imagine her ever showing off by going to concerts or eating fancy food. All of that was beyond her world. The two of them were completely different. My heart ached for her.

Sure, Momoko's mother had failed to mold her daughters into her ideal image, and now both of them hated her, but she'd never once had to worry about money. My mom was poor. She didn't own a house, and she didn't have savings. But maybe she was living a happy life, following her own path. And while I had complicated feelings for my mom, I didn't hate her like Momoko hated hers. So who was happier? Thinking about it put me on the verge of tears. Maybe I wanted to see my mom. I let the idea sink into me as memories from my childhood bubbled up, one by one.

Maybe I'll call her soon—yeah, right after New Year's. I felt awkward about being the one to call her, but it wasn't like we were fighting, and maybe Mom found it hard to take that step. *Come to think of it, I haven't told her anything about my life since I came here. Maybe she'll be relieved, happy even, to hear I'm working so hard at Lemon. Plus, it's the New Year. I can treat her to something she never normally gets to eat, sushi or sukiyaki maybe, wouldn't that be wonderful? Having a nice meal together. We've never done that before.* My heart beat faster, and I was on the verge of tears. *I'll work myself to the bone all through December, and then I'll give Mom a call with the fresh hope of the New Year. Yeah, that's what I'll do.* I fell asleep to those thoughts. But in the end, I never did end up calling her. Instead, out of the blue, my mom came to see me.

3.

"Aw, you look so good, Hana!" my mom said, her smile stretched across her face.

She launched into stories, talking with her whole body—a hostess friend of hers, well, her husband had died in an accident at work, and the salon in front of the station, well, the three sisters who ran it had a falling out and closed up shop. Finally, my mom paused to take a healthy sip of her iced coffee. She looked as full of energy as she had when last I saw her a year and a half ago, but she'd lost some weight. Her once round cheeks were sunken, and I couldn't help but notice the dark circles around her eyes.

We were sitting in a family restaurant in Sancha, across from each other at the table closest to the kitchen.

Dishware clattering, the voices of the staff as they called orders back and forth, and over it all, the ceaseless dinging of the chime on the front door. At the table next to ours was a loud, red-faced group of middle-aged men in baseball uniforms, their table crowded with glass tankards of beer. In family restaurants on a Sunday, the crowds never stop from sunup to sundown. Only two years ago, I'd spent all my time working at a restaurant like this, long enough that the very sights and sounds were a part of me, but now I felt like I was looking at someone else's hazy memories.

"Hey, Hana, sweetie, aren't you hungry?"

"Not really," I said. "I already had lunch."

"Ooh." Mom pouted and then opened her menu. "Well, I'm having something," she said, and hit the button. A uniformed waiter appeared, and Mom ordered omurice. I watched him take her order slip back to the kitchen, and then I went to the drink bar, filled a glass with oolong tea, and came back. Mom smiled at me, blinking, but I couldn't tell if she was being polite or actually happy to see me.

"The girls you were with before, are they your friends?"

"Yeah."

She was talking about Ran and Momoko. But I didn't tell her that I lived with them or worked with them—I just nodded.

"They looked like nice girls. Young, happy."

"I guess."

"They are. Young people are so cute," Mom said brightly. "But time sure does fly. I can't believe New Year's is already over! Did you have mochi? Oh, but Kimiko doesn't cook, does she."

"We didn't really do anything special, just the usual."

"Oh yeah, that's the best! Sleep, rest up, and the holidays are over before you know it. Might as well do nothing, right?"

She was right, New Year's had been over in the blink of an eye, everything back to normal and January already half-gone. *Wow, it's 1999*, I realized.

When I was a little girl, Nostradamus's predictions had been all the rage, and 1999 was supposed to be a big number, so it was stamped into my memories. There were lots of theories about some great calamity that would destroy the world—we'd all die before we were adults, the sun would turn into a cube, the next ice age, nuclear war—with each new story I grew more and more frightened. But one time, someone said, "What are we worried for? That's way in the future, right?" and I remember answering, "You're right." It had been a summer evening after a huge downpour, and we'd gone to a shrine to find someplace dry to sit. But as we talked and talked, I grew frightened, like I had nowhere left to run. I became convinced that the fat, black tuft of moss at my feet had moved. Remembering all this, I traced the seams of the cushion on my booth seat.

While we waited for Mom's order, her one-sided chatter grew more excited. I had no idea what to say, so I just fidgeted and hummed along.

I really had been planning to call her in the New Year, but she had shown up out of the blue, and I hadn't mentally prepared myself. Prepared for what, though? I didn't understand my own feelings. Was it that I didn't actually want to see her, or that I was nervous? What?

"You must have had plans with your friends. I'm sorry."

"I can catch up with them later. It's fine."

I checked my phone to see if they'd texted, but there were no new messages. Maybe they were still on the train. Last week, Momoko had asked, "Hey, why don't you guys come over to the Aobadai house next week? My parents are back in Karuizawa, and Shizuka won't be around." Ran and I were excited to see the place, so we picked a date—today—and had left the house only about thirty minutes ago.

"What's Kimiko up to today?" Mom asked.

"I think she's just home. She was there when I left."

"Oh."

Between my short answers, I remembered again the shock of spotting my mom by the train station. I'd turned around, and in a heartbeat, I'd known it was her. It was the fact that I recognized her right away, in a millisecond, that surprised me more than anything. The moment our eyes met, I sensed something between us that bound us together, plunked down like a giant paperweight so that no matter the violence of the wind, nothing beneath it could get blown away. That imposing indifference, that hugeness, that . . . I was so overwhelmed by it that I took a step back and very nearly started crying.

Maybe I shouldn't have picked up. When my phone had first vibrated, Momoko and Ran were already making their way down the stairs toward the gate. But when I saw "Mom" on the screen, I reflexively hit the answer button and put the phone to my ear. "Hey, I know it's sudden, but I've been wondering how you are. I was hoping we could meet up!" She spoke like she was picking up a conversation left off from yesterday. Ran and Momoko turned to me with a puzzled look, and I signaled them to wait. My mom told me she was outside Sangenjaya Station, and when I asked where, she told me she was outside McDonald's. That was where we were standing. My mind went blank. I turned around, and there she was, my mother.

When the waiter brought the omurice, Mom asked him for a bottle of ketchup, used it to make a red spiral on the yellow omelet, and then spread the sauce with the back of her spoon.

She split the whole thing in half down the middle, mixed everything together, and then started eating. While she ate her meal, I fiddled with my phone and tried to gather my thoughts. We never made an effort to see each other, but maybe it wasn't so strange that she'd come to see her daughter on a whim, right? What would we talk about when she was done? I followed my train of thought along. Come to think of it, she'd never called my cell phone before. When Yeongsu first gave me the phone, I'd put her number in, but I don't think I ever gave her my number. And yet she'd called me, so she did have it. Maybe I'd told her the last time she called Kimiko? No, I hadn't had a cell phone yet . . .

Mom finished her meal in a flash, and then she gulped down her water. "Mmm, that was yummy." She smiled. Her brown dye job was starting to fade, and white showed at her roots, but her makeup was the same as always. Even so, I couldn't quite look at her straight on, so I dropped my gaze to her sweater. It was oversized, and I couldn't figure out its pattern, but the overall impression was floral. Her cuffs were pilling, and on the tips of her bony fingers was a chipped, hot pink manicure. Mom started talking about this and that, complimenting my work at Lemon. She grinned as she told me she and Kimiko had talked over the phone not too long ago, and Kimiko had told her how much she'd come to rely on me. While Mom talked, though, I noticed a flash of nervousness across her face. That expression—I'd already known, of course, that she must have a reason for coming all this way to talk to me, but now I began to wonder if she was going to ask me if she could come live at the house with us, or else ask me to come back home. Maybe something had happened with her real-estate-agent boyfriend, and she was alone now? Either way, I had a feeling she wanted us living together again.

"Hana," Mom said, the corners of her mouth lifting again. But then she paused, licked her lips, and gave a troubled laugh. "The truth is . . . there's something I wanted to talk to you about."

"What is it?" I drew a slow breath and braced myself. *Here it comes.*

"You see, well, I was actually in the hospital for a bit."

"What?"

"I thought you'd worry if I told you, so I kept it quiet. What do you call it? You know there's the uterus, right? It's not my uterus, it's the place right before it, I got cancer there. It's called cervical cancer or something like that. I've already had surgery, I'm fine now. They got it quick, and it wasn't that serious, the cancer. It did hurt, though, for about a week."

"Cervical cancer?" I asked. "Cancer? You had cancer, Mom?"

"Yeah. I've had to take some time off work. And there'll still be more tests after this."

The word "cancer" shook me, and I didn't know how to respond. Mom had cancer—I repeated the word in my mind, and my chest grew tight. The sound of the word "cancer" had a particular weight and dread to it. How bad was it? Really bad? What happened to people who had surgery for cancer? My mind filled with questions. But at the same time, there was my mom, right in front of me, and while she'd lost weight, she was well enough to talk right over me, and she'd hosed that omurice right off her plate. Maybe I didn't need to worry much. That's what I tried to tell myself. But what if the cancer had spread and her case was worse than she was letting on? Like this was her farewell, her parting words, maybe she had come to say goodbye? My mind raced with everything I didn't know.

"And I . . . I wanted to talk to you. I mean, it's hard to ask . . . but you see, I, um, I was hoping you could lend me some money."

"Money?"

I stared at her.

"Yeah, money. I'm so, so sorry, Hana, super sorry."

Silence swelled between us, broken only occasionally by the coming and going of the bell tone the automatic doors made each time they opened.

So that's it; she came for money. I looked down at the cloudy dregs of my oolong tea. And then, I wanted to laugh. She wasn't here to ask if she could come live with us or ask me to come home. She wasn't even here to tell me she was really sick; it's good she wasn't, but . . . wow, she'd come here to see me about money.

But then, why else would she want to see me? Of course that was the only reason. She'd always scraped by, and she'd never had any savings, hadn't even kept an emergency supply at the tenement. We got by on her daily wages from the bar, and nothing else. Crumpled ¥1,000 notes and loose change. Of course her life had stopped when she got sick and had to stop working; how could it not have? I wanted to laugh at myself, tell myself to get a grip. I imagined water dripping from a tap, doing its best not to be noticed, but then someone came and twisted the faucet shut tight. I remembered our kitchenette, its flooring warped into ripples by humidity, the lime-scaled stainless steel of the tiny sink, the wrung-out dishcloth in the corner congealed like papier-mâché, the plastic bins stuffed with clutter. My mother, back home late from working at the bar, standing in the kitchenette making ramen.

"Uh, what about the guy?" I asked. "The real estate guy you were seeing. He won't, um . . . help you?"

"No, we broke up."

"But weren't you working for him, too, as like, a secretary or something? You're not doing that anymore?"

"Nope."

"But it was your job."

"I know, but no way," Mom said with a laugh. "I went back to the bar, Mama Junko's place, and started working there again. I'm on break right now, but I go back next week. Remember she and I had a fight when I quit? But I told her everything, and she agreed to let me come back. Isn't that great?"

Setting aside the health issues, at least Mom had a place to work. Which meant soon she'd be able to go back to living the way she always had, but she hadn't made any money while she was recovering, so she must be struggling with the rent and the bills and things.

But even so, I thought. I didn't want to know all the details of Mom's breakup, or what kind of relationship they'd had, but the bottom line was he hadn't helped her out. From what I could remember, he was the one who made her stop working at the bar, even though he'd met her there, and convinced her to come work for him instead. There was no way for me to know whose fault the breakup was, but I felt like I wasn't getting the whole picture. When she and the real estate agent had first started dating, Mom had been convinced her happiness had finally come. She was so excited, and I'd been excited for her, too. I wanted it to work out.

But it hadn't, clearly. You couldn't trust anyone for anything. Just because you started seeing a guy with money, that didn't mean his money became yours, and just because you started living with him in his big house, that didn't make it your home either. His house, his money, anything really, even if a guy let you use it like it was yours, all that meant was that he was *letting* you use it.

Marriage was probably the same, and parents and family, too. No matter the relationship, the person who earned the money never forgot that it was theirs. In their heart of hearts, it was always them *letting* someone else use the money. As a favor.

The money lender is stronger than the borrower. The borrower is weaker than the lender. The one with the money has the say, always. They get a sense of superiority, whether they're conscious of it or not, and the one with no money, they wind up groveling and kissing ass. The one with the power can always make the weaker one *go away*, as if they never existed. That's what happened to my mom, all bright-eyed, happy to quit the bar and go work at the real estate agency with her lover. She didn't even last two years. I don't know if they broke up before or after her diagnosis, but it didn't really matter. I remembered what En had said—*There aren't hardly any decent rich guys out there.* Of course, men have more money than women, so it's probably true that there are more shitty men than women, but the real question is: Who has the money? She'd said the best way was to save and save, and only when your cash overflows do you sip off the top—that was the best way. The money you make, that's yours, and no one else's money is going to protect you. Only your own.

I thought of my navy shoebox, hidden in the attic above the bedroom closet. Inside was the money I'd earned. ¥2.35 million. The money Kimiko and I had saved by working our butts off at Lemon. I could see the bundle of bills, holding its breath in the murky, chilly darkness. The thought that we'd have less made me miserable. No, not just miserable, it physically hurt. There was a little bit of "why me" in there, too. But I could work and work hard, and I could save even more money. I could help Mom out. This was my power. In my mind again, my mother in the dark kitchen, making ramen. I extended my fingertips toward the money, softly pinched off one bill, and then another and another. I imagined holding ¥30,000. The brown ¥10,000 bill transformed into our familiar room in Evergreen Hills, and there my mother leaned on the wall, drinking a can of beer, watching TV. My heart ached.

Even though my real, actual mom was sitting right in front of me, when I imagined her, she was alone, a lot younger, not the woman across from me. And the two of us laughing, sitting on the steps of a supermarket, maybe waiting for someone, something, and me so much smaller, playing with the toy that had come with the candy I asked her to buy me. I took another two bills in hand, a total of ¥50,000.

I suppose I can give her that much. What else can I do? It's only ¥50,000 out of ¥2.35 million, it'll be fine. That's how much we average off eight customers at Lemon. Six, if someone buys a whole bottle. If I work hard, I can make up the loss in three days. Yes, it's decided.

She probably still doesn't have a bank account, same as me, so I'll have to meet up with her again to give her the money. Mom was watching me closely, her lips pressed together, eyes darting down and up again. I exhaled and sat up straighter.

"It's fine," I said, putting my heart into it. "The money, I mean."

"Hana!" Mom exclaimed, her voice rising an octave, eyes wide. "Thank you!"

"Don't worry about it. But I'm glad you're going back to work at the bar."

The moment I gave my answer, my face relaxed. I guess I really had been nervous, seeing her again after so long. And there was the shock of finding out she had cancer—that must have been what made me tense up around the shoulders and jaw. Another long breath left me feeling refreshed, as if I were standing in the middle of a huge field, the brisk spring wind caressing my face. I felt like I'd accomplished something, like I was a truly generous person who'd done something good. My ability to help my mom through my own work gave me a newfound sense of confidence, and I was almost embarrassed by how proud I was to do right by her. It felt amazing.

"And . . . you don't have to pay me back. You've had a rough go of it. I'm happy to give it to you." I was thrilled that I actually managed to say those words out loud, and I smiled, pleased with myself. "But I don't have the money with me right now. I'll have to see you again to give it to you."

"Oh, do you think you could transfer it to this account?" Mom picked up the purse at her side and pulled out her wallet. She plucked out a card and set it on the table, sliding it across to me.

"Oh, you got a bank account!" I was honestly surprised.

"Yep! I mean, actually I had it all along. I found the card in an old clutch. I don't know where my bank book is, or my personal seal, but I figured my PIN was my birthday, and when I tried it, it worked!"

"Huh." I flagged down a waiter, borrowed a pen, and copied the branch name and account number onto a napkin, trying not to rip it. "Okay. I'll send the money here."

"Wow, Hana, thank you so, so much!" Mom said, clapping her hands together in gratitude.

"It's fine, don't worry about it."

Mom grinned big, and I did, too. But she didn't stop, just kept staring at me and grinning. A whole minute, she sat there, the same expression. I nodded a few times, trying to signal that it was really okay, and she nodded, too, still smiling, but there was something serious in her eyes. It was only then I realized we'd never talked about the most important detail: how much I'd be giving her. I started to say "About how much—" but right then, she talked over me. "Right! Hana!"

Still smiling, she flashed me a ridiculous peace sign. At first, I thought she was celebrating her success, so I flashed her a peace sign, too, but then I realized it wasn't a peace sign. It seemed like she was showing me how much.

". . . Um, two? Just twenty thousand yen?" I asked, my hand hanging in the air. Mom shook her head hard.

"What, two hundred thousand?"

"Um, no, not exactly . . ."

Her face creased so deeply I couldn't tell if she was still smiling or almost crying. She wiped her nose with the back of her hand and shrank into her seat. "Well, you see . . ."

"What?"

"I'll, I'll pay you back. I promise I will, but"—she started rubbing her hands together in supplication—"it's two, you know, oh, I'm just going to say it, I'll say it, the two is two, um, two million."

I squeaked, a sound I'd never made before, and blinked, dumbstruck. Mom froze completely, and we stared at each other. My mouth was hanging open, but no words came to me—it was all I could do to blink. When I didn't move, Mom laughed once, wryly, like she'd come to her senses. She thrust herself across the table like she was trying to take it into her arms, and said, "It's not like that, Hana. There are reasons, I can explain. So first, if you'll just listen—"

"What, no, what?" Finally I was able to speak, and I threw myself back and laughed. "What the hell, Mom, two million?"

"Don't look at me like that, Hana, I can explain everything."

"Explain what? What reasons could you possibly have, ha ha ha ha!"

"No, I do, please, if you don't lend me this money, I'm so done for. Seriously."

"No way, you've got to be joking, aha ha ha ha!"

Of course two million was no laughing matter. I didn't know if I was sad or exasperated or angry, but I sank into my side of the booth, twisting awkwardly, and laughed even though I wanted to cry.

I think I must have laughed because just sitting there would have been unbearable. But underneath my senseless roaring, I was disgusted with myself, almost furious. *Why am I laughing, what is there to laugh about? Two million yen? What the hell has that got to do with me? What am I supposed to do? She's asking for almost everything I've saved. What the hell is she saying? This is crazy, right? Absolutely insane? And what happened that she needs so much money? What's it for? What did you get yourself into, Mom?* Slowly my laughter was crushed under the trepidation that welled up from deep inside me, and I choked on words that only made my fear worse. When my laughter finally eased, it was replaced with the threat of tears—tears for what, I didn't even know.

"I'm so, so sorry, Hana, super sorry, I swear . . ."

Eventually I got ahold of myself, and for a minute, Mom let the silence sit between us, but then she launched into her explanation.

Mom and the real estate agent had already been dating about a year when I left home at the end of that summer—and after I left, their relationship was steady for a while, no real problems or anything. He was more than twenty years older than Mom, and he really did own a real estate agency, all of what he'd told her was true. After Mom quit the bar, she'd go with him either to his office in front of the station or to a satellite office in Saitama, where she cleaned, served tea to clients, and went with him in the company car to look at open properties. She kept the apartment at Evergreen Hills, but he told her she could use a studio apartment in one of the buildings he owned one town over, so she packed up the bare necessities, moved into the studio, and started commuting to work from there.

At first, he promised he'd make her a salaried employee, but three months, and then six, passed with no real change. Whenever they leased to a new customer, or he won a bunch of money gambling on horses or hydroplanes, he'd give her some cash, but that was it. When he was in a good mood, he'd give her as much as a hundred thousand, but sometimes he'd wrinkle his nose at her and hand over a measly ten thousand. There was no set amount, no set time, and it seemed like she'd never get a steady income. But he was letting her live in his studio apartment for free, and when they ate together, he paid for everything. Sometimes he picked her up in his own car. She figured that was enough.

But then one day, something upset him, put him off—she couldn't remember what—and he flew into a rage and told her not to bother coming in to work. It wasn't like she had a punch card or anything, so she figured, whatever, and stayed home watching TV. A few days later, she decided to give him a call and ask what was going on, but his anger had only gotten worse, and he lectured her for hours. Mom didn't talk back, just yes-ed along, but that only made him explode. He screamed at her that she was an idiot, worthless, useless, and then he hung up on her. She was surprised, but she still thought it would blow over, so she decided not to worry about it too much. When you work in nightlife, you meet all sorts. A guy who seemed decent from every possible angle would come in the next night and say the most unbelievable things or cause a load of trouble. Or there'd be a customer you thought you had a good relationship with, one who favored you, but he'd do a one-eighty and act like he hated you on the thinnest excuse—or no excuse at all. A man turning on you wasn't unheard of—it happened.

Though he'd seemed nice enough when they first started dating, the real estate agent was a difficult man—he was moody, prone to bouts of anger for no reason. If he had been a customer at the bar, Mom could have told him not to come back or asked Mama Junko to play referee, but he wasn't a customer anymore. He and Mom were involved—or to put it more bluntly, he was involved with her finances, so she wasn't quite sure what to do.

For a month, Mom did exactly as she was told; she didn't go into the office, just stayed quietly in the studio. But she was worried that if she didn't do anything, she'd make him angry again, so she called him a lot to show she was putting in the effort. No matter how much she called, though, he never picked up, and if she tried the office, they told her he wasn't in. He'd never done something like this before, and she was confused, but she didn't like the idea of forcing him to talk to her if it meant he was going to lose his temper. She kept telling herself maybe it was fine to leave things the way they were, even as her funds disappeared. Hoping to get more cash, Mom went to the pachinko parlor in front of the station and killed time winning and losing. That's where she met "Headmaster."

"I'd seen her around before, you know, she stands out in a crowd. Not actually beautiful or stylish or anything, but there's something about her, draws you in. One time, she sat down next to me for a game, and we got to talking. She gave me a few extra plays, and she was fun to talk with, nice. So then we started going out for lunch sometimes. She was about the same age as me, and we got to be friends.

"I think she told me her name once, but I forgot. She said everyone just calls her Headmaster. So, we traded numbers and started going out for drinks at izakaya and stuff. I was still keeping up with my friends from the bar, but things got weird with me quitting and that whole mess, so you know, it was easier to hang out with her. And then she started giving me advice about my real estate agent, stuff like it was probably good to lay off a little, call the office about once a week to show I was still thinking about him. Honestly, I felt better just being able to tell her about my problems, you know? And maybe her clothes weren't the latest or hottest, but she had bling—an expensive-looking ring, a Chanel wallet, fancy hair clips. Then she told me how she had her own business, and I was like, 'What, no way!'

"Oh, and when was that . . . I was wearing a T-shirt, so maybe September, maybe after. I was sweating buckets, that's for sure. Anyway, that's when he finally called me back. I think it'd been two months since I last heard from him? My money was gone, and I was like, '*Finally*,' but then he told me his wife found out, and she was so mad, and there was all this talk about suing or being sued or something. It was just a mess."

"His wife?" I asked. "He was married?"

"Well, yeah," Mom said with a laugh. "I mean, he was sixty, why wouldn't he be?"

"Well, that's not . . ."

"The wife, she was living in Saitama, he said. Neither of them could be bothered to get a divorce, but they couldn't stand each other, their relationship was basically over. It was a dead end, he said."

I put my glass to my lips a moment and only then noticed it was empty.

"Oh, Hana, your glass is empty—wanna order something, Hana, hmm? Doesn't your throat get creaky from all that oolong tea?" Mom opened the menu and glanced at me, but I had no intention of speaking. "I'll get you one, too, okay?" she said, ordering two floats.

"Uh, there's a lot going on here," I said, massaging my temples with my fingers. "Go back a minute, who is suing who about what?"

"Oh, you wouldn't believe this," Mom said, eyes wide. "The wife is threatening to sue him and me. I asked him how that works, and he said that there's a thing where if you know someone's married and you date them, the wife can sue you for a ton of money. He told me if she takes us to court, he'll have to pay, too, but there's no way I'd have the money for that kind of thing. So he said it's better if we just end it now before lawyers get involved. And then he told me I needed to get out of the apartment before the first of the month because his daughter needed a place to live."

"And?"

"And so I packed up my things and went back home. What else was I supposed to do? I was really lost, so I talked to Headmaster. And she cheered me up, treated me to dinner and drinks, and told me I could start working with her. I'd make enough to live on my own."

"When you say Headmaster, what does that mean? She works at a school?"

"No, not really a school. It's like a business team. She's the leader."

"Business team? What business?"

"Lingerie," Mom said. "They specialize in shapewear. It's all the rage right now. Have you heard about it, Hana?"

"No."

"Shapewear is . . . well, it's something you wear to correct your body. So that your clothes look good on you."

The floats arrived, and Mom used her long spoon to start scooping away at the ice cream. Each scoop made the ball of vanilla bob in its green melon soda. The way Mom moved her spoon reminded me of how she used to clean out my ears as a kid. I shook my head and looked down at the countless bubbles bursting in my own glass.

"Headmaster is, I guess you'd call her the founder? She started the company, the system. And shapewear, Hana, it's not anything like a normal bra and panties, it's more like a bodysuit. It's patented in the US, so you know it's safe, and it's made with these scientifically proven wires and pashmina, which is this amazing, luxurious material that's about five times more expensive than silk. And if you wear your shapewear every day, it'll take the excess from your stomach and upper arms and back and move them to your chest and your rear, you know, where they're supposed to be, and then your body will remember what's supposed to go where. Your spine and organs will move back to where they're supposed to be, too, which means stiff shoulders are gone, and you can breathe better. You can even wear it when you're sleeping. You can remake your whole body with just one easy step—"

"Hold on a second," I cut off her speech—it sounded like she'd memorized it off a script. "What does this have to do with you?"

"Right, so one piece of shapewear costs anywhere from three hundred fifty to four hundred thousand," Mom said as she ate her ice cream. "And for each piece we sell, we make anywhere from eighty to a hundred thousand. That's the job."

"Sell? You sell these things?" I asked, frowning.

"It's hard to explain . . . so first you go to Headmaster's apartment and take a training course . . . Because Sister has two different ways you can—oh, Sister is the name of Headmaster's brand, Siesta Sister, good name, right? Cute. The slogan is 'Shape while you sleep' . . . Anyway, whether someone's selling the shapewear or buying it, we're supposed to call them Sister, so Sisters sell Siesta Sister Bodywear, and then there are more Sisters."

"Okay . . ."

"So I became a Sister and started selling Siesta Bodywear. We all went through the training course."

"Okay."

"But I said there are two different ways. There are Sisters who pay every month for stock and then sell it, and there are Sisters who buy their own stock and sell it, and they get a bigger cut of the sale. Headmaster said I was probably better suited to the second way."

"Okay."

"So I went in on a trial basis and sold my first piece right away. It cost me two hundred eighty thousand, but then I sold it for *three hundred eighty thousand*, and then I sold another one.

A profit of two hundred thousand in no time. Headmaster was telling me I had talent, and I really thought I could make it work, so I signed a contract to be a Sister and buy my own stock. And there's a discount for buying in volume, so I registered for eight sets."

"Registered. You mean you bought them?"

"Yeah."

"*You* bought them."

"Right, you're supposed to buy up your own stock ahead of time, and if you buy them in a bundle, you get a discount."

"How much did it cost?"

"Well, bundled, they take thirty thousand off the base price, which makes each suit two hundred fifty thousand. Good deal, right? So much cheaper. And we still sell at the same price, so that makes our take a lot bigger."

"How much?"

"Well, two hundred fifty thousand times eight, so . . . two million."

I shook my head.

"No, Hana, you don't understand." Mom thrust herself across the table at me, spoon still in hand. "Since I'd already sold two bodysuits, Headmaster said it was okay for me to pay up once I'd sold them. But there was a time limit, and I did my best. After those first two, I just couldn't sell any more no matter how hard I tried, and my time ran out. I don't have that kind of money, and I didn't know what to do. But she introduced me to someone who would lend me the money, so I borrowed it from him."

I shook my head again, sighing long and loud.

"If she asked me now, I probably wouldn't become a Sister, but back then, my boyfriend had dumped me, and I didn't know what to do, I didn't have money. And I'm sure everything he told me about his wife and going to court was made up. He'd just found himself another chick and wanted to cut me loose. But back then, the only person who'd listen to me was Headmaster, and her training course was so fun, and the other Sisters were selling their shapewear and making a lot of money, it seemed perfect for me—I thought maybe I just needed some practice. It was the only option I had for making a living, and I felt like I had to try."

"Mom . . ." I pressed my hands over my face, my fingertips over my eyes.

"And that's right when I found out I had cancer and that I needed surgery. Headmaster lent me money for the procedure, and she was so nice, you know, listening to my problems, so I felt like I really had to make it as a Sister. So I borrowed the money. But the bodysuits aren't cheap, right, they're impossible to sell, and I was so embarrassed I couldn't show my face anymore. Not to mention the loan payments . . . Anyway, after I got out of the hospital, I ran into Mama Junko while I was out on a walk, and she heard me out and decided to let me come back, but that was after I'd already borrowed the two million and paid up to Siesta Sister, and my installment payments were already coming due. And the interest was so much more than I thought it would be. I'm paying everything I can every month, but it only goes toward interest. I told Mama about it, and she told me I'd been had. She told me I needed to pay back the money and cut ties as fast as I could, or else."

"So basically you went to a loan shark."

"I think, probably, yeah."

"You have documents? A contract, stuff about the interest?"

"They, they told me to just sign, and I did."

I slumped into the booth and slowly exhaled. I didn't know what to say, or even how to say it. No, maybe I did know, but I didn't have the energy. My mind was clear, but my limbs were limp, and I didn't know which part of my body to focus on to force myself back up again.

Mom fidgeted with her spoon, eyes brimming with tears. Her ice cream had melted, turning her glass into a muddled whirl of green and white.

At some point, the middle-aged baseball team had gotten up

and left, and now there was a group of three families. They were flipping through the menus indecisively. There were three kids, all little, but I couldn't have guessed their ages. They looked the same to me, and their moms had the same faces and haircuts, the same tones of voice—they sat there, chatting and laughing with their kids.

"Tell me something," I said hoarsely. "Why . . . why did you decide to ask me for the money?"

"Well," Mom looked at me with pleading eyes, "I didn't know what to do, so I called Kimi. And I wanted to know how you were doing, too, Hana, really."

"And Kimiko . . . she told you we'd been saving money?"

"Well, I told her I was in big trouble, and she said if I'm in so much trouble, I should talk to you, Hana. She just gave me a nudge. She's such a sweetheart."

We were silent.

Mom's lipstick was wearing off, and her wrinkled lips looked narrower. She picked incessantly at her nail polish. She'd done that ever since I was little, whenever she was feeling nervous or troubled or cornered. We'd only been talking thirty minutes, but in that time, my mom seemed to have shrunk. She had been dumped, tricked, robbed, gotten cancer, and now her only choice was going back to that run-down bar to entertain drunks. She had no money and no one she could rely on. Except her daughter, who had run away from home. And now she waited anxiously to hear if that daughter would give her the money. I knew she had no other options, that the only way she'd be saved was if I gave her the money. I knew that. I knew it well. But that knowledge made everything hurt, ache, and I shook my head uselessly, helplessly.

"Wait here," I finally said. "I'll go get it."

"Hana . . ."

I tottered out of the restaurant like I was drunk and headed toward the house.

My feet felt different as they struck the ground, and the town and people around me seemed flimsy. I thought of the paper dress-up doll I'd once had. Her clothes had tabs you could fold down so she could wear them—she'd had a lot of shoes and things, too. You could change her whole outfit. And I had other things—envelopes, stationery, stickers, things I kept because they were too precious to use, things that made me happy. I don't think I ever threw them away, so where did they go, I wondered, dazed.

The scenery before me changed matter-of-factly, like flipping through a faded magazine, and I realized I was in front of the house. It was locked, so Kimiko must have gone somewhere. I unlocked the front door and went in, climbing the creaking stairs to our bedroom. I took down the futons, climbed into the closet, slipped the board loose, and took down the navy shoebox. I counted out three hundred fifty thousand from the bundle and returned that to the box and then held the remaining two million in my hands. Bill by bill, month by month, everything that I'd worked so hard to save. All the money I had. The idea that it would now disappear felt unreal.

I went to the kitchen and found a rubber band, bound the money tight, and stuck it into the depths of a bag with a crossbody strap. Then I put my shoes back on and retraced the road to the family restaurant. As I climbed its steps, I wondered if maybe Mom had left. I imagined for a moment that she'd regretted begging me for the cash, hadn't been able to stand making me feel that pain, so she'd just gone off somewhere. But she hadn't. The automatic door belled as I stepped inside, and I saw that Mom was still there, toying with her phone. When she saw me, she half stood up, bobbing her head.

I sat down across from her, took out the two million, and handed it to her. She burst into tears, bowing deeply and apologizing, hair spilling over the tabletop like dried seaweed. A passing waiter glanced at us before looking away. "I can pay off the first loan with this, and then, once I'm done paying off the interest, I'll pay you back, Hana. I really, really will. I'm so sorry." Mom took out her cracked pleather wallet and tried to pay the bill, but I told her it was fine and paid it myself. We walked silently back to the station and parted at the stairs that led down to the ticket gate. She turned and waved at me several times, until she disappeared.

I went back home, took out my futon, crawled in, and cried. Well, not cried, really. Fluid flowed from my eyes, and it wouldn't stop. I don't know for how long. My body was hot and cold in turns. Eventually, I heard the front door open downstairs. I thought Kimiko must be back, but I stayed curled under the blanket. Then I heard someone coming up the stairs.

"Hana?" Kimiko called.

I fidgeted under the duvet to let her know I was listening but wasn't interested in coming out. She came closer and sat down next to me, laying a hand on me.

"Hana."

"Yeah?" My nose was stuffed, and it was difficult to breathe.

"Did you see Ai?"

"Yeah."

"Okay."

"Kimiko?" I asked, still hidden under the duvet. I was so stuffed it came out as Kibiko. "Kimiko, I have to apologize. The money we were saving, I gave it all away, to Mom."

"That's fine, Hana," Kimiko told me.

"No, it's not. I mean, she's my mom, but you got mixed up in it."

"It's your money, Hana. I'm not mad at you."

"That's not true. I know I keep the books, but it was money we saved together."

"Maybe so, but I already told Ai it was fine when she called."

"But Kimiko," I sobbed, finally sticking my head out onto the pillow, "I . . . I just, it's really, it hurts. I don't know, I don't know if it hurts because the money's gone, or because I feel bad for my mom, or because we worked so, so hard, and we still wound up like this. All of it, it's too much, just too, too much."

"Yeah."

"I'm trying so hard."

"Yeah."

"But I always wind up back here."

"Yeah."

"It was the same before, with Snoozy, when he stole my money from me."

"Yeah."

"And it wasn't stolen this time. I chose it. I gave it to her."

"Yeah."

"It was the only thing I could do."

"Yeah."

"But, I just, I don't know what to do anymore."

"It's okay," Kimiko said. "You'll save up more money in no time. Just keep working."

I curled into the futon and wailed. It rose from deep in my throat, a twisting, writhing sound like none I'd ever made before, and it drove through my chest and pierced my heart. Two million yen, half of it Kimiko's, and so much money had to be important to her, but she didn't scold me or blame me or anything, which made me even more miserable and wretched. My face was soaked with tears and snot and sweat, the whole mess dripping onto my pillow. Kimiko didn't say anything, just rubbed my shoulder through the duvet.

At some point, I fell asleep. When I woke up and checked my phone, it was just before 4 p.m. What time did Mom leave? What time did I come home? I couldn't remember. There was a missed call from Ran and a text from Momoko asking, "Are you coming, Hana? Everything okay?" I forced my heavy eyelids open and replied, "I'm gonna stay home. Some stuff happened. Tell you later." Two minutes later, Momoko sent an "OK!" I threw my phone on the tatami and closed my eyes. Each sniffle made my temples pound.

When I went downstairs to the living room, I found Kimiko the same as always, half under the kotatsu, watching TV and laughing. I remembered when I first met her at Evergreen Hills.

It was summer and the fan was on, and I had looked at her, lying just like this, watching TV and laughing, though there was no kotatsu then. Her pitch-black hair was like a living creature, and her eyes sharp, and I'd walked with her everywhere that summer, both of us soaked with sweat as we went to the convenience store, the public bath, the night market. She'd make me karaage, too. In the kitchen, I filled a cup with water and drained it in one swallow. Then I went back to the living room and slipped under the kotatsu. The two of us watched the variety show. I thought about our old friend, Loose Socks, with her bangs and hair like a water fountain, and wondered how she was doing.

"My eyes must be so swollen," I said, trying to make myself the butt of the joke to hide how embarrassed I was that she'd seen me crying.

"They are. All puffy. Like a three," Kimiko said, grinning.

"Like a three?"

"Yep! Like this." Kimiko drew a three in the air, and we both laughed. Then turned back to the TV. It had switched over to a cooking program, and a woman in an apron was stir-frying meat and vegetables as she explained each of the seasonings in her little glass bowls.

"Kimiko?"

"Yeah?"

"A while back—I guess it was last year, I had a long talk with Yeongsu. He told me a lot about himself, about how he grew up."

I hadn't meant to talk to Kimiko about this, but something about her face in profile made it flow right out of me. Somehow, I felt like I had been waiting for this moment to bring it up.

"He told me a lot of things."

"Did he?" Kimiko said, her eyes still on the TV.

"I found him in Lemon, doing some baseball gambling stuff. It must have been a Sunday. I kind of panicked. That's why he told me. About his work—about all of you, way back when."

Kimiko looked at me curiously.

"He told me about when you and Kotomi worked in Kabukicho."

"That was a really long time ago."

"You three have been friends all that time."

"Yeah."

A long silence. Everything was washing over me—these last six months, my nameless anxieties, the sleepless nights, and then today, all our money disappearing. I was adrift on the sea. I focused as hard as I could on the TV, trying not to let the ocean drown me. I imagined my mom, crying, smiling, the two expressions layered on top of each other, and then, though I'd never met them, Yeongsu's mom, the men of the tekiya, Yeongsu and his friends carrying his father's remains. Something rose within me, not misery or anger, but something I couldn't quite grasp, I didn't know where it was going. And then I started talking, as if I was trying to explain to myself how I was feeling, even though my thoughts were a mess.

"I was really surprised when Yeongsu first told me what kind of work he does. I didn't understand, and I was angry. I didn't like that he was using Lemon like that. I was afraid. I couldn't believe what was happening. But after he told me his story—I don't know how to explain, it made me think about a lot of things."

"Yeah."

"I mean, I left home as a teenager, same as him, and I'm working and drinking every day, even though I'm too young to drink booze. The cops freaked me out when they came to the bar. I'm still hiding my age. But if I want to survive, this is the only way I can, there's nothing else for me, and that's the truth. And I think Yeongsu is in the same boat."

"Yeah."

"I don't know if I can say that the things I'm doing or the things he's doing are right, you know, I can't, really, but if someone told me I was doing something bad, I think I'd disagree with them."

I scratched at my temples, unable to explain myself.

"Of course it's not right, there's nothing right about it, but it's not wrong either. That's how I feel. I'm a kid, so in that sense maybe there is something bad about it, but in the grand scheme of things, if you asked me if I was doing something wrong, I just don't think I am. I've been thinking about it ever since I heard Yeongsu's story. I'm hiding my age, which is lying, I guess, but—I don't think I'm doing anything wrong. At the same time, if someone asked me what I was doing with my life, I wouldn't know what to say."

"Your life?"

"Well, I mean, maybe what I'm doing isn't wrong, but what am I actually doing?"

"But"—Kimiko looked at me—"who's going to ask you that?"

"What?"

"Who's going to ask you what you're doing with your life?"

"Well . . ." I blinked at Kimiko.

"Why would anyone ask that?"

"Well, I don't know, but—"

"Then it doesn't matter."

"What?"

"It doesn't matter, because nobody's asking."

"I think . . . I think maybe I'm asking myself?"

"Then just stop asking yourself."

I met Kimiko's eyes. Stop asking myself? That had never even occurred to me. For a few seconds, I couldn't find words. Kimiko watched me with a curious expression.

"But, if I, I mean . . ."

"Uh-huh?"

"I'd be in trouble, well, no, not trouble, but—"

"Then it doesn't matter."

"Well, I guess maybe . . ."

"You always like to make things complicated, Hana." Kimiko laughed. I didn't know what to say to that. The cooking show was over, and now some shopping program was on—the screen was filled with pictures of some sort of face cream with real gold powder in it.

"So did Yeongsu tell you about his brother?"

"Yeah, he did."

"Huh." Kimiko nodded, still smiling. "Both their names have 'water' in them, you know?"

"Ujun, right? 'Rain' and 'greatness?'" I whispered. "Oh, rain!"

"And Yeongsu is 'reflection' and 'water.'"

"He told me about when he was a kid, too. About the street stalls. About his dad and his mom and his family."

"Uh-huh."

"Parents . . . What's the point of them?" I said.

"Yeah . . ."

"They piss you off, and you can never understand them, but then you still feel bad for them, you know, and sad, too. I just don't get the point."

"True."

"I really, truly don't get it."

"But what can you do?"

"What?"

"Your parents are your parents."

"You think so?"

"Yeah. I don't know a lot, but I do know that you just have to wait, wait for the end."

I met Kimiko's eyes and held her gaze a few seconds.

Then I remembered that her mother was in jail, and I had to look away. I felt bad for even thinking about it, uneasy, so I tried to change the tone, stretching and joking, "But anyway, who has time for this, right?"

"For what?"

"Everything. Eeeeverything! Who has the time? Saving all that money all over again? How many jobs do I need? Two? Three? We'll never get that kind of money back. And we'll only need more and more."

"We'll be fine. We have Lemon."

"Well, yeah, but—I know! I'll start helping Yeongsu out with his job." I laughed loudly. "I'll be his sidekick and work my ass off, make a shit ton of money that way, problem solved."

"That would be pretty tough." Kimiko laughed along.

That's when Ran and Momoko got home. They shouted hello as they came into the living room, spreading their hands wide, exclaiming, "Ta-da! We brought this back!"

It was a huge picture, totally bizarre—the overall impression was blue, but at first glance, I couldn't tell if the blue was showy or dark. As I studied it more closely, I realized it was a painting of the ocean. In the background a dazzling rainbow split the middle like a laser beam, and in the foreground plump dolphins leapt through the sparkling waves.

"It's a Christian Riese Lassen!" Momoko exclaimed. "It's super heavy, but we brought it anyway. You wouldn't believe how many looks we got on the way home."

"It was crazy," Ran laughed.

"What, this is amazing," I said, eyes wide.

"It's a Lassen. A real one!"

"A real one?"

"Really real. Hilarious, right?"

"Oh my god."

"Right? We could even sell it."

"Seriously?" I asked. "Is it expensive? Do you think we'd get a lot?"

"Probably. I think we could get a decent amount off it, right? It's signed, too!"

"But what if your parents find out?"

"How would they? They have so many."

"I don't know," said Ran, who'd been studying the painting. "I kind of like it."

"Seriously?" Momoko laughed.

"Yeah, seriously. We can always sell it, but why not hang it up here or at Lemon? I mean, I love the dolphins. They're super cute. And we brought it all this way, like you said."

"Well, I was saying that I think of all the Lassens in my parents' house, this one is the best."

The three of us stood in a line, staring at the Christian Riese Lassen. I'd heard his name before, and I'd seen his designs on posters or notebooks or something, but this was the first time I'd seen a real one, an actual signed print. The painting was bizarre—I couldn't decide if it was subtle or over-the-top, dark or bright. The painting was a night scene, but there was so much light, and the dolphins were leaping, but they were somehow lonely, and as I looked at them, a faint shadow clouded my mood. Even though the Lassen was filled with the ocean and waves and light and dolphins, it reminded me somehow of the back alleys of Sancha at night.

"Come on, let's not sell it, please?" said Ran.

"Well, I guess we don't have to sell it right away."

"Right? I kind of feel like it's fate. Look how the dolphins are smiling."

"They *are* cute," I agreed. We made cup ramen for dinner, and I studied the Lassen while we chatted over our noodles. We decided to put it in the living room or the bedroom for now, but eventually we wanted to move it to Lemon. Ran even declared that having a signed Lassen print at the bar would make the whole place feel more expensive, so customers would be more likely to buy top-shelf.

"Yeah," I said. "You know, Lemon's all I've got—I mean, it was all I had before, too. But I feel like I'm starting over again, and I'm more prepared than ever. It's Lemon or nothing."

Then I told Momoko and Ran what had happened with my mom that day—though I didn't tell them how much money there was, only that it was my entire savings. Once I'd told my story, Ran confessed that she'd been too embarrassed to tell us up until now, but her mom had called not long ago, and Ran had sent her mom a bunch of money. "You two are just too good, mad props," Momoko exclaimed, holding our shoulders and mock sobbing. "But now we've got the power of Lassen! Lassen all the way! Lassen till we die! Lemon, the bar where you can see a Lassen in the flesh! We'll charge people to see the dolphins, make a killing!" Momoko raised a fist in the air and shouted, "Let's do it!" and we joined her.

But Christian Riese Lassen never made his way to Lemon.

The last Sunday in February, at nearly ten o'clock at night, Jin-ji called Kimiko's cell. The four of us were under the kotatsu, watching TV, same as always.

"Hana. Hana!" Kimiko was louder than usual.

"What?"

"Lemon's on fire."

We yanked coats and jackets over our pajamas and ran as fast as we could to Lemon. Mindlessly we flew through the darkened streets, and when we emerged into the shopping district on the boulevard in front of the station, we discovered a line of fire trucks crowded against the curb. The huddle of their taillights dyed the night bloodred, and a crowd of onlookers craned their necks, trying to catch a glimpse of the fire. We excused our way through the crowd, pushing closer to Lemon.

The acrid smell of burning plastic, wood, and more wafted over us. There were puddles of water like the aftermath of a cloudburst on the asphalt, and hoses snaked in every direction. Finally we emerged at the front of the crowd, where we found yellow caution tape stretched between the streetlights a few meters in front of our building. Beyond that, we saw Little Heaven, fire-blackened. The glass door was shattered, and the entryway, the curtains, the exterior, all of it was as dark as the mouth of a charred corpse.

It looked like the firefighters had already put out the fire. There was no smoke, only the horrible smell. Black water trickled from the windows, the air-conditioning units, the signs, from every part of the building, and firefighters and police in silver and orange uniforms came and went in front of the building. One of them came up to me and told me to move back. I wanted to shout at him, "No! You don't understand. Lemon is here. Our bar is here!" But I couldn't speak. I sank back into the crowd and listened to them chatter—*oh my god, how terrible, it's completely burnt out, did someone die*—but all I could do was stare at the charred remains.

How many minutes, or maybe even hours, we stood there, I don't know. The crowd dissipated, and even when the firefighters finally began to leave, we still stood frozen. There was a single plastic bottle in one of the puddles, white against the black. I heard a cop say something into his radio. Kimiko was on my left, and Ran and Momoko clung to each other on my right. The stiff wind blew my hair over my face again and again. None of us spoke. We just stood, blinking up at Lemon.

EIGHT

INITIATION

1.

Yeongsu and I arrived twenty minutes ahead of time. We made our way through the crowds of Shinjuku Station to the east exit, climbed the stairs to get outside, crossed two big streets, and found the place where we were supposed to meet her without any trouble—it was the third floor of a building that had a CD shop on the ground floor.

Compared to the bright sunshine outside, the building was particularly dark. Yeongsu stepped inside the elevator first, then waited until I got in to press the button for the third floor. Under the bluish fluorescent light, I noticed the bumps and wrinkles on his face that were usually invisible, like a steep cliff that I'd never seen or visited. Yeongsu stood there with his arms crossed, holding a small bag under one arm, and stared intently at the glowing lights as the elevator moved up floor by floor.

When we got off, there was only one door, dark and wooden with an oval-shaped sign on it. I looked closer and made out the words "Gentlemen's Club—The Sirens." Yeongsu opened the door and went inside, and I followed him.

A woman stuck her head out from behind the counter. She was wearing an apron with large red and white polka dots, and her permed hair was tied in pigtails. *She must be in her fifties or even older*, I thought. She studied our faces with a disinterested look, blinking a few times, and then told us to sit down. She disappeared behind the counter again. Yeongsu walked over to a booth at the far end of the club and sat down, and I sat down next to him. In the kitchen, I could hear the woman at work—banging a plastic trash can against the wall to empty its contents, stacking up crate after crate filled with empty beer bottles, slamming shut the fridge door after checking the contents and making a note of what was missing. Those sounds were more than familiar to me—they overwhelmed me with an almost painful sense of nostalgia. Even from far away, the sounds made me feel like I was inside Lemon's kitchen again. The sensation was so vivid that I could feel my body moving along with each sound.

We sat in the booth in silence, not saying a word to each other. Yeongsu occasionally looked down at his cell phone or scratched his eyebrows. The chill from the outside had disappeared, and now, even sitting still, I was starting to sweat under my pullover. It was a beautiful, crisp day in mid-March, the winter cold still lingering in the air. Sweat trickled down my back and my armpits, but it had nothing to do with the weather outside or the heater that warmed the room. I wished I had brought something to drink. At that moment, I heard the door open behind me and saw Yeongsu stand up. Reflexively, I stood up halfway and turned around.

A woman had entered the room. Yeongsu bowed his head, and I did the same. He grunted so low I wasn't sure she heard him.

The woman walked behind me and sat down in the booth. She smiled and told us to sit down. Then she settled into the cushions, took off her black coat, rolled it up, and placed it by her side. Yeongsu let out another short grunt that could have been a greeting. We sat facing her.

The woman was smaller than I was, with dark hair that barely brushed her shoulders. She didn't seem to be wearing any makeup. She had on a dark gray scoop-neck sweater, similar colored pants, and no jewelry. All in all, she looked unremarkable.

"It's been a while, Yeongsu."

So this is Vivien, I thought to myself—that was the name Yeongsu told me earlier. I tucked my chin and straightened my spine.

"Yes, it's been a while."

As Yeongsu said this, Vivien lifted her lip slightly, almost a smile, and smoothed her hair back with both hands, tying it up in a bun. The woman before me was so different from the one I had imagined when Yeongsu described her to me, I was caught off guard. She was supposed to be older than Kimiko and Kotomi, well over forty, but she looked a lot younger. More than anything, I was surprised at how ordinary she looked—like she could be working in an office or a stationery shop.

"When was the last time we saw each other, Yeongsu? Has it been two years?"

"Yes, two years."

"Oh, I remember," Vivien said, with a smile in her eyes. "After the whole Muramatsu incident."

Yeongsu nodded.

"Have you been seeing Konno?"

"No, not anymore. I haven't seen him since then."

"Well, that's no surprise, I guess."

Vivien and Yeongsu mention several other names, sometimes with a chuckle, and talked about things I didn't understand—business matters I assumed. The woman in the polka-dot apron slowly made her way over to us, carrying a large bottle of beer and three glasses. I could see her better over here—she was a large, stout woman, and the glasses she held between her fingers looked unnaturally small in comparison. After placing the bottle and three glasses on the table, she disappeared into the back room again. Catching Yeongsu's eye and making sure it was all right, I poured beer into each glass, filling it to the top. Vivien took her glass and drank a big gulp without raising a toast. Yeongsu followed. I made sure to wait until he took a drink before I lifted my glass. I was so thirsty and nervous that I drank it down in one long pull.

"I thought you were bringing me a new source, Yeongsu, figured you'd heard the rumor that I was on the outs. But I guess it's the other way around."

"Well, not exactly. I heard you were short on staff."

"Ha, that's a way of putting it," Vivien laughed, looking somewhat pleased. "I'm not short on staff . . . I've got no staff. 'Cause I'm past my prime."

"Well, it's the same everywhere these days."

Vivien looked at me for the first time. We locked eyes for about two seconds. She blinked a few times, slowly, and made a sound that could have been a hmm or a humph.

"What's your name?"

"It's Hana. My name's Hana Ito."

"How old are you?"

"I'll be nineteen soon."

"You from Tokyo?"

"Yes, ma'am, from Higashimurayama."

"And where do you live now?"

"I live in Sangenjaya."

"Have a driver's license?"

"No."

Vivien nodded a few times, then turned the conversation back to Yeongsu. This time, they seemed to be talking about running the books.

I kept sipping beer, half listening to their conversation, which was full of baseball team names, nicknames, and words and phrases I didn't know the meaning of. They also talked about money.

"Okay, well, I'll call you later then," Vivien said when the beer bottle was empty.

"Got it."

"Hey, Yeongsu, by the way, that Kamazaki was talking shit about you."

"Oh, you can ignore him," Yeongsu said curtly.

"Got it." Vivien chuckled. "Well, we've both been through a lot, haven't we? I guess we're similar in a lot of ways."

"Please, you must be joking. You're not scum like me."

"Oh yeah? We might be more similar than you think."

Vivien laughed without making a sound. Between her colorless lips, I could see a gap between her two front teeth, so straight and clean it felt almost purposeful. The gap was beautifully aligned with the rest of her teeth, not one of them crooked, and it impressed me more than any other part of her face. From the kitchen, I could hear the sound of water hitting the sink, as if someone had turned the faucet on full blast. The three glasses were empty, so the conversation was apparently over. Yeongsu and I got up from the booth, bowed slightly, and left the club.

We walked back toward the station in silence for a while. Once we'd crossed the first street, I called out to Yeongsu, who was walking ahead of me.

"Yeongsu, wait!"

He turned around and looked at me.

"Um, I was so nervous," I said to him. "I mean, that Vivien—she was so different from what I expected."

"Uh-huh."

"I thought she was going to be more intimidating, you know? Like a real gangster."

"A real gangster, huh. I told you Viv was a woman, right?"

"Well, yeah, but . . . I don't know, I was imagining someone really scary, like out for cold blood, you know?"

Yeongsu turned back around and kept walking. I sped up to catch him.

"So . . . you think I made it?"

"Yeah, I'm sure you did."

"Really? How do you know?"

"I don't. It's just a hunch."

"Really?"

"Yeah."

"So . . . what happens next?"

"Well, she'll call me first, and then she'll call you. You just wait."

"What, she's gonna call me directly?"

"Probably," Yeongsu said. "Viv always hated having people

in between. She does everything herself. She usually doesn't do newbies either."

"Newbies?"

"New faces."

"Oh, so I guess it's not a done deal then," I said nervously.

"Well, she said it herself. Viv's not in the best spot right now. She doesn't have enough people working for her, and they've been rippin' her a new one. If she wasn't interested, she wouldn't have met you in the first place." Yeongsu sniffled and continued.

"She's always kept things small, so she didn't step on anyone's turf. And that hasn't changed. She likes to know who's working for her. But anyway, don't get too worked up about it. It'll be a job anyone can do . . . Hana, I got somewhere I need to be. I'll call you, all right?"

It was a Sunday afternoon, and the streets of Shinjuku were crowded with people. Rushing or ambling, smiling or frowning, dressed up or run-down, they went at their own pace going who knows where.

Supposedly everything that unfolded was by chance. But as I moved along with the crowd, I began to feel like every move, every direction, they were already decided—we just didn't know which way. But still we moved under the same sun and through the same languid spring air, tracing someone else's steps, following someone else's orders. That made me confused, and I felt like I was watching myself from a long ways away. Then, I heard the high-pitched honk of a horn and looked up to see that the light was about to turn red. I could feel the cars gearing up to accelerate all at once. On any other day, I would have stopped and waited for the next light. But in that moment, I took off running as if I had been struck, sprinting to the other side.

After Lemon burned down at the end of February, and we lost our work and our livelihood, I spent the next few days wading through an indefinable feeling. The four of us must have talked about so many things—on the way home from the fire, at home that night, into the next day—but somehow, I couldn't remember anything we'd said. I didn't lose my appetite, I wasn't paralyzed with shock, but for those few days, it was as if my head was covered with layers and layers of plastic bags. Maybe we just kept on the same as always, aside from no longer heading to Lemon for work.

I also found out that the fire started in En's restaurant. Who knows why En was at work on a Sunday, using the kitchen. She was hospitalized for burns and smoke inhalation. Fortunately, it sounded like she was going to make it.

I tried contacting Jin-ji to see if we could visit her in the hospital, but he said she didn't want to see us. That was a surprise to me—we'd been working under the same roof for a long time now, eating the food she'd cooked us, talking together, joking around, crying and laughing and singing. I didn't know how to process the fact that she didn't want to see us.

But reality gradually began to weigh down on us. Lemon was our lives. There was no trace of it left after the fire, and the four of us had lost our income. The money we spent every day at the supermarkets and convenience stores was small, but with every day, our savings decreased. Would we try to open Lemon again? How would we come up with the rent for our house? Jin-ji didn't say a word to rush us, but we could tell that he had his own troubles. After all, one of his buildings had burned to the ground. Had the building been inspected by the fire department? Had there been any code violations? As the owner, he would be asked a lot of questions. And we had plenty of other things to worry about. For example, what were we going to do about our laser disc rental? Would we have to pay damages? If so, how would we come up with the money? Come to think of it, we weren't even the ones listed on the rental agreement—that was Mama Atsuko. Did that mean we could get away with it? Should we get away with it? Even with something as small as this, we didn't know who to contact or even where to begin. There were so many things to think about and to talk about. The problems were piling up from every angle, and my brain didn't feel like it was working anymore—I was at a loss.

I wished the four of us could join forces, think things through together, and divide up the work—but that's not what happened.

If I didn't raise an issue, the others acted like they didn't see the problem. For some reason, Ran and Momoko, not to mention Kimiko, didn't seem to think that this situation affected them directly. When I tried to talk to them about it, they just said, "We'll figure it out." "Let's get Lemon going again." "I know—we'll make it an even bigger place this time!" Our conversations always turned toward the trivial and unrealistic, and we never came up with any concrete plans. In the moment, their optimism, irresponsible though it was, numbed my pain and cheered me up, but afterward, I always wound up back where I started, heavyhearted and resigned to the fact that I was the only one who could do something about our problems.

Anxious, I desperately tried to think of ways to get by. First, Momoko and Ran. Momoko had a family to fall back on. Ran, too, had a boyfriend who was somehow still around, and she could probably find a part-time job if she put her mind to it. The problem was me and Kimiko. I tried to imagine myself going back to Higashimurayama, with Kimiko by my side, and working at a family restaurant to support us—but that wasn't a realistic option either. Even working eight hours a day, my salary would only amount to a couple thousand yen, and we couldn't live on that.

And I couldn't go back to my mother either. Every thought of her tormented me. Whenever I remembered the two million I gave her that day at the family restaurant, it made me so depressed I felt sick to my stomach, and even now tears of frustration welled up in my eyes. I still couldn't quite believe I'd handed over so much money. But even worse than that was the piercing sadness, frustration, and sorrow that overwhelmed me every time I thought of my mother.

Sure, she was ditzy and careless, hopelessly irresponsible, but she didn't cheat or deceive other people; she was a good person, and the thought upset me even more. And it made me hate the people who'd taken advantage of her all the more. My faceless hatred and anger and bitterness, the complex cocktail assailed me every time I thought of her. I couldn't possibly live near her now, let alone in that lifeless tenement house.

We could go our separate ways, start our own lives? At least in terms of money, that might be possible. But what about Kimiko? No, she's a fully grown adult, and before she lived with me, before we started Lemon, she managed to get by somehow, so it's not like she can't survive without me. I mean, Yeongsu and Kotomi would be there to help. She was fine before, she'd manage fine again. Kimiko would be fine. She's not afraid of anything. If I said to her, "Hey, Kimiko, with everything that's happened, why don't we go our separate ways?" she would probably answer, "Okay." Same as always. And she'd disappear, leave without any hesitation, same as she did that summer day four years ago. She'd desert me. And I'd go back to my old life, the life I had as a child, alone in an empty room with dark, damp walls, where no one ever came to see me. I shook my head.

This is my house. I have to protect this house—this house I found all on my own. Kimiko and me, us, I have to keep this life I built for us.

I bought a magazine that had a listing of part-time jobs and carefully combed through the pages, including the nighttime ones. But what I found was that for someone like me—someone with no high school degree, no skills, and no talent—the amount of money I could earn was pathetic.

I seriously considered working at another bar or a cabaret club. But I also knew that I probably wouldn't be able to make it in those places. I just had to look at Ran. She was funny and pretty, interested in makeup and fashion, all around popular and a top earner at Lemon—but at the cabaret club right next door, she was a failure of a hostess who couldn't get a customer. She practically got fired because of it.

The only reason I managed at Lemon was because it was the kind of place where I could be myself, where I could act the same way I did at home with Kimiko. I didn't need to dress up or put on makeup, and I knew everyone because there were only four of us. There were no quotas, no competition—all I had to do was work with the people I lived with to entertain local regulars.

Because that's what Lemon needed from me. It was the kind of place where I got to make the decisions, do the cleaning, balance the books, close late at night, open again the next evening. That was Lemon. And above all, the money that Kotomi brought in every month kept us afloat. I had to get Lemon back on track somehow, so we could protect the house we shared. So we could survive.

2.

Around the end of April, I got a call from Vivien. Ran was out interviewing for a part-time job, and Momoko had gone to visit her mom about something important. Kimiko was up early that morning, which was unusual for her, and after finishing her usual wipe-down, she left the house without saying where she was going. I was alone at home, lying on my futon and staring at the ceiling, when my phone rang. I jumped. It was from an unknown number. Aside from my three housemates and Yeongsu, there was no one in the world who would be calling me. *Here it is.* I gulped and picked up the phone.

"Hello?"

There was a pause, and then I heard a woman's voice.

"Is this Hana Ito's number?"

"Yes," I answered. Though she sounded a bit distant and muffled, it was definitely Vivien.

"Yeongsu gave me your number. Are you in Sancha now?"

"Yes, I'm at home."

"Can you come out in two hours, say around two thirty?"

"Yes."

"Great. Come meet me in Shibuya, in front of the Tokyu Inn. It's just to the left of Miyamasuzaka."

"Tokyu Inn, got it," I repeated.

"It's a hotel. You'll see it right away. Wait there, and I'll call you."

When Vivien hung up, I felt as if the room had suddenly gone quiet, even though there weren't any sounds to begin with. I put my hands against my cheeks and exhaled deeply. Then I remembered that I hadn't taken a bath last night, so I went downstairs and took a shower. I didn't know where the specific Tokyu Inn that Vivien had mentioned was, but the station staff could probably help me once I got to Shibuya. *There's probably a map, too*, I thought to myself as I dried my hair with a towel. I didn't have much of an appetite, but I made myself eat an egg over rice. Then, as usual, I grabbed the feather duster and ran it across the knickknacks in the Yellow Corner.

The Yellow Corner occupied the shelf next to the TV in the living room. I hadn't added anything new in a while, but the shelf was always visible and had become a part of this house—a part of me. I didn't just look at it. I took care of each and every object, rearranging them from time to time, holding them in the palm of my hand, and cleaning anything glass with soap and water to make sure it sparkled. Despite the mess that I'd been going through—losing Lemon in the fire, my mom asking me for money—I believed that it was thanks to these yellow blessings that I was able to live like this. After all, I'd saved over two million yen before everything happened. As I gazed at the Yellow Corner, I remembered the dream I had more than a year ago, the dream that carved itself into me and haunted me.

The tennis court, the sandy beach, Kimiko's dustcloth, the bright red blood flowing from the stab wound in my stomach . . . I could recall every detail vividly, along with the words and phrases I had read in the dream dictionary. The images and the dream analysis were indistinguishable now, intertwined in my memory—so much so that they had become an undeniable fact. I hadn't had a single dream since. This helped convince me that the dream was something special. Everything that had happened and then the call from Vivien today, it all seemed to point to the fact that things were progressing just as the dream predicted. *It's going to be all right. There's nothing to be afraid of.*

This is what I have to do. Please let everything work out. I closed my eyes and repeated the words over and over. Then, exhaling sharply, I opened my eyes, reached for the yellow hairband that was hooked on the ear of the shiny yellow lucky cat, put it around my wrist, and left the house.

On the way to the station, I decided to give Yeongsu a call to let him know I was going to meet Vivien. He didn't pick up.

When I got to Shibuya, I asked the station attendant for directions and arrived in front of Tokyu Inn twenty-five minutes early. I wondered if I drew attention just standing around, and whether it would be better to wander or go into a store and pretend to shop—but in the end, I couldn't force myself to move. The thought of meeting Vivien alone and discussing details of the work made my stomach tighten. I looked at my phone thinking at least ten minutes had gone by, but it hadn't even been five. I stood there nervously gripping the strap of my purse, sighing, and glancing at every person on the street. At 2:30 p.m. exactly, my phone rang.

"Hey, over here, get in the car."

I looked up and saw a black car with the hazard lights flashing. I couldn't see inside, but somehow, I felt like it was looking at me. As I approached, I noticed that the whole car was coated in dust and that there was a semicircular ding in the windshield. Through the glass, I could just make out Vivien. I instinctively headed toward the back seat, but Vivien signaled me to get in the front, so I lowered my head and got into the passenger seat.

Vivien drove silently, and I remained silent, too. The floor of the car was littered with crumpled receipts, empty plastic bottles, and plastic convenience store shopping bags. There was no unpleasant smell though—no hint of leftover food or cigarette smoke. I realized that, aside from taxis, this was the first time I'd ridden in someone's car. Being in the passenger seat felt strange. Unlike the train or the bus, I could see everything from a lower perspective and feel the vibrations and sounds more directly. And everything loomed so large in front of me that each time

Vivien hit the brakes, my legs clenched, thighs tightening. After driving about fifteen minutes (I spent the whole time staring out at the large trees that lined the right side of the street), Vivien pulled into a large, deserted parking lot.

"So," she finally spoke. She sounded cheerful, which made me feel relieved. Vivien glanced up at the rearview mirror, then looked quickly to the left and right. She reached for a small pouch under her feet, unzipped it, and took out several cards. After checking them briefly, she kept three in her hand and put the rest of them back.

"This is what you use to get the money," Vivien said.

"What?" My voice came out louder than I had intended.

"Yeongsu explained everything to you, right?"

"Um, yes, but not . . . in detail."

"What do you mean? He didn't tell you anything?"

"Not really, no . . ."

"Well, what did he tell you?"

"He told me that I would be dealing with you directly from now on, and that you would give me a job that I could—"

"Look," Vivien interrupted and showed me one of the cards she held in her hand.

"I'm going to give you three of these today. You see the numbers on the back? There's another card with the PINs, so you memorize which PIN goes with what card. Each card has a daily limit of five hundred thousand yen. You wait three days before you use the next one. Three cards, 1.5 million total. I'll collect everything in two weeks."

"Wait, can I write that down?" I rummaged in my purse for a notebook. I was getting confused with all the numbers, and plus, Vivien spoke really fast.

"Write everything down?" Vivien raised her eyebrows. "We don't write things down."

"Well, I . . . I didn't expect that we'd be doing all this today," I told her honestly. "I'm sorry, it's my first time."

Vivien cleared her throat and looked into my eyes.

"It's easy. Even a kid could do it."

"I don't want to make mistakes," I said, and let out a deep sigh. "I'm sorry, I'm just so nervous."

"Being nervous is fine, but we never write anything down, got it?" Vivien said. "You know how Yeongsu does with his baseball, don't you?"

"I've never really watched him. I just catch glimpses here and there."

"Really?"

"Yes."

"Well, usually he writes everything on wafer paper."

"Wafer paper?"

"You know, that starch paper stuff they use for food. You write on it, and once you're done, you swallow it."

I nodded, not knowing how else to respond.

"We never use paper. Well, these days, we almost always know when the cops are coming for a raid, and they almost never do, so it's not nearly as bad as it used to be."

Just then, Vivien's phone rang. The ringtone was ZARD's "Don't Give Up." The up-tempo music jumped and echoed through the car, and I straightened in response. Vivien took the phone out of her pocket and glanced at it, deciding whether or not to answer. I glanced over a few times. The bright afternoon sun highlighted the dark circles and wrinkles underneath her eyes and the sunspots on her skin. She looked older than she had at the club. "Don't Give Up" kept on playing. After what seemed like an eternity, the song cut off right in the middle of the climax, right as ZARD sang "no matter how far apart we are." Then, it was silent.

"So . . . where were we?"

"Um, edible paper and destroying evidence?"

"I never said anything about destroying evidence." Vivien smirked though the smile didn't reach her eyes. The gap between her front teeth appeared, and its perfection eased my nerves.

"No, ma'am . . . but you did say to swallow it."

"It's not as easy as you think, you know. Sometimes there's no water to wash it down."

"So you've . . . eaten edible paper, Vivien?"

"Sure, I have. Not for the baseball stuff though. But we're off topic," Vivien replied. "You can call me Viv, by the way. Vivien's too long."

"Okay," I said, remembering that Yeongsu had called her that, too. "I'll call you Viv from now on. Got it."

"Well, anyway . . . Hana, right? Your job is to collect cash."

I looked at the cards in Viv's hand. I had to convince her that I was useful, someone she needed. Maybe I shouldn't have said that stuff about writing things down. But "Don't Give Up" had lightened my mood, and from the way things were going, it didn't seem like I'd done anything too wrong. But I couldn't be sure.

Viv's instructions were so specific and she spoke so quickly that the amount of information didn't seem to matter. Maybe she was testing me, my comprehension, how I reacted, how much I could figure out on my own. I couldn't let her think that I was no good. I had to show her that I was motivated and capable. I tried to look as calm as possible.

"So Viv, about the cards . . ."

"Uh-huh."

"Can I explain what I'm supposed to do in my own words, just to make sure?"

"Go ahead."

"Okay, here goes. Let me know if I get anything wrong."

I swallowed hard and tried to focus, to remember everything Viv had said earlier.

"So first, I take these three cards. I get the PINs from another card and make sure they match the cards I have. I memorize the PINs. I withdraw the money."

"Sounds right."

"Each card has a withdrawal limit of five hundred thousand."

"Yup."

"After you use one card, you have to wait at least three days. Three cards multiplied by five hundred thousand equals 1.5 million. Collection is in two weeks."

I thought I had gotten it right and waited for Viv to say something, but she sat there in silence. Uneasy, I decided to ask another question.

"So . . . where exactly do I withdraw the money?"

"An ATM."

"Which one?"

"Don't use the ones with security guards, you know, the ones inside banks. Go to the ones that are just ATMs, like in Shibuya or Shinjuku, where it's crowded and lots of people are coming and going."

"So it's okay if there are people around?"

"For these cards, yes. You're just withdrawing cash like everyone else. It's good camouflage if there's people around."

"Can I do it all at one ATM?"

"No, you'll want to change locations. Make sure you wear a hat."

"Should the ATMs be far apart?"

"As long as it's in Shibuya or Shinjuku, where there are lots of people around, you don't have to worry about that. Any time of the day is fine, too."

"Okay."

"I'm giving you three cards this time. Make sure you do it three days apart. Every two weeks, I'll come and pick everything up and give you the next batch."

"Got it."

"So that's three million a month."

Three million? I held my breath and nodded in silence.

"We'll swap the cards every time, so make sure you bring the cards with the money when we meet."

"Yes, ma'am."

"That's about it. Things may change depending on the card, but that's all you need to know for now."

"Um, what if . . ."

"What if, what?"

"What if I get caught?"

I looked into Viv's face. I was eager and ready to work, but this question was so important, I had to ask it no matter what, but to my surprise, Viv didn't seem fazed.

"Caught, like, you mean, by the police?"

"Um, yes."

"Well, then you say some foreigner gave you the cards in Kabukicho."

"What?!" My voice came out louder than I had intended. Viv seemed startled by my reaction.

"What do you mean, what?"

"I mean, um . . . well, I'm supposed to say *that*?"

"Do you have a problem with it?"

"No, I mean, it's fine. It's just so . . . simple."

"And?"

"The police will believe that?"

"Sure, why not?"

"Why . . . what if they detain me and I get questioned?"

"That won't happen."

"But . . . what if it does?"

Viv glanced up, then scooped her hair back using both hands. "Well, then you just tell the police that some foreigner came up to you on the street, and he wouldn't leave you alone, just wouldn't shut up, and it was so annoying, and the next thing you know, he showed you a card and said you can get a lot of money with it. Then he gave it to you, and you figured he was lying, but you tried it out anyway, and voila! It worked. Just say you spent the money already. Oh, and you can tell them which ATM you used."

"Really? I should say that? They'll believe me?"

"Well, you wouldn't be lying. Some foreigner or me—what's the difference? Kabukicho or in a car—it's all the same."

Was it really as easy as she made it out to be? I'd been nervous and anxious, but Viv's casual attitude toward the whole thing—her utter ease and composure—made me wonder if I could handle it after all. A different kind of anxiety washed over me, and unconsciously, I placed my hand on my stomach. I didn't know what to do. I was at a loss for words.

"You won't get caught though, I promise," Viv continued. "We only handle super safe, super secure products, with fast turnover. The three cards I gave you—they're from a reliable source, with actual accounts. No way they'll be traced back to us. Don't worry."

While I chewed over Viv's reassurances, I desperately tried to think of something I needed to ask her or something I should clarify—but all I could think about was the money and the directions I'd managed to get into my head. I nodded silently.

"What day is it today?"

"April . . . thirtieth. Yes, the thirtieth."

"All right, then the first delivery will be after Golden Week, around the fifteenth. I'll be in touch about the time."

"So, um . . . if I have any questions, can I call you?"

"Sure," Viv replied. "Just don't register my number on your phone. Memorize it. Delete your incoming and outgoing calls, got it?"

"Got it."

"Well, like I said, there's nothing to worry about. Just in case, make sure you only carry one card at a time."

"Okay. Any other tips?"

"Well, when you withdraw the cash, do it with confidence, like it's your own money. Take out the bills, put them in your bag, then go. Be natural. Don't look around, don't draw attention. Memorize the PIN."

"Okay."

"Oh, and since Yeongsu isn't involved in this, everything from here on out is between you and me. Don't mention this to anyone. You understand, right?"

"Yes."

"Okay."

Viv handed me the three cards and a card with the PINs on it. She watched as I put them in my wallet, then started the car.

My body felt oddly light, as if I were floating in midair, gliding along an invisible rail through the scenery that passed outside the window.

"Where do you want me to drop you off?"

We were back in Shibuya, where the streets were filled with people. "Anywhere is fine," I answered without thinking.

"I'll see you next month then. Around the fifteenth. I'll call you."

I got out in front of Tower Records, and Viv's car sped off with a roar, quickly blending in with the other cars and disappearing from sight.

I stood there for a few seconds, or maybe a few minutes. I heard a loud honk and suddenly found myself thrown into the bustle of the city. When I looked up, I saw a yellow signboard, and next to it a huge poster of some singer I didn't recognize. Her eyes were large, with white squares floating inside them. I walked to Shibuya Station, took a bus, and returned to Sangenjaya.

3.

On the morning of May 3, I caught the bus in front of Sangenjaya Station and headed to Shibuya.

Walking down the street, riding the bus, I was nervous the whole time, and everything I saw, everything I heard, somehow felt out of the ordinary. I kept pulling down the brim of my hat and then putting my head in my hands. "That hat looks great on you!" The shop girl's high-pitched voice echoed in my mind. I had picked up the bucket hat for a thousand yen at a thrift shop in an alley in front of the station. The hat was beige and boring, tired looking, and it covered my face well. Inside my purse, which was slung across my body, was a wallet, and inside the wallet was one of the cards that Viv had given me. I kept repeating the PIN in my mind, sighing after each repetition.

Because of Golden Week, Shibuya was so crowded that it took all the energy I had just to get off the bus and take a few steps forward. Maybe the crowds were a good thing, though. I imagined the heavy weight in my chest becoming smaller and lighter for every person on the busy streets, and as I became lighter, I managed to inch along.

I had already been to Shibuya and Shinjuku two days ago to look for ATMs that met Viv's requirements. Just the thought of going to an ATM today, inserting my card and withdrawing the cash, made my fingers tremble. Viv had trusted me with this. Even if I didn't get caught, I had the feeling that what I was about to do was going to change my life forever, and my stomach clenched with fear.

I had never used a cash card before, or even held one in my hand, so I had no idea if the card Viv had given me was real or a fake. But each card was shiny and solid, printed with the name of a real bank, plus a set of raised numbers and a name. The back side was also covered with official-looking fine print, and if Viv had told me the cards were real, I would've believed her.

But where did they come from? Did they belong to someone? How did the whole thing work? What I was about to do was probably risky, but just how risky? These questions had played on repeat in my mind ever since I got the cards from Viv. *We only handle super safe, super secure products, with fast turnover. The three cards I gave you—they're from a reliable source, with actual accounts. No way they'll be traced back to us. Don't worry.* Every time I felt scared, I repeated Viv's words in my head and tried to shake off the doubts that crept into my brain. But my anxiety always came back. As I walked through Shibuya, the crowd of people surged toward me—families, lovers, groups of girls, men in suits—and as soon as they passed, another swarm of people appeared. I struggled onward, feeling like I was dragging something heavy, something as big as me—but before I knew it, the ATM was there before me.

The ATM corner was located on the first floor of a long, narrow building. It wasn't very big, but it had a bright sign with the bank's name and three identical machines.

There were two or three people lined up in front of each

ATM—men, women, couples. Apparently, everyone needed to do some shopping over Golden Week. I walked over to the right-hand machine and got in line, waiting for my turn to come. My nerves ratcheted until I could feel my heart pounding. A deafening clanging rose within me until it was so loud I was sure it was going to knock me down—I felt like the ringing must be leaking out of my ears, my eyes, my skin, and I couldn't believe no one else could hear it. My fingers trembled inside my pocket, and to stop them from shaking, I clenched my fists tight.

My turn came, and I stood in front of the panel.

In the corner was a small, square, slightly curved mirror, and I could see my face in the reflection. Was there a security camera behind it, watching me? If I got caught, was the footage from the camera what would get plastered all over the news? Maybe everything—the people next to me and behind me, the number pad, the automated messages coming out of the machines, the door opening and closing behind me—everything was already watching me, and the moment I inserted this card, a piercing alarm would go off, and men would rush over and hold me down. The vivid scene unfolded in my mind. But there was no stopping now. I took a deep breath to contain the fear that threatened to overwhelm me, and just as I had practiced at home a thousand times so it would feel natural, I took the card out of my wallet and inserted it into the slot. I felt a slight resistance at first, and then the ATM swallowed the card. I wondered what would happen if the card didn't come out, or if an alarm started ringing. Did the machine send a signal the moment I put the card in? Were security guards going to come running? Or what if the person next to me was actually a plainclothes cop and they suddenly grabbed my wrist? As my fear reached its peak, tears welled up in my eyes.

I waited one second, two, and just as I was about to whimper, the screen asked what kind of transaction I would like to complete. With trembling fingertips, I pressed the withdrawal button and typed in the PIN. When the next screen appeared, before I could overthink it, I pressed the number five, followed by five zeros. The word "Processing" appeared on the screen. I waited a few more seconds, and then, all of a sudden, there was a loud shuffling sound, and I nearly stopped breathing. But then the cash slot opened, and I saw a bundle of ¥10,000 bills inside its gray walls. I reached in and took the cash, folded the whole stack in half, put it in an inner pocket in my purse, and zipped it up tightly. A cheerful voice urged me to finish the transaction, as the words "Please take your card" appeared on the screen, and the card reemerged. I pinched its corner and the receipt the machine had spit out and stuck them both in my wallet. I turned around as I heard the machine say, "Thank you for using our services."

Next in line was a young couple whose hair was dyed in different colors, chatting happily and looking at each other with puppy eyes. They hadn't even noticed I was done yet. No one was looking at me; no one seemed to be interested in anything around them—bizarrely, they didn't even seem to care about the money they were withdrawing, about to withdraw. For them, nothing was happening, nothing that caught their attention, nothing that would linger in their memories. I gripped the strap of my purse with both hands and put the ATM behind me.

I repeated the same process three times, with three days in between, just as Viv had instructed. The second time was in Shinjuku on May 7, and the third time was in Shibuya on May 11. In total, I withdrew ¥1.5 million.

I barely remember how I made it home the first day. I know I felt paranoid, like I was being followed or like someone was waiting on our doorstep to catch me.

I wasn't hungry in the least, but I hadn't eaten anything since morning, and I could taste stomach acid at the back of my throat—I was starting to feel woozy, too. When I got back to Sancha, I went into the first ramen shop I saw and ordered a bowl of shoyu ramen, but while I waited, my temples throbbed, my limbs tingled, and the weight of nerves crushed down on my chest. It was all I could do to sit on the stool. The woman sitting kitty-corner from me kept glancing over, like she thought I might be sick, and that made me feel even more trapped, cornered even. I only managed a few noodles before I had to set the bowl aside and leave.

The second run was the same—I was half-dead by the time I was finished. The third time, when I got home, I was so wiped out I could barely move. By then, I felt like things were going better, but in what way, I couldn't even begin to guess.

The work I had to do for Viv made Golden Week feel like it would never end.

The first day of the holiday, Momoko went home to Aobadai and called to say she was spending the rest of the week there to hash things out with her parents. Ran had passed her interview and was going to start working at a cabaret club near the station, a different one from where she'd worked before. That week, on a whim, Kimiko took Ran and me out for yakiniku a few times, using the money Yeongsu gave her every month that was supposedly for her mother in prison. When we went out, Ran talked about her new club, the way it worked and the customers and the girls, while Kimiko and I grilled meat and drank beer. We'd laugh and make jokes, and I realized it had been a long time since I last had a beer that wasn't from a can. When I was alone, I felt trapped and didn't know what to do with myself, so I was grateful for the time I got to spend with Kimiko and Ran. It was the only time I didn't have to worry about the cards or money.

A few days after Golden Week ended, I got a call from Viv. It was eleven in the morning. I pushed the talk button the moment I heard the phone ring. For a second, I couldn't hear her voice, so I pressed the phone to my ear and repeated, "Hello? Hello?"

"Hey, I can hear you. How'd it go?"

"Fine, I think."

"Good, good."

I thought I heard Viv giggle, and I imagined the gap between her front teeth.

"Can you come out in a couple of hours?"

"Sure, I'm ready anytime."

"Good, I'll see you at one then."

After she hung up, I stared at the closet door, still clutching my phone.

Above the ceiling, inside the navy shoebox, was the ¥1.5 million I had withdrawn using Viv's cards. I never got caught, no one was after me. I had succeeded in bringing the money here without anyone knowing about it. I took the futons out of the closet, climbed inside, and took down the cash. I bound the bills together with a rubber band, and after some hesitation, I put them inside a large envelope I'd bought at a hundred-yen shop. Then, I shoved the envelope into the bottom of my purse.

We met at the same place as last time.

The dusty black car arrived at precisely one o'clock in front of the Shibuya Tokyu Inn. This time, I ran up to the car before Viv signaled me, and with a bow, I opened the passenger door to get in. As the car started to move, through the window, I watched the same scenery as I had two weeks ago. We followed the same route, turned the same corners, and pulled into the same parking lot. Viv yanked the grinding gearshift into park, and the car grew silent. Everything was exactly the same as the first day we met. It was as if time had been rewound, and we were replaying the day all over again.

"Um, I have it," I whispered, gesturing with the purse I clutched against my stomach.

"How'd it go? Wasn't too bad, was it?"

"Well, the job itself wasn't too bad, I guess."

I sighed, releasing the darkness and weight I'd been carrying for the past two weeks.

"Where'd you do it?"

"Shibuya and Shinjuku."

"Good, good."

Viv nodded in satisfaction. She glanced quickly to the left and right, and then she motioned to me with her chin. I unzipped my purse and took out the brown envelope with the 1.5 million. I checked to make sure no one was around and then carefully handed it over to Viv.

"In an envelope and everything, huh? Look at you," Viv teased, laughing, and then she took the wad of money out of the envelope and started flicking through the bills with her fingertips. The ¥10,000 bills moved smoothly between Viv's fingers. The empty envelope fell to her feet, but Viv didn't seem to notice. It was trash now, just like the receipts and gum wrappers scattered on the floor. In no time, Viv had finished counting all 150 bills, and then she peeled off one bill at a time until she had 15, and she handed them to me.

I stared at the ¥150,000 in my hands.

One hundred fifty thousand. Fifteen bills, ten thousand each. That was my reward for this job. My reward for those three acts, for each time I felt like I was being hunted to death. At Lemon, if all four of us had worked ourselves to the bone, this would have been five days of work; for just me, it would have taken two weeks. At a family restaurant, I would have had to work two and a half months, from morning till night. I honestly didn't know whether ¥150,000 was worth my three runs, never mind the agony of these past two weeks. Was it a lot or not enough, I honestly couldn't say.

One thing I knew for sure was that right now, there was no other way I could earn this kind of money in just three days.

"Your pay is ten percent of what you collect. That's the base salary. So this time, it's fifteen. You okay with that?"

"Yes, ma'am."

"You up for another one?"

I nodded yes. "Um, can I use the same ATMs, or . . ."

"You can with these cards. You should take note of a couple good places, though, and rotate through them. Keeps things fresh, too." Viv laughed. "Oh, right, the cards."

I folded my stack of bills in half, bowed slightly to Viv to show my thanks, and put the money inside a yellow pouch I planned to use specifically for my pay. Then I handed Viv the three cards, the card with the PINs, and the receipts for each transaction.

"When we met, I forgot to ask about the receipts," I said. "I wasn't sure what to do with them."

"Oh, you can just throw them out next time."
"Throw them out? Where?"
"Anywhere. In the trash."
"Like in a regular trash can?"
"Yeah, sure, a regular one. Wherever."

Viv held up one of the receipts and studied it. "Some people don't even notice their money's gone." She laughed with disdain.

I remembered exactly what each receipt said. The amount of money in each account had made me gasp when I first saw. Viv hadn't told me not to look, so I studied each receipt intently, my eyes almost burning holes through each of them. The account balances had etched themselves in my brain—twelve million in the first, thirty million in the second, and five and a half million in the third. All three accounts had men's names on them, and each time I looked, there were so many zeros I could hardly process the actual amounts. *What was this money? Who were these people? Where did these cards come from?*

I wondered how it worked, this thing I was involved in. But of course, I shouldn't, couldn't ask Viv.

"All right then, let's try these next."

Viv took some cards out of the small bag at her feet and checked each of them quickly, as she had done last time. Once she knew the numbers, she selected three cards and handed them to me along with the PIN card.

"Same as before," she said. "Piece of cake, right?"

"Uh, not really," I said, honestly. "It's nerve-racking."

"Ha, a little nerves are good for you." Viv studied me, then chuckled. "You'll get over it soon, I promise."

Viv had some errands to run, so she offered to drive me halfway home. We went back the way we came, passing through Sancha's busy intersections, and once Viv had turned onto Setagaya-dori, she let me out and sped off.

Three whole months since Lemon burned down.

Although the four of us no longer worked together, on the surface, our lives looked the same as they always had. We ate ramen at midnight, watched TV, and sat around playing with the Tamagotchi that Momoko had stolen from her sister, Shizuka, and the whole time we laughed and exclaimed, "We don't have any money!" "Nope, we don't! What are we going to do?"

There was no word from Jin-ji either. There were things we were supposed to know, supposed to want to know—what happened with the building where Lemon used to be? En was probably out of the hospital by now, so how was she doing? But I had a feeling that those questions were losing patience with us, that they were leaving us further and further behind. On the other hand, we tacitly shared a vague, baseless conviction that we had to stay here, living together in this house.

We might not have had profits from Lemon anymore, but we still had rent and bills to pay. Ran had plenty of complaints about her new job at the cabaret club, but she still paid her share on time, and Momoko did, too, from money she got from her parents or grandmother. I didn't know where Kimiko was getting her money, but she had given me ¥70,000 twice in the past three months, which I set aside for the rent. Whenever we went out for necessities or food from the supermarket, we divided the costs as evenly as we could, and when I went out alone to buy things for the house, I paid out of my own savings. On the surface, we were holding it together somehow. But I knew it wouldn't last long. Kimiko's payments were irregular, and the situation wasn't much better with Momoko and Ran. Whenever I started to feel like we were doing all right, though, the conversation I once had with En came back to haunt me and pull me down to the depths of despair again. Because the truth of what En said hadn't changed: Everyone gets old, and getting old means you need money, and if you get hurt or get sick, that's it. Nobody's gonna come and save you, there's no security in this life, just misery. And thinking about En made me think about Lemon, and my heart ached.

We kept on like that, day after day, until one night, toward the end of June, we were watching TV together and Momoko blurted out, "God, I can't stand my parents anymore. They're seriously driving me crazy."

Momoko managed to graduate high school, in spite of almost never going to class her entire senior year, and she'd been arguing with her mom about her future ever since. Her high school had a two-year college attached to it, and Momoko's mom had enrolled her without Momoko knowing about it. To get around Momoko's absences so she could graduate high school, her mom told the headmaster that Momoko was having some mental health problems and was unstable, so they'd put her in counseling and would have her study and send her papers from home. The counselor who'd signed off on everything was some friend of Momoko's mom, and she'd even found some college student and paid them to write Momoko's essays. Momoko couldn't believe what her mother had done and was determined to fight it out.

"But aren't colleges, like, super expensive? Isn't that a waste?" Ran asked.

"Anyone can get in, it's a school for morons. But my mom can keep her pride so long as they're paying tuition. Plus, she can't stand the fact that I'm wasting my life doing nothing. She's worried I'm just gonna bum around forever and not get a real job."

"Why does she care? It's not like she's expecting you to start working so you can support her and your dad, right? I mean, they're the ones paying for you to go to college."

"It's not about money." Momoko frowned. "I told you before, my parents don't care about money."

"But isn't it kind of nice to have parents who do everything for you? Doesn't it make things easy?"

"Easy?" Momoko shot Ran an irritated look. "No way, it's not easy at all. First off, my mom's not doing it for me and my sister, she's doing it for her. All she cares about is herself. She can't bear it when her friends ask her how her daughters are, and she can't give them a decent answer."

"Can't she just say you're fine?" Ran laughed.

"Are you kidding? Of course not. Who cares if we're *fine*. It has to be something she can brag about, something that will make her friends say, 'Wow, that's *wonderful*.' Everything else is meaningless. For my mom, reputation is everything. She tells her stupid rich friends in stupid rich Karuizawa that I live in Shibuya with Grandma, that I'm too *artistic* and *sensitive* to study alongside mediocre classmates, so I'm being homeschooled with a special teacher, and that someday I might even study abroad. And she tells them that her youngest is so beautiful that TV and fashion agents scout her whenever she steps outside, but of course she'd never let her precious daughter go into the entertainment industry. That's why she never invites us out to Karuizawa. We'd destroy her lies in an instant."

"Huh . . . well, I'm sure it's hard for you, Momoko."

"Hell yeah, it's hard. Not like you could understand, Ran. Whenever I talk about this stuff, I feel like you and I are on different wavelengths. You just don't get it."

Momoko laughed and looked over at me, as if expecting me to agree with her. I met her eyes for a second, but I didn't pick up the conversation thread—I couldn't. I'd been listening to them talking, but I wasn't really paying attention—I was too busy running numbers in my head.

July was just around the corner. I'd done four rounds for Viv, and tomorrow, I was going to start my fifth. Each gig got me ¥150,000. If I did two rounds a month, that got me to ¥300,000. With four rounds, that meant I'd made ¥600,000 with Viv, and with Kimiko's extra money, that meant that even after rent, I had ¥300,000 to my name. And then there was the ¥190,000 I'd already had before I started working with Viv. (It had originally been the ¥350,000 left after I gave everything to my mom, but bills had chipped away at it.) In total, it came out to ¥490,000. That was everything I had to my name.

I hadn't told Ran or Momoko about my work with Viv. I hadn't even told Kimiko. I was worried at first that they'd be suspicious or ask what I was doing for money, but no one asked, no one even thought to ask, and no one seemed to care. I was glad I didn't have to explain myself though. After the first time I met Viv, I called Yeongsu, and I called him again a few days later, but that was the last time I'd talked to him about it. I wanted to tell him everything—but all I said was that Viv gave me a job, or at least a trial. *Yeongsu isn't involved in this, everything from here on out is between you and me.* Those were Viv's words. For his part, Yeongsu seemed to understand the rules of the game and didn't ask me any questions.

Three hundred thousand yen a month didn't feel like nearly as much as what we'd made with Lemon, but that was an illusion. Because now we didn't have Lemon's expenses or bills. Working with everyone at Lemon was fun and rewarding, but there were also times when I had to deal with mean, annoying customers. Lemon was fundamentally different from the family restaurant—the pay, the hours, the exhaustion—at the same time, even though I could hold my liquor, Lemon was uniquely draining. Plus, we were only holding our own because Kotomi brought her customers from Ginza, and I was always worried that those customers could stop at any moment, and then what would we do?

Sometimes I wound up crying in the bathroom after a customer said something awful to me. This job with Viv—if it could be called a job—came with a rush of energy, a vigor that blew away the kind of stress that had come from working at Lemon. The thought of starting a new round tomorrow, working every three days, made me tense and nervous for sure, but the intense dread I had felt in the beginning had disappeared. I noticed that my hands didn't shake in my pockets anymore. I had a purpose now, a goal. I wasn't doing this just for the sake of money or to have an easy life—I was doing this to protect my home. And to save up enough to get our Lemon back up and running. That's why I'd started this job in the first place.

Even the tiniest bar would cost at least three million to start up; five million for a more decent place. And no one in their right mind would lend me, with no ID or high school education, that much money—they'd laugh in my face. I could search the whole world and never find a place that was within my reach. Our regulars were scattered, and our business contacts vanished with Lemon in the fire. We were starting from zero—no, from less than zero. We needed money. If I didn't somehow come up with the funds, my life with Kimiko would be over.

I couldn't work for Viv forever. That would be impossible, I knew. It was only because I had a purpose and a deadline that I could do it in the first place. *All I have to do is save up enough to get Lemon back, and then I can quit and go back to my old life, to the way it used to be. This will not go on forever,* I told myself. I really believed that, wished for it with all my heart. But for us, that was never in the cards.

NINE

BUSINESS IS BOOMING

1.

"—somen noodles, bread crusts, and what else, potatoes? Boiled ones. Boiled potatoes." Viv used a pair of golden tongs to flip the meat, which was sizzling so loudly I could almost see the sound. She set a slice on my plate. "So what are yours?"

"I think mine might be somen."

We ate our yakiniku. I don't know how we wound up talking about foods we'd eaten so much we couldn't take them anymore, never wanted to eat them again.

"Me, too. I ate so much somen I thought I'd wake up one day and be noodles." Viv laughed. "No sauce even. Though if I had soy sauce, sometimes I'd use that. You?"

"I had sauce. Somen from the convenience store comes with a sauce packet."

"You kids have it so good these days. Go on, eat."

This was the second time she'd brought me to this restaurant. It was a yakiniku joint in the loosest sense of the term, like no other yakiniku I'd ever seen before. Meat, vegetables, sauces so glistening and perfect they were on a different level than ordinary food, and when I bit in, everything was so good my face went stupid, I just couldn't help it. And it wasn't only meat. They had things like uni, salmon roe, truffle eggs over rice. Each grill table was in a quiet private room, and the rooms were decorated with shelves bearing expensive-looking vases glazed in detailed patterns and highlighted with spotlights. Classical music played so softly I could only hear it when we weren't talking. Everything, from the floor to the table to the plates to the lighting, even the sound of the meat sizzling and the smoke rising, exuded cool luxury.

Viv had a glass of red wine, and I was drinking beer. A man in a black suit I recognized from the last time we were here entered the room to cook the thick slices of meat for us, but Viv told him with a smile that we were happy to do it ourselves. She made a show of saying things like, "The boss, well he's . . ." and "That new restaurant, have you . . ." and the man smiled at her and bowed in a manner I could only describe as elegant, before exiting.

Spring was long gone, and we were well into summer—after my fifth or sixth meeting with Viv, she started inviting me out to dinner sometimes. The first time had been this place. She'd said, "If you've got time after this, have dinner with me," and then she drove us to this building, which from the outside looked like a palace.

Viv pulled into a parking space, and I was surprised when a staff member from the restaurant appeared out of nowhere, greeted us, and started guiding us inside. Based on what I'd seen of Viv up till now . . . I mean, of course she had money, but her car was always covered in dust, and her clothes were always—there was no other word for it—boring. That she would eat at such an expensive restaurant like it was the most normal thing in the world seemed so out of character. I couldn't believe that *I* was eating at a place like this either.

I was already nervous from how expensive the restaurant looked, and even though I'd met Viv several times now, sitting across from her made me tense up. Platter after platter arrived, the meat so colorful it looked almost fake. Viv cooked as it came, toyed with her cell phone as the fat sizzled, and served me the finished pieces, urging me to eat. From the first bite, I knew that this was the most delicious thing I'd ever eaten in my life. The experience of the flavor was shocking, and my eyes widened as I chewed meat so perfect I didn't have words for it.

The first several seconds were pure astonishment, or maybe I was just startled and impressed, but soon my mood darkened, like someone had whipped a thick, musty curtain over me. I tried to prod at why I was upset, but I couldn't find any logical connections in the flow of my emotions until my mother's smiling face appeared before me. In my heart, a sharp clap and then a biting echo—my mother had never eaten a meal like this, would never eat a meal like this, might not even know meals like this existed in the world. Then came Kimiko's face. Suddenly, my eyes grew hot—with a start, I realized I was welling up. *Wait, not here, not now. This isn't the place. Get a grip, you're just having dinner. Think about how delicious this meat is! No, you don't even have to do that. You just have to think about chewing, like a machine. No, don't think about anything at all. Just be empty, be nothing.* But I couldn't. Everything I'd been bottling up since I started this job, all the stress and anxiety, whirled inside me like a typhoon until my tears spilled over and began streaming down my cheeks.

"Whoa, what's wrong?"

Viv was surprised. Of course she was, she'd thought we were just having dinner. I wiped my eyes with my hot towel—unbelievably, beautifully perfumed—and told her, "It's nothing. I'm sorry," over and over, shaking my head.

"This is definitely not nothing," she said teasingly.

"It's just, this meat, it's so good . . ."

"Seriously?" Viv said with a laugh. "That's clearly not it. What's wrong?"

"It's the meat, it's really good . . ."

"People don't cry over meat." She laughed and passed me her own hot towel. "Have some beer, it'll help you calm down."

"Okay. I'm sorry."

"Hurry up and drink, you're scaring me."

"Sorry."

Viv kept chuckling, and I wound up laughing, too, through my tears. Once we'd laughed ourselves out, I fanned myself with both hands and finally calmed down. I bowed and apologized again, and Viv shook her head, saying, "Seriously gave me a scare there." Someone knocked softly, and then the same man as before came in, wearing exactly the same smile. He checked over our table and grabbed the empty plates, poured Viv more wine, bowed, and exited.

We went back to eating, but soon, Viv demanded that I tell her why I'd suddenly burst into tears like that. We knew each other well enough to joke a little, but we'd never told each other about ourselves, hadn't asked either. All I knew about Viv was that she and Yeongsu were part of the same world and that she was older than Kimiko. I didn't even know her real name.

But haltingly I told her, about how I'd left home in Higashimurayama, how I lived with Kimiko and two friends, how we'd run a bar, how I'd lost my savings helping my mom, how Lemon burned up soon after. Viv sipped her wine and listened silently to my whole story. I explained how I needed money so we could reopen Lemon together, how I'd asked Yeongsu for advice, and he'd introduced me to her and to this job, and how when I'd bitten into this meat just now, it was so delicious it made me think of my mother, and I'd started crying, though I still didn't know why.

"Well, you're a bit of a strange one, aren't you," Viv said, laughing again.

"I'm strange?"

"Yes, strange. I'm a strange one, too, that's how I know," Viv said. "So you're living with Kimiko. Yeongsu hadn't told me."

"You know Kimiko?"

"I do. If you know Kimiko and Yeongsu, does that mean Kotomi's still around?"

"Yes. Kotomi has been very good to us."

"How old are all of them now?"

"I think Kotomi and Kimiko are maybe thirty-nine?"

"Time flies," Viv said with a smile, gathering her hair at her neck. "Guess that means Yeongsu's in his late thirties. He's aging like fine wine."

"I guess."

"What's Kimiko up to?"

"I'm not really sure what she's been doing since the bar burned down."

I imagined telling Viv that while Kimiko did go out sometimes, she mostly wiped down the house and cleaned. The thought of her made my heart ache.

"Is Kotomi still working the nightlife? Does she have her own business?"

"No, she works at a club in Ginza. She'd always bring her customers to Lemon."

"She's been doing that work a long time."

"Were you, um, friends with them?" I asked.

"We didn't hang out, but we did see each other from time to time, back in the day. Small world, you know? The last time I was with them all was, what year was it, '85? '86? More than ten years ago, I guess. The baccarat days."

"Baccarat days?"

"Baccarat. Have you played?"

"No." I shook my head.

"Well, maybe that's for the best," Viv said, crinkling her eyes. "Baccarat's heady."

"What do you mean?"

"Once you try it, you're hooked. All those little bets on ponies and pachinko and dice and baseball, they start to feel stupid, pointless. With baccarat, either the house wins or the player wins, that's all there is, nice and simple."

"The house wins or the player wins," I repeated.

"Right. You go to the tables, and there's lots of other players. Afternooners, evening gamblers, yakuza, self-employed, company men, hostesses, construction workers, prostitutes, people who you really can't tell what they do. They all swarm to gambling houses. That's where I met Kimiko, I think."

"Is baccarat like what Yeongsu does?"

"No, it's way more fast-paced," Viv said with a laugh. "Firecracker gambling. You buy a bunch of chips to play, right? So you bet on the banker or the player, whichever you like, then the dealer starts flipping the cards, and the closest to nine wins. That's it. If the side you bet on wins, you get double back what you bet. There's only one trick to baccarat. Whichever wins the first match of the day, banker or player, doesn't matter, you keep betting on that side. Then, it's not just double, it's four times, then six times, ten times what you originally bet. Everything goes your way. You'll think you're a genius."

"A genius?" I whispered. I wasn't sure, but I felt like genius was a word that belonged to music, art, that sort of thing. It seemed out of place here. "Is it genius to feel like everything's going exactly how you thought it should?"

"Yep. Genius."

"So you don't . . . it's not like feeling like you're god or something?"

"Nah, gods are cookin' the books. It's not like that, you feel like . . . you're on top of the world. You're still human, but bam! All at once you know everything, everything there is to know. You see reality as it is—or it's like, reality presents itself to you and unfolds before you. It's the best feeling in the world, and that? That's got to be genius, right? And the larger your bet gets, the more people will come to watch, dozens of people all around you. And once you're a genius, you can see everything. Logically, the odds are two to one, and that's always the same no matter what. Two to one, win or lose, scalp or be scalped. But once you're a genius, the odds are one to one, there's only one way forward, no matter how you look at it. Understand?"

I nodded hesitantly.

"You can win five million, ten million in a single night, and sometimes you get a winning streak for days. You stop sleeping, ha, it's impossible. A taste of genius makes playing feel amazing. Plus you can make some spending money. Wanna come try sometime?"

"Me?"

"I'm joking," Viv said with a laugh. "Anyway, that's what happens with newbies. I'm not talking about people like me. What we were after, what we saw there, it wasn't money."

"What do you mean it wasn't money?"

"Well, money is money, but what happens there, it's . . . how do I put it." Viv blinked a few times, thinking. "It's beyond money."

"Beyond money?"

"When I was twenty-eight, I bet a hundred million in a one-on-one. I gathered up my whole savings and took out loans from every single place I could find, and that was a hundred million. All for baccarat."

"A hundred million?"

"In one match. And I won."

I stared at Viv, awestruck.

"It's burned into my memory. Soldered out in perfect detail—the people in the gallery around us, their faces, what they were wearing, the men, the women, the way they gasped when I won. What happened then, that's what I mean, it was beyond money."

"You mean winning?"

"No." Viv touched the corners of her eyes, like she was trying to remember something. "Gambling is always win or lose. Nothing more to it. If you lose, the money disappears, and if you win, you get more money. Simple. But it's like, in the moment, at that table, money doesn't matter anymore. It's not just less important, it's utterly meaningless. In that moment, money becomes the most worthless thing in the world. Weird, right? Make no mistake, money is everything, but at the same time, it's nothing. There's nothing greater than money—you know that in your bones—but there, in that moment, what you have in your hand, that huge wad of cash, is greater than money itself. And *that's* your world. When you take that bundle of bills in hand, you can feel it. It throbs in you, the only thing you can feel—I'm not explaining it well, but that's what it feels like.

"And sure there are people who go deep into debt and sink, people who make themselves a nice rope necklace, people who get offed. One after another, bang, bang, they die for money. But death is one thing, you know, and money's not the cause. Not the cause of death, I mean. You don't die because you lose at baccarat and you can't pay up. That's not what kills you."

Viv slumped down, crossed her arms, and went silent. I waited for her to continue.

"The ones who play for fun, for a little spending money, they're different, but serious gamblers, the ones who play for genius, they've been dying little by little from the start."

"What do you mean?"

"Like they're killing themselves one bet at a time. On the outside, they wear clothes, eat food, live their lives. They look normal enough. But they're making themselves die one breath at a time. Beat by beat, they keep on dying. Those are the ones who come to play for real, the ones trying to go to a place that's beyond money."

I turned Viv's words over in my mind, trying to understand.

"Hah. What am I saying. Even I don't know."

"Wait." I adjusted my posture and looked at Viv. "What you said, 'trying to go to a place that's beyond money . . .'"

"Yeah?"

"When you get there, you feel better about dying little by little, or you figure out a way to not die?"

"No, you've got it backwards. It's horrible, living while you're dying. Sometimes you just want things to be black and white. See, serious baccarat players, sooner or later they find a way to die a perfect death."

"But you . . ."

"Me?" Viv said with a smile. "What does it look like to you? Do I look like I'm living?"

"You do."

"Hmm." Viv grinned. "Anyway, I've been going on and on about stuff that doesn't even matter. Baccarat or not, we all die, no matter what. We have different words for it—an accident, illness, natural causes—but it's the same as being killed somewhere along the way. Don't you think?"

Again, there was a knock, and a different man in a white uniform came in bearing a fresh grill plate.

I'd seen waiters at yakiniku joints change out a charred grill plenty of times, but what this man did looked nothing like those other restaurants. The polished grill plate he held in his hand looked like some Roman shield, and the way he set it into place was almost ceremonial. When he finished, the other man returned, poured Viv more wine, and asked me if I'd like another beer. I said I would, and he bowed again, a perfect bow. I put a slice of beef in my mouth, slowly chewed, and swallowed. A few minutes later, he came back with a sparkling amber beer. Once I'd had a sip, I asked, "Do you still play, Viv?"

"No, I quit," Viv said. "Well, not quit. It's just that I'd stopped feeling anything. I didn't care anymore."

"All of a sudden?"

"I'm not sure—I think it must have been just after that big win."

"What happened after that??"

"Well, this," Viv laughed. "No dough, no scams, stuck on the outs. In time, everything changed, the way money moved, who moved it, the people, the turf—so now I run credit cards, just an old biddy scrounging around earning chump change."

"But what about the hundred million?"

"Ha! That didn't last a month. Gambling halls don't let you leave with the money you've won. They eat it back up in your next bet, and that's that. The house always wins. The players always lose."

I silently drank my beer.

After a pause, Viv said, "About your bar. Are you getting the start-up money by yourself?"

"Yes."

"Why?"

"What do you mean why?" I asked reflexively.

"What about Kimiko and those friends you're living with?"

I didn't know what to say.

Why *was* I doing it? Why was I trying to get the funds to start up Lemon on my own, when all of us would be working there? It wasn't like Ran or Momoko or Kimiko had asked me to get the money, or like we'd put our heads together and made a plan. I just wanted to keep living with Kimiko, to protect our home, those were the things I wanted, that meant I had to be the one to get the money. But even knowing this, I started to feel anxious, unsure.

"Hey, don't think too hard about it," Viv said, chuckling. "In this world, the people who can do everything end up doing everything, so there's no point in dwelling on it. It's a waste of time. Smart people are the ones who end up working their asses off. But that's okay."

"It's okay?"

"I'm not saying it's a good thing. I'm saying it can't be helped. It sure beats being a moron who can't take care of herself. Idiots might be happy, but they're still idiots. Is that what you want?"

"I don't know. I don't know what happiness feels like."

"There are happy people out there, for sure. But they're not happy because they have money or a job. They're happy because they don't think," Viv said. "You can use your brain, Hana, right? So that's okay. That's enough. Just use your head and earn money. If you live a normal life, and don't get into that gambling shit, then money is the easiest form of power. That's not a bad thing. When you rack your brains and work your body and finally get your hard-earned cash, you understand how stupid and disgusting those jerks are, the ones born with money who never had to suffer for it. So you're better off."

I looked down at my hot towel, at the dents left by my eyes and nose.

"Have you told Kimiko about what you do for me?" Viv looked straight at me.

"No. I haven't told anyone."

"Not even your happy, cheeky little friends?"

"No. No one."

Viv held my eyes as she raised her wine and sipped. We gazed at each other in silence. In the background, I could hear a soft, familiar piano tune.

"You're making, what, three hundred thousand a month now? Not enough, right?"

I nodded.

"So make more." Viv laughed loudly, looking pleased with herself. Maybe it was a trick of the light, but the gap between her front teeth looked somehow wider.

2.

Viv and I started meeting up regularly when she came to collect money, and sometimes even when she wasn't collecting. She started giving me more details about what she did—all about her "waning fortunes" and how her old friends and business partners split ass (this apparently meant left town). She always made her stories funny, with a lot of jokes, but I never knew if I should laugh or not.

Viv had a lot of channels for making money.

She also ran a few businesses, but I couldn't work out if they were real places or just fronts. Sometimes I overheard her talking money on the phone with people she called chief.

I often heard her talk about locksmiths and roofers, too. I figured that she must be letting someone from that world, the underworld, use one of her places, or maybe letting them keep something there, but mostly what Viv told me about had to do with the cards. Things that were directly connected to my job.

I was using forged debit cards to withdraw the money I gave

to Viv. But those cards felt real, just like I'd thought when I first held them—in the realm of forgeries, they were the best of the best.

"When it comes to forgeries, you've got the whole gamut, right. Cream of the crop on down to the dregs. I'm handing you the cream. I change up who's doing the withdrawing and where they do it, just in case, but those cards are durable, the good shit."

"The good shit?"

"Mm-hmm."

"What makes a card not good?" I asked.

"Well, recently most of the shitty ones are from China. You put info in a blank, use it once, and then toss it."

"A blank?"

"A blank card. It's empty, just the magnetic strip. A fresh piece of plastic with no information on it. You put in the stolen info, and you usually use cheap info, too, data you can't trace. A shit ton, whatever you can get. But if you're not careful, you'll get caught, just like that. Plus, with blanks, you end up with a bunch of flagged cards—the ones already reported missing and stolen. And of course, blank cards are getting expensive, so some daredevils are using karaoke cards or hospital cards for scams instead. They're the same size and thickness, so why not?"

"Karaoke cards? Wow."

"I've even seen cards from a yakiniku joint. You put in the data and slap on the magnetic strip. And then just like magic, those cards are someone's debit card or credit card."

"What's the difference between a debit card and a credit card?"

"What, you don't know?" Viv frowned down at me.

"I mean, sort of, but how are they related?"

"So a debit card lets someone access money they've put in the bank, right? Like a key to a lockbox. But a credit card you can use to buy stuff, even if you don't have the dough. Some even let you withdraw cash, depending on the contract—meaning, you can borrow money. All the money you put on credit gets added up, and they send you a bill a month later."

"Can you get as much money as you want?"

"Depends on the person. I mean, not just anyone can get a credit card. The credit card company looks into you—how many years you've worked and where, how much you have in savings and income, how much rent you pay, how long you've lived wherever you're living, if you have loans, if you have family. If the company decides you'll be able to pay back what you borrow, then they give you a card."

"So it depends on income?"

"Right. Most cards give you a starting line of three hundred thousand, and if you use it a lot and always pay it off on time, after a while, the company will give you a bigger credit line. Five hundred thousand, a million, probably three million at most. If they think you won't flake out on them, they start asking if the rest of your family wants credit cards, too. Credit card companies always want more customers."

"How do the companies make money?" I asked.

"Oh, through fees," Viv said, tilting her head. "You really don't know anything about credit cards, do you."

"Sorry."

"It's all good." Viv nodded. "So for example, say you have a credit card and you use it to buy something somewhere."

"Okay."

"You pay with the card at the store. The amount you used gets sent to the credit card company. Then the company pays the store. Whatever you paid minus a fee. Then you pay the credit card company after. The credit card company is the middleman between you and the store. Did people pay with credit cards at your bar?"

"Oh." I blinked. "Yeah, they did."

"So you get it."

"Well, no."

Sure, there had been a few customers at Lemon who paid their bill with a credit card. Now that I was thinking about it, one of the big landowner guys once told me his family made him use one. "My son's wife, she's a shrew, she wants to keep tabs on how much money I'm using and where," he'd told me with a pained smile. And the powerful customers Kotomi had brought, a lot of them used credit cards. But Kimiko was always the one who handled cards and ran them through the machine. It had been that way from the start, so I never needed to know anything about them, and only a few customers paid with a card anyway. If a customer told me they were using a card, I took it and handed it to Kimiko. Then she'd take down a rectangular machine from the shelf next to the register, run the card, and do whatever she did. The customer would sign a receipt, and then we'd give them back the card and another receipt, and that was that. Come to think of it, the customers who paid by card, especially Kotomi's customers, always spent a huge amount, and sooner or later, Yeongsu would stop by and give us their payments in cash, and that cash got added to the take later. I remembered him and Kimiko talking sometimes about picking up the cash payments from the bank.

"People could pay by card at the bar, but I never used the machine. It always made this huge 'klunk' noise, so after a while, we started calling it klunk. 'Just klunk it.'"

"That's an imprinter."

"I never used it."

"Most machines now, you just run the magnetic strip, but the principle's the same," Viv said. "Up until now, my job's been easy, but it's going to get more difficult. In a couple years, every store will have a CAT, credit cards and debit cards will merge, and it'll take more work to read the data. But that doesn't even matter, because you know how everyone's got those computers now? Apparently, people will start using those, and we wouldn't even use physical cards anymore. Then all the young, sharp crooks will take off, and our glorious age will end, ha!"

"What's a cat?"

"A CAT system. Places that accept credit cards either have CATs or they don't," Viv said. "With CATs, when they run your card, the information goes straight to the credit card company. The company and the shop have a direct connection. So if you use a flagged card, they know right away. But shops that don't have CATs aren't connected, so it usually takes about a month for the credit card company to get the information because everything happens by mail. So you get about a month before the card gets flagged. That's a good chunk of time to make money."

I nodded, organizing the information she'd given me in my head.

"I don't usually use flagged cards, though, so it doesn't much matter to me if a place has a CAT. But you know, the places that don't have them, they're precious, especially department stores. You can make a lot that way, so long as you have the people and the legs. But that requires endurance. Because you have to be able to run, literally. I don't have legs anymore, so I don't do that. Like *Attack No. 1*."

"*Attack No. 1*?"

"You know it? It's an anime."

"I've never seen it, but I've heard of it. It's about volleyball, right?"

"Right. So I'm the coach. The young, strong people who need money are my players. I make them run, they sweat, and they earn. It's all about teamwork."

"You work in teams?"

"Of course."

I turned it over in my head—*teamwork, Attack No. 1*.

"Right now, I've got my people working alone, but there are times when it's better to have teams. Anyway, what I'm saying is that cards are convenient. You can use them a lot of ways. We made a killing on forged telephone cards, and prepaid pachinko cards were moneymakers for a while. You could get all the balls and coins you needed and then turn them into cash, which was great. Seriously, if you teamed up with a good player, you could put a pachinko parlor out of business just like that. Oh, and another thing guys did was fish white-collar girls, get her to take out a bunch of credit cards in her name. You'd get her to do whatever, buy stuff, max out her cards, and when they were done, they'd have her declare bankruptcy. Another popular one is to report a card stolen or missing and then hand it over to an accomplice and have them use it as much as they can until it stops working. You get about a month with those."

"Do the card owners not have to pay?"

"Of course not. They filed the card stolen, right, and no one can prove they were using the card themselves. And the stores that get hit are technically victims, so the credit card companies still have to pay them. Every last yen. The card companies have these fat insurance policies, so they never take any damages either. And the insurance companies? Well, they cheat people all the time—making insane amounts of money year in and year out, telling people they're going to die or get sick or get in accidents—so they're just fine. The money goes around and around, and everyone comes out on top."

"Um, what I'm using, the forged cards, they're debit cards, right? Not credit cards?"

"Right. Only the best."

"What do you mean by best?"

"I mean they're basically real. Sure, they're fakes, but they're more or less the same as real ones. They're clones. Do you know what that means?"

"No."

"So the clone is connected to some guy's bank account, and he keeps all his money there, but he's still got his own debit card. Nothing's been stolen, except his information. You put the stolen information on the clone. One card becomes two cards, but the second card's a copy. Think about a telephone, there's a main line and a second line, right? Well, not exactly, but close enough. The card is made to look like the real thing. Of course there are flaws, but nothing that would make anyone at an ATM take a second look, and security cameras sure can't tell."

"I was thinking they were real."

"Sometimes the card and its data are two different things, the names and numbers are different from what's inside. But the cards you're using, they're clones. They're embossed with Roman letters, right? Those names are real. Now, some people are making fakes with their runners' names. Just on the off chance someone asks to see their ID, it'll match. So it's all good that way. Credit card fraud is one of those crimes where they have to catch you in the act, so the most important thing is to get away with it in the moment."

I nodded, impressed.

"Anyway, it doesn't matter if it's a credit card or a debit card. Even if the wrapping is a lie, the data is real. There's no difference between you and the actual owner making a withdrawal. Like sticking a straw in their savings and slurping it up. It's my favorite method."

"But then," I said slowly, "they're gradually losing money from their accounts, right? Don't they notice?"

"That's the thing about top-of-the-line cards. The data is expensive."

"What do you mean?"

"Well, basically the data belongs to doddering geezers who don't think about their account balances or keep close track, 'cause they're filthy rich, and senile, too. They've been carefully selected, and we know exactly who they are. That's the data we use to make the cards."

"And those people, don't they get in trouble?"

"Why would they?"

"Well, their money disappears, right?"

"So?" Viv replied immediately. "Why would they be in trouble?"

"I don't know, I mean they probably worked hard and . . . saved for years."

"Fuck no," Viv said with a laugh. "Listen. The kind of rich

people who don't even know how much money they have in their accounts, the kind of rich morons who don't even notice their money's disappearing, they've never had to work hard for it. They don't need to work hard for it. There's no real reason they're rich."

"Really?"

"Really. If you use your brain and body to earn cash, then you give a shit about your money. You care just as much as poor people. But people who are protected by their family's money, their parents' money, their ancestors' money, there's no reason why they should have it. They've never worked hard once their whole lives. You've been breaking your back to make money since you were a kid, right? So was there any reason you should have been poor, that you should have no money? Was there?"

I didn't know what to say.

"Of course not. There's no reason you were born poor. This is the same. Some people are rich because they were born that way. And those stupid fuckers, they make systems so they can keep having their stupid money, and it just goes on and on. They make their fucking systems, make them stronger and stronger, so that from their parents' generation, their granny and grampy's generation on down the line, they never have to suffer, and they never have to be scared. They can just keep sipping that cool, sweet nectar. All for their fucking selves. You think you've got nothing to do with some rich person over there, with all their money, right?" Viv caught my gaze. "But you know what, there's only so much cash out there. If the rich have the money, that means you'll never get it. Ever. It's simple. Rich people die rich and poor people die poor because that's the way those fuckers want it. People with money make the rules to help themselves, and poor people get sucked dry. And when you're all dried up, when you're nothing but dregs, they make you think it was *your* fault you failed at life. They make it sound like you had a chance. Well, fuck that. We get wrung out by the system, and all we are, all we can ever be, are dregs."

I hummed, trying to process everything.

"Money is power, and poverty is violence," Viv said. "Poor people are beat down from the start, which means they don't even know they're being beaten. They're trampled and brutalized until their minds and bodies are wrecked. They're raised to believe that's just the way things are. That's why they don't know anything. But you still get hungry, right? And if you're hungry, you need food. To get food, you need money. And what do you do to get money? Do you work? Where? How?"

Viv smiled and flashed her gap teeth.

"Those are *their* rules. It's got nothing to do with me. Nothing to do with you either. So you don't ever have to think about rich people's money. All you have to do is imagine how fucking stupid they are. Just keep on taking. Their money is different than ours. Think of it as data. Because that's what it is."

"How do you find a rich person's data?"

"You work together." Viv grinned. "Former insurance brokers, former bank employees, former securities brokers, former real estate agents, tax advisors and accountants, people who worked for credit card companies. And of course, the lovers—hostesses, mistresses, sometimes even members of the family. With these old rich men, there's always someone in their pocket, someone at their expensive retirement home or the golf club or in Ginza, who's willing to sell their data, so that's where we buy it. And that data includes their family tree, their hobbies and personalities, estimates of their assets, and reports on their fucking stupid lives—that all comes with their personal information and PIN. That's why it's so expensive."

"But how do you steal the data you put in the magnetic tape?"

"Skimmers. They look exactly like normal bank terminals. There's a channel and everything, so you just run the card through. Doesn't take more than three seconds. Once you've got enough information in the skimmer, you take the whole thing to a vendor overseas. You pay them money, and after a while, you get back the clones."

"What about the PINs?"

"You get those, too. It's easy if you're there when they make a withdrawal. But ninety percent of people use their birthdays. Or they'll write it somewhere easy to find, a little notebook or something. Hell, some operators even take them to the bank to make a new account. Lonely old geezers are so ready to trust anyone who'll spend time with them, and the banks usually don't bother to investigate as long as you have a bank card and a personal seal. They're happy to trust their finances to someone else, it makes them feel good. Like they're too good to handle their own money. Especially the ones out in the countryside, those guys are real idiots, a dime a dozen." Viv smiled. "That's why there are so many different kinds of cards. But it's only a matter of time until clones go out of style. Like I said, computers are the future. You'll never have to leave your house to go shopping. Can you believe? Your card info travels over the computer. Ha! I can't keep up. I can't even imagine. Plus, once the government passed the anti-cri, the scene completely changed, these dumbasses are popping up all over the place."

"Anti-cri?"

"The anti-gang something something law—whatever it's called. Laws to put pressure on the yakuza. Land sharking, protection rackets, shakedowns, fronts—the things the yakuza used their power to do have gotten harder."

"Is that a bad thing?"

"Who knows? Maybe normal people feel relieved, but in the long run, I think it'll strangle the city." Viv whistled through the gap in her teeth. "Make no mistake, yakuza are not nice people. I hate 'em. They always make things harder, and they're *so* loud. The way they order people around pisses me off. But with the yakuza, at least you know who you're dealing with. The cops know who they are, everyone does. Plus, they're a family right—so the Oyabun takes responsibility if anything happens. The moment a kid takes the pledge, raises his cup, and puts on the family crest, he swears absolute obedience to the

Oyabun. They have rules, they're a real organization. No matter how big and powerful the yakuza family, they've got discipline, everyone knows who hits the brakes, outsiders and insiders alike. But after the anti-cri, their sources of income dried up, they've been slapped with fines, cornered, pushing money around got more difficult, and people disappeared. They got weaker. Then came the motorcycle gangs, and the strongest Chinese triads, too—they all sensed an opening. They've got a lot of young, impulsive guys who have nothing to lose and no one to protect. Those guys'll do anything. If the yakuza have a strict vertical hierarchy, then the triads are all lateral. They stretch out and out, and they're carving up the territories and the dough. Like you wouldn't believe. At least with the yakuza, if they're trying to steal rival territory or if there's a shoot-out or someone makes a mistake, everyone knows exactly who did what, but with the triads, you have no idea who's giving orders to who, or even if there are orders to begin with. It's all invisible. You can't figure out who's tied to who, who's in or out, it's all loosey-goosey. It's a pain, not being able to know who you're facing.

"That's why I always say I'm on the outs, because of stuff like this. Those foolproof debit cards you're using right now, my favorite thoroughbreds, they're probably on the way out soon, too. There are always booms and busts. Computers are the next thing, so computer scammers are the hottest commodity now. Soon the world will be run by nameless, faceless crooks. Take the loan shark, for example. With the yakuza, even if they were the worst of the worst, even if they charged a ten-fifty interest, at least they actually lent you the money. But soon, it's gonna be swarms of rats who force you to give money you don't owe to places you don't owe. They won't even bother forging cards. It'll probably be more direct, more damaging," Viv sneered. "So we have to get money while we can. Because the world changes just like that."

. . .

August was almost over. Every day was blistering, and no matter where you looked, summer was in the air, but that year, summer didn't feel like it had always felt. Huge white clouds filled perfect blue skies, cicada song screamed over every surface, and from time to time, wind gusted through, ripe with the sun's heat. And I sweated my way across the city. But a deep dark canal had carved its way between my sense of self and my sense of summer, and though it was silent, I could sense something flowing violently through it. But I had no way to look down and see what exactly that something was.

Viv started giving me more cards.

My monthly take of three hundred thousand doubled. I started switching out the hats I wore when I went around to the ATMs, and I always wore a yellow hairband on my wrist for good luck (though it was hidden inside the sleeve of my hoodie). I'd climb on the train and go to parts of the city I didn't know, blazing trails to new ATMs. No matter the neighborhood, there was always a bank, and there was always an ATM. Just like there were always vending machines and houses and parking lots.

Each ATM was filled with cash. How much was inside them? I wondered. I couldn't even imagine. It seemed strange to me, knowing that each ATM was chock-full of money. And it was amazing, too, that people came one after another to withdraw that money. Inside the machine, that money didn't belong to anyone, but the instant it was withdrawn, it became someone's property. Well, maybe not. Because even if a person put that money in their wallet, it wasn't long before it went off somewhere else.

So what did it mean for money to become someone's, to become yours? If you bought something, that thing became yours, but I sensed this was different with cash. Money is only ever moving. Here, there, from someone to someone, from somewhere to somewhere. Maybe the true form of money is movement. And when you needed money, it was only ever moving through you—my thoughts wandered incoherently as I walked through the oppressive late-summer heat from one ATM to the next, withdrawing cash and stuffing it in my purse.

From my monthly earnings, I took only enough for rent, utilities, and food and saved the rest of what I made in the navy box in the attic. In that murky space, the money waited. When no one was around, I'd hold it softly in both hands, feeling it, its weight, and when I wasn't holding it, it waited within me, invisible as numbers. No matter how often I looked at it, my money never moved. Its stillness calmed me. The thought of it unshrinking, unmoving, here, secret from everybody, working silently toward my goal, made something within me loosen. If I could just keep on saving like this—if I could keep going, four hundred thousand to the box every month, in a year I'd have some breathing room, and I could start working toward reopening Lemon. Every morning, I held and wiped down every object in the Yellow Corner and prayed to them that everything would somehow turn out okay.

One day, coming home from a meeting with Viv, I bumped into Kimiko on her way out. We were living in the same house, so maybe "bumped into" is the wrong phrase, but it felt right somehow. Her billowing black hair formed a cloud on either side of her face, and she wasn't wearing makeup—she looked the same as always, but I could tell she was flustered.

"Kimiko, what's wrong?"

"Hana." Kimiko blinked several times, as though she was surprised to see me. She pushed open the gate, came down the steps, met my gaze, and took a breath. "Hana, Kotomi is hurt."

"What?"

"I'm going to see her."

"Kimiko, wait."

"What?" Even though she was dashing off, her expression when she looked back at me was somehow vacant.

"Just wait," I said, running after her. "What's happened? How did she get hurt? An accident? Did someone call?"

"She called me."

"So what happened?"

"He hit her. He finally left her alone today, so she was able to call me."

"He who?" I was shocked.

"A guy, you know." Kimiko put her thumb straight up.

"What guy? What are you doing with your hand?"

"This."

"Yeah, but what is that?"

"A guy, a guy, anyway, I'm going."

With that, Kimiko headed toward the station. "Call me if anything happens," I yelled after her. Kimiko nodded, rounded the corner, and disappeared.

I stood motionless in front of the house. Two minutes, three minutes, I don't know how long I was there. When I came back to myself, I was staring at a dog bounding toward me from across the street. It was a midsize brown dog with a collar a little darker than its fur, and it took me a moment to realize an older woman was walking it, leash in hand. After they passed by and disappeared, I shook my head and went inside.

Kotomi was hurt. As I took off my sneakers in the entryway, I replayed everything Kimiko had said. She was hurt, and when she was finally alone, she'd called Kimiko. A guy had hurt her. Who was this guy, and why had he hit Kotomi? How badly was she hurt? Was she okay? Was the guy her boyfriend? Her man? Or maybe he was yakuza. Or a customer. If he was, maybe he'd come to Lemon. I remembered the necktie and leather shoes I'd seen when we went to her housewarming party. The shoes had been black and glossy, like they were covered in a layer of wet lacquer. The necktie was a dark shade of blue. In my head, my questions and worries and fears warred with the image of those shoes and tie.

Did Yeongsu know anything? Maybe I should call him. I hadn't seen him in quite a while. Only once since I'd started working for Viv—the four of us had been having dinner at an izakaya, and he'd stopped by and chatted with us for a bit, and that was it. He'd looked tired at the time, which bothered me. I wanted to talk to him about some things, about the work I was doing, but with everyone there, I ended up not saying much at all. Yeongsu had only stopped by to give Kimiko her usual envelope, and in twenty minutes he was gone.

Eventually, I realized someone else was home, and I looked up. Was it Ran or Momoko? A glance at the clock on the Yellow Corner shelf told me it was just after four in the afternoon. Momoko had said she was going to see Tommy-cat in Shibuya—it'd been a while since last she saw him. I didn't ask for details, but Momoko said he was organizing a party or something, and that's what she was going to, even though it was probably going to be boring.

I went upstairs and found Ran in the room we used mostly as a closet. Ran lay on her side with her back to me, tucked among the scattered drawers and colorful boxes, the magazines and the drying towels we never bothered to put away, the clothes we left lying whenever we undressed. The brilliant light of the setting sun filled the room. It bathed our off-white Seiyu curtains with light, making them glow until the room became the setting sun itself. A huge sunbeam cast a puddle of light at Ran's feet. Music played softly. X Japan's "Endless Rain." It made me think of Lemon—my heart ached as waves of memory washed over me. "Ran," I called.

"Hana."

Ran slowly turned over until she could see me. With the sun behind her, her face was in shadow, and her voice sounded slightly muffled.

"Were you asleep?"

"No, I was just . . . laying here."

"Kimiko just left. Apparently, Kotomi's hurt."

"What? Seriously?" She sat up, and even with her face in shadow, I could tell that she was frowning. "When?"

"She called. We won't know more until Kimiko gets back."

We fell into silence. "Endless Rain" ended, and the next song started up, but Ran hit the stop button, and the room went silent.

"I think she's probably okay. Well, I'm not really sure, but she called, so Kimiko's going to her," I said. Ran nodded a few times and then lay back down on her side.

"Are you sick, Ran? Tired?"

"No, I'm okay. I'm just . . . thinking about everything."

Ran turned her head toward me, then rested her head on her arm. I went in and sat down, leaning back against one of the boxes.

"Did something happen?"

"Yes and no. I don't know. Maybe I'm like this *because* nothing's happening. But I've been so tired lately. How about you, Hana? I feel like we haven't talked, just the two of us, in so long."

I felt that way, too, now that she'd said it. These past few months, I was always out in the afternoons, doing work for Viv, and more and more, I'd been spending my evenings with her, too. By the time I got back, Ran had already left for work, and by the time she got back, I was already asleep. And when I got up, she was still sleeping.

"It sounds like Momoko's working hard at her karaoke job. How about you, Hana? How's it going?"

"I guess . . . it's normal. I do the same thing every day."

"Yeah."

I hadn't told anyone about the cards—instead I told them I was working three days a week as a temp at a packing plant in Gotanda. I'd jotted down the information from a part-time job ad so I'd be able to answer questions if anyone asked (I'd even gone to the plant and checked out the neighborhood and the atmosphere), but Kimiko, Ran, and Momoko didn't seem particularly interested in the details, and they never asked about it. I was relieved I'd gotten by on such a weak lie, and after that, I did my best not to be in any conversations about work.

"When I think about the fact that I'll just keep on living, having days like this, I start thinking everything is impossible."

"What do you mean 'impossible'?" I asked.

"Well, I mean, when you think about the future, don't you

feel weighed down? Like, you wonder if anything will ever change. Like, so many things feel impossible, right? That's what I think." Ran smiled. "I don't know how long I can keep working at the club, but what other work could I do, right? I don't have money. I can barely do nightlife. It scares me so much there are times I freeze up. I can't go back home, and there's nobody who'll help me if I'm in trouble. I mean, my parents call asking *me* for money. They think because I'm living in Tokyo, I must be doing well. My mom has no idea. I guess they can't help it, they're flat broke. I feel like I should do something, but I can't. Not too long ago, my boss told me off. I'm not meeting my minimum quota, it's pathetic. And some of the other girls are freezing me out. They laugh at my clothes and stuff. Every place is the same. If they think you're a loser, they don't hesitate to treat you like one, and they have a ball making sure you know you're trash. But it's the only club around here."

I didn't know what to say.

"It was good when we had Lemon. I didn't know about my future then, either, and I know it burned up in a fire—but we were together. It was fun."

"It was fun," I said.

"Right? It really was. I . . . I just don't know if I can keep living like this—I mean, it sounds over the top, but I feel like I'm just going to keep getting older and nothing good is ever going to happen to me again."

"That's not true."

"You think so?" Ran smiled, forlorn. "Oh, you know how I had a boyfriend, right? The guy I was living with?"

"Yeah."

"Well, apparently, he's got a new girlfriend. I mean, I left him. Because living with him was the worst, it was suffocating. But it never felt like we actually broke up. We were still seeing each other sometimes, and I thought maybe we'd kind of keep going. But lately, he never answers the phone, so I asked him about it, and he said he met someone." Ran sighed. "It hit me harder than I thought. And the fact that it blindsided me surprised me even more. We were together a long time, and I kind of thought we'd be together no matter what, even though things had gone sour. But he's a different person now. Like he has amnesia or something. He's totally changed. He's obsessed with his new girlfriend. I don't even know him anymore, seriously."

"Oh wow."

"Yeah. So tomorrow, I'm going to get out of my phone contract and find a different company so I can get a new number, maybe a phone that has i-mode."

"Really? Maybe I'll go with you."

"Seriously? That would be nice. It's been a while since we hung out together."

We started reminiscing about Lemon. Our stories went on and on—about the time a customer did this, or the other time when we all got drunk and Momoko did that. Before we knew it, the room had darkened from golden twilight to pale blue, the contours of things somehow more substantial than they had been before.

"Hey, what about En? I wonder how she is. Do you think she's gotten better?" Ran asked.

"We wanted to go see her, but she said she didn't want to see us, and that was that. No calls from Jin-ji either. I keep paying the rent, though."

"The building is still ruined, charred black. I go look at it sometimes before work. Nothing's changed."

"Yeah, just a big piece of plywood over Little Heaven's door. I go look at it, too, sometimes."

"You do?" Ran said, surprised.

"Uh-huh."

"You kind of feel like you have to, right? I've been thinking about En lately."

"Me, too. I wonder how she is," I said. "I remember when she told us about that customer of hers who died, Yosshi, and she always said she was all alone in the world, no relatives or anything, so where did she end up? I wonder if she's okay."

"And . . . I couldn't believe she didn't want us to see her, right?"

"Me neither."

"At first, I thought maybe she felt bad about everything because the fire started in her restaurant, and that was why? Like she didn't think she could face us."

"Yeah."

"But then I thought maybe, well, maybe she actually hated us and that was why."

"What?"

"I think . . . En really hated us," Ran said, meeting my eyes. "I do."

"But why?"

"It took me a while to realize, but I think she hated everything. Little Heaven, the drunk customers, the booze, all of us squawking and complaining, I think she hated every last bit of it. I kinda get it. Like—and I'm speaking hypothetically here—say the fire wasn't an accident, say En started it on purpose, which I know is horrible, super scary to say, but say she did start it—I'd be glad, if she did. That's how I feel."

"You think the fire was on purpose?"

"Yeah. I think En wanted to burn it down, and if she did, then I don't know, I think I'd be happy for her."

I blinked at Ran.

"Sorry, I'm saying weird stuff. Sorry, Hana. Are you mad?"

"No, I'm not mad," I said. "It never crossed my mind. I'm surprised, is all."

"Don't mind me, I'm just saying whatever pops into my head. Sorry. But . . . that is what I think."

Silence fell on us. Beyond the window, I heard the faint gonging of a bell. I noticed it sometimes, in the evening. It wasn't a low, clear bong, like the kind you hear at a temple, but rather a clatter of repeating high tones, so maybe it was from a church or something. I didn't know how far the bell was or what direction it came from.

"Hana?"

The silence had given Ran time to perk up, and she grinned at me. "I think you're the most amazing person I've ever met."

"What? Where's this coming from?"

I'd never imagined Ran might say something like that to me. "Don't act so surprised."

"Why wouldn't I be?"

"Because you're amazing, Hana."

"I'm not." I shook my head. "Seriously, where is this coming from?"

"I've always thought so. And I wanted to tell you." Ran smiled. "You always go all in. You're the real deal."

"I'm not."

"No, you are. I feel better just looking at you. When bad things happen at the club, all I have to think is, 'Hana's here, so it'll be okay.' I know we don't have Lemon anymore, but you, you left home, you ran Lemon like clockwork, managed us, pulled us up when we were down, you even found this house for us. I lost my boyfriend, and I know my parents wouldn't take me back. If it wasn't for you, I'd be out on the streets. I think about that a lot," Ran said. "I've talked with Kimiko about it, too. She agrees, you're amazing."

"Kimiko said that?"

"Yeah. She said you've got a good head on your shoulders, that you're kind," Ran said. "Sometimes I feel like I'm just going through the motions, but when I see you, I start to feel okay again. Because you've got your shit together, and no matter what happens, I know you'll get us through it somehow. There was even that thing with your mom. So many terrible things happened to you, but you don't give up. Which is amazing. You have this strength in you. I'm a year older than you, but I feel like you're my older sister, like I can always count on you. I think that's what having an older sister is like, anyway. So long as you're here, everything will be okay."

I didn't say anything, couldn't say anything, but Ran's words moved me. So much so I could almost hear it. True, bad things had happened to me, and even now, I was filled with a kind of loneliness and anxiety I couldn't tell my friends about. I was in over my head. But Ran saw me. Really saw me. She knew how hard I was working. And not just Ran. Kimiko saw me, too. My heart was singing, my eyes hot.

"Thank you, Ran, for saying that."

"Of course. But I'm not saying it just to make you feel good, Hana. I'm serious." Ran smiled. "But I'm glad it made you feel good."

"I feel the same." I scratched the side of my nose, embarrassed. "It's only because I have you guys that I can do any of this. I want us to keep going like this forever, and I've got goals to make sure we do."

"What goals?"

"Well, reopening Lemon, of course. So we can work there together again," I said. "I want to work with you guys."

"Oh, Hana . . ." Ran's eyes were shining. "It feels real, when you say it like that, like we can actually do it. I know we talk about it sometimes, running the bar again. But even just getting through each day is so hard, and I don't know what we'd need to reopen, so part of me thought we could never make it happen, but when you say it, I feel like we can. You really are amazing, Hana, with you I feel like we can do anything."

"I'm not. I'm really not." Under my fingertip, I felt my nostril flare. "But I have confidence. Confidence that we can work hard enough. We did it before, so we can do it again. It'll be okay. Just leave it to me."

"Hana . . ."

Ran and I were both kneeling on the floor, facing each other, and there was so little distance between us. When we realized how close we'd gotten, we both laughed. Ran asked if I was hungry, and I said yeah, so we went down to the kitchen, but there were no leftovers in the fridge, and the ramen and snack baskets were both empty, too.

We walked to the convenience store and picked up some

karaage, salad, and onigiri, a few bento and cups of ramen, and some beer and snacks, and we carried it back home. We chatted, ate whatever we wanted from the spread, and turned on the TV, but that got boring fast, so Ran found the blue bag of video rentals we kept next to the TV stand. Neither of us were much interested in movies or books, but Momoko went to the Tsutaya in front of the station all the time to rent movies and CDs, which she watched or listened to alone in the middle of the night. She also kept a row of books and magazines she'd brought from home on a shelf in the corner of the second bedroom upstairs. They were mostly novels, manga, and magazines, but some of them had titles that gave me pause—*The Manual for a Perfect Suicide*, for example.

In the blue bag, there were three videos. Their cases and tapes were bare—no photos or anything to give you a hint of what the movies were—just the titles. *Nights of Cabiria, Reservoir Dogs, Breaking the Waves*. Ran picked out *Breaking the Waves* and said, "This one's got 'Breaking' in the title. Probably a good cry, right?" So we decided to watch it. At first, we kept talking, drinking beer, eating snacks, and laughing, but as the movie went on, we quieted down. We didn't know what the movie was, but the camera moved in a shaky, nervous way, and the characters were all—well, I was terrified for the main character, the woman being driven to madness, and before I knew it, I was sucked in, but also skeptical. I frowned at the screen, and by the halfway point, I was exasperated with the baffling plot, grimacing at parts that were too weird—the whole film kind of irritated me. And it was so long. After it finished, neither of us had words to describe the jumbled emotions and horrible aftertaste it had left us with.

The VHS player rewound the tape automatically, and when it clunked to a stop, Ran returned the tape to its case, smiled wryly, and said, "So that sucked."

And then Kimiko came home. We immediately went to the door and waited for news of Kotomi. I was relieved but also bothered to see that Kimiko didn't seem very upset. "I'm sweating buckets. Let me take a shower first," she said and headed for the bathroom. Ran and I sat restlessly in the living room until she came back.

Kimiko sat down, hair wrapped in a towel, cracked a beer, and told us what had happened to Kotomi. I understood each individual word she used, but there were moments where I couldn't follow what she was saying, and I kept having to double-check or ask questions. If I were the one telling the story, it'd go like this—Kotomi had a boyfriend named Oikawa. Well, a man she was involved with, both in terms of time and money. (This was the man Kimiko had meant when she stuck out her thumb; the thumb meant her patron.) It turned out he was a member in a gang, in the yakuza.

Oikawa was forty, maybe a few years older. He first showed up at the club in Ginza about five years ago and immediately got obsessed with Kotomi. He started coming every day, dropping insane amounts of money on her, made her the number one hostess in the club, and eventually, they ended up lovers. Oikawa was a yakuza, but he wasn't old guard, more the kind of guy who ran real estate scams for big money. His front business was boat sales, plus a bunch of booking agencies for celebrities coming from overseas. According to Kimiko, Oikawa was good looking and clean-cut, and he was powerful and charming, so Kotomi liked him a lot. Their personalities meshed well, and sure they had a few fights over the years, but mostly their relationship was good.

But Oikawa started doing more and more drugs, which made him unpredictable. The drugs started to affect his work and relationships—he started jumping at shadows, causing trouble everywhere. Oikawa and Kotomi had fights from the beginning, but Kotomi was no slouch, so if he slapped her, she'd slap him right back, but these past couple of years, he kept getting worse and worse. He was convinced that everyone, including his own gang, was out to frame him, that they were already making their move. He raged how any day now, any time now, they'd come for his balls (and everything else, too), so he took more drugs, drank more booze, became terrified and violent.

The only person he could trust was Kotomi, and when he was in his right mind, he'd even tear up and tell her he was only alive because of her, that he'd leave her all his money, he'd get off the drugs and start over from square one, he'd wash his hands of everything and go legit, but then something would set him off, and he'd change completely, vent his paranoid fears to Kotomi, break things, raise hell.

Then, three days ago, he got caught up in his delusions—he convinced himself that Kotomi was informing on him to his enemies and rival yakuza, that she was screwing one of the higher-ups in his own gang, that even their first meeting had been a honeytrap—and he came at her like a heart attack. He took her phone, and when she tried to take it back to call work, they got into a scuffle. Kotomi's elbow found its way to Oikawa's eye, and he lost it, kicked Kotomi in the stomach and punched her in the face, up one side and down the other, and then for two whole days, he locked her inside the apartment and wouldn't let her out of his sight. Finally, he calmed down and left for Kyoto, a work trip planned well in advance. He would be gone for two days, so after he left, Kotomi called Kimiko.

"Shouldn't she run?" My voice was quavering. "Shouldn't Kotomi run? How bad is she hurt?"

"A split lip and two black eyes. I'm glad it wasn't that bad."

"Wasn't that bad?" I repeated. "You think that wasn't bad?"

"That's what I said."

"Hold on. That's definitely bad, Kimiko. What are you saying?"

"I'm saying her injuries aren't that bad." Kimiko looked at me, puzzled, like she had no idea what I was asking.

"I'm not talking about her injuries here," I said, shocked at Kimiko's response. I pressed on. "That's not the real problem, is it? Because this is bad, right? I mean, why . . . is Kotomi home right now? Because if she is, won't that Oikawa guy just do the same thing all over again when he comes back? You should have brought her here. Why did you come back without her?"

Kimiko stared at me for a long moment and finally said, "What?" There was no feeling in her voice, her tone completely robotic, but her eyes burned with an unfamiliar menace that lanced straight through me. I scooted back from her, and not knowing what else to say, I shut up.

Still, she glared at me. I dropped my gaze to my lap and licked my lips repeatedly. Had I made her angry, said something wrong, something I shouldn't have? I'd never seen Kimiko like this before, never sensed this kind of indescribable tension in her. Instinctively, I clenched my fists.

Eventually, Kimiko stood and went into the bathroom, and I heard her start up the hair dryer. Its mechanical droning drew an invisible circle around me, and I could feel it slowly shrinking, hounding me. Ran and I were silent. I could feel my own trembling with each slow exhale.

"Did you guys eat?" Kimiko asked when she came back, as though nothing had happened. My heart was pounding, and my head was filled with Kotomi, and I couldn't answer. I glanced at Ran and our eyes met. She looked frightened, uneasy.

"Wanna go for yakiniku?"

"No, thanks though. We already ate."

"Okay."

The three of us watched TV in silence. There was a variety show on, but I didn't process any of it. More than anything I wanted to make an excuse to go upstairs, but something kept me from speaking. Kimiko laughed at the TV. Her laugh was loud and full, like she couldn't help herself because it was too funny. She turned a grin on me, her old self again. Seeing her, I dropped my shoulders from where they'd hunched. I looked at Ran. She nodded slightly, as if she, too, had sensed the change. The TV switched to the weather report, so Kimiko started flipping through channels and said, "Kotomi wanted to see you guys."

"I'd like to see her, too," I said. "It's been a while."

"It has, hasn't it," Kimiko said.

"Remember how we used to go out to eat together all the time?"

"Karaoke, too," Ran added. "What did she like to sing, again?"

"I don't think she did sing," I said. "She said she wasn't good at it, and she wouldn't let us hear."

"Oh yeah. But if we're talking karaoke, it has to be Momoko, right? She told me she's been singing in the karaoke booths during her breaks at work. I suppose anybody would if they had a voice like hers."

"Where is Momoko, anyway?" Kimiko asked.

"She said she was going to a party."

From there, we were back to our usual selves, joking, laughing, drinking beer, eating snacks. I looked at the clock—it was well past eleven. Kimiko yawned and stretched languidly. I was afraid to ask, but I couldn't help myself.

"Kimiko?"

"Yeah?" she said, rubbing the corners of her eyes.

"Should we maybe . . . tell the police? About Kotomi?"

"The police? What would we tell them?"

"You know, what happened."

Kimiko frowned at me, lines forming between her eyebrows. "You mean tell them Oikawa beat her?"

"Yeah," I said, nodding.

"Come on," Kimiko said, shaking her head and laughing like she couldn't believe I was bringing this up again. "What do you think the cops would do?"

"I don't, I don't know, but—"

"There are no cops. Not for us."

"But aren't you afraid he'll beat Kotomi again? I don't know, maybe they could do something with that Oikawa guy so he couldn't get her, or—"

"There are no cops for me, no cops for Kotomi."

"But—" I persisted, and Kimiko interrupted me.

"There are no cops for us. If you want to talk to them so bad, you do that. But just know that if you do, it's going to get messy, especially for Kotomi. If you want to do that to her, go right on ahead."

I stared at Kimiko, wide-eyed.

"Would they arrest Kotomi?"

"They would."

"But why?"

"Why? Well, if they get him, they get her, too, they live together. That's why no cops. I mean, come on, Hana. What about you? Would *you* be okay going to the cops?"

My heart thudded in my chest. Viv's face appeared in my mind, clear as day, superimposed with Kimiko's face there in front of me.

Would I be okay? Going to the cops? Why would Kimiko say that? I looked away for a moment, and my eyes found the Yellow Corner. I tried to calm myself, but my thoughts ran me round and round. Did Kimiko know about my job? Viv said she and Kimiko weren't in contact. So had Yeongsu . . . But he didn't know the details of what I was doing. Maybe he told Kimiko that he'd put me in touch with Viv. So did she know where my money was coming from, even though I'd told her I had a factory job? If she did know, she'd never said anything about it. Why? Because she didn't care or because she didn't think it was any of her business? Was she waiting for me to say something? Or did she have a reason for keeping quiet? Or maybe she wasn't talking about the thing with Viv at all, and she was just trying to remind me I was a minor who'd skipped out on my mom. My unsettling thoughts whirled and warred in my head, and my hand found its way to my throat.

"Well, I'm going to bed," Kimiko said.

Her futon was folded neatly in one corner of the room, so she spread it out and slipped inside. She rested her head on her arm, yawned hugely, and in a sleepy voice, told us both we ought to go to bed.

At the beginning of autumn, a bunch of things happened all at once.

First, Momoko's sister, Shizuka, showed up at the house. It was the middle of September. One evening, the doorbell—I don't think anybody had ever rung it until then—chimed in the entryway. For a moment I had no idea what the bell meant or where it was coming from. Momoko was asleep upstairs, and I was downstairs with Ran, who was getting ready to go to work.

When I opened the door, I found three high schoolers, still in their school uniforms: one girl with hair dyed light brown and two boys.

"Is my sister here?"

This must be Momoko's sister. As the thought crossed my mind, I was shocked by how perfectly proportioned Shizuka's face was. Between her flawlessly parted bangs, her forehead was smooth, and her straight, cute nose crowded close to her mouth, bracketed tightly by her jawline. Her eyes were so big that they nearly took up half of her face, no exaggeration, and her huge pupils shone out at me. Her double eyelids were deep and long and lined with thick eyelashes. At the same time, her whole face was so small. I blinked at her, dazzled. But then I realized something was off. While from the neck up, Shizuka was even more beautiful than Momoko had led me to believe, her body seemed too large for that petite face of hers. Her neck, shoulders, and arms were rounded with flesh, and her school uniform was bursting at the seams, blouse straining as her breasts and stomach threatened to escape. The legs that emerged from her miniskirt were short and rocky with muscle. For a moment, I thought the boys to either side of her were tall, but then I realized that they were the same height as me. They just looked tall because Shizuka was so short. Both boys wore their uniforms in ways that were probably against school rules—one had a black hoop earring threaded through his ear, and the other wore his ochre hair tousled like steel wool. From the way Momoko described Shizuka, I'd always imagined her as a willowy, tall model, so her actual appearance surprised me.

"Do you . . . mean Momoko?"

"Yes," Shizuka said, putting her weight on one leg, jutting her jaw out, and nodding.

"Wait just a second."

I closed the door, went upstairs with Ran, and together we woke Momoko. She tried to go back to sleep, pulling her summer blanket over her head and turning away, but when we told her that Shizuka was here and was asking for her, Momoko looked at me with eyes wide open and leapt up.

"Hana, tell her I'm not here, for real, please."

"Oh no, I already said you were," I said, panicking.

Momoko groaned and pressed her hands to her forehead. "Oh god, what is she here for? What does she want?"

"I don't know. What do you want us to do?" Ran asked. "We can tell her you're not here after all?"

"I don't know."

While we debated, the doorbell rang again, and when we didn't answer, they started ringing the bell incessantly. The chime made a kind of cute tinkling sound, but as it rang on and on, the noise grew overbearing, and it started to drive me crazy. Momoko sighed, realizing she didn't have a choice, and went downstairs.

Ran and I followed her to the entryway, where we cracked the door to listen in and figure out what was going on.

"Gori, what the hell do you think you're doing?" Shizuka demanded angrily.

"What is it, Shi? Why are you here?"

"Because you don't answer your fucking phone. What the hell?"

"I, I'm not . . . I'm busy."

Momoko was nervous—it was clear Shizuka had the upper hand.

"The fuck you are. Why else would Tetsu be coming after

me, messing with me? He won't buzz off, follows me around, keeps asking, 'Where's Momoko, Where's Momoko?' So fucking call him already. Right now. Now! Why should I have to put up with that dumbass just because of you. He's fucking annoying. Like, just go and die already."

So Shizuka called Momoko "Gori" and Momoko called Shizuka "Shi." And someone was bothering Shizuka because of Momoko, and Shizuka was fed up with it.

Her rant only grew louder and more belligerent, and sometimes the boys laughed, but I couldn't make out what Momoko was saying. That worried me, so I opened the door and poked my head out. Over Momoko's shoulder, Shizuka's gaze met mine. She glared at me with her big, sharp eyes and barked, "What?" I couldn't quite figure out if she was smiling at me or threatening me, her shapely lips peeled back until I could see her teeth. Even from the doorway, I could tell that the edges of one of her front teeth were stained black, and the stain drew attention to her gap tooth. Ran poked her head out, too. Momoko turned to look at us, her expression worn down in a way I'd never seen before.

"Sorry, it's just we have plans. Why don't you call Shizuka after we're done, Momoko," I directed this to Shizuka as I urged Momoko back inside. Black Hoop Earring and Steel Wool stood behind her, grinning like idiots.

"Gori, seriously, call him. Oh, and Zucchi says he can't get ahold of you either, so call him, too. Stop screwing around already."

With that, Shizuka left, her whole body swaying back and forth between the boys on either side of her.

That day, Ran skipped work (she'd been doing that a lot lately), and we both decided to ask Momoko what was going on. She looked exhausted, crumpled in on herself as though she'd shrunk a size or two.

Long story short, Momoko was in big trouble. A high school classmate of hers had turned into a real party girl at college, going to clubs all the time, and she'd taken Momoko with her several times. But it wasn't just clubbing—she got tangled up in helping the organizers sell tickets to exclusive parties. When we asked for more details, Momoko was reluctant to say, but eventually she told us her friend had introduced her to a team that planned parties and raves, and there was a guy—he called himself Uno—and he was really nice, and well, she just, no, she totally fell for him.

Uno was twenty-six and lived in Minato-ku, and even though he was always surrounded by beautiful girls, he was still nice to Momoko and paid her a lot of attention. It was the first time a guy had ever been nice to her like that, and so she started getting involved in his party business. At first, she'd just buy a ticket for herself, even if she didn't actually go to the raves. But soon Uno started calling her, asking her to bring along friends from high school and college, telling her he wanted to hang out with her, and Momoko couldn't bring herself to tell him she didn't have any friends. She started buying more tickets, three, then five, using her grandmother's money. Uno complimented her on how popular she was, and Momoko was over the moon. Soon enough, he wanted her to help him out with work, nothing big, just help, and she went along with it. Uno introduced her to the other people he did the events with, and she started handling tickets for him sometimes. But with no friends or even acquaintances, Momoko had no way to move the tickets. She still wanted Uno to say nice things to her, she wanted him to think she was cool, so she started stealing cash from her grandmother's bank account. That was two months ago. Ten tickets became fifteen, twenty tickets became thirty, then fifty, and in the middle of it all, Momoko's grandmother got sick, so her parents started talking about whether or not to put her in a home, which meant they checked her bank account and discovered what Momoko had been doing. They took back her grandmother's bank book and debit card, and they reduced Momoko's allowance until she was just scraping by. Even then, she still wanted to see Uno—she wanted him to keep paying attention to her, and she couldn't let it go, so she ended up begging her grandmother for the cash.

Then, last month, Uno and his team told her they were doing a huge blowout event at a club in Roppongi and asked her to move a hundred tickets. One ticket was five thousand yen, so basically they were asking her for five hundred thousand. Momoko knew there was no way she could come up with cash for a hundred tickets, but she couldn't bring herself to tell Uno because he'd been so nice to her. Momoko took the stack of tickets with a smile and, not knowing what else to do, threw the whole bundle in a park trash can.

When she finished her story, Momoko glanced back and forth at Ran and me. After a moment, I asked, "So the people your sister was talking about out there, those were guys from the club?"

"Yeah. Uno's teammates. We know each other from school and stuff, so they know Shizuka's my sister. She goes in and out of the popular circles, goes to all the clubs, and she's flashy, right. I dipped out, so I think that's why they went to her."

"Can't you just keep dodging them?"

"I don't know."

"And you don't have the tickets? You threw them away?"

"Right."

"Which means you have to give them five hundred thousand? To pay for the tickets?"

"Yeah. Yeah, I think so. I think that's why they're after me."

We all exhaled in unison.

"Could you ask your grandma, or maybe your parents, to do something?"

"No way. I can't tell them."

"But don't you think they'd help—" I started to say, but suddenly Momoko let out an odd wail. Surprised, I looked at her only to see she'd grown bright red, eyes and mouth quivering, fat tears dripping down her face. In a hollow voice, she said, "Not anymore, Hana." Momoko wasn't a smiley person, but I'd never seen her this miserable, either, and I couldn't respond. Ran didn't speak either.

Once she'd had a minute to calm herself, I asked, "How did

they know where we live?" Momoko guessed that they'd seen the receipts for when she'd sent books and clothes here. That or they'd tailed her home.

I supposed it didn't matter anyway—they already knew where Momoko lived, and Shizuka might not be a real problem, but the guys Momoko had gotten mixed up with, Uno and his lot, if they came to the house themselves . . . my mood darkened. They wouldn't stop until they got their money. When we asked for the rest of the story, Momoko admitted that she'd quit her job at the karaoke joint last month. Ran asked her what she did when she told us she was at work, and she shrugged. "Usually, I just wander around Shibuya or the park or Tsutaya. Sometimes I do karaoke by myself."

I know we hardly ever see each other, I thought to myself, *but I had no idea Momoko was this low. We sleep in the same room, and still I don't know anything important happening in her life.* I had mixed feelings about the whole thing. But then again, it was the same with me. Kimiko might or might not know about my real work, but Momoko and Ran both thought I had a factory job. The fact that I was running fake cards for Viv, to the two of them, that was outside the realm of possibility. I felt ashamed and helpless. Momoko went to take a shower, and Ran and I sat and listened to the drumming of the water.

Eventually Ran said, "What was her sister's name? Shizuka?"
"Yeah."
"She was gorgeous."
"Yeah."
"But her teeth were so gross."
"They were disgusting."
"And Momoko said her room's like that, too, and her *panties*. A face like that, money like that, and she's still a total nutjob, huh. Like she's sick in the head."
"Yeah."
"And the boys were the same."
"Yeah."

"Makes me think of that trio, Dreams Come True. Oh, and their song, 'Map of the Future II'—*in hell*," she added, making a hilarious face, which relieved some of the tension.

We didn't manage to come up with an actual plan for what Momoko could do about the tickets. We were all too freaked out. But neither Shizuka nor Uno's guys came to the house, and they never called either.

The Roppongi event was supposed to be in three weeks. Maybe it wasn't as bad as Momoko imagined; maybe as far as Uno's team was concerned, a hundred wasn't that many tickets. We tried to put a lighter spin on the whole thing, but the fact that Shizuka had come all the way to the house to press Momoko meant that, no matter what we wanted to believe, the problem wasn't going to go away. It boiled down to money. We needed to do something about it.

And then we stopped being able to get ahold of Yeongsu.

I tried calling him at different times of the day, but his phone just rang and rang until it switched to voicemail. I tried texting, but I had no way of knowing if he got any of the messages. Kimiko told me he'd disappeared like this before, and it was nothing to worry about, but I was worried. And I couldn't do anything about it.

Then there were the envelopes of money—I didn't know how much Yeongsu gave Kimiko, but however much it was, that money had dried up. He'd told me it was for Kimiko's mom in prison, that she needed it to pay off her mom's debts. At the time, I hadn't thought about it much, but now it bothered me.

Every few months, Kimiko handed me fifty thousand or a million, like an afterthought, but where did that money come from? She went to Kotomi's a lot, so I'd thought maybe she was making money there somehow or other. But ever since the incident with Oikawa, Kimiko hadn't gone to Kotomi's as often. Instead, she stayed around the house, going out maybe once a week. She was either watching TV in the living room or wiping everything down with her dustcloth, and the last time she'd given me fifty thousand had been two months ago.

Kimiko didn't talk about herself much, and she didn't ask people about themselves either, so I rarely knew what she was thinking, but I began to notice a change in her demeanor. Like maybe she *knew* there was no money in this house, that there'd be no money going forward, and that even she was growing nervous about it.

About a month after we last heard from Yeongsu, Ran quit her job. She had a few reasons. Her manager had cornered her about the fact that she didn't have any regulars, and while she was welcome to sit and work alongside one of the girls who did have customers, when she did, she was bullied into drinking by the other girls and even the customers. One time she even got alcohol poisoning (Ran could really hold her liquor, so I can't imagine how much she must've drunk). Then a ¥30,000 pot of Clé de Peau Beauté foundation disappeared from one of the other girls' handbags, and people started to spread rumors that Ran was the one who stole it. She was angry and heartbroken.

We were screwed.

I was the only one earning any money. Momoko and Ran and Kimiko just watched TV or played with makeup (even though they had nowhere to go) or watched movies or slept.

When we first came to the house, we'd been so bright, so carefree, but now that spirit was dead silent. Even when Lemon burned, we were more optimistic. Ran and Momoko were lethargic and downcast as they sat watching TV. Kimiko was the same as ever, tidying every nook and cranny of the living room and wiping down the walls, but compared to before, she seemed more listless, too. Money, rent, our next actions—there was so much we needed to talk about, but we were on thin ice, and I thought that if one of us actually dared to start talking about it, everything we'd been silently balancing and holding in would burst out. And then it would be over.

My agony only grew as I watched the three of them.

That agony carried a lot inside it. I was saving the money I earned from my job with Viv not because I wanted some luxurious life for myself but because I wanted to reopen Lemon for all of us. But I was the only one with a job while the others were unemployed, which meant we all tacitly understood I was the only one bringing in any money. When we went to the supermarket or the convenience store together, Ran and Momoko could only put up chump change, so I had to pick up their slack. While I did feel bad for lying about my job, I was also torn about the rest of it. I knew none of them felt any sense of danger or urgency about the finances, and I knew there was no quick fix, but were they planning on doing *anything*? Everyone was miserable, which made it harder to talk about money, but we still had rent and utilities to pay. If push came to shove, I could pay from my secret savings, but I couldn't exactly tell them how I'd gotten that money.

Maybe they were all secretly panicked about things, but none of them ever bothered to bring up the rent. I waited for days, but still no one said anything, so finally I just said, "I'll spot you the money for this month's rent," and nothing else. They responded by shaking their heads: "Oh, you shouldn't do that." "But that's so hard on you, Hana." They acted like they cared, but not one of them asked where the money had come from. In the end they just thanked me and accepted my offer.

I was hounded by visions of being trapped, by my anxiety, by the knowledge that we couldn't go on like this, by fears about what to do next. Like when we sat together with our legs stuck under the naked kotatsu, watching TV. We didn't speak, and from the outside we probably looked normal. We were spending our time, the time where we couldn't do anything, together at home. But sitting there, I felt the bands around my chest draw tight, until I was terrified, sweat pooling in my armpits, and I couldn't sit still anymore. I became paranoid, thinking that everyone—Ran and Momoko, and Kimiko, too—they were blaming me.

"If anyone could make it work, I figured it would be you, Hana." "I was counting on you." "I thought you were amazing." "Guess I expected too much." "Ugh, really?" "You said you had this, and I believed you." "Guess not even you can fix everything, huh, Hana." "I thought you had a good head on your shoulders, that you could do anything." None of them had actually said those things, but I could hear their words surging over me all the same—I felt hunted.

Something had to be done. I had to do something. I became obsessed.

Cap pulled low over my brow, I walked from ATM to ATM in neighborhoods familiar and unfamiliar and racked my brain for a solution.

I figured that Ran and Momoko were both recharging their batteries, and once they'd shaken off the tickets and the club, they'd find part-time jobs and start bringing in money again. But how long would that take? And how long would they last at those jobs? Ran and Momoko each had flaws. Insecurities. I knew that Momoko sometimes fell to brooding, and that Ran cried in the middle of the night, though she tried to hide it from us.

But I was most worried about Kimiko. Kimiko, who could no longer get ahold of Yeongsu, whose mother was in jail, who only knew the nightlife, who couldn't quite seem to get her act together and be a real adult. I pictured the blue mark on her right hand. There she was in my mind, gripping the dustcloth, blank-faced as she wiped down the walls and plastic storage bins. Kimiko as a child, Kimiko as an adult. What if we all started working at a factory or something, started over from zero. But no, there was no way. Even if we got by this month and the next on the hundred-yen-an-hour pay, we wouldn't be able to keep it up for long. I couldn't let go of my job with Viv. I couldn't quit. And that work, too, our only lifeline, would soon disappear, I was sure. So in this moment, right now, while I still had the job, I had to earn as much as I could, no matter what—suddenly, I remembered En's words. How hard it is to live without money, how miserable. En, who always had a smile for us and basically let us eat for free. Always so kind. We'd sung, we'd laughed. I'd liked her. But maybe she'd hated me.

Maybe she'd started to hate everything, or maybe she hated

everything all along, maybe she set the fire so she could lose everything, including herself. I would never know. What I did know was that, with Lemon and Little Heaven charred ruins, I'd probably never see En again. That made me sad. So sad I started to think, *If only I'd had money, En wouldn't have had to burn Lemon and Little Heaven.*

How did people go on living? People I passed on the street, people reading newspapers in the cafés or drinking booze in the izakaya, eating ramen, going out with friends to make new memories, people coming from somewhere, going elsewhere, laughing, raging, crying, people who lived for today and would wake up and do the same tomorrow. How did they do it? I knew they had honest jobs, earned honest money. But what I didn't understand was how they'd first obtained the qualifications to live within that honesty. How had they made it to that side? I wanted someone to tell me. My nights were sleepless, filled with worry, tossing and turning, and my thoughts grew distorted, so much so that I almost called my mother. *Hi, Mom, Mom, I'm in trouble, I don't know what to do.* On the borders between dreaming and waking I spoke to her. *Hey, Mom, how did you make it this far, how did you keep going, when I was a kid, when I was really little, how did you survive, we had no money, how do people do it, how do they go on living day in and day out, I just don't understand, hey, Mom, how are you, have you been suffering this whole time? Were you scared? Hey, Mom, was it hard to keep going? Like, really, really hard? Isn't it hard, making a living, having to keep earning money, not being able to eat or pay rent or go to the hospital or even drink water because you're broke? Hey, Mom, I just don't know, I don't know what to do, and it's really hard, so hard, I don't know what to do, hey, Mom, can you hear me? Hey, Mom*—Mom stops eating her instant ramen and turns toward me, some summer day, always summer, Mom sitting on the tatami in her white heels, smiling at me, *What's this, Hana, why are you crying, don't cry, don't cry, sweetie, nothing good will come of crying.* She smiles at me again, and when I was a kid, that smile made me so happy; it made me come running home from school whenever I thought I might get to see it, *Hey now,*

Hana, don't cry, you've got to keep your head up, you'll be okay, it's you, you're smart, you can do anything, I know you'll be fine, you're not like me, Hana, I'm no good, I only cause you trouble, no good, no good, but you're different, Hana, so, so much better than I ever was, you're amazing, I'm so proud of you, I know you'll be okay, I just know it, Hana, thank you, thank you, I think about you so, so much, I promise I'll pay you back, I'll pay back every yen, I'm working so hard, and I'm so, so sorry, super sorry, things will get better, I promise, don't cry like that, Hana, I know you'll be okay no matter what, no matter what, you'll be all right, Hana, you will, everything will be okay—I pressed my face to my pillow and tried to hold back the endless flood of tears, squeezing my eyelids together so tightly they hurt. I locked off my throat so I wouldn't start wailing, so that Ran and Momoko wouldn't notice, and I repeated my mom's words over and over.

It's all right, I'm all right, I can work harder, I'll be okay, I'll just work harder—a faint round light appeared in my mind, the light from some refrigerator, from some unforgettable summer, that warm light pouring from the crack in the door, the fridge Kimiko had packed full just for me. I remembered her. I remembered Kimiko, in that tiny kitchen, the scent of garlic on her fingers, our cones of shaved ice from a festival stand, kids grilling squid, the scent of sweetly spiced smoke rising into the night air, laughing so hard I was in tears, walking, dripping sweat, our futons lined up side by side, returning my uniform to the restaurant, the billowing hot wind, Kimiko standing inside that breeze, calling my name, calling me, scrubbing Lemon, just the two of us, making it our own, our sign with the Lemon logo, *It's all right, I'm all right, I'll be okay, I can do this, I can make this work, it'll be okay, I'll protect Kimiko till the end*—I repeated until I cried myself to sleep.

The next morning, we all got up at the same time—we hadn't gotten up together in so long—and went to the convenience store, bought breakfast, and ate together. I waited for afternoon to come, and then I called Viv.

3.

I couldn't believe it, but our *Attack No. 1* went off without a hitch. Ran and Momoko were both quick studies. Their first day, we were all so nervous that not one of us spoke or ate or drank anything, but that evening, after we had ¥550,000 cash in hand, our nerves and fear transformed into excitement and pride.

"Holy shit," Momoko said, shaking her head, her face glowing. "Like, holy shit."

"I think we were at it less than three hours, right? And we got five hundred fifty thousand! Insane! Like, unbelievable!" Ran said breathlessly, unable to hide her excitement.

After our first attack run in Shibuya, we went back to Sancha and had a breather at the McDonald's in front of the station. The three of us drained our Cokes, trying to cool our excitement, and then we went silent, each recalling the day's accomplishments. Momoko had the cash. She clutched the bag in her lap, and each time someone came up to the second floor, she watched them suspiciously from the corner of her eye. "It's fine," I told her, and both of them nodded, relieved, and put their lips to their straws again.

"Wow," Momoko said, "Just wow. I didn't know. I had no idea you were doing something so amazing, Hana."

"Me neither. I had no clue."

"Yeah. I didn't mean to lie or keep you in the dark, but this job has to be top secret, so I couldn't tell you."

"I get that. Totally!" they exclaimed, still bubbling with excitement. We finally noticed our drinks were empty, and Ran went to buy us refills. Momoko kept her grip on the bag, like she was holding hands with somebody precious. Ran came back a few minutes later, and she'd even picked up some burgers, fries, and chicken nuggets for us to share. When I tried to pay her back, she grinned and said it was her treat.

"So you've been doing this job alone all this time?" Momoko asked through a mouthful of hamburger, clearly impressed.

"Yeah. The work I was doing on my own, it's not completely the same, but pretty similar. A card is a card."

"Wow. I still don't really get it, but it's amazing."

"So the person who's actually our boss, you don't know who that is, right?" Ran asked, trying to gauge my expression.

"Nope, no idea. A different person comes to the spot every time, and we just do what we have to do."

"You don't know if it's a man or a woman?" Momoko added.

"I don't."

"You don't know their age or anything, you've never met them?"

"No. Normally I just get a call. So if I get followed, I won't lead them to anything. I think that's why."

"Got it. I guess that does keep it secret, makes sure you're both protected," Ran said with a decisive nod.

"It's like, like being a spy, or being in a movie, like mysterious and so totally cool, and it's kind of scary, but kind of exciting, too. I feel like we've made it to the next level. Oh my gosh. The fact that we can earn this much money? I mean, how did you even find this job, Hana? You said it was Yeongsu?" Momoko kept talking, clearly enjoying herself. I had a feeling she was just going to keep asking questions, so I tried to hint to her that she should drop it already. Ran noticed my expression and tried to change the topic, but Momoko couldn't control herself and kept flapping her gums at a million kilometers an hour. She didn't actually want to know the *truth* behind this job, though; she was just excited that she'd made a couple hundred thousand in only a few hours. I had no sense that she wanted to know just how dangerous or safe the work was. Ran was different in that respect—she was more astute, or at least sensed this wasn't the kind of thing you just asked about. So while Ran read the air, Momoko was still totally wired, and I gave vague non-answers to Momoko's mix of stories and questions. We spent several hours sitting there in that McDonald's, high on our success.

"So when is the next time? When can we do it again?"

Momoko waited until we'd left McDonald's and were on our way home to start badgering me again, turning her sparkling eyes on me.

"We wait. They'll call and tell us when, and that's when."

"But Hana, this five hundred fifty thousand, it's not all ours, right? The boss takes a bunch? How much?"

I hadn't expected her to ask for an actual figure, and I hesitated. "That's . . . that hasn't been decided yet."

"Humph." Momoko frowned mightily. "Well that just means we've got to work harder."

"What?"

"I mean, we don't know how much we'll have after the boss's take, so if we want to make real money, we've got to do this again, the more times the better. What I'm saying is that if we work more, our take'll get bigger, right? So let's do it. Like, at first, to be honest, I was seriously scared, but it was totally fine. If it's always like this, it'll be a breeze. I'll work so hard, so so so hard. We can do it, right, Ran?"

"I guess." Ran said hesitantly, catching my eyes. Momoko had locked her arm with Ran's, and Ran staggered a little. I felt a little weird about the fact that Momoko wouldn't shut up about the job, was so happy she was acting like she'd found it herself—never mind that this was her very first day—but honestly, it had been my first attack run, too, and I was relieved it had gone well. Our approach was different from my usual gig, and I'd been nervous all day, but once it was done, I started to feel a sense of accomplishment swell within me. And I was glad Viv had given me this kind of promotion, that she believed in me enough to give me this new work.

Full dark had fallen, and it was chilly, so we huddled close together and waited for the walk light to change. The different colors each shone their own light, dancing, shrinking, and swelling before me. Following their movements, it occurred to me that on the other side of this street, just down that alley, was our Lemon, or what had been our Lemon—there in my mind, and maybe the memory of it alive in Ran's and Momoko's minds, too, but none of us mentioned it.

I called Viv two weeks before our first attack run and asked to meet with her. She listened to my whole story, and when I was done, she said, "Now it's common sense, but don't mention me. Don't involve me. This is all on you. There's no backing on this one. If you think you've still got what it takes, we'll go ahead."

"So does that mean you'll give us more cards?"

"I told you before, I only work with the best cards. I'm not just going to hand them over to help your idiot friends," Viv said with a laugh. "But I suppose I could give you some lower quality cards, some small fries. Of course, the risk goes up with those. But what you're saying is that you're in a bind 'cause you're not making enough, that's why we're here, right?"

"Yes."

"Okay then," Viv said. "But remember that this is totally separate from what you do for me. We'll keep doing our thing, got it? But for your little friends, I'll send you on a new job, a different one."

"Understood."

"You're young, but it's like I said before. *Attack No. 1*. Now you're the substitute coach, and the captain, too. Remember, teamwork is life."

I nodded firmly. *Attack No. 1*. Manga. Volleyball. Of all the things Viv told me about her past, this story, being young and working as a team, was what stood out to me the most. I didn't know what the job was yet, but I sensed that this was the only way we could survive, so I called up Viv to ask for help.

That alone had taken courage. Viv had made it clear that I was never supposed to tell anyone that I knew her, let alone that I worked for her, and I was terrified that asking her to help people she didn't even know would be the end. All the trust I'd accumulated would evaporate, Viv would cut me off, and I'd lose my only means of earning money. But I didn't have any other ideas. Resigned, I decided asking Viv was the only way. I had to try.

"I'll have the cards ready by next week. When I give them to you, I'll explain what you need to do and the conditions for your employment."

"Viv," I said, "thank you so much. Really."

"It's all good." Viv grinned, flashing the gap between her front teeth. "Although, it is work. I'm not doing this out of the goodness of my heart, so no need to thank me. Just make sure you tell your friends they need to keep their mouths shut. If they can manage that, they'll earn their living with their legs and their heads."

"Yes, ma'am."

"Well then. You know, you're . . ." Viv smiled, her tone playful and teasing. "Never mind. If it goes well, you'll make money. Good luck."

The following week, I met Viv at the designated spot and received five "small fry" cards from her. They were different from the cards I usually used at the ATMs, because they were the flagged cards Viv had told me about—stolen and missing cards, cards people sold off because they were so deep in debt they didn't know what else to do—the kind the credit card companies wouldn't hear about for a month.

I spent nearly half a day asking Viv the same questions over and over—what exactly were flagged cards, how exactly did we use them, what should we be careful of, what was the same and what was different about these cards compared to the fakes, what should we do if something went south? I asked until I was sure there was nothing I didn't know about the job. Viv grew exasperated. "If you're so worried about it, don't do it. Your eyes are all bloodshot. You look totally crazy." But I was desperate. And even if this work went okay for a while, I knew that the time was fast approaching that it would dry up—Viv told me often enough. We had to make as much money as we could while we still could. If we didn't, Kimiko, me, none of us could keep going. Viv didn't let me take notes, so I beat every single word she told me into my head one by one.

Our targets wouldn't be ATMs this time; they would be department stores. Department stores without CATs—the ones that couldn't instantly share information with the credit card companies. We'd buy gift cards from the stores and then sell them to a ticket reseller who paid in cash. But even without CATs, department stores still had rules around gift cards. If anyone tried to buy a card worth more than twenty thousand, the clerk had to call the credit card company and make sure the buyer was good for it.

So the upper limit for each gift card was fifteen thousand, which meant we had to go looking for gift cards at every counter and vendor in the department store. Beer, books, rice, restaurant vouchers, gift cards you could also use in other department stores—we did round robins with our flagged cards, until we'd each gotten gift cards from all the different counters. Once we were done with one department store, we went to the next CAT-free place and did the same thing over again. Each time we ran a card, we were terrified the clerk would think something was suspicious, but the amounts were small, and the English signatures we'd practiced over and over to sign the receipts looked real enough, and none of the clerks seemed to care. They ran everything with a businesslike flow and sold us the gift cards without a problem, without even looking at us.

The flagged cards Viv had given me had a short shelf life. We had to use them within three days, and once we'd used them, we could never use them again. We weren't allowed to throw them away, either, just in case. After our first attack run, when I went to get the next cards, I brought the whole of the five hundred fifty thousand we'd earned. Viv studied the bills in my hand for a while, just thinking, and finally said, "You keep that," taking none for herself. For a while, all the money we got from the cards was ours. I kept working the fake debit cards, and that did go to Viv. Our attack runs were steady. A lot of department stores still didn't have CATs, and we started campaigning in more distant neighborhoods, doing the same runs over and over. We felt so free, so alive, in what we were doing, like we really were in *Attack No. 1*. Our runs were just as organized and exhausting as playing volleyball in the manga would have been.

When winter began, Viv started giving us forged credit cards in addition to the flagged cards, which meant that even if a department store had a CAT, we could still safely take a run at it. These credit cards handled basically the same as the debit cards. The only real difference was whether I went to an ATM or a store. There was still the twenty-thousand-yen limit if you were buying gift cards at a department store, but unlike the flagged cards, these lasted more than three days, which gave us time for more strategy and freedom.

Viv gradually transitioned us from flagged cards to credit card forgeries, which was also when she started collecting half the take. Apparently, the market rate for runners like us was ten percent, so I think Viv was giving me special treatment, looking out for me; fifty percent was astonishing. We started handling multi-trip vouchers for the Shinkansen, too—they were worth a lot more money than the gift cards.

We took Viv's advice and wore white T-shirts, plain jackets, and black or navy skirts, and we put our hair up in ponytails—a costume designed to make us look like young women working at some drab office. We called this our uniform, and the sight of each other in those clothes doubled us up with laughter. Momoko and Ran bought a more natural chestnut hair dye at the drugstore and started wearing only light makeup for the attack runs. In uniform, we went to travel agency ticket counters and asked for fifty sets of Shinkansen tickets for Tokyo to Shin-Osaka. It was worth six hundred thousand, give or take. So long as the forgery card's limit was a million, we didn't have any problems, but sometimes we got cards with five-hundred-thousand-yen limits, or even three hundred thousand. With those, we had to be careful never to overcharge, because if we did, we had to pay what was left in cash. If a charge wasn't approved, we got the hell out of there. At the ticket reseller, we got almost all of the six hundred thousand back in cash—the resellers only took off about twenty or thirty thousand.

There were a million travel companies selling Shinkansen tickets, so sometimes we split up for attack runs, and on those days, we could make more than ¥1.5 million. The ticket resellers around town lay in wait for people wanting to sell tickets, no matter how few. No one noticed what we were doing, even though we were always outside the resellers, even though the money changed hands so fast. We were obsessed, sleeping less, running around town with wads of cash, invisible. Our money grew and grew. In our house, in the closet, there was only ever more.

"First time we've had a day off in forever," Momoko said, though I couldn't tell if she was happy about that or not. We were sprawled under the kotatsu watching a talk show.

"Our next batch of cards seems late. I wonder if something bad happened," Momoko said uneasily, though she kept her eyes on the TV.

"No, I don't think so. That just happens sometimes."

"If you say so."

Time had gotten away from me—it was already mid-December. Soon, 1999 would come to a close, and 2000 would follow on its heels. On TV, they were talking about the Y2K problem—the commentators were fired up, discussing how when the clock struck midnight, massive errors would crash the system, how there might be worldwide problems. We watched in silence. The talking heads jumped from topic to topic—the end of the century, the end of the world, the start of a new century, a new era, the kinds of scientific advances that might be made in the next hundred years—but I didn't process any of it.

As the commentators laughed and chatted on TV, I thought about how Nostradamus had been wrong, and the world hadn't ended with 1999—in fact, nothing happened.

Some weeks, Viv had cards for us every time I saw her, and

sometimes, we'd go a week without getting new ones. Those weeks, we curled in on ourselves, nauseous, wondering if the whole scheme had been found out. When new cards came, though, our fear transformed to excitement, and we went all out, doubling the energy we put toward earning. We planned our attack runs carefully and thoroughly, blazing trails to travel agencies and department stores, balancing the frequencies of our visits. In months where we got a lot of cards, I think our take cleared three million. While Tokyo was lively and carefree with Christmas and the end of the century, our fever pitch kept growing and growing. Spurred on by an indefinable energy, we kept earning.

Usually, Kimiko and I handled the money.

When I first asked Viv for help, one of her many conditions was "You can involve Kimiko, but she must never ever do a card run herself." I didn't need to ask why, but Viv still added, "You understand, right? Kimiko's not all there." She laughed. "You should have her be your treasurer. Then she only needs to sit around."

I followed Viv's advice, and one day, I sat down with Kimiko and explained to her the situation we were in and our new jobs. Ran and Momoko were out, so it was just me and Kimiko. She sat with her legs under the kotatsu, back hunched, watching TV. I put my legs under, too, and turned toward the TV. On top of the kotatsu was the dustcloth and a half-eaten Yuki no Yado rice cracker. Kimiko listened to everything I told her in silence.

"—so I can't tell you who our boss is, but I can tell you that things are going well."

"Okay." Kimiko looked thoughtful, but she didn't ask for any more details.

"There's a lot we have to do, but we're making it work. And we're saving plenty of money. So you don't have to worry about the rent or the cell phone bills or food, because we're going to make as much as we can. And I know you wouldn't, but you can't tell anyone about this, about the job or the money. Oh, and we need a, what do you call it, minister of finance? Someone to keep everything nice and safe, and we were hoping you could do that."

"Okay. Got it."

"Kimiko?"

"Yeah?"

"Are you okay?"

"About what?"

"I don't know, you just seem kind of down."

"No, I'm fine." She thrust her fingers into her hair and scratched her scalp. Somehow, her movements seemed too slow. She used to go to the salon all the time, but her hair had grown out and lost its luster. I felt like I could no longer sense Kimiko's essence, like her life force was just gone.

"If you say so."

"I still can't get ahold of Yeongsu," Kimiko whispered, eyes still on the TV.

"Yeah."

Silence fell. It had been nearly three months since Yeongsu disappeared. At first, I'd tried to call him all the time, but once we started our attack runs, I got caught up in everything, so I hadn't even tried to ring him lately. Yeongsu. Kimiko had said he'd disappeared before, and he was a grown man, so part of me felt like there wasn't any point in worrying, especially given his line of work, but maybe three months without contact was too long. Maybe he wanted to call us but couldn't, or maybe there'd been an incident, or maybe he was caught up in something really bad.

"But my cell phone is still working, right?" I said brightly. "It's the one Yeongsu lent me ages ago, so that means someone's still paying the bill, which means, even if we can't get ahold of him, he's still doing his thing somewhere, same as always, right?"

"Your cell phone?" Kimiko said, glancing at me. "Well, yeah, but I don't know if he actually pays the bill. I don't think he does. I don't know whose phone it is."

"Seriously?" I was taken aback.

"Seriously. It's changed hands so many times."

Our conversation stalled, but after a moment I continued. "How's, uh, how's Kotomi doing? Is she better? I haven't gotten a chance to see her yet, and I'd really like to."

"I'd like to see her, too," Kimiko whispered, almost to herself.

"You haven't? That guy—that jerk, what about him? Are they still together? Can you not see her because he's around? Do you think that's what's going on?" My mood darkened as I imagined Kimiko's delicate face, black and blue, bloodstained, eyes swollen, lip split and bleeding. Maybe I shouldn't have said anything. I sat up, trying to get ahold of myself, and smiled at Kimiko.

"Well, anyway, I'll give you our take from this month. I know I said minister of finance, but there's not much to do, really. When you're home make sure no one comes in and steals it, that's all. You'll get a salary out of this, too, and you can use that for whatever you want. I'll save whatever's left over and—"

Suddenly, the words caught in my throat.

I was going to say, *I'll save whatever's left over, and we'll use it to reopen Lemon, so we can work there together again.* When I started, that was my biggest goal, and I still believed it would happen, but somehow, I couldn't say it.

Why? Why couldn't I tell her? I still loved Lemon with all my heart, and I was sure Kimiko did, too. It was important to both of us. That hadn't changed. And besides, our work for Viv was on a time limit, I knew that, which made reopening Lemon all the more important to our livelihood. So why couldn't I just say it?

"Hey, Kimiko?"

"Yeah?"

"What do you do when we're out at work?"

I wanted to change the subject, so I tried for something I thought would be trivial.

"What do I do?"

"Yeah, I was just wondering how you pass the time."

"I don't do anything."

"You don't do anything?"

"Yep. Nothing."

"What about TV? Or cleaning?"

"That's about it."

"Oh. Well, from now on you're going to have a salary, and you can use it however you want. You should give Kotomi a call, go see her. I want to see her, too. I've been worried about her. And we can take some time to talk about Yeongsu. Soon."

"Okay."

Staring at Kimiko made me think about Kotomi, and about Yeongsu, too. I wondered if I should ask about the payments she was supposed to be sending to her mother in jail. But I wasn't sure, so I decided not to. I'd first heard about Kimiko's mom from Yeongsu—she had never mentioned it herself. Maybe she wouldn't mind that I knew, but I couldn't be sure.

And there was that time—I still remembered the scent of fear and nerves in the air when Kimiko got back from seeing Kotomi after she'd been beaten, Kimiko's menacing air, the way she glared at me with unfathomable eyes. I didn't want to remember that night. I wished I could forget it completely.

"Oh hey, you know, we've had so much going on, I feel like we haven't had any time to talk. We should go out for dinner, just the two of us. And then maybe we can go for a haircut? We could do yakiniku?"

"Yeah."

"Are you listening? Kimiko?"

"Yeah."

She fidgeted herself into sitting and snatched the dustcloth, using it to wipe the kotatsu in big circles, like she'd forgotten to do it earlier.

"Hey, Kimiko," I said, "you know what we should do? A kotatsu burrito! Remember?"

"Kotatsu burrito?"

"Yeah, you know, you take the kotatsu blanket and burrito up in it?" I grinned, pleased I'd remembered. The first winter

Kimiko and I had lived together, she would take the blanket, still warm from the kotatsu's heater, and wrap me tight in it. It felt amazing, so that winter, I'd asked her to wrap me up again and again.

"What's that?"

"You don't remember? You know, like this, burrito up?"

Kimiko mumbled a non-answer, tilting her head to the side. I pursed my lips together and looked down at the kotatsu blanket. Again, I tried to change the subject, but Kimiko, unable to keep up a conversation, stood and shuffled to the bathroom. She hadn't lost any weight, but as I watched her retreating back, I felt like there was less of her, like there was something *lacking* in her, and it made me nervous. Feeling helpless, I went upstairs to our bedroom and slumped down against the wall, staring at the door of the closet.

There was money. In there.

The thought came from nowhere.

A lot of money, money that would just keep growing.

All the loneliness, the yearning, the dejection I'd been feeling—just like that, the money banished that maelstrom of emotions. Like a magic trick, like someone had snapped their fingers, and everything before me disappeared.

Every month, I handed Ran and Momoko their salary of a hundred fifty thousand—I didn't ask them for rent anymore. To Kimiko I gave two hundred thousand. The rest, I told them, I was saving for the future, and Ran and Momoko seemed satisfied with that for the time being.

Our attack run earnings went into the box in the closet. I had everyone watch as I arranged the money neatly, putting ten-thousand-yen notes in stacks of ten, doing the same with thousand-yen notes, and then putting the lid back on the box. This was a ceremony to savor the fruits of our labor, yes, but it was almost like the world's biggest . . . excitement, like touching possibility itself. We had an unspoken rule that no one would touch the box unless we were together. But I told Kimiko to wait until we were out working and then, every day, count the money and make sure it matched the total we were supposed to have. It wasn't that I didn't trust Momoko and Ran, but I thought it was only natural to have Kimiko count the cash; it was her job.

As the world raced toward the end of the century, everything heated up, ballooned. People vibrated with enthusiasm, and here and there throughout the city, vortexes had begun to form, and when these forces collided, they gave birth to a new kind of mania. Momoko, Ran, and I threw ourselves into the flow—or against the flow, we couldn't tell—of excitement and cheer and desire, running attack after attack after attack.

TEN

BORDERLINE

1.

It was the New Year. We spent the first few days of January watching TV with our feet stuck under the kotatsu, all of us distracted and listless. We felt like we ought to do something at least a little holidayish, so we went to the supermarket on New Year's Eve and bought a two-tier Osechi set. But every dish in the Osechi was cold and tasted more or less the same, and I couldn't tell if it was actually good or not. We also drank more than we usually did. On some days, Momoko and Ran would get up and start the day by making splashy cocktails, drinking them, along with sake, until they were plastered. I went along with it, but no matter how much I drank, I never got drunk.

It was the second New Year's we'd spent in this house. How many had it been since I first met Kimiko? Four years, or could it be five? It would be easy to count the years if I put my mind to it, but whatever number I'd come up with wouldn't feel right anyway. *How time flies!* or *Has it only been that long?* These expressions weren't enough to describe the time we'd spent together, the things we'd done. A simple number like that had nothing to do with us.

"Hana, are you awake?" Ran asked one night, long after we'd turned off the lights. Momoko was already snoring.

"I'm awake."

"I'm so wide awake." I could hear her turning over in the faint darkness. "Doesn't the holiday feel long?"

"It does."

"Sooooo long."

"How long does it go this year? For the people who have jobs, I mean," I asked.

"I don't know, but I think we have a few more days after the weekend. The shops are already open though."

"Mm-hmm."

"I feel like we've had this conversation before, a long time ago. 'When do you start work again?' You asked me that, remember? We were on the street. It was freezing!"

"We did, didn't we. You always wore that white bomber jacket."

"Yeah, they always made me stand outside. We were so young."

We were silent for a moment.

"I wish the holidays were over already." My eyes had grown used to the blue of night, and I saw Ran turn toward me. She blinked. "I feel like we're wasting time, you know, like taking a loss right now."

"You mean our attack runs?"

"Yeah."

"I suppose we are," I agreed. "I start thinking, 'In three days we could've made this much.' Stuff like that. Once the New Year holiday is over, we'll have to put our backs into it."

"For sure. We . . . we've saved up a lot, haven't we?"

"Yeah, it's coming along."

"Is that . . ." Ran paused a moment to make sure Momoko was still asleep behind her, and then she lowered her voice, "I mean, you've got plans, right. For the setup and everything . . ."

"For the money?"

The air changed between us.

"Well . . . you said you wanted to reopen Lemon, right? So we could work together again. That's what we're saving up for?"

"Yeah, that's the plan," I said.

"Right . . . hey, remind me, how much is it going to cost, to reopen?"

"A lot." My voice was lower than I'd intended, and I cleared my throat. "The first time around, with Lemon, we were really lucky, because we just took it over from the previous owner and could start right away. But now we have to do everything from square one. We'll need real IDs to rent a space. Not those fake insurance cards we're always using right now. We need actual forms of identification, and a guarantor. We'll have to jump some major hurdles to make it happen, and for that, we have to be prepared."

"Yeah."

"That's why we're doing everything we can right now. First, we have to save up our earnings from the attack runs, and I've been checking the ads in real estate agents' windows. I go to the bookstore sometimes and look up stuff, like how you can rent a space, how you get the qualifications to run a bar, that sort of thing."

I explained everything to Ran like I'd actually been doing those things, but in reality, I'd only thought about them vaguely.

"Wow, it takes a lot, huh." Ran sighed like she was both impressed and disappointed at the same time. Then, she carefully asked, "So does that mean we still don't have enough?"

"Enough money, you mean?"

"Yeah."

"Um, opening a bar costs about eight million, sometimes ten million if it's a high-demand spot. Down payments and stuff. It's different from just renting an apartment."

"Seriously? It costs that much?"

"It does. And the costs don't stop there. You probably know this already, Ran, but you're in the red until you hit your groove, and even after that there's still loads of expenses. We have to save up enough to cover those, too. It's no easy thing to open a bar. You need a whole lot of money. And remember, we lost all our customer contacts. We're not starting from square one, we're starting from, like, negative square."

"Hmm, right" was all Ran said. I couldn't tell if she'd understood or if she was thinking of something else, and that feeling made me unsettled.

What was Ran actually asking? She didn't seem to be particularly invested in the idea of reopening Lemon, not in any real sense. Maybe it was just the money she was interested in. That was my guess. I sensed what she was actually saying was this—*We can reopen Lemon, if that's what you want, but once we've paid off the expenses, how much will be left? How much of that money will be mine?*

If that's what she was thinking, well, I couldn't blame her. It had been two months since we started our attack runs. It wasn't unreasonable for her to compare her cut with the amount of money we added to the savings with each run, and to think that maybe she was getting short shrifted. It made sense that she would want to know if her cut would increase or if there were any long-term plans.

But I didn't know what the future held either. What I knew was that we had to earn money while we could. Whether we reopened Lemon or not, we needed to have as much money saved up as possible, in case worst came to worst. We could talk all we wanted about splitting the savings or spending it—but that was nothing if we didn't have the money in the first place. Why was Ran asking me about this now? I found myself getting irritated.

After all, Ran and Momoko might be working hard, but I was the one who'd made our attack runs possible in the first place. And how had I done that? By bowing down my head and begging Viv to help me. And why did she give me what I asked for? Because she trusted me. I had earned that trust by working for Viv for nearly a year, perfectly carrying out my duties, sometimes even surpassing her expectations.

I could still remember how nervous, how terrified I'd been the first time I took the cards from Viv and stood before an ATM. I was so scared even the memory of it made my heart jump. I'd stood alone against that terror.

And what had Ran and Momoko been doing while I faced that boundless terror? Ran had technically been working at the cabaret club, but she'd make a bunch of excuses not to go, to take it easy. As for Momoko, she hadn't been doing anything, just using her family's money to screw around and get into the whole mess with that ridiculous guy and the tickets. The only reason the two of them got to loaf around this house was because I'd been holding the line, and only barely at that. In fact, it was because I'd asked Jin-ji for help that we even had this house in the first place. The only reason the two of them could have it easy, could laugh and hang around and have this carefree life, was because I was doing all the caring.

I knew our attack runs were risky, that they were putting themselves out there, too. But I was the one who paid attention to every little detail: the card supplies, the orders, our work rotations, planning out places where we couldn't be traced, taking care of the fake IDs Viv supplied for us, the payoffs. All Ran and Momoko had to do was to put on their uniforms and stand at the service windows, making sure the security cameras couldn't see their faces (and only because I told them to). With just that, they were earning a hundred fifty thousand a month. They didn't even pay rent or utilities, so they could use their money however they wanted. How was that not enough? Momoko was clueless when it came to money, so that was that, but Ran of all people should know how hard she'd have to work to earn that kind of money anywhere else.

Maybe when I wasn't around, Momoko and Ran were talking behind my back about the attack runs and how I was managing the savings. Which might mean that the conversation Ran and I just had was her testing the waters, sounding me out. What if Momoko was faking it? What if she wasn't really asleep? I imagined the two of them laughing and making their secret plans—at McDonald's or in the living room or wherever. My cheeks grew hot.

At the start of the new year, our savings was ¥5,753,000. (I remember this perfectly, because the next morning, I waited until the two of them were out and counted the whole thing.) That was everything we'd earned these past two months from me planning, directing, running around, saving everything I possibly could. What if . . . what if Ran and Momoko teamed up and took the money in the cardboard box, just disappeared with it? It was a slim chance, one in a million, but the thought suddenly came to me, and my heart lurched.

Would they? No, no way, I thought, *absolutely not, they wouldn't, they couldn't, but . . .* My hand was pressed against my throat. I took several deep breaths, trying to calm myself—but I couldn't. My thoughts carried me down darker and darker paths. Instead of shaking it off, I blinked and blinked, trying to rid myself of the overwhelming anxiety that filled my body. *It's okay. Nothing bad is happening. We're in the clear. Totally clear. You're just overthinking things. The money is right there. Let's look on the bright side.* I kept on breathing deeply in and out, trying to relax the tension in my shoulders. *Ran and Momoko are your friends, more than your friends. They're your comrades.* But terrible visions came to me, one after another, and my anxiety smoldered and crackled within me. My temples began to throb as thoughts whirled in my head. *Maybe I should be trying to figure out their parents' addresses while I can. And that cardboard box—we've been using it as a kind of proof that the money is all equally ours, but is that really a good idea? Maybe I should make up an excuse and put the money in a safe . . .* I didn't realize how much time had passed while I was asking myself those questions. When I finally called out to Ran again, there was no answer. She'd fallen asleep, and I could make out the faint sound of her breathing.

2.

On January 4, the long New Year's holiday finally ended, and we went back to our normal lives. Or, I wanted to believe we did, but I could feel that something had changed. I couldn't shake the crawling sensation that something was off. First, I couldn't get ahold of Viv, no matter how many times I called. She never called me back either. I'd met with her just before the holidays began, and we'd made a plan to get in touch sometime after the holidays ended so we could set a date to exchange the next set of cards.

We'd never had a real schedule for the days we made our attack runs, and there wasn't a set number for how many cards we'd get or how often we'd use them. But this was the first time I couldn't get ahold of Viv. I didn't have any other way to get in touch with her—all I had was the phone number she made me memorize.

Momoko and Ran were out shopping in Shibuya. Kimiko had gone out that morning, too, saying she was visiting her father's grave. She was in a cheerful mood, and while she put on her makeup and got ready, she chatted about so-and-so's new hit song and asked if we wanted her to bring back anything—but I was too paranoid to listen. Once I was alone, the silence spilled into the house until it sank into my very pores and expanded within me. I felt like I was being chased out of my own body.

Could Viv be in the hospital? But if she was, surely she'd let me know, even just a quick call. Could she have been in some kind of accident and died? The thought filled me with dread, but the most likely scenario was the possibility that Viv had been caught by the police. The idea of it made me feel nauseous. Suddenly, the heat of the kotatsu was too much for my legs, so I got up and went to the kitchen to drink some cold water.

Waiting for Viv's call made me feel physically ill. My phone almost never rang, so there was nothing special about the fact that it wasn't ringing now—but the realization that I was suffering made me feel it even more acutely. *Viv, where are you? Did something happen?* I called out to her again and again in my mind, as if I were pounding a heavy door that refused to budge.

Viv's disappearance unnerved me completely. I lost my appetite and ate nothing, just spent all day curled upstairs in the bedroom. Ran and Momoko were in the living room eating snacks as usual, and when I told them I was feeling beat down with a cold, they quickly agreed to sleep downstairs and give me the bedroom. Kimiko brought home a bowl of rice porridge from the convenience store and warmed it up for me.

Up on the second floor, I lay still in my futon with only my face exposed to the cold air and stared unblinking at the corner of the closet's sliding door. I imagined the worst-case scenario and simulated every possibility that could unfold.

One: Viv had been arrested for something unrelated to us. I didn't know the exact details, but from the way she talked on the phone while we were together, I knew that Viv didn't only operate the cards. She had several sources, some similar and some very different to our card grift. Maybe she'd been caught for one of those.

Two: somewhere along the way, the three of us had unknowingly made a huge mistake, and Viv had noticed. To keep herself safe, she'd cut off contact with us entirely. This seemed entirely probable, almost certain even, and it made my body tremble.

But if we had made a mistake, what could it be? We'd carefully switched out the fake insurance cards Viv had given us, and we'd kept up a rotation so that we never overlapped the places and times we were visiting. And I'd staked out the ticket resellers long enough to realize that it wasn't unusual or noteworthy for people to come and sell bundles of Shinkansen tickets or huge stacks of gift cards for no apparent reason. There was a mutual level of indifference between the resellers and the customers, like even though a person was manning the counter, they were simply going through the mechanical steps of their work. That's why we'd prepared work clothes—not only the uniforms—just to visit the ticket resellers, to fit into the atmosphere of their shops. Even with security cameras—originally it had been Viv who told me this, but the good quality cameras were expensive, so the resellers usually used the cheap ones with fuzzy recordings, and most of the time they were just dummies. We needed hats when we were visiting the ATMs, but we didn't need to worry about that sort of thing at the ticket resellers. Viv had also said a lot of resellers kept a tacit understanding with their customers. The tickets were their bread and butter, and without them there was no business. Their goal was to get as many tickets as possible, and so long as the tickets were real, they didn't care who was selling or where the tickets had come from. Even if they thought a customer was suspicious, there was no need on their part to make a fuss over it. The time they would spend making a report was better used buying and selling even just one more ticket, plain and simple.

And most importantly, I thought, *even if someone had realized what we were doing, we had to be caught "in the act."* That was why Viv always reminded me that if, on the very slim chance we were caught, we should break loose and run and run and run until we'd lost them, because that was the only absolute way to get away with it. ("If you're the lookout, you just stay where you are and pretend to not know anything," she'd said.) So if we'd made a fatal mistake somewhere along the line, we would have been caught then and there. But we hadn't been. Which meant any mistake we had made wasn't enough to get us arrested.

But there was a possibility that the police had let us go and were watching us. Although Viv had said the police needed a good reason and a lot of prep before they'd let someone slip, so unless it were a major crime—like big real estate scams or elaborate deals where yakuza were involved—the police usually didn't waste their time and resources watching people. Say, for example, there was someone selling speed, and the cops let him keep working and put a stakeout on him. That wasn't because they were aiming for that person individually. The plan for their investigation was to strike at the smugglers and traffickers backing him. Normally the single arrests were people who got caught in the act purely by chance, either because they'd been acting suspiciously or because they screwed up when the police were questioning them. According to Viv, something like our modest grift with the cards, where money only moved in the tens or hundreds of thousands, and where there were only a few people involved, was like child's play, so insignificant that it wasn't worth their time. Even at this very moment, there were people running half-assed scams on pachinko parlors that were easily moving several times the money we were. If you just stopped to think about it, you could see that there were countless bigger and more obvious crimes in this world—and for the people doing the arresting, there were plenty of juicier cases for them to follow up on. They didn't have the time to worry about a piddling scam like ours. Of course we shouldn't be careless, but so long as everyone did exactly as Viv said, there was no need to be afraid. Sleep well, eat well, keep up our strength, and keep calm—that was all there was to it.

That's right, the only way to get caught was to get caught in the act—that realization made me relax, and my courage slowly seeped back in. The fact of the matter was that at this very moment, I was here inside my futon, and nothing bad had happened. I was free. I just couldn't get ahold of Viv. She wasn't answering her phone, but that didn't mean something had actually happened to her. I was just caught up in my own mind, anxious and letting my anxiety carry me away with worse and worse scenarios. This agony was meaningless, the product of my own negativity, my own imagination. The only concrete fact was that I hadn't been caught in the act. That was unmistakable—and solid proof that nothing bad was happening. Energy returned to me, and after staring at the corner of the closet a little longer, I shook off the futon and got up.

When I went downstairs, I found Momoko, Ran, and Kimiko lazing around, feet under the kotatsu, laughing at some variety show. Something funny must have happened because they sat with mouths half-open, same as the B-listers and talking heads on the TV, laughing along. None of them noticed me, asked me how I was doing or if I was hungry, even though I'd been telling them I wasn't feeling well and had spent several hours in bed that day. They didn't care. They just kept giggling with stupid looks on their faces.

I passed the living room in silence and went into the kitchen, filled a glass with water, and drank all of it at once. I realized I was starving, so I checked our stock for ramen but found it empty. The wakame ramen I'd bought before I'd started feeling sick was gone.

We didn't have explicit rules about the food in the house, but we more or less understood that if someone bought something, that was theirs, and if we wanted to eat something that wasn't ours, we usually asked for permission first. But my wakame ramen was gone. I didn't know who'd eaten it, but whoever it was hadn't asked me. I was irritated, but I shoved that down and opened the fridge. Inside, there were only bottles of soy sauce and barbecue sauce, canned cocktails and beer. That didn't come as a surprise—we never had food in the fridge anyway. With no other options, I decided to have the Pino ice cream bon bons I'd bought. I'd wanted to have them for dessert after I finished my ramen, but I didn't feel like going to the convenience store to get food first. *The Pino won't get me full, but whatever.* When I opened the freezer, though, I found that my Pino, too, had disappeared.

"Where are my Pino?" I asked out loud, reflexively. But just then, there was an explosion of laughter on the TV, which was quickly drowned out by the three of them laughing. None of them heard me. I slammed the freezer door shut with more force than I'd intended, and it made a bigger thunk than I'd expected. But again, none of them noticed. I stood before the fridge, waiting for someone to notice me standing there in the dark and call out to me, but a minute passed, three minutes, then five minutes, and still there was only the stupid, obnoxious sounds of the TV and their idiotic laughter.

I grew impatient and went back into the living room, but they still wouldn't look away from the TV, their faces slack. Finally, after a long while, Ran noticed me standing there in the corner.

"Oh hey, Hana, this is so funny, come watch."

"Funny, my ass," I spat. Ran looked at me, surprised, and sat up, correcting her posture. Momoko was still laughing, but she must have noticed something was off, because she looked at me, blinking in confusion.

"Where are my Pino?"

"Huh? Your Pino?"

"That's right. And my ramen."

For a moment they were both silent, and then Ran looked to Momoko as if to say, "Do you know anything?" But Momoko looked back at Ran, blinking cluelessly.

"What, so neither of you ate them?"

"Well, I don't really remember," Ran said, shuffling in her seat again and looking at me. "Wait, the ramen . . . I'm sorry, I might have . . ."

"It's not just my ramen. I'm talking about my Pino, too."

"Pino . . ." Momoko copied Ran and sat up and frowned as if searching her memory. "Which Pino? From when?"

"My Pino, the box I was going to eat."

"Maybe they got mixed with some other ones and . . . someone ate them?"

"Someone? The only people here are you two."

"Well, Kimiko's here, too," Momoko said quietly.

"Did you eat them, Kimiko?" I asked. Kimiko was still watching the TV, laughing silently, so I asked her again, and she hummed vaguely.

"Did you hear that? Kimiko didn't eat them. Kimiko doesn't eat ice cream, remember? So it had to be one of you. Why are you blaming her?"

"We're not blaming her. I just . . . um, you know, don't remember."

I glared down at them, silent. Sure, I was mad that they'd eaten my ramen and my ice cream without permission. But I could feel something much bigger boiling up—my anger, my displeasure, all my negative emotions from these last few months, no, maybe from these last few years. They were filling me up from every direction.

"Hey, Hana? I'll go buy some, okay. You're hungry, right? I totally get it. Just wait a few minutes, and I'll come right back." Ran hurriedly got up from the kotatsu and smiled, trying to ease the tension between us.

"Hold on a second, that's not what this is about."

"What?"

"The way you phrased it, it makes it sound like I'm hungry, and I'm just being selfish about it, so you'll go buy food, and that'll be that. But that's not it. The problem here is that someone ate something that was mine without my permission. That's the point I'm making here. Me being hungry has nothing to do with it."

"Oh, um, yeah, you're right . . ." Ran said, nodding again and again from where she half stood.

"But one of us probably did eat it, even if we don't remember who, so we'll go get more, okay?" Momoko followed, forcing a smile. I kept glaring down at them with my arms crossed, saying nothing. They both glanced up at me a few times, faces frozen, but then they dropped their eyes to the kotatsu and stopped moving.

"Well, whatever, it's done. But don't do it again."

I remained silent for a few seconds, enough to make them feel uncomfortable, then turned to go back to the kitchen and see if there was any other food. But as I turned, I caught sight of the Yellow Corner next to the TV. It looked off, so I drew nearer and shouted at my discovery.

"It's filthy over here!" I turned back to them. "Look at this. Look at all this dust! Why? Isn't anyone cleaning it?"

Both Ran and Momoko stood up at once and came up behind me to peer at the shelves.

"Look, here. And here! Our Yellow Corner! Why . . . why isn't anyone looking after it?"

The two of them stood behind me, flustered, trading remarks about how dusty it was and what they should do about it. In the Yellow Corner, grime clung to every surface of every yellow object. The feelings I'd only just shoved down roared up again. They were overwhelming, like mercury rising in a thermometer, going clear past the last ticks and exploding out of the glass. *What the hell is this?* I thought to myself. *Seriously, what the hell is going on? What do they think they're doing? I've been stretching myself so thin worrying about our future, our savings, our money. I even made myself sick over it, and they've just been sitting here, not a thought in their heads, cackling at the TV, doing whatever they want, leaving all the important shit to someone else. They eat when they want, whatever they please, and they've always been that way. How could they not even notice that the Yellow Corner was covered with dust, right under their noses? What the fuck?* I closed my eyes and clenched my fists.

"Um . . . Hana?"

I took a deep breath and then raised my eyes.

"This is completely fucked-up. How come no one's looking after the Yellow Corner, when you spend all day staring at the TV? We've talked about why it's important. Right? The Yellow Corner, it's so important. And this, all this dust, this is unacceptable. Can't you see? Don't you understand? What were you thinking?!"

"We were . . . um . . ."

"Huh? What were you thinking? Why don't you care?"

"But"—Momoko spoke softly, peering up at me like she was trying to figure out how angry I was—"normally Kimiko does the cleaning for us. I mean, she's always dusting, so—"

"So what you're saying is that it's Kimiko's fault? That she's not dusting enough? That's your excuse?" I glared at Momoko.

"No, that's not what I'm saying, I just . . . didn't know."

"Didn't know? And when you don't know something, what do you do about it? You figure it out, isn't that the normal thing to do? You go back and—"

"Hana, these things, right? We use these things to dust?"

At some point, Ran had gone to the kitchen and grabbed the pack of dusting cloths and was now waving them around. "I found them, right? We dust with these?" She yanked two cloths from the pack, hurriedly pushing one into Momoko's hands.

"Come on, Momoko, we'll dust them one by one."

"Not just the front, you have to do the back and the sides, too."

"Got it."

"Don't waste the cloths, make sure you use every corner of them."

"Got it."

Kimiko had always used the same old dustcloth to wipe down everything—the walls, the shelves, the kotatsu table—even when the cloth had become filthy and ragged. But the last time I was at the drugstore, I'd found these all-purpose disposable dusting cloths, and I got Kimiko to start using them instead of her usual one. The disposable cloths didn't need water and picked up even the smallest speck of dust—they even polished things. They seemed to be the most useful thing to have—you could use both sides and clean almost everything in the house, except the food. Of course, it would have been cheaper to get a reusable dustcloth from the hundred-yen store—disposable cloths were a luxury. But it was the color that had caught my eyes. These dusting cloths were yellow—so bright that once I'd noticed them in the drugstore, I couldn't keep my eyes off them. I had to have them for the house.

As I watched Ran and Momoko pick up each item on the shelf and carefully rub every surface until it was free of dust, it suddenly occurred me that maybe this was why I couldn't get ahold of Viv.

We had neglected our precious Yellow Corner, had stopped taking care of it, had forgotten what it was originally for and ignored it until it was covered in filth. Maybe that was why our luck had run out.

Because yellow was the color of fortune. And fortune meant that money flowed to you. Of course, our finding this place to live, our earning money, that was part hard work, but I also believed that it was fundamentally thanks to our lucky yellow.

Yellow was how this all started. I met Kimiko, who had yellow in her name, and she was the first one who'd taught me about yellow bringing fortune, and that was how I was able to leave Higashimurayama and find my own place, my own life. Of course, there was Lemon. Lemon had burned, and my mother had made off with my savings, and yes, terrible things had happened. But I'd also found a home I could share with Kimiko, a way to earn money, a way to live my life, our lives. I couldn't help but feel that yellow fortune was deeply intertwined with our path. Of course I couldn't prove it. But then again, I also couldn't prove that yellow had nothing to do with our luck either. So who got to decide? Me. I had to decide, in my own heart, what was important for me, and I'd come this far believing in yellow. That was a fact. And the moment we'd started neglecting the Yellow Corner, we'd been cut off from Viv, cut off from our good fortune, and wound up where we were now.

Yellow, that was it. Yellow. No matter what, we had to do right by yellow—and in that moment, I had a realization, as if someone had clapped their hands right in my face and turned me back into myself again. It had been forever since I'd last gone to the bookstore, hadn't it?

That fateful dream, the one I still remembered with perfect clarity even now. It was the only dream I remembered from these past few years, and the fact that my life had gone exactly as it predicted meant that it was also a prophecy. It had been ages since I last checked that thick, lavish *Dictionary of Dream Analysis*, the one that had told me exactly what the dream meant.

Back when we still had Lemon, I sometimes stopped by the bookstore before work and picked up the book, rereading the sections I'd already memorized and feeling energized by the familiar words. The combination of that dream and the color yellow had protected me, allowed me to be certain in my good fortunes, and that was how I had made everything happen. But not only had I forgotten our Yellow Corner. I'd forgotten all about the precious *Dictionary of Dream Analysis* as well. It wasn't only that our yellow luck had run out. The neglected book had made everything worse, doubled the negative. Stricken, I checked the clock and found it was 7:10—I could still do it. I would make it in time.

"I'm going out. Make sure you clean everything," I blurted, then grabbed my purse and dashed out the door, running as fast as I could for the bookstore in front of the station. I was panting as I entered, going past the aisles until I found the shelf. I scanned the spot high on the right-hand side of the display where I'd placed the book to make sure no one bought it. Gone. The book was thick and heavy, impossible to miss. Gone. I ran my eyes over the shelves, up and down, side to side, but it wasn't there or anywhere. My dream dictionary, the book that had recorded my fate, had disappeared. I took a few steps back, studying the entire shelving unit, but the result was the same. The once glossy, sparkling sign that declared "Learn to Love Yourself! The Age of Healing!" had faded to nothing and now hung crookedly.

I panicked. I panicked so much I had to lean against the shelf. *This is it. We're finished. What do I do? What can I do?* I crouched forward, arms wrapped around my stomach, and froze in that position. *Our luck is used up, it's abandoned us, everything's going to take a turn for the worse, we'll suffer the most violent ill fortunes and fall straight into the pits of hell. Now, this moment, this is when it begins.* I nearly collapsed to the floor. From the next aisle over, a middle-aged woman appeared carrying a heavy supermarket bag. I felt her glance at me several times, but it was all I could do to force strength back into my shoulders, willing myself not to be carried away by each and every doomed vision that came over me. It took everything in me to keep standing. There in the aisle, those memories—feelings and scenes, scents and ordinary conversations—formed a wave, and their force rushed through the cavern that was now my body, abandoning me, like I had become some sort of sewer pipe or something—yes, the core of me was hollow and flimsy, like the empty core of a toilet paper tube, and I felt helpless and weak. Tears welled over my lower eyelids, and my nose stung. But I shook my head violently and managed to shake it off. *No, no, you have to think. There must be something. Come on, think, something yellow, something that can balance the books, something yellow that can bring the luck back. You've got to find it, you've got to think,* I told myself, trying to drum up my courage. *There must be something, there has to be. You've made it this far, haven't you, so you have to find something for the road forward.* I wrung my brain like a washcloth until it ran dry. *Yellow, yellow fortune, yellow, yellow fortune,* I repeated the words, almost desperately.

But as my mind tried to tie one thought to the next, a huge steel plate descended from the ceiling, ready to crush me flat, and when I threw myself sideways, a hair's breadth between me and the plate, I found that the walls, too, were now closing in. I had nowhere to run; this was it . . . and at that moment, something flashed before me, inside my head, and I opened my eyes wider than I ever thought possible. *That's it, the walls! The walls! I've got it, I know where to find it.* I ran out of the bookstore at full tilt, crossed the street, and headed west on Setagaya-dori.

I was headed for a hardware store I'd gone to many times when we were setting up Lemon. It was kind of famous, located right before Kannana-dori, and the lineup was so good that pros went there all the time for construction supplies. Some of Lemon's regulars were also devoted fans and had sung this store's praises. I ran as hard as I could for five or six solid minutes and slid into the store, grabbing the first guy in uniform I found, almost collapsing against him as I demanded yellow paint. "Oh yeah, over here," he said and led me to shelves at the back of the store. I realized that he didn't actually work for the store but was a customer himself. I was still panting hard as I stood before the shelves. There were so many different kinds I didn't know what to get, but I found the can with the brightest yellow on it. In massive font across the front, the can declared "Fast-drying! Long-lasting durability!" I took every can they had, which was four in total, grabbed three paint brushes from the display next to the cans, and carried the whole load to the register. The bill came out to ¥8,300, a huge amount—but I paid it and walked out of the store. My pace was slower than before, but I ran all the way home.

"I'm back!" I shouted, kicking my shoes off from where they'd caught on my toes. I tried to dash into the living room, but I tripped, my knees slammed into the floor, and I landed on my jaw. "Ow!"

"Oh my god, Hana, are you okay?" Momoko and Ran rushed over to me, picking up the paint cans and brushes.

"I'm okay, I'm okay."

"Hana, what is this? Where's . . . where's your ramen?" Ran asked, holding a paint can in one hand, her other hand wrapped around my shoulder.

"Never mind the ramen, we have to do this, this."

"This?"

"Paint! We have to make everything yellow! Now!" I said, shoulders heaving.

"Make what yellow?"

"The house!"

"The house?"

"We're going to paint our house yellow!" I said, glancing between them before turning my eyes forward. "We'll do the downstairs rooms first. Let's start with the west wall—yeah, over there. Everybody grab a brush. Hurry up."

"Okay." They nodded, mouths hanging open.

"Kimiko, you go upstairs. I'll call you when we're done. Ran, you move the TV and the shelf so we have room, and we'll start painting from there, from that corner—Kimiko, come on, stop watching TV, go upstairs or go take a bath. Now."

"Yeah, yeah," Kimiko mumbled, scratching her head as she exited the living room.

We spread trash bags on the floor, set out the paint cans, took up our brushes, and started painting—painting yellow all over the walls, dripping paint on the floor as we went, painting with abandon. In truth, the most experience the three of us had with painting anything at all was our nails, or maybe watercolor—so the walls were patchy and uneven, with drips of paint hardening here and there. The whole thing was a sight. Plus, I hadn't known that different paints had different uses. The paint I'd bought was oil-based and was meant to be used outdoors, and there was a warning label on the side that said if you did use the paint indoors, you needed to ventilate the space properly.

It was cold out, so we kept the windows closed as we smeared on thick layers of paint, which meant, of course, right in the middle, we started to feel sick and nauseous. We were ready to give up, but I was so determined to get our luck back as quickly as possible that I hounded Momoko and Ran to fight through it, and we kept painting.

Just after two in the morning, the mood changed, and we started feeling giggly. No matter what anyone said, we laughed helplessly, unable to stop. It felt different from being drunk, but we were acting strange in ways we'd never do if we were sober, spouting meaningless gibberish and doubling over until we were nearly falling down. We laughed so hard we couldn't breathe when someone said, "A little dab'll do ya, do ya!" and we were on the floor laughing so hard we were crying. "Muscle, muscle, triple decker" and "Udon till we're done" nearly finished us off. We rolled on the floor, paintbrushes still in hand, bright splatters of yellow paint flying all around us. The yellow stretched and shrank like a living thing, leaping, trailing like an obi, drawing spirals in the air. An arc of yellow passed between Ran and Momoko in slow motion, glistening like a shooting star, coming straight toward me. I spread my arms and offered my heart, taking the paint in, and then I laughed out loud. We lost ourselves in wielding our paint-soaked brushes, and whenever paint flew onto our faces or into our hair, we exploded with mirth. We draped our yellow-spattered bodies over each other, twisting and contorting in never-ending laughter.

By the time the deep hue of a winter morning began to glow beyond the curtains, Momoko and Ran were spent, asleep under the kotatsu. I was fuzzy with exhaustion and paint fumes, but still I felt a sense of accomplishment and relief as I took in the yellow walls. Sure, the paint was uneven, and parts of the walls weren't fully coated where we'd run out of paint, but we'd done what we needed to do. I was exhausted. *I'll think about tomorrow tomorrow.* I closed my eyes and sat without moving, finally succumbing to stillness—but somewhere in the distance I heard a ringing, a sound that was coming nearer and nearer. As I rubbed at my drooping eyelids and raised my head, the yellow walls jumped into my vision. For a moment, I didn't understand where I was, what I was looking at.

Right. This yellow, it's the yellow we just painted the walls. This is the living room. This is our house. It took a few seconds to remember each one, as if I were counting each fact on my fingers. Momoko and Ran were dead asleep, their faces and hair covered in flaking yellow paint. Morning light now filled the room. I thought I'd only closed my eyes for a moment, but I must have slept plenty without realizing it. Then I noticed my phone was ringing, so I extended my heavy arm to drag my purse closer until I could grab it. Looking down at the phone screen, I saw Viv's number. The moment I saw it, my drowsiness fled, and I pressed the phone to my ear.

"Viv!"

"Hana?"

"Where have you been?! What have you been doing?!"

"What have I been doing? I just got back yesterday."

"From where?"

"Korea. Didn't someone tell you? Togashi was supposed to call."

"What, Togashi? Who?"

"I had to leave in a hurry, so I told Togashi to call you and let you know. You must have heard from him, right?"

"No, nobody called."

"Seriously? I'll kill him."

"Oh, I'm so glad you called. I was worried sick about you."

"You were? I mean, yeah, it was sudden this time, but . . . it's fine now."

"So . . . it wasn't just vacation," I said, to make sure.

"Of course not. It was work. One of the young guys got gun-shy, and there was nobody else, so I had to go and pick up the skimmers myself, honestly way below my caliber. Well, I managed to get a new terminal and some other good stuff, too, so it wasn't all bad. Oh, and a ton of blank cards, too." Viv laughed. "You're going to be rolling in the dough! The magnetic strips and tech are way better. I was honestly surprised—you can even access the data remotely and send it long distance. Once we can use that, we won't even have to send runners to get the skimmers and take them back to Korea. Amazing, right?"

"Uh-huh."

"Of course it's expensive shit, and you'll need someone to manage the technical side. I'm on the outs, so I probably won't be involved with that," Viv said, laughing again. "Oh, speaking of, you must be out of cards by now, right?"

"Yeah, we've been through this whole round. We were waiting for new ones."

"Right."

"And you and I had talked about meeting up after the New Year, so I got really worried when I couldn't get ahold of you. I thought maybe something bad had happened."

"Something bad?"

"Well, you know, like—" But the words caught in my throat. "Anyway, I'm glad everything's good."

"Yeah," Viv said noncommittally. "Let's meet up on Friday. I'm getting a new shipment of insurance cards on Thursday, so it'll have to be after that. Oh, and in addition to the usual cards, I have some things I want you to keep at your place, so I'll bring those, too."

"Our place? So should I bring something to carry whatever it is?"

"Yeah, a big bag should be fine. It's just cards we've already used up, and a bundle of ones where the magnetic strips didn't work right, so it won't take up much space. Just put them with the used cards you've already got."

"Understood."

"Okay. I'll call again soon then."

"Oh, Viv," I said, stopping her before she could hang up. "I just wanted to ask, I haven't heard from Yeongsu in quite a while. Have you?"

"Yeongsu?"

"Yeah. At first, Kimiko said we didn't need to worry, but we haven't heard from him since last fall. It feels off. So I wondered if maybe you'd heard anything . . ."

"Yeongsu," Viv said thoughtfully. "Hmm, I haven't heard anything about him lately. But I also haven't heard any rumors about him getting caught or being on the run. I'm sure he's just doing his thing."

"I suppose so," I said, sighing. "I was just worried he was never coming back."

"Ha! If he's alive, he'll come back. No guarantees if he's dead, though," Viv said. "All right, I'll call you soon. Now that it's a new year, you're gonna be hella busy again! Earn every yen you can."

After Viv hung up, I kept holding the phone in my hand, staring into the distance. I could hear a bird chirping, kids playing and shouting as they took off running. I was struck suddenly by the choking scent of the paint, and I rubbed at my nose.

ELEVEN

BLACKOUT

1.

It was just as Viv said—with New Year's behind us, our sources of income picked up. We were on a roll. A day, a week, a month—time passed like a raging storm, and there was no room for anyone's emotions, no room for slacking off, only room for the violent force of the ATM spitting out bills. We were out in the winter cold all the time earning our keep, but I don't remember feeling cold. Spring came, and I turned twenty. I don't remember feeling much about that either. When I finished an attack run, I went home, slept, and then went on the attack again. Repeat, repeat, repeat.

It had been a few months since Momoko and Ran joined me. For a while, any little thing would balloon my anxiety into a tsunami and swallow me in waves of fear and compulsion until I couldn't tell up from down. But by the time early summer came, I'd grown more stoic and steadier on my feet.

Of course, I was still extremely careful. I found myself watching my surroundings more, and I think I became even more deliberate and discerning with how I divided attack run rotations, monitored our behavior in ticket resale shops, and handled the forged debit cards. At the same time, I loosened up around other things. Imagine a washbasin. Before, when I filled the basin to the top and tried to carry it, I was always desperately trying not to spill any water. I'd move slowly and deliberately so that I didn't trip and lose everything at once. But now, I never cared about the water. *If it spills, it spills.* Or maybe I just figured it never would. Or maybe the water was already gone, and I didn't realize or care that the washbasin was empty. Whatever it was, the more I loosened up, the more our money seemed to fall in line, growing and growing and growing.

I paid off Momoko's debt. Five hundred thousand, all in one go. Right before Golden Week, in 2000, Shizuka showed up at the house for the first time in a long time. Momoko and Ran were out in Shibuya, so it was just me and Kimiko in the house. I opened the front door to discover her there. Shizuka was just as stunning as the first time I'd met her, but today she was alone, not wearing a school uniform. The legs that poked out from her miniskirt were just as stout as I remembered, so burly they looked out of place with her top half, and there were shockingly prominent dark circles under her eyes. Though she still glared fiercely, her eyes were also dull, and it was clear she wasn't doing well.

Shizuka explained that no matter how many times she called, Momoko never picked up, and these past few months, Uno and his gang of ticket sellers had been hounding her, driving her crazy, and she was at her limit, and even though Gori (which is to say Momoko) was the one who had fucked-up, Shizuka was getting harassed because she was Momoko's sister. Once she finished her explanation, she told me she was thinking about going to the police.

"I mean, I'm the victim here. Uno is batshit crazy, he even cornered my friends, made them date for fucking cash. It's too fucking much, I mean look at me. And the whole reason Uno's after me is Gori. If she's gonna keep ignoring me like this, I'm gonna rat on her to my parents, have them file a missing person's report or some shit. It's a fucking pain in the ass, but I'll bring them here, I swear. What else am I supposed to do? They think Gori's still fucking around in Aobadai with me and Gramma, but she's living here, with you assholes."

I didn't think the police would do anything, even if Shizuka did file the report, but I still felt unsettled. I was twenty now, but Momoko was underage, and if her parents got involved, that would be a giant pain. And on the off chance the cops did show up, they might get suspicious and search the house. As I slowly started to panic, I sensed someone behind me and turned to find Kimiko standing there. Maybe she'd heard us talking and wanted to see what was up. But the fact that Shizuka had seen her left me shaken. Kimiko had on a worn, stained T-shirt and shorts, and she still hadn't gotten a haircut. She looked totally normal inside our half-painted yellow house, but under the light of day, even just in the entryway, she cut a bizarre figure. In her hand, she held a bright yellow cloth, and she ran it once over the front door, as if it was simply the next step in her cleaning routine, before going back into the house.

"Oh, so it's not just you. You've got a lady in there, an old hag," Shizuka said as I ran her off and closed the door. But I couldn't get her smile as she turned around out of my head, her expression that said she'd found something good. The next night, I handed Momoko the five hundred thousand and told her to go and give it to Shizuka and to tell her to never come here again.

I was mostly free of the fear and nerves I'd first felt toward our attack runs, but after Shizuka's visit, I started to grow more and more irritated with Momoko and Ran.

Even Momoko, who was a clueless dunce, started giving me more respect after I gave her the money to pay off her debt, but she still did plenty of things that pissed me off. It wasn't just when she and Ran had clearly done something wrong—it was their fundamental way of thinking, or rather not thinking at all, that put me eternally on edge. Take Lemon, for example. I knew by now that there was no way we would ever reopen Lemon. I had no ID, no bank account, and no respectable form of employment. There was no way someone like me could open a bar. I knew better than anyone that it was impossible. And this realization came with so much pain and shock that I honestly didn't want to think about it anymore, let alone talk with Ran and Momoko about it. But the fact that neither of them asked a single thing about Lemon, the fact that neither of them seemed to care—that pissed me off.

But then there were also times when I was on top of the world, and when I was like that, I'd take them out to McDonald's or Yoshinoya, and we'd hang out around the station together. Momoko and Ran liked going to Shibuya and Shinjuku, but I never wanted to go anywhere other than Sancha. It was enough for me to go on the attack runs in the busier parts of Tokyo. When I walked around Sancha, in the residential and the shopping areas, I always saw people enjoying each other's company—friends, families, lovers. There were plenty of girls around the same age as me. They wore carefree smiles on their faces, and they looked happy. I was sure that this happiness sprang from the fact that they had someone looking out for them—parents, families, boyfriends, I didn't know—someone stronger than them that gave them relief and comfort. Every time I saw those girls, I felt a dark vortex whirling in my chest.

In my heart I cursed them: their parents probably gave them money to go to school, buy things, eat things, and they probably spent their days fooling around with poser boys and friends who grew up just as spoiled as they did. They all wore the same brainless expressions. But each time I got mad at them, I thought about the money in the box. *It's fine. I have money. I have more money than any of you spoiled rich brats who don't know the first thing about protecting yourselves. This is money I earned myself, money I fought for, money that's my own*—that helped me calm down.

Money gives you time. Time to think. Time to sleep. Time to get sick. Time to wait. Maybe most people didn't need to earn that sort of time for themselves. Maybe most people already have time from the get-go. But Kimiko and I were different. Of course, I knew that we led the sort of lives we couldn't tell anyone about. That's why I'd spent sleepless nights trembling with fear, and I knew that if anyone found out about our operation, we'd get arrested and make the news, and every single person in the world would blame me for everything I'd done. We all need money, and that's why we sweat our asses off working, they'd say. But I wanted to tell everyone that I was sweating my ass off, too. With a half smile on my face, I wanted to ask every one of them—*And you, who are you to judge what's good sweat and what's bad? Where do you spend your time sweating your ass off? Bet it's some place real nice, right, so why don't you tell me how to get there?*

May came and went, and in June, I got a call from Yeongsu. It had been so long since I last heard from him that when I saw his number on the screen, I couldn't move. When I finally picked up, it was his familiar voice on the other end. Even though my mind wasn't processing what was happening, I remembered how when I'd first met him all those years ago, I'd thought he had a truly beautiful voice. We decided to meet at the reggae-inspired izakaya where we'd gone together one time, where we'd talked for hours just the two of us.

Yeongsu was already drinking a beer when I arrived. I thought he'd lost a little weight, but he looked healthy enough, which was a relief. The moment I sat down, I started telling him excitedly how worried we'd been when we couldn't get ahold of him, but he told me to calm down and ordered a beer for me. I drank the first one nearly in one gulp and ordered a refill. "You haven't changed," Yeongsu said with a wry smile.

"So why did you disappear like that?"

"Oh, you know, the baseball stuff."

"Did you get caught?"

"No, though that would have been bad, too. You remember that one time when you came to see us at the bar, right?"

"I didn't come to see you. I saw you guys by accident and wished I hadn't."

"Right. Well, our baseball thing, the whole thing was supposed to be under the table, so things got rough for a while when the boss found out."

"Under the table?"

"We were poaching the boss's customers. So it was the boss

that was after us, not the cops—and we had to hide until the heat died down. It took us a while to make amends."

I told him he could have at least called us, but Yeongsu made excuses, saying he was caught up in all the other gigs he needed to manage. Then I told him everything that had happened these past few months, as I remembered them. I talked mostly about Viv and me—how I couldn't get ahold of Viv either and how that had scared me, and everything Viv had told me up till now. I hesitated to tell him about our attack runs, so I settled on a shortened version, telling him that I'd gotten Viv's permission to expand the enterprise, and Momoko and Ran were in on it, too. "Kimiko's not involved, is she?" Yeongsu checked, but that was the only thing he asked.

"Well, there's one other reason it took me a while to come back," Yeongsu said, about an hour into our conversation. We'd just started in on our third beers.

"Remember Jihun?"

I blinked at Yeongsu. Before I could answer, he went on. "Jihun, the one that went missing?"

"Yeah, he was your brother's friend, right?"

"He was before my brother died. But I found out Jihun's alive."

My eyes widened.

"He lives in Osaka."

"No way! Seriously?" I flinched at how loud I'd been. "Sorry."

"For the longest time there was nothing, no sign, you know, but if you keep an eye out, sometimes you get lucky. The stars aligned, and I heard a rumor that there was a guy that might be Jihun."

"Did you see him?"

"Yes and no. When I got the info, I found out he'd gone clean. But I wanted to make sure it was really him, so I had to go, just to see." Yeongsu scratched his shoulder. "He's in east Osaka, is that what they call it? Lots of factories, and he's working in one of 'em. Had a little one, too."

"A kid?"

"Still in grade school, from the looks of it. Buzz cut and everything."

"So Jihun's married and living a normal life, huh," I said, getting excited. "That's amazing . . . I'm glad, you know, that he's alive."

"Well, it looks like the little one's mom got sick and died."

"What?"

"I looked into it. Three years ago, give or take."

"So he's raising the kid alone?"

"From what I found out, yeah." Yeongsu dropped his gaze to the table and smiled faintly. "He's put on the miles, got a kid, wears this raggedy factory uniform, everything about him's changed, but I knew with one look. 'That's Jihun.' Couldn't believe it."

"So . . . I know you had to keep your distance this time, but you're going to go see him again, right? Talk to him?"

"I don't know."

"What?" I asked. "Why not?"

Yeongsu's expression grew thoughtful, but I couldn't help barreling on. "He'll be surprised, no doubt, but I bet he'll be really happy. He'll be so glad to see you again. I just know it. You should go see him, Yeongsu. You have to."

Yeongsu didn't look at me and just said, "Maybe." Seeing his face, I thought I might have said something wrong, but I didn't know what or how much. We lapsed into a strained silence, half listening to the izakaya's reggae music.

"Oh, Yeongsu," I said, trying to lighten the mood again, "I wanted to ask, why did you call me instead of Kimiko? You told me you'd call her after you saw me, so I haven't told her anything."

"Couldn't tell you," Yeongsu said. "I just thought I should talk to you first, before I called Kimiko or Kotomi."

"So I shouldn't tell them I saw you?"

"No, I guess not."

"Well, they're both really worried about you, so you better call them soon . . . Oh!" I remembered what had happened with Kotomi and Oikawa, so I told him about that, too. Yeongsu listened in silence, and when I finished, his face twisted with disgust, and he spat, "That rotten piece of shit."

"She's apparently back at work now, and Kimiko's seen her a few times since then. But Kimiko's been weirder than normal lately, too, kind of out of it."

"And you three are bringing in the money, right."

"Yeah, and I make sure to give some to Kimiko. She has enough to send some to her mom, I think."

Yeongsu nodded a few times in understanding and then glanced at his watch. "It's late. I need to get going. I'll call Kimiko and Kotomi soon. And about Jihun—well, don't tell Kimiko or Kotomi yet. I suppose I'll have to tell them, but I need to think about the timing."

"Okay."

"If you've got time, you should stay and have some more beer. I'll call again, soon."

With that, Yeongsu stood and left. I stared at the corner of the table and thought about Jihun. I'd never met him, or even seen him, yet I felt like I could somehow remember him. Jihun was Kotomi's lover. How would it feel, to find out a lover you'd thought died more than twenty years ago turned out to be alive after all. Would it feel different from a family member or a friend? I couldn't imagine it—I'd never had a boy I'd even liked—but I thought, even if the news came as a shock, or made you feel confused or frustrated, you'd still be glad to know they were alive. Whenever I thought about Kotomi, I always got a wistful feeling, and today it was particularly poignant. I drained the rest of my beer and left the izakaya. Yeongsu had already paid the bill.

When I got home, Kimiko ran to the entryway to tell me Yeongsu had called, looking cheery in a way she hadn't lately. "Seriously?" I said, putting on a surprised face as I followed her into the living room. There, I nearly had the wind knocked out of me from what I saw. Momoko was watching TV, and sprawled next to her, laughing, was a girl I'd never seen before.

While I gaped in disbelief, Momoko introduced the girl as so-and-so from high school. Before I knew what I was doing, I had come up behind Momoko, grabbed her by the shoulder, and yanked her up, and ordered the high school friend to get out.

My sudden outburst was frightening enough that the friend grabbed her bag and ran out without hesitation. Momoko made to follow, but I stopped her and pushed her back inside.

"What the hell were you thinking, Momoko!"

"What? I was just hanging out with a friend," Momoko replied, waving her hands as if to deny any wrongdoing and looking confused.

"And just what do you think is in this house? What the hell were you thinking!" I yelled. "And you, Kimiko, how could you let this happen? Where's Ran?"

Without waiting for an answer, I raced up the stairs and yanked open the door to the bedroom to find Ran lounging on the floor with headphones on, her back to the door. I snatched the headphones and hurled them aside, and Ran jerked upright with a shout, shocked.

"Ran, did you know there was a stranger downstairs, inside the house? What are you doing up here?"

"Wha, what, what are you—"

"Shut up! Go downstairs!"

I dashed back downstairs and into the living room, glaring at Momoko and Kimiko. I couldn't believe it. This couldn't be happening. My hands shook with anger, and I could feel a scream building up in my chest. Ran had followed me down. I ordered them to sit and explain to me what exactly they were thinking, letting someone into the house. Ran and Momoko tried to look at each other, but I yelled at them to look at me. They both nodded and sank onto the floor. First, Momoko explained, faltering, how her friend had given her a call, and it had been a while, and they wanted to hang out, but they couldn't think of anywhere to go, so they ended up coming to the house. Ran said she and

Momoko had eaten lunch together in the room, but then she'd gone upstairs to listen to music and read magazines, and if she'd known, she would have put a stop to it.

Kimiko said that Momoko had introduced the girl as her friend, so they'd all had a beer and watched TV together. The way they spoke, what they said, the way their eyes moved was so idiotic that it made me dizzy. At the same time, I was so angry that I thought my rage would explode and my body would be blown to pieces. I told the three of them not to move and ran up the stairs again, checking the contents of the box. There was no trace of anyone touching anything, no change in the box where we kept the cards from Viv either. My shoulders heaved with a mixture of relief and rage, and clenching my fists, I made my way back downstairs, slowly this time.

2.

"But I'm clueless about machines, and I've never even been to Ginza. And aside from the attack runs, Momoko and Ran are totally useless, and . . ."

"And?" Viv said when I didn't continue. "Why do you need to think about it? How's this different from your usual gigs at the ATMs? There's nothing difficult about it. What's up with you, Hana?"

Viv had come all the way out to Sancha, which was unusual for her, and asked to meet me in an old café in the shopping district. The moment we sat down, she started talking about a new job. She seemed off from the start. She talked as fast as ever, and nothing looked different about her, but she seemed somehow anxious, unsettled.

Up till now, I'd only handled debit and credit cards that already had information loaded on them, but Viv said this time she wanted me to start collecting data so she could sell it off. To do that, I would need to attach skimmers to card readers and steal PINs as people used them. The cards had to be carefully selected, to make sure they were reliable. That's what she wanted me to do, and on top of that, she wanted me to do it at the club in Ginza where Kotomi worked.

"The skimmers just snap on. They're both black, the machine and the skimmer, so no one will know. Then all you need to do is stick a camera up on the ceiling where it can catch people's hands on the PIN pad. You don't need to know anything about machines. You leave it there a week and then go back and swap the skimmer with a new one. Another guy will pick up the camera footage through wireless. You'll just be a liaison, basically. Kotomi can take care of the club side."

"Oh, so I can tell Kotomi?"

"You're funny, Hana," Viv said, looking right at me. "How exactly do you think you'd manage this without telling her?"

"But . . . what if Kotomi says no?"

"That's not an option. You're going to persuade her. You're going to make it happen." Viv sighed dramatically and adjusted her posture several times. "First, you have her get you a key, then you go in the afternoon and bribe the person manning the register. That's it. All done. Listen, I'm not asking for your opinion, we're doing this. Our card operation is just about spent. When you're neck-deep, you better start bailing, and we're neck-deep."

These past few weeks, the number of cards we'd gotten from Viv, and the frequency with which we got those cards, had both gone down significantly. Our ATM attack runs were becoming few and far between, and I was starting to feel anxious, too. We had the money we'd saved till now. But if that was all we had going forward, it would disappear like that. With the four of us, the money we'd scrimped and saved would be gone in a few years just on ordinary living expenses alone. We had to ensure we still had a way to earn. That was true of anybody out there. But I didn't want to get Kotomi involved. Maybe she already knew a few things about us through Kimiko, but I didn't want to be the one to explain and ask her to get involved with this.

"Hey, Hana. Wake up. I don't know which way you're facing, but there's only one way forward," Viv said, baring the gap in her teeth and looking visibly irritated.

"If you're worried about setting up the camera, you can pull Yeongsu in on it, too. It sounds like he's basically dried up, so he'd probably jump at a job. And Kotomi, well she and Yeongsu and Kimiko are thick as thieves, so she'll fall in line. Kotomi isn't that innocent, you know, she'll know what to do. Mention my name, too, when you talk to her. I'll tell you about the take later. Same for the camera and the skimmer, I'll give them to you when they're ready. Okay? Are you listening? Don't sit there like a lump, Hana. Get Kotomi and Yeongsu on board and up to speed, so you can move as soon as I've got everything ready."

Once she'd spilled everything, Viv sat in silence for a while, then suddenly stood and walked toward the register. When I realized she was leaving, I scrambled to follow her out the door. As we were walking toward the main boulevard, Viv's phone rang, but she glanced at the number and ignored it. She hailed a taxi, got inside, and let the door close without looking at me. Then, she was gone.

From the way Viv acted at the restaurant and the way she took off just now, I sensed that it wasn't that she was frustrated with me—she seemed hounded by something with no space to think about anything else. Maybe things were worse than I knew—our attack runs and ATM scams, Viv's own sources of income. The way she left—I'd never seen her act that way before. It darkened my mood.

When I got home, Ran and Momoko had their legs stuck under the bare kotatsu, and they were watching TV. When I walked into the living room, they both stiffened—I could feel the mood change immediately.

"I'm calling a house meeting."

At my announcement, the two of them sat up, dropping their eyes to the table. It was the end of June. The muggy, cloying air of the rainy season filled every corner of the room. The patchy yellow paint job on the walls seemed even murkier than usual.

I sighed, exasperated, and started explaining why we hadn't had any decent attack runs these past two weeks.

I had started this new routine of "house meetings" after that fateful day—when Momoko had let a complete stranger into our house. Since then, once a day, I'd set aside time to talk to them about work and our current situation and lecture them about things I'd noticed around the house. And the two of them would listen. I was shocked, absolutely livid that they'd been so careless, that they didn't understand even the basics of what measures needed to be taken to make sure we could keep working. I needed to make them thoroughly comprehend the situation, and to stamp out any naivete and thoughtlessness they had going forward. During our "meetings," the two of them naturally spoke to me in a more formal, respectful way.

"—which means for this next job, the two of you won't be involved. So just wait in place until we can start doing attack runs again. I'll talk to Yeongsu and work things out with him. Momoko, when are you next going out?"

"I don't have any concrete plans, Hana," Momoko said.

"Okay. Ran?"

"I don't either, Hana."

"Okay. Grocery shopping on Saturday afternoon, same as always. We'll go together. If you go out for any other reason, make sure to leave a clear note. Don't forget to keep to curfew. And the Yellow Corner. Do we still have dusting cloths?"

"Yes, Hana."

Sometimes the "house meetings" only took a quick ten minutes, but sometimes they went on late into the night. When I got talking, I would remember what happened, and my anger and fury would explode again, and in those moments, the two of them curled in on themselves, bowing their heads to the floor and apologizing with everything they had. But their apologetic attitude was only proof to me how ignorant they were, and it made me angrier. My tirade would go on with even more force. *Do you really think apologizing will help us get by? That it'll bring in money? Do you have any idea how we make a living? What would happen if someone found out? One careless mistake, and everything could come crashing down. If that happens, how will you answer for that?*

Their apologies meant nothing to me if they were going to forget about it a few minutes later. *Why don't you try using your heads, even just a little!*—the two of them hung their heads as I unleashed on them. But that didn't accomplish anything either. In the end, we had money that needed to be kept secret, our lives depended on that money, and each of them owned part of that money.

I worried more about Momoko than Ran. Momoko was the kind of moron who'd been fooled by some smooth talker into investing hundreds of thousands of yen in those stupid party tickets. I blamed myself, too, that we'd been living together, yet I hadn't even noticed what was happening. Without our attack runs, Momoko would have more free time, and I had a hunch that she would restart her relationship with Uno and fall into debt again—there was a chance the money here would even be put in danger. I didn't know what might happen. That's why I'd made the notes mandatory: if the two of them were going to leave the house, they had to write it in a notepad in the living room—when they left, where, why, with whom, and when they'd get back. If they were going to be late, they were required to call. I explained that these rules were necessary in order to protect our money and our secret jobs, and that even if Ran and Momoko had no ill intentions, even if they didn't make mistakes, there was every chance someone might get an inkling of what we were doing and set a trap for us to take our money. They were surprised at first and grumbled about it, but eventually they nodded in agreement. To me, it felt like common sense. This was to protect our way of life. Ran had nowhere else to go, and Momoko was now basically in the same boat. And even though our attack runs did take a certain toll on the mind and body, they made a handsome salary of a hundred fifty thousand a month just by following my orders, and now, with the attacks put on hold, they could lounge around the house all day and still keep the same living conditions. They had no reason to complain. To make sure our lives and money were completely safe, I started checking their cell phones every night, too.

"—so that's everything for today. Where's Kimiko?"

"Upstairs, I think."

My words didn't get through to Kimiko. I knew that was impossible. That day, even though Kimiko understood the facts of why I was furious—that she'd not only let someone into the house but then gone and offered them a beer—she didn't seem capable of understanding why I was angry. I knew that was the kind of person Kimiko was, but that day, I gave in to the momentum of my anger and questioned her just as thoroughly as I had Momoko and Ran. When I did, though, she looked troubled and whispered, "I don't understand that kind of stuff." It was the same answer she gave every time—when we were about to lose the apartment, when I used to try to talk to her about our finances. She'd sound totally detached and indifferent, as if it was someone else's problem. "Then what exactly do you understand, Kimiko? Give me one thing, even just one thing, that you actually understand," I railed, voice rough. Kimiko went silent, but two days later, when I was in the upstairs bedroom arranging and counting the money in the box, she came in and sat cross-legged next to me.

She watched me work in silence for a while, and then she asked if I was hungry. "I have other things to worry about," I spat, still irritated, and in response, she said, "That's the kind of thing I understand."

My hands paused, and I looked at her.

Seeing her so close, I realized that I'd almost completely lost the larger-than-life image I'd had of Kimiko's existence, the impression of strength in her eyes I'd had when I first met her, that I'd carried all this time. It was like a punch to the gut.

"Hana. See, I get when someone's hungry or when they look sad. Then I know what to do. That's it, Hana."

My chest ached, realizing that even though she was incapable of any serious thought, she'd spent the last two days doing her best to think about the question I'd shouted at her, and now here she was, trying her best to explain. The anger that had smoldered within me the past few days slowly died down, and I grew tangled in my own wandering thoughts—*Why does she look so old, beyond her years? When did her eyes grow so vacant? Maybe she was always like this, and I've just never noticed . . . no, that can't be, Kimiko is more . . .*

As I turned over Kimiko's words—about someone being hungry or sad—I remembered that summer when I was fifteen, when she filled up the fridge with food, and that memory thrust me into a pit of sadness and heartache.

"Hana?"

"Yeah, I know, Kimiko, that's who you are," I said. "It's not your fault. That was on Momoko. Momoko brought that girl to the house, so you were nice to her. She said she was thirsty, so you gave her a beer. But from now on, Kimiko, I don't care whose friend they are, you can't let anyone into the house, okay? There's something very important in here that no one can know about. You know that, right?"

"I know."

"You'll do what I say, won't you, Kimiko?"

"Yeah, I promise."

"You're such a big help. You're so good at cleaning, and it's thanks to you that everything's going so well."

"You think so? I'm not really good at anything," Kimiko said with a smile.

That was three weeks ago. I was remembering our conversation as I climbed the stairs, and when I got upstairs, I found Kimiko sitting in the dark bedroom in front of the closet, clutching her knees, acting as a guard. The house had felt different since that day, and it seemed that even Kimiko could sense the faint nervousness that wafted through the rooms. She'd apparently grown a new sense of responsibility—sometimes she'd lounge around and watch TV, but once she was done wiping everything down, she'd taken to sitting for hours every day guarding the money. I sat down next to her and said, "Hey, Kimiko, do you know Viv?"

"Viv?"

"Vivien. I don't know her last name, but she's the boss who's been sending us on the attack runs. She told me she knows you, and Kotomi, too. She said you used to work together at a casino or something like that."

"Vivien . . . Vivien . . . I can't remember right off the bat." Kimiko stuck her hands in her hair, tussling it and twisting her head. "Yeongsu got you that job, right? So I've probably met her at some point, a long time ago."

And then I told Kimiko everything about the new job Viv had brought to me, basically ordered me to do. And that I had to ask Kotomi for a favor to make it work.

"Oh . . . the last time I saw Kotomi, she was saying she was sick of both the club and her guy. She was laughing about it, but still. I hope this new job works out."

I didn't know how Kimiko would react to the idea of involving Kotomi, and I'd been nervous, so I was relieved that she seemed calm. I'd half expected her to give me that same scary look she gave me after that whole conversation about Oikawa. Feeling relieved and relaxed, I soon found myself telling Kimiko things I never told Momoko and Ran at the house meetings. Like how worried I was about the whole thing, even though Viv insisted things would keep going on the way they had, and that this was the only stream of income left open for us. Or how Viv had given us a really good take with the attack runs, but maybe that hadn't been because she cared about me; maybe it was meant to sweeten me so I couldn't say no to her no matter what—these were things I'd kept to myself. Kimiko sat silently, clutching her knees and listening to me talk. And just as I was thinking how nice it was to be able to talk, just the two of us, the way we hadn't in a long time, Kimiko looked at the clock and abruptly stood and went downstairs. Apparently, time was up, her guard shift was over.

That night, I called Yeongsu and explained the situation. His reply was immediate—it took less than two seconds for him to say he'd do it, and the speed spooked me. If he was so willing to be on board without even knowing what his share would be, he must really be at the end of his rope. It reminded me of how anxious Viv had seemed at the café that afternoon, and my hand went weak around my phone. It hadn't even been six months since our income picked up at the start of the new year, but I sensed that all at once, everything had changed. Yeongsu said he'd talk to Kotomi first. I told him that would be a big help, and then I hung up. He called again two days later, and apparently, he'd talked with Viv, too, because he said the arrangements for the skimmer and camera pickup were already in place. Then we made plans to meet, Kotomi and Kimiko and Yeongsu and I, on Wednesday afternoon the following week.

"The lady who works the register, her name's Chie, and I've known her a long time." Kotomi slowly exhaled a stream of smoke, and then, in a tone that sounded even more drawn out, continued. "She's got three grandkids, and her daughter who's divorced took up with another guy and disappeared, so she's been looking after the grandkids. Who knows how much she's had to work since she was young, but I guess her luck hasn't changed. Well, anyway, this Chie . . . she's a real nice lady, she gets it."

"I've prodded and poked, but Viv still won't give me an actual number. I suppose no matter what, we've got to cut the old lady in, too. Have you talked to her?"

"Yup." Kotomi nodded. "She's in."

"She'll have to unlock it for us, too."

"Yeah . . . I'll have her make an extra key, just in case."

Yeongsu nodded approvingly and drained his beer. We were at a little bar down an alley not far from Shibuya Station. It was a place Yeongsu had known forever, and there weren't any other customers besides us.

How long had it been since I last saw Kotomi? We'd talked on the phone after Lemon burned, but it'd been over a year since we'd seen each other face-to-face. Kotomi had always been slim, but she'd lost even more weight, and in the dim lighting of the bar, the edges of her silhouette were covered in shadow, making her look even smaller.

"One of Viv's guys—Togashi—will take care of the recording and matching the PINs and card numbers. Once I have the key, I'll go with the guy to the club on a Sunday afternoon and decide where to put the camera. According to Viv, he checked the building two days ago and made sure there's no camera at the club entrance, and he thinks the signal will reach through the emergency exit."

"Perfect. More customers pay with credit cards nowadays," Kotomi said, smiling. "I still can't believe it's Viv. I almost wouldn't have guessed she was alive. Sure she feels the same about us, though."

"Hey, Yeongsu, is Viv in trouble?" I wasn't sure I should be asking, since Yeongsu seemed like he was in even worse trouble, but I couldn't help myself. "She seemed really nervous the other day."

"Management is squeezing Viv dry," Yeongsu said. "And that's just from the big boss. There's a load of shit from those faceless gangs, too—they just creep out of the cracks, taking territory and people right under your nose. Those guys are young, and they aren't yakuza, so they have no crest, no Oya, and they do whatever they want. There's no way to talk business with them. Viv's got no chance. Everyone's coming at her from all sides."

"So . . . what's going to happen?" I asked.

"What'll happen will happen. If things keep up, there'll be nothing left for Viv, or for us. Even this gig's just a stopgap—by next year, the card companies will have stepped up, and there'll be some new fiddly system. But money now is money now. We've gotta do what we can." Yeongsu rubbed his head with the palm of his hand. "Anyway, Viv says the skimmer paired with the PINs from the video will still sell for a shitload in Korea and China. And you can spread them out to Malaysia, too, for a cheaper price. So here's our operation: Togashi and I will set up the camera in the club. The old lady will put the info on the skimmer. I'll have Togashi deliver the new skimmers every time. Hana, like I said, there's no camera at the club entrance, but there's one on the first floor, so Togashi and I will go in through the back. The club is called C'est la Vie, and it's on the third floor. Once you decide on a day of the week, you go there and pick up the skimmer. There's a barbershop on the second floor, so you can go in the building pretending like you're a customer. It would be too dangerous for Kotomi to take it herself. Kotomi, you cool with that? The old lady can do it?"

"Chie's the only one who runs the register. The manager, the owner, the girls, all of us have to drink and entertain the guests. There's a guy on the lowest rung who closes up every day. For opening, half the time it's the guy and half the time it's Chie. I think it'll work." Then, Kotomi added, laughing, "Hey, make sure to pay her nicely. She can use all the help she can get."

"The buy-in is a hundred thousand—Hana, you got that?"

"What? I do, but not on me."

"It doesn't have to be now, but when you go see Chie the first time, give her the cash and tell her she'll be getting her cut of the take from Kotomi. Reassure her that we're not gonna screw her."

For a moment, I wondered if and how I would get that hundred thousand back—but this wasn't the time to be worrying about that. I could feel Yeongsu's nervous energy. Everything had to go well, and that was that. At the same time, I was worried about Kotomi—her eyes looked dull, and she seemed less spirited than usual. She didn't look sick, but she was so thin, even for her. While we were talking about this, Kimiko kept pouring us all beer, never saying a word. But being around Kotomi seemed to relax her, and even though we were talking about this job, I was happy to spend time with Kimiko and Kotomi after so long apart.

Our new mission—aka, operation C'est la Vie—went smoothly, despite my worries. The register lady, Chie, was completely plain and unremarkable save for her incredibly droopy eyes, and she'd hand me the skimmers in plastic bags, the same way you'd give a neighbor a souvenir.

Kotomi's club processed even more credit cards than we'd imagined, so we ended up collecting twice a week. It had a kind of refreshing, exciting air to it, like doing a water relay or something. I felt none of the nerves or exhaustion that came with running the ATMs or doing the attack runs. This job was so simple, like putting a stamp on a postcard that was already written and sticking it in the postbox. I think that was because I had other responsible people with me, Viv, Yeongsu, and even Kotomi. Also, the fact that I never had to handle cash was a big part of it. Of course I picked up our cut in cash from Viv, but on site, all I handled was a black, rectangular piece of plastic that would fit in your palm—if I didn't already know what it was, I would have had no idea.

Once operation C'est la Vie was set in motion, Viv's good mood returned, and she started to smile again. Yeongsu seemed to be enjoying the work of ensuring that we'd get the maximum profit from the data we obtained. Viv started inviting me to meals like before and would sometimes even give me a few cards for attack runs. Our fifty percent cut dropped to twenty. Apparently, everyone wanted to buy up the cards before the security system changed, and prices were skyrocketing. But when I decided to resume the attack runs with Momoko and Ran like before, I noticed that the mood wasn't the same. The ambition and drive they'd had before was gone, but neither of them seemed sick or worn down—and even when we weren't in a house meeting, I could sense a distance and a coldness between us that hadn't been there before.

I soon knew the reason. At the end of a particularly lackluster attack run, we decided to have a drink together, which we hadn't in a while, and as we sat around in the living room, Ran and Momoko brought up the subject of money.

During our house meetings, I naturally acted as the chair, and I'd often get irritated with them in real life, too, but we also just chatted and hung out the way you normally would with roommates. That night, Ran was talking about new cell phone models, and Momoko was talking about a manga she'd read lately, and I was just listening to their chatter. Once they were done with the lengthy pleasantries, Ran asked me, with hesitation, "Oh hey, about the money we saved up so far, what do you think will happen with it?"

I was caught off guard since I hadn't been expecting to be asked about money, but I managed to feign calm. "That's work-related, so shouldn't we talk about it in the next house meeting? Plus, we're back to doing the attack runs again."

"Well, we used to talk about money outside of meetings, right? We don't talk like that anymore. All we do now are meetings."

Ran looked at Momoko as if to say, "Right?"

"Oh, I've been wanting to ask for a while, but, Hana, we're not reopening Lemon anymore, are we? You haven't brought it up lately."

"I haven't brought it up?" I frowned. "You two never seemed to care about it. You never asked. So why should I bring it up?"

"That's not true. We just didn't want to step on your toes," Momoko said. "You always make the big decisions . . . so there's not much we can do. We're both just on standby right now."

"What? Are you talking about the house rules?" I glared at her. "After all the trouble I went through explaining things, I thought you finally understood. Momoko, you know what you did, right? How much danger you put us in?"

"Hey, we're not in a house meeting right now, and we're drinking, so I'm just gonna say this . . . you've been dragging me for one mistake this whole time, and honestly, I'm fed up with it," Momoko said. "I'm sorry, I was naive like you said. That was my fault. But I've apologized so many times, and I haven't made any big mistakes like that since, right? I know you're the leader on the attack runs, but aren't we equals here? You look at our phones and make us write down where we're going—it's insane. We've been going along with it because you go crazy when you're pissed. But seriously, you're way out of line."

My eyes widened with shock at this unexpected speech from Momoko. Hadn't she reflected on what she'd done and cleaned up her act? Did she not understand that my rules were meant to protect our home and our money? Me, out of line? I go crazy when I'm pissed? What was Momoko saying?

"Listen, I think you've got the wrong idea," I said, doing my best to rein in my temper. "I paid back your ticket debt, didn't I? Aren't you grateful for that? Your sister and her friends know where this house is. If they wanted to, they could smash right through a window, hell, the front door, and make off with our money! Then what would we do? What if they started to suspect something and blackmailed us? That's why we need to be careful."

"No, I think *you've* got the wrong idea. I'm tired of you talking about those tickets. That's why I'm saying you need to tell us how much money we have. You can take the stupid five hundred thousand I owe you, and there'll be plenty left over. Five hundred thousand, my ass. Let's split up the money, straight and even, between the three of us and go our separate ways. Then we don't have to worry about break-ins or being badgered. Let's just split up."

"Split up?" I demanded. "What do you mean split up?"

"It's easy. We each take our share and go live our own lives, that's what I mean."

I gulped and looked at Ran.

"Ran, this . . . what Momoko's saying, you two decided this together?"

"Well . . . I mean, we never talked about splitting up or anything . . ." Ran looked back and forth between me and Momoko. "But we do think it's about time we talked about the money."

"What the fuck?" I could tell my voice was shaking. "Talk about the money? Time to split up? What the hell are you saying? There's no way we can just split up!"

Momoko and Ran were staring at me. I exhaled so violently my shoulders rose and fell, and I tried to quell the anger rising up in me. "Do you know everything I've done, everything I had to go through to get us this far? And then you just say, what, we've saved enough so we should just split up and act like none of it happened? You think you can just get off so easy, Momoko?"

"Well, then let me ask this." For a moment, I thought Momoko would back down, but she regained her footing and glared at me. "We worked our share, too. What about everything we've had to go through?"

"What the fuck do you think your salary is?!"

"But that's not all the money, is it! None of this makes sense. It's crazy."

"You're the one that's crazy."

"What? No, you're definitely the crazy one. Even the way you talk is nuts." Momoko sneered at me. "Whatever, just split the money fair and square, there's no reason to be here anymore. We should end this now."

"What are you . . . I told you we can't, we can't do that."

"Why not? It's not like we're reopening Lemon. So what's the point of us staying here like this? How long do you plan to go on? When will you stop?"

"Momoko," I said, looking her straight in the eye, "do you know how long you're going to live, when you're going to die?"

"What?"

"Do you know how long you're going to live, how much money you're going to need to make it until you die? Have you thought about that?"

"What? Nobody's talking about dying. That's got nothing to do with this."

"Of course it does. You're asking me that very question. When will I stop? You asked me that. So what's your answer, Momoko—how long are you going to live, and how much money do you need to make it until you die? Can you honestly tell me you know, because you're asking me the same thing."

"Oh hell, you've really lost it," Momoko said, her face twitching.

"Ran," I said, looking at her, "you get what I'm saying, right? What I mean?"

"There are," Ran said carefully, "some parts I understand."

"Stop being so polite!" Momoko demanded. "There's no way any of this makes sense! Seriously, you've both gone mental. Ran, we are not Hana's minions or slaves. I'm telling you this is crazy. I don't know what your plans are, Hana, but I'm telling you, I'm out. So let's count the money upstairs, and we'll take it from there." Momoko stormed out of the living room and started running up the stairs.

"Where do you think you're going!" I screamed, running after her. I dashed into the bedroom and grabbed Momoko's shoulder as she was trying to grab the closet door. She lost her balance for a moment, but then she tried to shake me off, wriggling from side to side.

"Don't you fucking touch it!"

"Ow! Let me go, the money's not just yours!"

Momoko flung me off, and I landed on the tatami flat on my ass. I couldn't beat her one-on-one—that realization hit me as the shock of the fall ran from my tailbone to my skull. Momoko's body was thick and sturdy, and she was stronger than me. If we fought for money here and now, I couldn't possibly win. And if Momoko took the money and ran, I'd have no way to get it back from her. The money we'd worked our asses off to earn was in the box—but at the same time, it was money that didn't exist.

"Momoko," I said, catching my breath, still on the floor, trying to speak in a calm tone. "What, are you going to take the money?"

"What? I'm just saying we should count it, so we can split it . . ." but her expression changed, as though she only realized just now that she *could* take the money and run.

"If you're going to take it, then take it," I said quietly. "But Momoko? If you do, they're gonna come after you, no matter what. We're in way worse than you can imagine. Where do you think those cards come from? They're not legit. It's all yakuza, the underworld, and the money, that's crooked, too, it's not just ours. We don't get to just use it however we want. But fine. You go ahead and take everything, Momoko. Remember, though, it's not your money, it's the family's. The yakuza's. It's so much worse, so much more fucked-up than you can imagine. The Oya—you know, the boss—he knows exactly who we are, you, me, Ran. He knows where we are, and he knows exactly how much cash we've got, too. Try and run off with the money, and they'll find you. We're not talking about your stupid fucking club tickets here, Momoko."

Ran had come upstairs while I was talking, and she and Momoko stood side by side, frozen, looking down at me.

"I'll count the money. But it'll take time. And if you want to split, we'll split, but I'm asking you for time."

After a long silence, Momoko asked in a low voice, a voice I'd never heard before, "How much money is in there?"

"Twenty-one million, six hundred fifty-nine thousand." I answered honestly. I heard them both gasp. This was the money we'd earned running our attacks, single-mindedly, from morning to night.

"Of course, the money I'd saved before we started our attack runs is in there, too. Because I was saving it for Lemon. But it doesn't matter how much money we have, we can never reopen Lemon. So we'll take the money we worked hard to earn and split it fair and square."

"Yeah, that's a great idea, Hana," Ran agreed, rushing to talk before Momoko could. "There's no use in fighting, right, Momoko?"

"And if the two of you want to quit the attack runs, fine," I said. "We can end that here, now. Just wait until I've talked to the Oya. But until I've cleared the money with him, follow the house rules. Do your part and don't screw around. Oh, and I was gonna wait until the next meeting to say—you've been doing pretty good with the Yellow Corner, but you've been slacking off on the entryway and bathroom. Yellow's important, but in feng shui, you're supposed to keep the entryway and bathroom spick and span, too, remember? And like we said in the last meeting, you only keep two pairs of shoes in the entryway. There's one pair too many right now—a pair of mules. They must be yours, Ran? Anyway, make sure to look after the house. I'll clear the money soon."

Momoko and Ran stood silent, staring at me.

3.

I started feeling a heavy weight on my shoulders every time I went to Ginza, even though I'd been there dozens of times and should have been used to it by now. No matter how sunny the day, the train was dark and gloomy inside, and I felt like I'd been blindfolded and was being taken to some distant, strange location against my will, even though I knew exactly where I was going. I didn't know what Ginza was like at night, but Ginza in the afternoon was barren and filthy, with trash scattered here and there, and I felt like I was walking through the giant dregs of the city.

Whenever I walked into C'est la Vie, Chie was always waiting with her overkill smile, and our interactions, brief though they were, filled me with melancholy. July was drawing to a close, and it seemed ridiculous to me that high summer hadn't even started. But what did the seasons have to do with me anyway? Nothing. Absolutely nothing.

Ever since that fight, Ran and Momoko had stuck to the house rules, going out less than they had before. They'd been so demanding with their talk about tallying the money and splitting up, but now they didn't seem to care about any of it. Instead, they just lazed in the living room and watched TV all day. But I couldn't let my guard down. I explained to Kimiko what had happened and told her to monitor them and to never leave the house empty.

The tally. I had to think carefully. ¥21,659,000 was what we had, and we couldn't just split it evenly four ways and call it quits. That didn't make sense. There was money in there that I'd earned on my own, and the pressures and responsibilities of the job had been completely different for me. But as I tried to think about how I might distribute the money more fairly, I was sure I was missing something essential—something I should be thinking about instead. There was something else, something about us, that was the real issue at hand. The thought harried me, but I didn't know what to do about it. Almost everything I'd told Momoko had been made up on the spot. I wasn't lying about the yakuza or the underworld. Viv was definitely a part of that, but we'd always paid our dues, and the money we had was ours. What was it that Ran and Momoko wanted, exactly? Where would they go if we split up? This was our house—our home. Was it money they wanted? But money in what sense? Having money, earning money, spending money . . . they might seem similar, but they were very different things.

Sure, it's natural to want money, but what exactly did they hope to get out of it? And what about me? What did I hope to find in money? Well . . . for me, it wasn't the money itself. It was . . . a house, a home. My muddled thoughts twined around me until I couldn't move, and whenever that happened, inevitably, my thoughts turned to Kimiko. Sometimes, that inevitability felt heavy, dark. But she was the only clear image in the confusion of my thoughts, the person who made me remember who I was. *Kimiko can't live on her own—Kimiko needs me.*

On the way home from Ginza, I got off at Shibuya to make a transfer, and that's when my phone rang. It was Kotomi. The roar of the trains was deafening, so I went aboveground to call her back. It turned out she was in Shibuya, too, so we made plans to meet at a hotel lounge café in the Mark City Building in twenty minutes.

Kotomi called my name and waved when she saw me. Even from far away, a glance was enough to tell anyone that Kotomi was beautiful. I rushed through the café, feeling my heartbeat, and sat down across from her. She was drinking a beer, so I ordered one, too.

"You look good, Hana."

"You, too."

"What lucky timing. I called Kimiko, too, but she says she can't leave the house for a while. Did something happen?"

"I'm not sure . . . I'll be sure to ask her when I get home. But she's doing well."

Kotomi told me she'd been staying at this hotel since last week. She was smiling, trying not to worry me, but there were shadows in her expression, and I suspected Oikawa had done something terrible to her again. Kotomi didn't bring up C'est la Vie and instead asked how everyone was doing at the house. I told her that everyone was getting along, all laughter all the time, it's so great living together with friends, same as always.

We talked about everything—the clothes Kotomi had been wearing the first time we met at Lemon, how I couldn't believe such a beautiful person existed in this world, how surprised I was by the amount of money she brought in every time, how the huge glistening black car she'd ridden away in seemed to me like a living creature on the sea of night, and how every time I saw the Christian Riese Lassen painting Momoko had brought home, I thought of that car. I was so happy to spend time with Kotomi, but I was also nervous, so I drank beer at double the pace I normally would. Kotomi laughed and smiled along with me as I gestured and babbled on.

We spent about two hours in the lounge café. I knew I was really drunk, but I felt good. Kotomi, too, had drunk more than she usually would have, and I was happy that she seemed to be enjoying her time with me. She'd grown so thin these past few years, but she was still beautiful—so beautiful that whenever our eyes met, I had to look away. Somewhere, piano music was playing, and the summer sunset made the twilight blue stretch on and on, heading slowly into the night. Eventually, we both felt like it was time to go, so we stood up together.

I figured she'd go back up to her room, but Kotomi said she

wanted to go to the drugstore so she would head out with me. As Kotomi stepped into the elevator, she stumbled, and I held her up. The two of us crowed with laughter, completely drunk. I went with Kotomi to the drugstore, where she bought eye drops, and then she said she'd walk me to the train station. I felt like I didn't want to leave her yet, and maybe she was feeling the same way. We walked down the boulevard, laughing and hanging off of each other, passing through the press of people, and a karaoke parlor appeared in front of us. Kotomi pointed at the huge neon lights shining on the building and asked if I wanted to do a few songs with her before I went home. I happily agreed.

Once we got our karaoke booth, we kept drinking beer. No matter what I said, Kotomi laughed as if it was the funniest thing in the world, so I just kept talking. About the summer day when I first met Kimiko. How she disappeared suddenly, and I felt lost and alone. How we met again. How even though Yeongsu had such a beautiful voice, I'd never once heard him sing. That made Kotomi laugh and say, "That's right! I've never heard you sing either. Sing something!" I told her I was terrible at singing and ordered another beer. Then I asked her to sing something. At Lemon, it was always Momoko and Ran who sang, so I'd never heard Kotomi sing either.

"Oh, I'm not very good," Kotomi said, leaning against the sofa to flip through the fat songbook.

"It's okay. It doesn't matter if you're good or not, sing whatever you like," I told her excitedly, and peered at the page she'd paused on. *This is nice*, I thought. *How long has it been since I last laughed like this, let go like this?* And with Kotomi, whom I adored. I felt that in this moment, right now, it was okay to forget everything and just have fun. I drank more and more beer.

"You're bottomless!" Kotomi laughed, and then, having decided on a song, she punched in its code. We grinned up at the screen as we waited for the song to start. Soon, a wistful melody, the sort that tugged at your heart, started to play, and Kotomi stood up, mic in hand, to bow jokingly to me. She was so beautiful that I found myself totally mesmerized, enraptured.

Kotomi's voice was delicate but clear and seemed to embrace every note, every word, with tenderness and care. I followed the lyrics as though trying to imprint them into my memory, and when the interlude played, I turned my eyes to study Kotomi's profile, unblinking. The disco ball overhead turned and threw sparkles of light onto her cheeks and forehead, and the light also danced in her dark, moist eyes.

Time unfolds in continuous links
There will never be an end, you think
The universe is right here,
infinite and clear, holding you tight

You're still Cinderella,
climbing those stairs to full bloom
Believing that someone
Will carry happiness to you

One day, you'll look back
And think—I was just a girl

When the song finished, Kotomi gave a little cheer, twisting like she was embarrassed, and then clapped. Kotomi's voice, the lyrics, the fact that the two of us were here together, the whole night—I didn't know why, but I was on the verge of tears, and it was all I could do to ask what the song was called. "This song is called . . . 'Full of Memories'!" Kotomi said, still talking through the mic, and then she put up both hands and called out, "Hanaaaa," laughing. As she did so, the slit in her skirt opened with the movement, and I saw a blue-black bruise on her thigh. It was so huge and such a dark color that at first, I thought it couldn't be real. Kotomi fixed her skirt right away, but I was dumbstruck by what I saw.

She tried to bring back the jokes and the laughter, but I couldn't go along with it anymore. When I didn't say anything, Kotomi told me "Full of Memories" had been popular when she was about my age, and then she started talking about when she was young. I was really drunk, and the images and words in my brain went round and round, and my eyes grew hot, and Kotomi's voice seemed to recede and then come closer. Kotomi talked about how she and Kimiko had never fought about anything, how the two of them had once lived together, how she'd only ever been to the ocean once.

"You go way back, right? Yeongsu told me that, a few years ago," I said.

"Yeah. Yeongsu, too, he's like a brother to me. He makes me worry with the way he disappears sometimes."

"Me, too, the last time he disappeared I was worried sick."

"But you know, he always comes back. Always."

We fell into silence. The faint sound of songs from various rooms filtered in, and with them, singing voices droning like echoes.

"Hey, Kotomi, your guy, Oikawa, we should really do something about him," I said. I never would have said it if I weren't drunk. I couldn't forget the bruise I'd seen. "Let's do something about him, Kotomi, it isn't right, we've got Yeongsu, we've got your back, we can do something."

Kotomi gave me a troubled smile and took a sip of beer.

"I'm serious, Kotomi," I said, tears starting to flow from my anger and hatred for Oikawa. "It's not right."

"Thank you, Hana. But there's no way," Kotomi said and laughed. "It's not gonna happen."

"We can though!" I said. "I'm sure Yeongsu told you, he found Jihun, right? He never gave up, because you never give up, and you've been friends for so long, so if we all put our heads together, there's nothing we can't do. We love you, Kotomi, we care about you so much, so—"

"Jihun?" Kotomi asked, with a smile still on her face. "Did you say Jihun?"

"Yes, Jihun. He's in Osaka, right? That's where Yeongsu saw him."

"Yes—yes, that's right." Kotomi kept smiling at me, staring at me, and then she nodded. "I actually . . . Yeongsu didn't give me a lot of details."

"Then you should ask him about it, and then we can work together. You have Kimiko, you have me, okay, Kotomi? So don't say it's impossible. It's not. Please don't say it is." I was crying now, overcome with emotion, and talking her ear off. Kotomi put her arm around me to comfort me.

"Kotomi, I mean it . . . please."

"Yes, Hana. You're right. There's nothing we can't do."

After that, we both sprawled out in the booths, drinking beer and talking about our memories. I told Kotomi I wanted us all to hang out again, go to a family restaurant, and Kotomi smiled and said that sounded nice. And then she thanked me for looking out for Kimiko. *I love her, you know? I love her, too. She saved me, she's always been so kind, and it's thanks to her that I met you, Kotomi. That's right, isn't it? Yeah. Hey, Hana? Hmm? Look up, that disco ball is so pretty. Yeah, it really is.*

We left the karaoke parlor just after ten o'clock at night. Kotomi said, "Let's do this again with Kimiko next time," and then she squeezed my fingers and let go. I set off toward the station, but I turned back again and again to wave. Kotomi waved at me until I could no longer see her through the press of the crowd. Let's do it again soon, with everyone next time. But that was the last time I ever saw her.

Still drunk, I replayed what lyrics and melody I could remember from "Full of Memories" in my head as I swayed with the bus on my way home. The summer night felt nice, and I thought about Kotomi as I walked. The way I felt about her was different from any other person. I'm not sure why, but I'd always felt that way. From the moment we met, there was something of sadness, of heartache, of loneliness about Kotomi, and she was precious and dear to me even when we weren't together. I didn't know why. I wanted her to be happy. I didn't know what happiness was, but I wanted her to have it. But it would be okay. She had Yeongsu, she had Kimiko, and now she might even have Jihun again. Viv was on her side when it came to work, too. We were here for her. I was choked up with emotion and grateful for the fact that I had friends, that I could be so lucky, having them by my side. Our house, our home. Right now, we were going through a rough patch, and there were things that pissed me off and irritated me, but couldn't we start over? I didn't have anyone else I was close with like Ran and Momoko. They were my friends. We could talk it over, set things right, put everything back on track—I made my way home on unsteady feet, and when I arrived at the front door, my hopes were dashed. I found Momoko there, trying to run with the money.

TWELVE

BACK TO SQUARE ONE

1.

Momoko stood on the doorstep, wearing a huge backpack and holding a paper bag in one hand. For a moment, I didn't understand what she was doing there. Her expression transformed, and she ran back into the house, but then she whipped around and tried to shove past me to run out again. The money—I was moving before I realized what was happening. I planted my feet, intent on restraining Momoko as she snarled and tried to bowl me over. We brawled and grappled, not saying a word, and then I saw my chance and wriggled in behind her, grabbing the straps of the backpack and yanking with all my might. Momoko lost her balance and tumbled backward with a thud. She'd hit her head on the step of the entryway into the house. She twisted on the ground for a moment, but then, with a sudden shout, she scrambled back into the house with the paper bag clutched to her chest and bolted up the stairs.

"Momoko," I yelled, chasing after her, "what the hell do you think you're doing?"

"I'm not doing anything!"

"Give me the bag."

"Shut up!"

Locked in each other's arms, we spilled into the bedroom,

grappling for the bag between us. Our momentum slammed Momoko into the closet door, and she slipped, banging the side of her head, maybe her ear, on a pillar. She cried in pain and loosened her grip on the bag, and I took the chance to yank the bag away, hugging it tight. I panted as I looked down at Momoko where she lay curled in a ball, moaning, "It hurts, it hurts." It was then that Ran clattered up the stairs, her hair still soaking wet. On her heels came Kimiko, looking as though she'd only just woken up.

"What the hell are you two doing?" Ran noticed Momoko clutching her ear and darted to her side. "You're bleeding. She's bleeding!"

"Who cares! She was taking the money, Kimiko, she was about to run away with it. What were you doing, Kimiko? I told you to watch her!"

"I'm sorry. I fell asleep," Kimiko said, uncharacteristically flustered, stomping and turning on the spot. Ran yelled, "You've gone too far, Hana." For a moment, the shrillness of her voice made me hesitate, but then I clutched the bag tighter. It was true that Momoko was bleeding, but only a little, not enough to make a big deal about it. She had been trying to run off with the money. What was Ran so worried about? Did she not understand what was happening? As I tried to catch my breath, I peered into the bag to make sure. The money was wrapped in a towel, but at a glance, it looked to be about the same size as the stack of money in the box. I knew instinctively since I counted it regularly. This couldn't be happening. I couldn't believe it. I'd explained about the yakuza and the underworld, warned them what would happen if we dared to run—and still Momoko had tried. What the hell was she thinking?

Ran was still shouting. "Hana, are you listening to me? This is—"

"Shut up!" I screamed. "Momoko was taking our money, all of it, and I'm trying to stop her. What were *you* doing?! After everything I told you, after everything . . ."

Momoko lay curled and bawling on the tatami, Ran crouched by her side glaring up at me, and Kimiko stood there motionless. As I stared at them all, a clamor went up in my head, and I tore at my hair. *What the hell is this? What is going on?* I thought of Kotomi, of my friends, of how sentimental I'd been feeling only moments ago. My heart began to pound, layering over the clamor in my mind, and I shook my head violently, trying to banish it.

I raised my voice and said, "Momoko, I told you, you can't just run off with the money. Are you fucking stupid?"

"Oh, fuck off! Who the hell would believe that story, the yakuza or whatever, I know you're full of shit. There's no way some underworld boss is gonna come after a shitty team like ours, don't make me laugh. It's just you with your fucking stories, and we all know it," Momoko screamed, her hand still slapped over her ear. "And we know you want the money all for yourself, but I'm not going to let that happen. You're gonna pay me what's mine, you're not gonna steal it from me."

"Oh, fuck off! I would never take your money. This is the money we've been saving together, it's all of ours, and I would never—"

"Shut up, stop talking, just give me my share!"

"Momoko, is that really all you care about, the money?"

"Like you're one to talk!"

"I don't care about the money, that's not—I mean, I care about the money, but that's not what I'm trying to say."

"Oh, cut the crap. Just look at everything you've done! You fucking used us, you used us! You used us so you could get this stupid money! You have no right to talk!"

I didn't know what to say to that.

"So don't act like we're in this together." Momoko blew out a long breath and glared at me. "You've trapped us with this money, made it so we can't leave, pretended like we were friends, but you've got it all wrong."

"What have I got wrong? None of you had anywhere to go,

any money, and I went out and looked and looked until I found us work, and that's what you've been using to live, isn't it? I've been busting my ass for you—"

"Nobody asked you to!" Momoko yelled. "Maybe you think you did it for us, but you didn't. No way, you are so completely full of shit. You did it for yourself, decided for us, started this whole thing without asking us. And now that we're here, if I were you, I'd make a clean break, split the money four ways between us, end it once and for all. Why don't we do that? Why?!"

I was silent.

"Ha! It's not that you won't—you can't. Do you know why?" Momoko continued. "Sure, part of it's the money, but deep down, you just can't stand to be alone. You have nothing, no one, so you control people with money, force everyone to stick around. Well, wake up. You should know by now what a loser you are."

"I . . ." I gulped once and continued, "What exactly do you mean I can't stand to be alone."

"Exactly what I said."

"Don't make me laugh. Who's the one who can't make it on her own? How can you say that, knowing everything I've done up until now, Momoko? While you were here, clueless, mooching off your parents and your grandma, bitching about how beautiful your sister is, fucking around and being useless, I was working my ass off, always working working working. I found us this house, found work for you, since you apparently can't do it yourselves, and now you have the nerve to say that to me, after everything I did for you, to say that I did it for myself? Let me say again, don't make me laugh, because you'd be nothing without me. You're the one who can't make it on your own. Where do you get off saying that to me?!"

"See, that's exactly what I mean." Momoko shot a glance at me. "You acting like you're the only one who worked hard, the only one who suffered. Well, guess what. Everyone works! Everyone suffers! If you can't understand something as simple as that, then why the hell do you even bother? What's the point?

You're so proud of your own damn suffering. Fine, fine, you're right, you win, so sorry I used my parents' money, so sorry I've got a complex about my sister. But you don't want me to apologize, do you. You want me to tell you how amazing you are? You want me to kiss your ass? *Oh, Hana, you're so brave, so thoughtful, so smart, turning every problem into a lucky break. You make our lives better with your hard work.* What a fucking joke."

There was a huge lump in my throat, and I could feel my cheeks growing hot.

"I can go on and on. I'll say it as much as you want. *No one has ever suffered as much as you, no one has ever worked as hard as you, you're amazing, compared to you, we're pampered babies, sheltered idiots, so sorry!*" She laughed bitterly. "But you know what? You wanna know the truth? You're nothing special. You were just unlucky, just pathetic. You didn't have anything but your stupid fortune-telling. That's all you are. Get it? You use your friends, you live in a shit house, you earn your dirty money stealing from credit cards, and now you have nowhere left to go, no way out. You're nothing but a bar hostess, you didn't even go to high school. You pretend to be generous, putting yourself out for your friends, but all you really want is to make yourself feel better. Do you understand now? You can't survive if you don't have someone to boss around, someone to kiss your ass, because that's who you are, and don't you forget it."

My body suddenly hooked forward, as though the world itself had cracked in two, and in the next second, I was on top of Momoko. "Stop!" cried Ran, throwing herself between us and trying to pull me off. And then there was a scream like I'd never heard before—the three of us froze in our grapple and turned toward the voice.

It was Kimiko. She had grabbed the Christian Lassen print that was propped against the wall, raised it high above her head, and in that moment, she crashed the print straight through the sliding closet door. The latticework fractured, and Momoko, Ran, and I cowered. Kimiko yanked the Lassen print out of the door, raised it above her head, and brought it down again and again until the door was nothing but splinters and paper. None of us moved as we watched the glistening blue sea in its sharp golden frame tear into the ruins again and again. Kimiko's explosion looked simultaneously involuntary and also completely volitional. I couldn't understand what was happening. I was dumbstruck, but at the same time, I felt I had to calm Kimiko down, had to stop her, so I came up behind her and grabbed her in a full nelson. The Lassen frame kept banging me in the head as I tried to calm Kimiko, to restrain her. Then, in the confusion, Momoko rammed into me, and I dropped the bag from where I had shoved it under my arm.

Momoko snatched the bag and tried to run from the room, but I managed to grab the hem of her T-shirt. Still, she didn't stop, dragging me into the hallway. Then Ran came out, followed by Kimiko. "Ow!" "Both of you stop it!" "Give it back!" "Let go!" Our shouts rose over each other as we struggled on the landing above the stairs. We were grabbing, pushing, yanking, locked together like dumplings on a skewer. I couldn't let Momoko run, couldn't let her get outside. I needed to get her back in the bedroom, take the bag away from her. Ran was screaming as she wheeled around, and Kimiko planted herself, her mouth pressed in a thin line as she tried to keep Momoko from escaping. It was coming to a head, all the energy climbing toward a climax, when suddenly time slowed—in the next instant, I saw Momoko falling down the stairs. She was facing me, and for a moment, she seemed to float, her arms outstretched, and then she fell, less a tumble than a swift descent. The next thing I knew, Momoko was at the bottom of the stairs, her body sprawled and twisted at an odd angle. None of us could move, frozen on the top landing looking down at her. But we had to move. Slowly, the three of us descended the stairs and stepped over Momoko into the hallway, where we called her name over and over.

After a few seconds, Momoko scrunched her face, shook her head, and spoke: "My leg, my leg, it hurts . . ." She was glaring at me as tears leaked from her eyes.

"You, you're all crazy," she said, holding her ankle. "I'm telling my parents everything, this is insane."

"Your parents?"

"Yep. I'm telling my mom. The cops, too."

"The cops?" My voice came out oddly shrill, and I gulped.

"That's right, I'm gonna tell them I got roped into it, you made me do it. I'm gonna tell them everything, come clean, and they can decide. I don't care about the money, I don't want it. You're all fucking crazy. Oh god, my leg hurts so bad. I'm going to tell them the truth."

"You can't do that."

"I can, and I will. I'll tell them everything."

"But if you do," I said, trying to calm myself down, "what'll you do then?"

"Don't lump me in with you. I'll go home, I'll tell my mom, and she'll help me. You're the one who'll be in trouble. How do you think you'll survive? You think you have a future? Ha, you don't. This is it for you. And I've always wanted to say this—what the hell is up with you and Kimiko? She's creeped me out from the beginning, fucking loser, but now, she's a freak. Seriously. Fucking crazy. Oh god, my leg. God, it hurts so bad, I need a doctor. What are you gonna do about this?" Momoko turned her eyes on me, babbling without pause. "Oh, I know, when I get home, I'm gonna tell Tommy-cat about this, he'll have a blast writing an exposé. All of it, you hear me? No, I know. I'll call him right now, this kind of shit is his favorite, it'll make a huge splash, teenagers make a killing with credit card fraud, it'll be way bigger than compensated dating—all right already, get out of the way. I'm going home."

I stared at Momoko, eyes wide. How serious was she? Was she making this up, or did she actually have a plan, an ulterior motive? Would she actually do what she threatened to do? I didn't know. I didn't want to know. I felt like if I let my guard down for even a second, I'd explode or just collapse on the spot. *What do I do, what do I say, think, come on, think, figure it out, what's the right thing to do here . . . That's it, there's one thing I do know, it doesn't matter if Momoko's serious or if she's bluffing, I can't let her leave the house. That's the only thing I have to think about right now—stop her, stop her right now, so come on, you idiot, do what you have to, do the thing you know you have to do.*

"Kimiko, make sure Momoko doesn't leave. Ran, come here."

"What, you think you can stop me? I won't—"

"Oh, shut up and stay still. Kimiko, keep an eye on her."

Ran was on the brink of tears as I took her to the kitchen. I told her there was no reason to worry.

"What do we do, Hana? Are we gonna get arrested?"

"We're not gonna get arrested, it's okay."

"I don't care about the money anymore. Let's just stop."

"They'll definitely arrest us if we stop, we can't."

"Then what do we do?"

"First, we have to get Momoko to listen to us. She's upset right now, so if we can just keep our cool and tell her we'll give her her share, I think she'll believe us."

"But she's saying she's gonna go home, what do we do about that?" Ran started crying.

"We'll keep her here for a while," I said. "Until she understands what needs to be done. Ran, everything is riding on this. So pull yourself together. Just do as I say."

When we came out, Momoko's face was twisted as she complained about how her ankle hurt, how it might be broken. Sweat was beading on her forehead, but I couldn't tell if her ankle was sprained or actually broken. I told Kimiko and Ran to hold down Momoko, who continued to wail, and I collected her bags and cell phone from where they'd fallen into the entryway. Her blubbering only got worse as I explained to her that we were going to have a house meeting upstairs. It was the middle of the night. If someone got suspicious of the noise and called the police . . . Beginning to panic, I told Kimiko to grab some packing tape and used it to tape over Momoko's mouth, telling her I'd take it off once she calmed down. Then the three of us took her by the arms and supported her on either side as we dragged her back up the stairs to the other room. It took more than twenty minutes just to get her there. Kimiko tried to restrain her by holding both her arms behind her back, but Momoko struggled, trying to wriggle the tape off, which left me with no choice but to grab some nylon rope and bind her wrists tight.

Momoko was screaming from beneath the tape, her eyes bloodshot and her upper body writhing. The more I gave orders and acted to control the situation, the more my mind went blank. What was I doing? I couldn't retrace the logic of the actions I'd taken even a few seconds ago, or figure out what I should be doing next. It was all I could do to still the shaking in my hands. I was terrified by the sight of Momoko, mouth taped, arms bound, tears running down her face, yet I was the one who'd done it.

I took several deep, long breaths to calm myself, and then I crouched in front of Momoko, and as calmly as I could began to explain: "Let's just talk, together, to make sure we're on the same page, so we can put all of this behind us. Let's forget about the police, okay?" But she wouldn't listen. Instead, she thrashed her uninjured leg and kicked me hard across the jaw. I shouted and tumbled backward. Kimiko flew forward, thinking Momoko had attacked me, and slapped Momoko loud and hard across the cheek. "No, Kimiko!" Ran and I rushed to stop her and explained that Momoko had kicked me by accident, not on purpose. We both apologized to Momoko, but she continued to cry and flail. I didn't know what to do. Momoko's ankle looked more swollen than it had been before. It might really be broken. But what to do? What could we do?

The clock in the Yellow Corner read 3:30 a.m. It'd been a few hours since we put Momoko in the room upstairs—she kept trying to crawl out again, so we had to bind her calves and knees together with more packing tape. I explained to her, carefully and patiently, that we'd give her her share of the money, split it four ways and let her go, but first she had to promise that she wouldn't go to the police or tell anybody about any of this. This time she listened but wouldn't nod in agreement. We stared at each other for a long time, unmoving, and eventually, Momoko tumbled herself onto her side and closed her eyes.

I remembered that we had some stick-on cold compresses in the refrigerator, so I brought one up and put it on her swollen ankle. I thought she might kick me again, but she didn't move, and after that, she looked like she fell asleep.

Ran, Kimiko, and I went downstairs to the living room, where we sat in silence. Ran buried her face in her knees, and Kimiko stared vacantly into the distance. I wanted to ask her why she'd done that with the Lassen print upstairs, but I didn't have the energy for it. The patchy yellow on the wall seemed to darken, then lighten, then darken again before me. So what were we supposed to do now? Momoko would have to use the bathroom at some point, and she'd need water, and food, too. She had threatened to go to the police and tell them everything about the cards. But what was I doing to her? I couldn't believe the situation we were in.

After a while, Ran and Kimiko fell asleep with their heads on the kotatsu table, but I was up until morning, not a wink of sleep. I grabbed a cup of water and carried it upstairs, where I found Momoko awake. Her eyes met mine. I asked her if she'd be willing to talk without raising a racket, and after glaring at me for a while, she nodded.

Once I'd removed the tape from her mouth, she exhaled and said, simply, "Bathroom." I removed the tape from her calves, helped her to stand, and then grabbed scissors to cut the rope around her wrists. She was limping, and her ankle was swollen, but I didn't think it was broken. For the time being, Momoko didn't look like she was going to make a run for it—maybe her leg just hurt too bad. Once she was done, Momoko calmly returned and took her time drinking the water.

"Momoko, I know you said a lot of things, but I think you're smart enough to know that if you tell anyone about this, you'll be in hot water, too. You used the money from this to pay off those tickets, and you were getting a salary from it, too. You were completely on board. Do you really think they'll believe I *made* you do it? You know they won't. Because they'll interrogate me, too. And besides, you said you were going to go home, but you don't have a home either. If you did, why would you be here?"

Momoko was silent.

"Five million," I said. "I won't know for sure until I do the math, but if we split it four ways, that's about what you'll get. And like I told you before, first I have to clear it with the Oya, and if you and Ran are out, I have to think about what the next steps are, too. You don't have to do anything for now, but until I hear back, you'll stay here with Ran and Kimiko. I have to go to work today. I have responsibilities. I can't call it quits. I can't make a clean break like that. It's work, Momoko, not just money. A lot of people are involved. You can't get out just like it's nothing, just because you feel like it. Honestly, I don't even know how I feel about it anymore either."

Momoko kept glaring at me for a long time, but then she huffed and looked away. I didn't know if that meant she'd accepted what I had to say, but finally she dragged herself into the bedroom, unfolded her futon, climbed inside, and pulled the covers over herself.

"I'm going to hang on to your phone for a while. Don't leave the house. Kimiko and Ran are watching you. Just hold on until I get the math squared away."

Momoko just lay there with her back to me, silent.

We spent a strange few weeks together after that.

I'd told Momoko that Kimiko and Ran were on guard, but they couldn't be there all the time. Momoko could have run if she really wanted to, but she never did, just stayed in the house. I think she'd realized that going to the police wasn't a good idea after all and that she really did want her cut of the money. We stopped talking to each other except when we absolutely had to, and the only thing that remained between us were the rules I'd decided for the house. Everything was stagnant. With operation C'est la Vie, I called in sick twice, and after that, I didn't hear from anyone. Maybe they were continuing the job without me. I didn't know. I wondered about my cut, what I should do going forward. I felt anxious, but at the same time, I couldn't bring myself to ask either.

I was exhausted. But there was the rent and the bills to pay, and everyone's salaries, too. I had to take care of everything. Momoko wouldn't like it if I started drawing money from what we'd saved. She—probably Ran, too—wanted her cut, and then she wanted out. If they got tired of waiting, if we had another night like that first night . . . Even just thinking about it made me want to vomit. Everything had turned to shit.

August came. The heat was oppressive; the sun burned down relentlessly and mercilessly on everything, every day. Momoko was holed up in the other room upstairs, and Ran and Kimiko listlessly watched TV downstairs. I shoved aside the broken fusuma, checked the money, and grabbed the bundle of cards. There were stacks and stacks of fake credit cards and debit cards in the box, each bound with rubber bands. I took the cards out and piled them up on the tatami. Between the ones we'd used for our attack runs and the ones Viv asked me to hold on to, there were a lot. Then I took the money out of the paper bag and piled it into a mound, same as I'd done with the cards. ¥21,659,000—if I didn't think of it as money, then it was just bundles of paper, but it was money all the same. The pile was small enough that, if I wanted to, I could easily hold it in my hands. I began to lose sight of what I was even looking at. I—we—had worked our asses off these past few years to collect what lay before me now. But what was this thing that we'd been gathering? Yes, it was money. For sure, we were collecting money—this thing that could transform into whatever we wanted, just like that. This thing that allowed us to protect and satisfy ourselves and our loved ones, this thing that could become time itself, possibility itself. A future, security, strength, fear, power—all the things I'd thought of as I'd grasped for this money. The words came to me one by one now as I stared at the pile, and I sensed that they were all true, but at the same time, they were all irrelevant. I didn't understand. *What is it I'm even looking at right now?*

As I sat before the closet thinking, my phone rang.

It was Yeongsu, but I couldn't bring myself to answer, so I just let it ring. When I came downstairs, I found Kimiko and Ran facing away from each other, both napping. Their sleep looked strained, not restful in the least—I knew the feeling well. They were sleeping the way people do when they don't have anything to do or anywhere to go, when all that's left for them is to simply stop being conscious. I put my phone in my purse and went out.

I waited until I could see the station before I called Yeongsu back. He answered before the phone even had a chance to ring and told me he'd call me back in a second from a different number.

"Hana," he said when he'd called again. "Viv jumped ship."

For a moment, the world went silent, as though the rays of the sun had swallowed up all sound, and then it came roaring back.

"Hana, did you hear me? Viv jumped ship."

"Viv what?"

"She took off with all the money from who knows how many sources, and now it's our problem—the biggest loss was the advance for the skimmer guys. From what I know so far, that alone was eight million. She disappeared with it."

I blinked again and again.

"Hana, are you listening to me?"

"I heard you."

"Hana, if, by some miracle, Viv calls you, pretend like you don't know anything, and do whatever you have to to get the story out of her. If my usual number's not working, use this one—it's a burner. If someone calls and you don't know the number, don't answer. Talk soon," he said and hung up.

I stood frozen in the middle of the street, phone still in hand. I could almost hear the sweat roll down my forehead, my temples, my neck, the small of my back, my armpits. I startled when a car honked its horn behind me and sped by once I was out of the way. I began trailing the car, cutting my way through the heat.

Viv. Viv jumped ship. Disappeared. To jump ship means to disappear, but where to? *To a place where no one can find her.* At first, I thought it was Viv saying those words, but then I remembered that it had been Kotomi. A long time ago, the night I first met her, she'd taught me that. Yakiniku. The gap between Viv's teeth when she smiled. Yakiniku. "Well, you're a bit of a strange one, aren't you." That's what Viv had said to me when I took a bite of the grilled meat, and it was so good that I thought of my mom and started crying. Then she'd laughed and told me to eat more. "I'm a strange one, too, that's how I know."

I turned right at the big intersection in front of the station and walked in the dark-blue shadow cast by the Shuto Expressway. I had no destination in mind, but I couldn't just stand still. I crossed the Mishuku intersection, walked through Ikejiri-ohashi, and finally wound up in Shibuya. When I came in sight of the station, a wave of people and sound suddenly washed over me, and I shrank away. I walked through the street where we'd carried out our attack runs countless times, turning corners again and again until I found myself in an unfamiliar place. I bought water from the first vending machine I saw, tucked in the corner of a parking lot. Then I sat down on a low wall in the shade of a building to drink it.

On the other side of the narrow one-way street were buildings that contained a multitude of shops. Shops selling cell phones, knickknacks, clothing—they butted up against one another. In front of the shops, girls passed by, laughing loudly, then a moped, then a truck came along and stopped so a man in uniform could drop off boxes, and then they were gone. I could see a short man with a phone to his ear loitering near a telephone pole. I wondered if Yeongsu was okay. I wondered if Viv was gone for good. If I would ever see her again. And what about the money? Were we in danger? Maybe Viv had her reasons for going off the radar; maybe something terrible had happened to her. The thought frightened me. But Yeongsu had been clear:

she jumped ship. And knowing Yeongsu, he probably had good reason to think so. Viv—I wiped at the sweat dripping down my face with the back of my hand.

It took several minutes before my eyes settled on the face of the man on the phone across the way. In that instant, I knew I'd met him before. I knew his face. Who was he? I wasn't sure exactly, but I knew him.

He was short and scrawny; he wore jeans and even from a distance, I could tell his T-shirt was worn and wrinkled. He looked tired and run down, middle-aged. Maybe he'd been a customer at Lemon. I focused on his face and searched my memory. No, not a customer. Then who, who was this man? This man I knew, this man, this feeling—in the next moment, something clicked, and I felt as if I had been punched in the head. It was him—Snoozy.

I didn't give myself time to think or ask myself why he was here or if it was really him. Before I knew it, I had gotten up and crossed the road. It didn't even occur to me to take stock of the situation. This was Shibuya, anyone and everyone could be here. *I* was here, so why would it be strange for Snoozy to be here. I was here, he was there. Just like back then. Everything came into focus, and I walked unblinking down the sidewalk toward him. He was leaning against a building, his back to me, rocking as he talked on the phone. I paused a few steps away from him and watched. This voice. This build, this hair, short in front and long in back . . . I looked down at his feet. The feet that had trampled my cushion. It was him. It was Snoozy.

"You."

My heart was beating out of my chest, and my hands and voice were both trembling. But at the same time, a different part of me was wide-awake, and it was from there my voice came. "You."

"Huh?" Snoozy turned toward me, phone still pressed to his ear, and studied me with a blank look. "What?"

"You. Snoozy."

"Wha . . . who are you?"

He was thinner than the last time I'd seen him, shrunken

somehow, and shadows like crags had carved themselves into his cheeks.

His bizarre hairstyle was the same, but I could see hints of his pockmarked scalp through his thinning brown hair. He smiled for a moment; then his face grew serious again. He whispered something to the person on the other end and hung up, putting the phone in his pocket.

"Who the hell are you?"

"It's me, the one you stole from."

"What?"

"Don't pretend like you don't know. You stole my money. Give it back. You were dating my mom. And you took my money, you asshole! Five years ago, in Higashimurayama."

Snoozy frowned, peering more closely at me. Then he slowly tilted his head and said, "No, you've got the wrong guy."

"Cut the shit. You know me. You stole the cash out of a box in my room. ¥726,000. You were there. Don't play dumb!"

"No . . . I never took any money. I remember the place . . . I guess she did have a daughter, but it wasn't you."

"Stop lying!"

"I'm not lying!"

"Whatever, just give me back the money." My left hand was strangling the strap of my purse, and my right hand was crushing the water bottle. "Give it back."

"I'm telling you, you've got the wrong guy."

"Oh, fuck off, give it back, all of it!"

"Crazy bitch, I'm telling you it wasn't me! Keep this up and I'll kill you!"

The sudden force of his threat shocked me, and I took a step back. I gritted my teeth and gulped. *No, don't back down now, he's full of shit, just shout right back at him, give him a taste of his own medicine*, I ordered myself, but the words wouldn't come. The tighter I clutched the water bottle, the more the back of my throat trembled, until my whole body was shaking.

This coward, this nobody, this faltering pipsqueak, smaller

even than me, small enough that I was sure if we got into a fistfight, I could beat him, this piece of shit who stole from a *high schooler* . . . And yet I was afraid of him. Countless times, I'd imagined what I'd do if I found him again, if I could go back in time, how I'd batter him with my anger and shame, beat him with my rage and bitterness, as they had beat me down so many times. In my imagination, I'd bawl him out, fly at him, kick him, beat him with the pickling stone, make him kowtow and cry and beg me for forgiveness. But now that he was here, right in front of me, all this pathetic fool had to do was threaten to kill me, and I froze on the spot, unable to utter even one word. *Do it, hit him, stop being a coward, rip him a new one*—I glanced around, looking for something I could use as a weapon. But there was nothing, and even if there had been something, I knew I wouldn't be able to use it. My eyes began to well with tears of fear and frustration. All he had to do was threaten me, say he'd kill me, and I turned dumb as stone, unable even to throw my lukewarm, crumpled bottle at him. The very fact of it threatened to take me out at the knees.

"Know your place, bitch," Snoozy said.

"Give it back . . . just give it back," I managed in a strangled voice.

"Fuck off! Who gives a shit about your chump change, just forget it."

Snoozy hawked up a loogie and spat it on the street in front of me. "God, you look different. Back then you were more . . . normal looking," he said, sounding fed up, and then he turned and walked away toward the station.

Even after I couldn't see him anymore, I still couldn't move. Agitation and fear twisted and twined within me, swelling up, and I had to force myself to breathe deeply, in and out, in and out.

I was soaked with sweat, so I bought a fresh bottle of water, but my hands were shaking so badly that it took me several tries to extract it from the machine. I kept telling myself that I needed to process what had just happened, make sense of this encounter, calm down, be cool, and I pressed the bottle to my forehead and breathed some more. Then a man came over to me and took up an over-friendly tone, *Hot today, isn't it, so hot, too hot, wanna come have a cool drink with me?* His smile disgusted me as he came closer still, and I jumped back, dropping the water bottle. I didn't even bother to pick it up, just ran. When I got back to a more crowded place, I turned to make sure he wasn't following me. I clutched the strap of my purse with both hands, clutched it tight, like it was a lifeline, so tight I couldn't hold it any tighter. Standing in the middle of the crowd, I didn't know where to go. But to stay where I was was too frightening. I started walking, one step at a time, letting myself be carried by the wave of people. I made it through Shibuya Station to the other side, where I followed the highway, turning strange and unknown corners again and again. I could taste my own stomach acid. I hadn't eaten since this morning. I went into a convenience store, bought an onigiri, ate it standing, and then walked on. It didn't matter where I turned or when, the road continued and I kept walking.

I arrived at a small park just as the layered clouds at the far edge of the sky were beginning to darken toward the blue of evening. I sat down on a stone bench. My feet were heavy and numb from walking, and my whole body felt feverish. A bunch of kids were playing on the playground, while their moms with the toddlers were packing up and trying to get them to leave, calling out their names again and again, a mixture of laughing and scolding. Inside my purse, my phone rang. It was Yeongsu. Maybe he'd heard more about Viv; maybe he'd found her. I stared down at the glow of the liquid crystal screen. The phone stopped ringing only to start again right away, so I exhaled, hit the call button, and raised the phone to my ear.

"Kotomi's dead," he said.

2.

When I got home, Kimiko was gone. Momoko and Ran were in the living room, eating bento from the convenience store and watching TV. A crowd of people was laughing on the show, sound effects ringing over them. Momoko glanced at me, then quickly turned back to the screen. Ran quietly said, "Hey." I went upstairs to the dark bedroom, put my right hand to my stomach, lay down, and closed my eyes, cell phone still in my left hand. It was so hot, but I felt like a ball of ice had sunk deep inside me, and I broke out in goosebumps. Even though I was motionless, my head was trembling, and I started muttering, counting out the numbers.

Kotomi was dead. Yeongsu had told me so. But those words simply floated in my head, voiceless. Kotomi's dead. I tried to say it out loud. But it wouldn't come. Kotomi's dead. *And "dead" means*—I blinked in the dim room—*right, "dead" means dead.* But that didn't move anything inside me either. Nothing followed. *Kotomi's dead, but where?* I hadn't seen it. Her death existed only inside the short call from Yeongsu, and maybe his information was wrong, or maybe it was a case of mistaken identity, and someone else was dead; maybe I shouldn't believe it just yet—but I sensed somehow that what he'd said was true. Kotomi was dead, just as Yeongsu had said. But if she was dead, then where had she gone? That, I couldn't understand.

Eventually I heard noise downstairs. Someone was here. Then the creak of the stairs as they came up, and when I turned to look, Yeongsu was there. Behind him was Kimiko. They both entered slowly, as if they were dragging along something as big as themselves, and they sat down in front of me. Shadows from different corners of the room fell on them, turning their eye sockets pitch-black.

"I'm turning on the light," Yeongsu said. I slowly sat up, and the three of us formed a circle in silence. Yeongsu's eyes were bloodshot, his complexion ashen gray, and he looked as if he'd aged ten or twenty years since I last saw him. He seemed completely spent. Kimiko's hair was tangled in places, and her eyes were puffy from crying, her face gaunt. It was after nine at night. How long had I been lying there? I had no idea.

"About what I said on the phone . . ."

Yeongsu finally managed to speak, but neither Kimiko nor I could say a word. We were silent again. I heard the sound of a passing car outside, the window flashing with its headlights for a moment before blackening again.

". . . Kotomi died a week ago, in her room, with Oikawa."

I looked up.

"I don't think it has anything to do with our operation," Yeongsu said. "I don't know the exact order of events, but Oikawa was on speed, and he hung himself. Kotomi was high, too, and her throat blocked up. She choked to death on her own vomit."

"Kotomi was . . ."

"To be honest, I don't know how she's been the last few months," Yeongsu said. "It'd been a while since we last hung out, and I didn't even know she and Oikawa had made it official, tied the knot. But I never thought she'd do speed. It just . . . doesn't seem like her."

I grabbed my elbows and squeezed.

"I heard rumors Oikawa had died a couple of days ago, and I heard there'd been a woman, too. So I looked into it, and the woman was Kotomi. Oikawa's guys took care of the cleanup, so I don't even know what's been taken care of on Kotomi's side."

"I didn't get to see her," Kimiko whispered.

"I think Oikawa killed her," Yeongsu continued.

"What?"

"There's no way to know what happened, and we'll never know for sure," Yeongsu said, sighing and rubbing at his face with both hands, "but Oikawa was high and knew it was only a matter of time till he got busted or offed by somebody, and Kotomi knew he was a useless fucking junkie."

"He hit Kotomi," I managed to squeeze out. "Did you ever meet him?"

"A long time ago," Yeongsu said, "back when he was flush with cash, when the yakuza were still backing him. But before you knew it, he was strung out on speed and whatever else he could get, and these past few years, he's been in bad shape. No one would back him anymore. He knew that, too, and he resented it. I heard he even started fights in the gambling dens and got banned. And not too long ago, he stopped leaving the house."

"Why didn't they arrest him?" My voice was quavering. Yeongsu didn't answer.

"My sources say he was like that even at home. Always high, always violent, always losing his temper. So he probably hit Kotomi, dragged her into it. And then he fucked up the dose or something, and Kotomi started foaming at the mouth, but he couldn't call an ambulance. And he knew there was nothing left he could do, and he was out of his mind on speed anyway, so he hung himself," Yeongsu said. "Murder-suicide."

Kimiko shut her eyes, pressed her hands over the tears that ran down her face, and sobbed. Yeongsu put his head in his hands and stopped moving. No one said anything. Yeongsu's phone rang. It kept on ringing, the bell shaking our silence. It kept ringing, then stopped, then started up again. Again and again. *Why doesn't Yeongsu answer? What if it's Kotomi?* For a moment, I was sure it was her, but then I had to shake my head.

The calls finally stopped coming, and Yeongsu said, "I'm heading out. Hana, you haven't heard from Viv, have you? Or gotten any other calls?"

I shook my head no.

"The ones who'll come for the skimmer money only know about me, they don't know anything about you, but all the same, be careful. Like I said before, don't answer any numbers you don't know."

Then Yeongsu turned and looked at Kimiko. He seemed about to say something but thought better of it, pressing his lips together. Then he left.

After a while, the stairs creaked again. It was Momoko and

Ran. They slowly entered, peering at Kimiko and me with meek expressions.

"Hana, we overheard a little. What happened?" Ran asked. It was all I could do to shake my head, but they wanted to know.

"Hana, please tell us."

"Kotomi is . . ."

"What about Kotomi?"

"She's dead. That's why . . ."

"What?" Momoko cried. "No way. What? But she . . . why?"

"We don't have the details yet."

"Are you serious? She's really dead?"

"What . . . I can't . . ."

Ran and Momoko met each other's eyes, and then both hung their heads. Momoko frowned and asked, "Does it, I mean, is it . . . does it have anything to do with our attack runs? With our source?"

"I don't know, but . . ."

"But?"

"I don't, I don't think so."

Momoko exhaled deeply and nodded, relieved. Kimiko slumped against the wall, staring at nothing, occasionally rubbing her eyes like an afterthought. Ran and Momoko looked back and forth between the two of us, their expressions a mixture of unease and worry.

"We'll sleep in the living room tonight, so why don't you two sleep here," Momoko said and then went back downstairs. Ran stayed a little longer, glancing worriedly at both of us, but then she went down, too.

Kimiko and I spent the entire night in a stupor, the lights still on above us. Sometimes we shifted, and sometimes I heard Kimiko crying, but neither of us spoke. The soles of my feet throbbed like my heart was beating there, which reminded me that I'd spent the entire day walking. Right. Viv had disappeared. Then I'd found Snoozy in front of that building in Shibuya. I could feel the sweat dripping down my skin, the fear that had frozen me completely—the scenes of the day were seared into my mind, but somehow it felt like it had happened to someone else. Kimiko lay down, sat up like she'd remembered something, lay down again. As dawn began to break, we both finally fell asleep.

From that day onward, Kimiko and I kept to the bedroom.

We lay in our futons staring at the ceiling until one of us got up, and if we got hungry, one of us would go downstairs and go out to the convenience store for whatever we could find. When we went down to the living room, Ran and Momoko went upstairs, and when we went back upstairs, they moved back to the living room. They seemed to be taking care to leave us alone. Sometimes when Kimiko and I were lying in bed, I could sense them checking on us from the hallway. Every time I looked, they'd disappear, but I'd stopped caring about any of that.

Lying next to Kimiko late at night, I thought back on my old tenement house in Higashimurayama. The sleeping room. One morning, I woke up and there she was. Kimiko. Her futon folded neatly, her pajamas folded just as neatly and set atop the duvet. Floating amid the clutter of the room, the freshness of that order had mesmerized me. I ate the ramen she'd made, and we walked around town drenched in sweat. It was summer. How many years ago now . . . I was still in junior high then. Many years passed, and I was twenty now. Five. Five years had passed, and in that time, in those years I'd . . . suddenly, I was frightened by what was to come. A whole five years, and in those five years I'd . . . "Kimiko," I'd called out for her before I realized what I was doing. No answer came, but Kimiko slowly turned toward me and looked into my eyes. I heard a moped pass by outside. In the dim of the room, Kimiko's eyes were sunken, carved in deep shadow, and every time she blinked, they became darker still.

"Hana."

Even though we'd been here together the whole time, I felt as if we hadn't met in ages. Her voice was husky as she called my name again.

"Kimiko." My voice was dry, too.

"I don't think Yeongsu's coming back."
I studied her eyes.
"He won't come back. I don't think he can."
I remained silent and still.
"And I was thinking," Kimiko said. "The last time I talked to Kotomi, she was talking about going to Osaka."
"To Osaka?"
"She said she was going to see Jihun," Kimiko said. "She found out he was alive, and she wanted to go, even just to see his face from a distance. But she asked me not to say anything to Yeongsu. If he found out, he'd stop her. She made me promise."
"What . . ." I couldn't breathe.
"I think someone found Jihun and told Kotomi about it."
". . . and you don't think it was Yeongsu?"
"Kotomi made me swear not to tell Yeongsu, so I don't think it was him."

But it was Yeongsu who had found Jihun. Had he never told her? At karaoke when I mentioned Jihun, Kotomi didn't seem surprised, just listened to me like nothing was wrong, nodded like she already knew. Or maybe she had been surprised. I didn't know. I'd been wasted, and I assumed that Kotomi already knew about Jihun, but then I remembered how Yeongsu had asked me to keep a lid on it until he talked to her, found the best timing for it, which meant he hadn't yet told her? And that meant she'd heard it first from me, looked into it on her own, and decided to go see him, go all the way to Osaka? Because I'd told her? But that meant . . .

"Hana."
I had been staring at the ceiling.
"Hana."
I couldn't answer.
"She made me swear not to tell Yeongsu, so I didn't. But I think she was about to go see Jihun, and Oikawa did her in before she could."

. . .

Little by little, I stopped being able to sleep. My appetite disappeared, and I spent most of my time in my futon. I must have napped in fits and starts, but scraps of consciousness disrupted me, and day or night, images came to me one after the next—I couldn't work out if they were dreams or reality or memories, but I found myself in all sorts of places. My mother was there, too, and her hostess friends, whose names I couldn't remember.

Someone laughing through cigarette smoke, the faded letters of Evergreen Hills, chatting with the manager of that family restaurant, the sound of men in baseball uniforms clanking their beer steins in a toast, being self-conscious about my dirty school uniform. Kotomi with her chestnut hair, so beautiful as she turned to smile at me. The chips of light reflecting off the disco ball, falling on her shapely forehead and cheeks. I couldn't believe, only a few weeks later, the woman before me was now dead. *Hey, Kotomi, Kotomi, is it true? You didn't know about Jihun, you heard it from me first, didn't you, even though Yeongsu told me to keep it quiet, even though he said he'd tell you when the time was right, but I'm an idiot and I just wanted you to be happy, so I told you thinking it would cheer you up, but that's why he killed you, isn't it, he found out you were going to Osaka, you told him you were, and that's why he did it, your crazy stupid boyfriend, and it's all my fault isn't it, I forgot my promises, I just wanted to cheer you up, and you ended up dead because of it.* Kotomi said nothing, simply held the mic and smiled, and on the screen the lyrics flowed, changing color as Kotomi sang along to them, and then Momoko and Ran and Kimiko and I were walking down the road, in the evening, to Lemon. En stood at the door of Little Heaven and waved to us, and suddenly Lemon burst into flames, and I saw Snoozy writhing and thrashing in the fire. Look at your face, look at your face, he said, laughing, pointing at me, and I looked in the mirror only for a moment before I cried out and looked away. It wasn't me. That wasn't me. *Kimiko, you filled the fridge before you disappeared, and it made me so happy, so so happy, ham and hot dogs, melon buns, to keep me fed,* but when I opened the door and peeked inside, it was suddenly filled with money, so much money I couldn't see the back, and fat stacks of cash dropped down, falling to the ground with the force of their own weight, and no matter how hard I tried to close the door, the money just kept growing and spilling out until I had to run, carried away on its current. The wind picked up, and bills plastered themselves to my face. I tried to peel them away and run toward the gate, but it was only after I was already through that I realized the gate was the gap between Viv's front teeth. *Hana, he's not coming back, Yeongsu can't come back, do you know why? I don't know, Viv, why did you disappear like that, did you hate me, did you think I—hey, Viv, why did you disappear, hey, Hana, it's always poor people who want to die, 'cause when you get rich, you want to hang on to life, but you know what, money lives longer than any human, hey, Viv, hey, Kimiko, yellow is for good fortune, the color of happiness, there's yellow in your name, Kimiko, that's right, put yellow to the west, it'll protect us, yellow will bring us happiness . . .* I opened my eyes and sat up, soaked in sweat. It was the middle of the night. Kimiko had her back to me and was completely still, asleep, but even so I knew she was staring at me. *It's all your fault. You did this. Kotomi's dead because of you.* I didn't know whose it was, this voice I could hear so clearly, this voice that had grabbed hold of me and wouldn't let go, so I picked up the box cutter next to my pillow and went downstairs, and far, near, the splotches of yellow grew and began to chant, *It was you, it was all you—*

"Hana?"

I turned and found Momoko and Ran standing a few steps away.

"Hana, um," Ran spoke quietly, "maybe you should put that away."

I looked down at the box cutter in my hand, pressed my thumb against the button, and pushed the blade back in. The blade made a squeaking sound as it moved, and Momoko took a step back.

"Hana," Ran said. "Hana, do you understand what I'm saying?"

I nodded.

"Hana, we don't mind if you're awake at night or asleep during the day, but when you make all this noise in the middle of the night, we're starting to go crazy, too. It's been a week? Ten days? Don't you think it's time to stop?"

I mumbled vaguely.

"And, I mean, the walls, what were you trying to do to them?" Momoko asked.

"I don't, I don't know," I said, the box cutter still in my hand. "I don't know, but... but the yellow, this yellow..."

"Are you carving words or something?"

"No, I..."

"Then what were you doing?"

"I'm trying to scrape off the yellow."

"What?"

"The yellow, the..."

"You're trying to scrape off the yellow paint?" Momoko frowned. "Um, I don't think that's possible. With a box cutter? Are you serious?"

I nodded.

"What exactly are you trying to do, Hana?"

"I..."

"Hana, you haven't been sleeping, you walk around at night, and when you come down, you're scraping away at the wall. I haven't seen you eat in days. You don't make sense when you talk. Do you even hear us? You're in pretty bad shape. It's seven in the morning right now. Did you know that? And what about the trash upstairs? You gotta take it out. I saw a ton of plastic bottles up there. And what about the bento I brought you yesterday? Did you eat it? And Kimiko, is she okay?"

"I had a little."

"She's still upstairs, sleeping, right? I haven't seen either of you bathing, and that's really not okay," Momoko said.

"I, I don't know, she's just been lying there, the whole time."

Momoko and Ran stared at me with impenetrable expressions—I couldn't tell if they were fed up or angry, if they were considering the situation carefully or completely at a loss. I wanted to run from their gaze, so I turned, put out the box cutter's blade again, and started scraping at the yellow. The paint at the tip of the knife crumbled into powder and fell to the floor, so I held my breath to keep from breathing it in. But the yellow dust was alive, all the specks I couldn't see with my naked eye, and they were falling onto my skin, burrowing inside my pores, blaming me, pressing me on. I cried out and crouched away, and then I began to wail.

"It's all my fault . . ."

"Hana, you're talking about Kotomi, right?" Ran said. "About the fact that she died. You haven't been the same since. But Hana, it doesn't have anything to do with you. It didn't have anything to do with the work we did."

"That's right, Hana, you're not making any sense. You're really starting to scare us."

"It's not just . . . not just Kotomi," I said, hiding my face in my hands. Tears spilled down between my cheeks and the palms of my hands, and every time I felt a trickle, I wailed and cried even harder. I didn't mean to cry, I could hear what Momoko and Ran were saying, but I was being pushed again and again by the waves that rose up within me—I could neither give myself completely over to them nor stand my ground against them.

On sunny afternoons, in the dark nights, the waves came crashing toward me. I was terrified of everything, everything I'd done in this house up to this point, of what I'd told Kotomi, of all the things I didn't know, of disappearing, vanishing. It was impossible to think anymore.

"I'm, I'm scared."

"Of what?"

"Of everything, all the things I did."

"Hana, what did you do?"

"What do you mean?"

"What do you think you did?"

"I . . ."

"What?"

". . . like, like you said before, Momoko, I . . ."

"You what?" Momoko pressed.

"I mixed you up in this."

Momoko studied me and then the wall. Then she went into the kitchen and came back with a trash bag, shaking it open in front of me.

"Hana, take everything from the Yellow Corner and throw it in here."

I looked to the Yellow Corner, tears steadily trickling down my face, and then I did as she said.

The keychain, the piggy bank, the giraffe sculpture, the pencil case, the yarn, the nail polish. I stared down at each dusty object and then put it in the trash bag.

"Hana, it's not your fault," Ran said softly. "They used you, Hana. And me and Momoko, too."

"Used?"

I looked up at her.

"That's right. Those people, all those people, they used you until you went crazy, Hana. They did it to all of us."

"Kimiko's still down, right? Asleep?" Momoko said, now rushing me along. "Now's our only chance, Hana. If we're going to put an end to it, this is our only chance. Nobody knows we've been living here. There's no proof. Except the money. So let's do what you said we would, split the money and get out. That'll be the end of it. Just forget everything that's happened, don't think about it, start over."

"Start over?"

"We can make it like none of it ever happened," Momoko said. "Because nobody knows. The second we're out, that's the end of it."

"But . . ."

"But what?"

"What about Kimiko?"

"Who gives a shit about Kimiko," Ran spat. "I thought she was crazy from the beginning. From where I'm standing, Hana, both Yeongsu and Kimiko are messed up. You've always talked like you think the world of them, but when they brought you in, you were a high schooler, right? I always thought that was sketchy. And on top of that, they had you work at the bar, made you drink yourself to death, do all that stuff with the fake cards. They made you think it was so amazing, but they were using you, Hana, using all three of us. Am I wrong?"

"Kimiko was the one who pushed me down the stairs," Momoko said, glancing first at me and then at Ran. "And when you bound my wrists, made sure I couldn't get away, those were Kimiko's orders. And after that she went crazy, smashed the door to pieces and punched me in the face."

"That's right," Ran said. "Kimiko did that. That's a fact. Do you understand, Hana? These are the facts as we know them. Nobody knows about this house, nobody knows what happened here, nobody will ever know—these are the facts. After this, if someone ever asks you about any of this, just remember that. Okay? *We* didn't do anything. *They* made us do everything. The adults were pushing us around, and we didn't know what they would do if we tried to defy their orders. These are the facts. Got it?"

"I . . ." I slumped to the ground, pressed my head against the floor, and sobbed. "Ran, Ran, I, I, I thought I was doing good, I thought we had no other choice, so I did it, all of it, and now—"

"I know."

"I wanted us to make it through, together, and I thought this was the only way, that's why I was so—"

"I told you, it's okay, Hana, here." At this, Ran signaled to Momoko, who put the paper bag on the floor between us and started pulling out the money. Each bundle was a million, and Momoko piled them each in front of us.

"Let's hurry—see, Hana? Four equal parts, just like we

planned. We'll even leave Kimiko her share, we don't want her coming after us. Five million each. More or less. I split it evenly, I promise. Each bundle is a million, and we each get five. Okay? Okay, Hana? We already packed our bags, so we're gonna go now. You should, too. It should be okay, but if there's anything here that would tie you to this place, take it with you. Oh, and the money is a secret between us, right, and the fact that we split the money and left. There was never any money to begin with, okay? Now you try and say it, Hana."

"There was, there was . . ."

"There was never any money to begin with."

"There, there was never . . . any money . . . to begin with."

"That's right. They made us work, but only gave us allowances. The adults controlled the rest. They did it. So there was never any money here. Okay? Do you understand, Hana?"

"Yeah," I said, nodding and crying.

"Stop crying already," Momoko said, nudging me. "We don't know what'll happen if you see Kimiko again, so we're going to wait right here while you go up and get your wallet and phone and stuff. Go now. Hurry up. And don't make a sound, you've got to be quiet, so quiet."

I didn't even bother to wipe at the tears streaming down my cheeks as I crept back up the stairs like Momoko had told me to. The curtains were glowing with morning light, and Kimiko still slept, her back to me. No, I didn't know if she was asleep or not. But she didn't move. I did as Momoko had said and put my wallet and phone in my purse. With no door now to guard it, the navy shoebox sat naked in the closet, its lid askew. I crept closer until I could pick it up. At the door, I slowly turned to study Kimiko's back. And then I put my hand to the wall and went back downstairs and into the living room.

"Was she asleep?"

"Yeah," I said, unsure even who or what I was answering to. My head hurt so badly I thought it would split open, and with each throb, a wave of nausea washed over me. The tears kept falling one and then the next.

"Okay, well, we're going," Momoko said quietly. "You leave, too, Hana. Within the next ten minutes."

With that, Momoko and Ran went out the entryway door, taking care not to make a sound. I stood in the middle of the living room, the navy shoebox clutched under one arm and my other hand tight around the strap of my purse. The money was strewn carelessly at my feet. I stared down at the small, messy pile of bills, my tears falling onto them. And then I crouched, reached out, picked up one bundle, and stuck it in my purse. For a moment, I thought the crumpled paper bag would topple over.

Then I left Kimiko behind and walked out of the house.

THIRTEEN

YELLOW FALLING

"Long day, huh, Ito-san? Oh, the manager wanted you to stop by his office on your way home."

"Oh, okay."

"That tofu steak is past sell-by, so you can take it home with you."

"Thank you."

I took off my rubber gloves and apron, went to the changing room, and got ready to go home. The time card machine made a big clunking sound, imprinting "8:15 p.m." in blue ink. The manager's office was a two-minute walk, located on the second floor in an old office building. I knocked.

"Ah, Ito-san. Sorry to have you come in when you should be going home."

When I stepped in, the manager looked up from the paperwork he'd been reading. The office was stuffed with piles of cardboard boxes and only had room for a mini-fridge, a flat-pack shelf, and a table with two chairs. Four people would've filled the room to capacity. The manager pointed to the chair in front of him, rubbing his hand over his graying hair. I bowed my head and sat to face him, putting some distance between us.

"About the shop," he said, looking tired, "I've done everything I can, but with the whole corona situation, it's just impossible. We're going to have to close temporarily starting next week, and from there, we'll have to wait and see."

"Okay."

"I'm sorry. I know it's sudden, but we're asking everyone to take a leave. We can't give you a full remuneration or anything like that, but we're hoping to give you a little something if we can manage it, at a later date. Unfortunately, the ward office still hasn't told us anything about applying for benefits or remunerations, or anything solid, really, so I can't guarantee anything. But when we get a clear answer, I'll contact you. Until then, if you find another job, please take it. We won't blame you. I'm very sorry."

"It's fine," I said. "I'm sorry, too."

"Why are you apologizing? We should be the ones apologizing. I really am sorry."

If the shop was closing starting next week, that meant today was my last shift. We'd had basically no customers over the three-day weekend, so almost all the food went to waste. I wasn't surprised by his announcement—with the way things were going, I'd expected it. When the manager was done delivering the news, he looked almost relieved. And then he and I chatted a while. He was in his mid-fifties with a daughter in college, and now everyone was stuck at home because of corona, and he was having a rough go of it because their place was small, and everyone was at each other's throats. When our talk wound down, I quietly thanked him and asked him to call me when things calmed down, and then I left the office.

It was the middle of May. Everyone was nervous and angry and panicked, and even a little excited about corona's spread, not knowing when it would be over or exactly how serious it was. The word "corona" was plastered across TV and the internet, and people were getting scared. But ever since I'd first found that article about Kimiko at the beginning of spring, reality no longer felt relevant to me. I was floating somehow, and even though I understood the words and voices emanating from the news, they seemed to unravel before I could grasp and make sense of them in my head. In the same vein, I didn't know what to think or feel about being let go from my only source of income, the deli I'd worked at for three years.

After I left that house in Sancha, I walked all the way to Higashimurayama, back to Evergreen Hills. It was around noon when I arrived, and I remember I was drenched in sweat. When I turned the doorknob to the sleeping room, I found it unlocked, and when I peered in from the entryway, I saw my mother fast asleep. I hesitated, then went inside, set the navy shoebox on a shelf, and stood for a while on the border between the kitchenette and where she slept. Maybe she sensed me there, because a few minutes later, she cracked her eyes and said, without any hint of surprise, "Oh, hey, Hana," and went back to sleep.

And then we went back to how we'd always been. The only thing that had changed was that I was no longer a teenager, and my mother's hostess friends didn't come by anymore. When evening came, Mom rode her bicycle to the next station over, to a bar where she'd found work. She came home right after midnight and slept straight through to the afternoon the next day. We were back where we'd started—it was as though the few years I'd been gone had never existed.

For a while after I came back, though—for one week, two weeks, I'm not sure, I was out of my head, disoriented—yes, the same as I'd been those last days in the house when I first heard Kotomi had passed away.

When I tried to sleep, I started to hear voices, Kimiko and Yeongsu blaming me, and I saw images of Kotomi, dead, her face smeared with vomit. I couldn't get away from any of it. When I was awake, I was on pins and needles, expecting the police to come and arrest me because they'd sniffed me out, or someone from the underworld to come find me. I had countless horrible dreams about my cell phone suddenly exploding, blowing my body to bits, or Kimiko, completely mad, hunting me down and attacking me. There were days when I just couldn't stop crying, no matter what I did.

But even though I was out of my mind, the things Momoko and Ran had said to me that morning in the living room were burned into the dark corners of my brain.

We had been used, they'd said. I'd been brought in when I was still a teenager. Kimiko had brought me in. That's what Ran had said. I'd always believed Kimiko had saved me. And the more I got to know her, the more I became convinced that she couldn't live without me, either, that there was no other way. That was why I'd been so desperate. But I was wrong, Momoko and Ran had said, looking down at me.

Our attack runs, Lemon, even Kotomi's death—all of it had been the doing of those crazy adults around us. We were kids who didn't know better, and they gave us booze and made us work and used us, end of story. We were powerless against their authority. There was nothing we could do except meet their expectations, succumb to their control. Nobody knows about this house, nobody knows what happened here, nobody will ever know—these are the facts, they had said.

Were they right? In that moment, their words were the only thing I had to cling to. If I didn't, I would have fallen apart, lost my mind completely. Through the sleepless days and nights, I tried to force myself to believe what Momoko and Ran had said. At first, I really did try to believe it. But the more I thought about it, the more I started to wonder if what they said was actually true, and there were even brief moments where I couldn't believe otherwise. I'd left almost all the money I'd gathered, so I suppose it belonged to Kimiko and Yeongsu now. I left it because I was afraid of them. I was afraid of Kimiko. No, that wasn't it. I shook my head. I was never afraid of her. I had to be honest with myself, with the truths I knew in my own heart. But what was truth? Was it what I believed to be true, what I could comprehend? Had I really never found Kimiko frightening? I must have. Maybe I never realized it, but I'd always been afraid of Kimiko, and maybe Kimiko and Yeongsu had made up stories to manipulate my feelings, use me for their gain—no, no, that wasn't true. I always decided everything for myself. I left the money behind of my own volition. Because that money terrified me, I didn't know what to do, and I needed to run away—no, that wasn't right either, hadn't I left it for Yeongsu and Kimiko, so I could help them? For Kimiko, who couldn't make it on her own? All that running around I did for Viv, didn't I do that for Kimiko, for us, so that we could go on living together? No, no, no, I left the money there for me, for myself, because I felt guilty for doing as Momoko and Ran said and leaving Kimiko behind, because she'd been so kind to me, that's why I left the money. But no, that wasn't it . . . what was it then?

I thought my mind would just go on churning like that forever—terrified, agonized, thinking about that house and Kimiko and Yeongsu, and about Kotomi. There was no way I'd ever forget. And for a few months, that was true. In ordinary moments, memories would rise and tangle up and leave me paralyzed—Momoko and Ran, the scenes from the days we'd spent together in the house, laughing together, enjoying ourselves, and the moment I'd lost everything. But in time, the memories began to fade. Autumn came, changed to winter, and then spring was almost over, and I realized that the space between my recollections was growing longer. Slowly but surely, a curtain drew itself over my raw emotions, and I found a job at a factory thirty minutes away by bicycle. I worked morning to night, and the exhaustion made me sleep like the dead, until I stopped remembering even to remember. I forgot it all.

Two years after I went back to Higashimurayama, my mother hooked up with a customer from her bar and went off to Kyushu. I lived alone for a while at Evergreen Hills, but the factory I worked at announced it would be closing its doors and moving to a new location, so I quit and left Higashimurayama.

There were plenty of places hiring. Most of them barely paid a thousand yen an hour, but for someone living alone on purse strings, it was enough. I started working as a cleaning lady at a big hotel in Yugawara in Kanagawa Prefecture. The hotel had one-room staff dormitories that didn't require any up-front costs, and our utilities were free. My days were spent going back and forth between the dorm and the hotel, but in my sixth year at the job, I grew close to one of the women who'd just started.

She was two years older than me, originally from Kochi Prefecture, and she was cheerful, quick to laugh. A year later, after much wheedling on her part, she and I rented a nearby apartment and started living together. I don't know if the thing between us was friendship or romance. For a while we had fun, but soon, she stopped going to work, and we started fighting all the time, and one day she walked out, putting an end to our two years of living together.

Not long after, I noticed that the thirty thousand yen I kept in one of my drawers was gone. I was hurt and betrayed, but I realized I was also relieved. I put in for a transfer to a hotel in Hakone and moved back into the staff dorm there—still a cleaning lady. In winter, the custodial company that employed me occasionally sent me to Nagano to work for the ski season.

When I was thirty-six, my mother passed away. It was winter. She'd just turned fifty-nine, and I hadn't seen her in years. I thought she was still living in Kyushu with her man, but when she died, I found out that somewhere along the line she'd moved back to Tokyo, where she'd lived alone in a tiny apartment.

Her death was sudden and unexpected—a heart attack. She hadn't been seeing a doctor or anything, and according to her landlord, who was also occasionally her drinking buddy, she had gone out drinking at an izakaya the night before with several friends from the dry-cleaning factory where she worked part-time. She'd been the same as always. Someone from city hall explained to me how to hold a funeral, and with the help of many people, I managed to pull it off—but I can hardly remember it now. It didn't feel real to me, even after I got the keys from the landlord and entered her apartment to take care of what she'd left behind.

It was a studio, only six mats total. A few clothes, some half-used makeup in a box, a TV, a few plastic storage bins, a futon left out, the bedding unmade.

There was a cheap-looking picture frame on top of one of the plastic bins, and inside it, an old picture: me, still little, wearing a checked dress and making a peace sign with a grin, sitting in my smiling mother's lap. Next to it was a drawer made of pasteboard, and in the drawer was a white envelope, written in faint pencil in cramped writing: "For Hana." In the envelope were crumpled thousand-yen notes: ¥73,000 total. I squeezed my eyes shut.

When was the last time I'd seen her? What did we talk about? What did her face look like? Sometimes, when she called, I didn't pick up. Maybe she had something she wanted to say, maybe she wanted to hear my voice. There were so many chances, opportunities, so much time we could have shared. I could only remember her smile, and I clutched my knees and wept.

I decided to quit my job in Hakone and move into my mom's apartment. I thought the landlord might refuse me, but she said it was hard to find a tenant for a place where someone had just died, and if I was willing to rent the place, it would honestly be a huge help. So I put on my mother's pajamas, slipped into her futon, and spent sleepless nights crying.

My body began to shut down until I could barely leave the apartment, only dragging myself to the shopping district once a week for food. Looking back, I know I was depressed, but in the thick of it, that never occurred to me. My body felt so heavy that I could barely manage a shower. I couldn't even summon the energy to care. I spent all my time in bed, but my nights were restless, and my days were spent staring vacantly at nothing. Sometimes I wondered what would happen if I let myself die, but that was neither here nor there.

I never saw anyone, never used money for anything but rent, food, and utilities, and it seemed like I could carry on that way a few years more, just living. But one day, while I was out shopping for food, I saw a hiring notice pasted to the glass of a deli.

It'd been so long since I last read any words, and while I was gaping at the notice, an old woman emerged from inside, a plastic bag in hand. Our eyes met, and she smiled at me.

It was nothing, the kind of exchange that happens everywhere all the time, but it somehow sent tears flowing down my face, and I rushed back to the apartment. Sadness and joy and regret whirled together within me, so tangled that I couldn't pick them apart, and I kept on crying that day, unable to discern the source of those tears. When I was finally done, my head and eyes ached, but that ache felt incredibly real.

After that, I started passing by the deli on purpose, and I began to come back to life. I started showering more, I bought new underwear for the first time in years, and I even managed a trip to the salon to get a long-needed haircut. And one spring, after three years working as a salesclerk at the deli, I found Kimiko's name in an article on the internet—and I remembered her. And it was only then that I realized I had forgotten those days living with Kimiko in that house.

My insomnia came back, the same as when I'd heard Kotomi died, and when I left the house, and after my mother died. Every hour of the day, I'd find myself reading the screenshots I'd made of the article about Kimiko, and I started spending most of my days remembering the things she and I had done back then.

The first time I'd met Ran, handing out flyers in her white bomber jacket and sandals on her bare feet; Momoko, who at first had been so shy, but her singing voice had been so beautiful, and before I knew it, the three of us were going out together all the time. Their faces, laughing, crying, talking through the night. Then I'd sigh and look down at my phone again. The article said Kimiko had locked away a woman in her twenties, beat her, hurt her. That she'd used her words to manipulate the woman and that she'd been arrested when the woman broke free and told the police.

When I first found the article, I was shocked that I'd forgotten Kimiko, and then I got scared that the things I'd done in that house would come to light. I couldn't stand to bear that fear alone, and so I'd gone to see Ran. But Ran only repeated to me what she'd said in that house, in that living room, that day.

Over the next several weeks, with each passing day, I hashed over my memories of that house, of us, of the things that had happened to Kotomi, of Kimiko, and the more I thought about it, I couldn't accept the idea that the things written in that article were true.

Of course I didn't know the truth of what happened. But I couldn't shake the feeling that what had really happened, the facts, must be different from what was written here. From the outside, the article made perfect sense—the woman who'd run was young, and the description was written in a way that people could understand. And Kimiko was silent, offering no explanation. The Kimiko I'd known was just like that. And just like that, the three of us, Ran, Momoko, and I, had created facts we could stomach and then run away. I could no longer separate what had happened twenty years ago with what I was reading, the things that might be lurking, flickering behind the dozen or so lines in the article.

I wondered how Kimiko was doing now.

May came to an end, and even into June, I kept thinking about her. I couldn't bring myself to look for a new job. The incident had happened in May of last year, and the trial had been in January. I never found more information about it on the internet. I didn't know if Kimiko had been found guilty or innocent, or if she was in prison. I kept searching, trying to figure out if there was a way for a person to find out the results of the trial.

What I did find said that a case like this usually wouldn't make its way into a case database, and that it was impossible for a non-specialist to find out any more using the internet. According to one blog I found, it was also impossible to find out information about who was involved in the case, and even if you submitted an information release request, you'd only get documents that were almost entirely redacted. The only other way was to figure out the name of the lawyer who handled the case and meet with them to ask for information, but say you did manage to find them, most likely, they wouldn't tell you anything unless you were directly involved with the case.

Should I just forget Kimiko the way I had before, the way Ran said I should? Should I leave those memories behind? And if I did discover where Kimiko lived, what exactly would I do with that information? I couldn't explain to myself what I wanted to do or why I felt such an urgency to do something. All I knew was that I couldn't keep going like this.

One afternoon, I picked up my old cell phone, opened the contacts list, stared at the names in there, and then jotted down a number. It was a number I'd never dialed once in twenty years, and I didn't know if it would work.

And if it did, what then? I didn't know, but it was the only option I had left.

The line rang for quite a while, then switched over to voicemail.

I took a breath, and then I gave my name. I said, "If you get this message, if you'd like, give me a call." The number might have belonged to someone else by now. Maybe I'd left a senseless message on the voicemail of a complete stranger. I probably had—it had been a long time. I shook my head.

My apartment was bursting with the inescapable humidity of June, the thick air flowing through every corner and crack. I curled up in my futon to try and escape. The afternoon light turned the backs of my eyelids red, and as I chased the patterns there, I fell asleep. From far away, I heard a phone ringing, and the ringing came closer and closer—the moment I opened my eyes, I reached for my phone and hit the answer button.

"Hello," I said. "Hello?"

"It's been a while." The sound was muffled and distant, but it was Yeongsu's voice. I gripped the phone tight.

"Yeongsu, it's Hana. I'm . . . I'm sorry I called you out of the blue like that."

"You still had the number, huh."

The tone of Yeongsu's voice hadn't changed, but the core of it had grown thinner, and his words occasionally wavered like they were blowing in the wind.

"I thought it might not work anymore, but I've been thinking about a lot of things, and I remembered you'd given me a number that I wasn't supposed to tell anyone else about, so if anything was going to work, I thought maybe this one..."

We were silent a moment, and I gulped. "Actually, a while ago, I found an article about Kimiko going to trial, and I keep thinking about it, thinking about her, about how she's doing..."

"Kimiko's trial?" Yeongsu said, almost as if he were talking to himself. "That made the news, huh."

"Yeah, and I read about it and didn't know what to do."

I was nervous. Even though it had been my idea to call him, I couldn't believe I was actually talking to Yeongsu after twenty years. I didn't know if I was making any sense. Yeongsu hummed noncommittally and then coughed heavily several times.

I had so many things I needed to say, so many things I wanted to ask—what had happened with Viv in the end, did they find the money I'd left, did they have any trouble after the three of us left, what had he been doing these past twenty years, what had really happened with Kimiko and that girl? But something lay between us, preventing me from speaking, and I wetted my lips again and again.

"Yeongsu, how, how is Kimiko, how's she doing?" I pressed the phone to my ear. "I want to know, and I've searched and searched, and nothing."

"Kimiko... her sentence was suspended, so she's not in the clink," Yeongsu said, taking his time to release each word carefully, one by one. "Anyway, she didn't do anything to that girl, to any of them."

"She... didn't do anything?"

"Nope."

"Nothing like what was in the article?"

I heard Yeongsu take a breath on the other end of the line.

"Yeongsu, do you think maybe you could tell me, where Kimiko . . ."

"What, you planning to go see her?"

"I don't know but—"

"I wouldn't bother, wouldn't make a difference."

"I don't know what exactly I want either. I'm not even sure I should have called you, but I . . ." I moved my phone to my left hand. "I thought, if I got through to you, there was something I wanted to say to you, something I needed to say to you. I won't say it's been on my mind all these years, I can't say that. See I, I, forgot about everything, didn't remember it. I only remembered how I wanted to remember, and I made it like none of it happened. I'm sure you're mad about everything I did, leaving like that, everything half-finished, disappearing, leaving you to clean up after Viv, but I was scared. I thought I'd live with Kimiko forever, I made her promise not to disappear, but even though I had told her that, I just abandoned her."

"Hana—" Yeongsu laughed, faintly. I imagined his face, and my heart ached. "You're the same as ever."

"I messed up, messed everything up, and then in my heart I blamed Kimiko, even though she didn't do anything wrong, even though I was the one who did it, I told myself, convinced myself that she made me do it, and then when it was convenient for me, I left her and ran for it."

"No," Yeongsu said, "anyone would've in your shoes."

"But I—"

"No one blames you."

"But—"

"Kimiko is . . ." Yeongsu exhaled slowly. "Well, Kimiko's in Higashimurayama. Living in that bar."

"In Higashimurayama?"

"She didn't have anywhere to go, so Mama Junko agreed to let her rent a room on the second floor. I can't visit her, and she doesn't have a phone."

"Where are you, Yeongsu?"

"Oh, you know, here and there. I'm feeling my age these days. Lymph in my kidneys, my liver—water building up in my gut."

"Are you sick?"

"You could say so, the time's coming."

I couldn't breathe.

"It is what it is," he said. ". . . So are we good?"

"Wait, Yeongsu, wait," I said. "I have some money, Yeongsu. I've been working ever since then, as a cleaning lady, working from morning to evening, and I have a little savings, so if you need anything, right now, Yeongsu, I can—"

Yeongsu chuckled and said, "Oh, keep it, use the money for yourself."

"Yeongsu, um, I said there was something I needed to tell you, something I need to apologize for," I said, barreling forward like he was walking away and I was trying to grab his arm. "About Kotomi, it's about Kotomi, maybe this isn't the time, but I have to apologize. I need to tell you, because you told me I shouldn't say anything, but I wanted Kotomi to be happy, I wanted to cheer her up, so the last time I saw her, I told her over karaoke, I told her, Yeongsu, like an idiot, I told her about Jihun, and then she tried to go to Osaka, and then that terrible thing happened, and I never told you about it, but it's my fault, if I hadn't, if I hadn't broken my promise to you, Kotomi might've . . ."

My tears welled over, and my throat closed, and I couldn't get the rest out.

Yeongsu was silent a long time.

And then he said, "Yeah, she was there, too," and laughed shortly. "Stop worrying yourself about it. It's over and done with."

After we hung up, I remained frozen, my eyes pressed to my folded knees.

When the train stopped, I was the only one who got off.

It had been more than fifteen years since I last came here, and though this town was the first place I'd ever known, though I'd lived here such a long time, though my earliest memories were tied to this place, I felt no pangs of nostalgia for the shabby ticket gates, the worn-down and stained gray of the stairs, not even the scent of the wind.

Maybe this was because I'd spent my entire childhood waiting for my mother at home or walking around the neighborhood while she was sleeping so I didn't bother her. I never once got on the train to go anywhere.

The shopping district in front of the station was fairly deserted, too. I passed a middle-aged woman on a bicycle with huge crates strapped to the front and back, and then an old man walking a dog. It was only then that I noticed the din of crying cicadas. Glancing over the shops, I saw that about half of them had their shutters drawn, and even the ones that looked like they might be open didn't seem to have anyone inside. I saw a yakitori place where I'd been a few times, and in front were stacks of beer cases with several glass bottles covered in white dust. There was a new orthopedic clinic next to the yakitori place, and its light-up sign glowed with kanji. It was so bright and colorful, and though I studied it a long time, I couldn't make sense of what was written there.

The late August sun beat down oppressively, like it was trying to send every person on the planet a message. Nothing moved. The pitted asphalt, the telephone poles, the crooked signs, the store awnings—they each had their own colors, but the unrelenting, glaring sunlight had somehow turned everything the same hue. It was surreal. With each breath, my eyes grew heavier, and sweat poured from me, soaking my armpits and back.

The building that had once been the family restaurant where I worked was gone entirely, transformed into a parking lot that was almost empty. I had come here by bike every day, working from morning to night, school or no school. There was the manager who liked to make everyone laugh. He always wore his hair neatly parted and teased up, no matter if it was early in the morning or late at night. He was always nice to me, but at the end, I didn't manage to see him and say thank you. I wondered if he was doing well, wherever he was—I wiped away at the endless sweat.

I'd come all this way, and still I didn't know what I was trying to do.

Yeongsu had said Kimiko was there—living on the second floor of the bar where my mother had worked.

If she was there, if I saw her, what would I do? Did I want to explain myself or apologize, ask her about her life? Or did I want to remember something I'd forgotten? I didn't know. And even if she was there, that didn't mean I'd get to see her. I didn't know how she was feeling, how she was doing. The heat ratcheted up second by second until I could practically hear it sizzling in my ears, and I exhaled again and again, trying to release whatever was in my heart. But the more I tried to get ahold of myself, the faster my pulse raced, and when I tried to pause to put my thoughts in order, somehow my feet just wouldn't stop moving.

Soon, I saw a worn wooden door on my right.

This is it, I thought, gulping, and I drew back a few steps so I could take in the whole building.

It seemed to have shrunk one or two sizes smaller than it had been in my memory, and cracks ran over its walls, some parts crumbling away. The stained-glass window next to the door was chipped and spidered here and there, its four corners sunken black. The pillar to the right of the door had a doorbell attached to it. I took a deep breath, put my finger to the button, and slowly pressed. I couldn't tell if it had rung or not.

I waited maybe half a minute but there was no answer. There was a small window on the second floor, but its curtains were drawn and didn't move. It felt like no one was living there. I pushed the doorbell again and waited. But just as before, there wasn't a trace of sound.

For several minutes, I waited in front of the door, dithering, but then I made up my mind and knocked. Three loud knocks. I waited a few seconds and then knocked again, even louder this time. But still nothing.

The sun was high in the sky, and its light and heat gave no sign of easing. I stood sweating. I realized I hadn't had any water today. My ears began to ring.

I don't know how many minutes I lingered there. It could have been one minute, five minutes. Maybe Kimiko had moved away. I glanced up at the second-floor window, looked at the cracks in the stained glass, then looked at the door again. I exhaled and started to turn away to walk back to the station. But then, I heard the door open behind me, and with a jolt, I turned around.

There was Kimiko.

The moment I met her eyes, a strong breeze blew between us, and her thick black hair billowed, just like it had that day, that summer day, that moment when I'd found her here—but it was an illusion conjured from my memories, because Kimiko's hair was gray now, clipped short, and she wore a threadbare T-shirt and faded shorts and no shoes at all.

"Kimiko," I blurted. Her hand rested on the doorknob, and she watched me. "Kimiko," I said again. "It's Hana. It's me, Kimiko."

"Hana."

Kimiko slowly blinked her sunken eyes and scratched under her ear, staring at me curiously.

She was completely changed.

Her cheeks were hollow, her skin spotted and carved with wrinkles, her limbs skin and bones, and she didn't look like she was sixty—she looked like an old woman. I looked at her right hand. The blue tattooed dot was still there, just as it had been so long ago.

When I saw that spot—tears spilled from my eyes before I knew what was happening, and I couldn't stop them. I didn't know what they were for, for bitterness or fear, for sadness? It was an indescribable feeling, and my tears gushed forth. I couldn't even wipe them away. Questions appeared in my mind—Do you live here alone, Kimiko? What do you do for food? Are you all right?—but I couldn't voice any of them.

Instead, I said, "Kimiko, I'm, I'm sorry. Coming like this, crying like this."

"It's okay," Kimiko said, her expression puzzled.

"Kimiko, are you here all alone?"

"Yeah."

"What about Mama Junko?"

"She's in a nursing home."

"So you, you're really all alone?"

"Yeah."

"And you don't have a phone, right?"

"Right."

"What do you do for food? Do you have money?"

"I have some. My friends give me some."

"You mean, Yeongsu? Yeongsu, right? He, he told me you were here, so I—"

"You know Yeongsu?"

My eyes widened, and I looked at Kimiko.

She looked at me. My eyes were clouded white from the endless tears, and I kept wiping them and sniffling.

"Yeah, I do, I do know Yeongsu. Hey, Kimiko, I used to live with you a long time ago, a really long time ago. I first met you when I was fifteen, right in this town."

"Yeah."

"You were so kind to me."

"Yeah."

"You made me karaage, and we went to the night market together. You filled my fridge with food, and you helped me so much, Kimiko, when my mom wasn't around, you always were."

"Your mom?"

"Yeah, you were friends with my mom, but you and I lived together, for years, together."

"We did?" Her wrinkles deepened as she smiled. "Is your mom doing well?"

"My mom, well . . . Mom died."

"So that's why you're crying so much." Kimiko nodded with understanding. "I cried when my mom died, too."

"Your mom died?"

"Yeah. In jail."

"Oh." I nodded, still crying. "Um, Kimiko, I did something terrible to you, I don't know how to explain, to you and Yeongsu, and to Kotomi, too, something really awful. I wanted to give you my everything, but in the end, I did something terrible, and then I ran, even though I'd promised, promised you and Yeongsu both."

"Yeah."

"And then I just forgot about everything, but I think maybe, because of what I did, you got into so much trouble, even though you didn't do anything, Kimiko, you really didn't. It was what I did, that's why terrible things happened to you, I think. I guess I don't know for sure, but now, now you're here, like this . . ."

Kimiko remained silent, staring vacantly at me. Her eyebrows were patchy, and her eyes were sunken, there were deep lines around her half-open mouth, and strands of frizzled white hair sprang here and there from her close-cropped scalp.

"Hey, Kimiko, why don't"—I pressed both hands to my face—"why don't you come with me."

I didn't know exactly what I was offering her or if I was even capable of offering anything. But I had to do it. I had no job, my apartment was tiny, I was barely scraping by just taking care of myself, and I didn't know what someone like me could do for someone like Kimiko. But Kimiko took me with her that day; I was alone, and she took me with her, and the years passed, and now here we were, like this, but the time we'd lived together, it wasn't all bad, not bad at all.

In Lemon, in that house, eating together, walking together, Kimiko had taught me how to laugh from my heart, she had made me happy, she had accepted me as I was, and now, this was what I could do for her—here, between us, there were so many things I could never repay, and Kimiko stood before me, alone, weak, no one to rely on. I was the only one who could support her, useless though I was, but if I could do it all over again, with

Kimiko, if I could do that, if I could save her—I sobbed and sobbed and said, "Kimiko, come with me."

Kimiko continued to stare, her mouth half-open.

"Let's go, Kimiko. Together."

"Don't cry like that."

"Kimiko, come with me, let's go."

"No," Kimiko said slowly. "I won't go."

"Kimiko—"

"I'll stay here."

And then, for a long time, we stared at each other.

"Hana, did you hear me?"

"I heard you."

I stared unblinking at her face. Kimiko scratched a spot above her ear.

"I'll stay here, because I can see them."

"See them?"

"Yeah. My mom and Kotomi. Yeongsu, too."

"You can see them?"

"Yeah."

"Kimiko, I . . ."

"Yeah?"

"I'll come see you again."

"Yeah."

"I'll see you again."

Kimiko smiled. And then she went inside and slowly shut the door.

I retraced my path through the shopping district, passed the station, and kept going down a road I didn't know. The pavement gently curved, crossing more and more roads, and if it turned into a dead end, I backtracked and picked a different path. I kept walking. Somewhere along the way, I found a park and sat on a bench, staying there until my tears dried. All the while, I could smell the familiar scent of a summer's day turning toward evening.

I walked until I arrived at a little station and got on the first train that came through. It was headed west, and fragments of light filled the car, dropping quivering shadows on the floor, the seats, the doors, and the passengers.

I was asleep before I knew it, dreaming a little dream. Someone was laughing, though I couldn't make out their face; the two of us were running, sweating, incredibly happy and incredibly nervous and incredibly sad, all at once, but still, we were laughing. *Hana, hey, Hana, Hana*—from far away, someone was calling me, but when I looked up, I saw a sunset spread across the whole sky beyond the window. I had no idea how long I'd slept. It was a sunset that seemed to flow directly into my heart, a color I once knew but had forgotten, could no longer remember, then it became a form, then a voice. I held my breath, taking it all in, and then I closed my eyes, and for a time, fell asleep once more.

MIEKO KAWAKAMI is the acclaimed author of the internationally bestselling novel *Breasts and Eggs*, a *New York Times* Notable Book of the Year and one of *Time*'s 10 Best Fiction Books of 2020. Her other novels, translated by Sam Bett and David Boyd, include *Heaven*, shortlisted for the 2022 International Booker Prize, and *All the Lovers in the Night*, a finalist for the 2022 National Book Critics Circle Award for fiction. In 2024, *Sisters in Yellow* won the Yomiuri Prize for Literature. Her books, translated into over forty languages, are known for their insights into the female body and philosophical questions surrounding gender, class and ethics in modern society. Born in Osaka, Kawakami lives in Tokyo, Japan.

LAUREL TAYLOR is a translator, poet and researcher. She has translated works by Kaori Fujino, Minae Mizumura, Tomoka Shibasaki and Aoko Matsuda, among others. Her first book of poetry, *Human Construct*, was published in November 2024, and her translation of Maiko Seo's *A Blessing for a Wedding* is forthcoming. Taylor researches the intersections of technology and literature in the early internet age and teaches courses on translation, Japanese literature and Japanese language at the University of Denver.

HITOMI YOSHIO is the translator of Natsuko Imamura's *This Is Amiko, Do You Copy?* and the co-translator of Mieko Kawakami's *Ashes of Spring*. She has also published translations of works by early twentieth century Japanese authors such as Ichiyō Higuchi and Midori Osaki. Her academic work focuses on the intersection of modern and contemporary Japanese literature, gender studies and translation studies. She received her PhD from Columbia University and teaches Japanese literature at Waseda University.